SECOND
STORY
WORK

JOSHUA
CYBULSKI

WESTRAY READS

Published by arrangement with Westray Reads

Second Story Work

ISBN: 9798686618480

Westray Reads paperback published: September 28th 2020
Westray Reads Kindle edition published: September 28th 2020

This is for my girls and my old man

Force always attracts men of low morality.

– Albert Einstein

September 28th, 2009
ONE

Derek Sierzant pulled his mask over his long brown hair and tucked his heavy beard inside. He adjusted the eyeholes and leaned back against the cold brick wall in the alleyway next to the Renfrew Post Office. His three accomplice's voices chattered on his walkie to let him know that they were in position as well. Their plan was to rob the armoured truck that would be pulling up to the bank in just a few moments.

Derek's three accomplices were his roommates – Hecky, Messy and R-Luv. They shared a house together in a posh Vancouver neighbourhood, but on this day, they were on the other side of Canada committing a felony.

Derek leaned against the wall for what felt to him like an eternity; in reality, it was just six minutes. He was early and he was nervous. He didn't have ice in his veins like Messy. Messy had been in combat, Derek had been in classrooms. This was new for him.

At 11:01 a.m., Hecky whispered into his walkie, "They're here."

Derek muted his walkie and began to creep down the alley toward Raglan Street. At the end of the alley police sirens began to ring out. He peeked around the corner and spotted two cruisers speeding down Raglan Street. The police sped toward the truck that Derek and his accomplices were targeting. *Fuck, someone spotted me!* - he thought. He took a step back and cocked his gun.

The police continued to speed toward the bank; they weren't slowing down. They sped through the intersection past the alleyway Derek was standing in. The police created a distraction to onlookers.

Amongst the chaos, the tin can pulled up in front of the bank and an armed guard exited the passenger side. He walked around the armoured truck and opened the back door to walk inside. Derek stayed perfectly still; out of sight in the shadows of the alley.

Moments later, the guard opened the back door and stepped outside. He was pushing a dolly cart stacked with bags of cash.

Derek watched his accomplice, Messy, mask up and exit the getaway car that was parked three cars back from the armoured truck. Messy stayed low and crept toward the guard. Derek took his cue and snuck onto Raglan Street using parked cars to shield himself. He popped his head out and saw Messy moving toward the guard.

As the guard lifted the cart onto the sidewalk, Messy jumped out of hiding and maced him in the face. The guard reached for his eyes and released the cart into Messy's waiting arms.

Derek peeked his head out to see if the truck's driver was aware of what had just happened. He was reading the paper!

Messy grabbed both the cart and the guard and pulled them behind the truck out of the driver's view.

Derek darted across the street, through traffic, to the back of the armoured truck. He crouched down beside Messy, who was holding the armed guard to the ground.

The second accomplice, Hecky, pulled the getaway car out of his parking spot and drove over to Messy and Derek. He parked in the armoured trucks blind spot and opened the front passenger door.

Derek and his crew drew stares from curious onlookers as Derek tossed the money into the car and shut the door. The armed guard grabbed his gun and took hold of Messy's foot. Derek saw the guard at the last second and hit him in the face with his gun. Several of the onlookers screamed as the guard's blood splatter filled the air.

Derek opened the back door of their getaway car and they jumped inside. "Go, go, go!" yelled Derek.

Hecky eased on the gas and made a right on Renfrew Avenue; Derek could see that the truck driver was still reading the paper! Hecky raced down Renfrew Avenue and passed cross streets Argyle, Lochiel, and Bonnechere Avenue. He then passed a high school where students were leaving early for lunch. They were doing 120km/h in a 40km/h zone. Hecky raced onto Ross Avenue, hopped the curb and flew through the gates that blocked the Millennium Walking Trail. He began to decelerate as he and the boys neared their switch car. They nearly lost control of the car on the loose gravel. Hecky fought to regain control of the car as it fishtailed.

Derek could see the switch car and a third accomplice in the distance. It was R-Luv; he was masked up and ready to go. Hecky raced to the switch car before skidding to a stop next to it.

He popped the trunk for Messy and Derek to retrieve two cans of gas. R-Luv transferred the money from one car to the other while Derek and Messy doused the getaway car in gas. Derek lit a book of matches and the three other boys watched from a distance as he threw the match in the car and ran. The gas ignited as Derek jumped into the driver's seat of the switch.

Derek floored it blowing both stop signs on Lisgar Avenue before turning left onto the road out of town. A dark sea of smothering smoke filtered into the sky covering the tiny town of Renfrew. The matches and gas had torched the getaway car.

October 4th, 2009
TWO

There it is. There it is lined up perfectly. Lined for him on a filthy glass coffee table in a seedy run-down motel. There it is lined up like little white soldiers saluting the man in charge. Derek Sierzant is not in charge. He's a soldier too, and he's being run into the ground by what is on the table. The soldiers are in charge and they have been for a while.

The soldiers have been running him for the past two years. They have run him into the ground, to rock bottom, and he has let them. His home, his life, even his diet, all of it is tainted and gone. The little white soldiers have taken his morals, his convictions and left him a shell of what he was.

He has undergone a physical and psychological transformation that has left him unrecognizable. No longer is he the lean, clean-cut preppy kid with piercing blue eyes who left home in chase of a dream. He has become a tanned, muscular, tattooed monster, with shoulder length whisky coloured hair and a beard fit for a caveman. His mariner-blue eyes have been left sunken, emotionless and beady. Derek Sierzant is twenty-four years old and he has nothing – nothing but money and his crew. Nothing inside of him but cocaine, beer and Doritos.

He holds up his hand to shade his eyes from the morning light piercing through the torn motel curtains. It's 6:00 a.m. and he has been at it for too long and he's not stopping. He rails more rackit, sits back on his unmade bed and kicks off his shoes to let his feet breathe. He's lost his sense of smell from too much junk, but he knows they stink. He loves high-tops and ball caps and usually pairs them with jeans and a t-shirt. He is the kind of man you'd notice on the street, his wrestler shoulders draw stares, but his clothes make him less memorable.

Derek sits back on his bed and reflects on how the last two weeks of running have been a microcosm of his existence. He has run from everything in his life. He's burned money and friends. If you want to create separation you have to burn bridges. Derek has had to create and improvise without any help. No friend wants a cokehead sleeping in their living room, especially one that has heat on his trail and another cokehead for his sidekick. Lucky for Derek he doesn't need a place to crash. He is the richest man no one knows about. He leans forward and breaks off another line with his credit card. Back to it he goes.

There it is. There it is in a perfect little line. He fills his nose through his fifty-dollar tooter. It has put him where he is – holed up, scared and struggling to survive. He's using a fifty because he and his boys are flush with cash they can't spend. It would bring heat to their door if they did.

Up, up, up his nose, up his nose their money goes, up his nose and in his head. What a rush! The adrenaline hits him and he feels it immediately. He'd be ready to take on the world if he could take on the day. For him the kick feels the same as it did earlier in the kitchen, off the coffee table before that, or off the glove box in the car. That feeling hits hard and Derek feels fantastic, he'll feel good for the next twenty minutes. He has done more today than ever before. He started the day with an eight and then Messy showed up with an additional ball.

Derek takes another bump and his mind begins to wonder about all the time and money he has let dope and women take from him.

Drugs have become too easy to get in Canada. Messy and Derek rolled into Canmore and within an hour of arriving they were bumping out lines in the bathroom. Derek's three and a half grams are nearly done and it's early yet.

He is startled by a loud knock outside the bathroom. He knows who is outside the door. He can hear his dog tags bouncing off the wood of the door. Seconds later it swings open and there stands Jyoshi Masih, or Messy, as he likes to be called. He steps into the bathroom and smiles a mouth full of perfectly carved out dazzling white teeth. His glossy brown eyes lock with Derek's; he's fucked.

Messy is twenty-seven, and much like Derek, he is a lost soul. Messy is lost for reasons that are similar to Derek's. They met four years ago in college and quickly realized they were much the same. Messy is lost, as is Derek. Messy is fucked up, Derek too. Messy admits he points his finger at society and God for his problems, ditto for Derek. They don't feel accountable for their actions. Helicopter parenting will raise an entitled child and entitled children make shitty adults. Derek and Messy are as shitty as they come.

Messy grew up as the only brown kid in a very white area of the country. His parents moved to Pembroke when he was five and he has spent his entire life standing out in a room. He spent two years in Afghanistan, but he wasn't welcomed back. He can use a gun, but he's always been shitty at taking orders especially when the order is to kill other brown people. Messy stands in the bathroom doorway in his pink dress shirt and sweater vest combo. He is built like a bullnecked brick shithouse. Messy's acorn coloured eyes are bloodshot and his curly black hair has a layer of grease on it. He hasn't showered in days. His jeans have white powder on them from his daily activities and he has beer dripping from his chiseled jaw.

"Jesus Christ, Messy, try getting some of that shit in your nose."

"I had a spill," replied Messy.

Derek looked Messy up and down. "Why are you dressed so nice?"

"I decided earlier that I wanted to look nice for our dealer."

"Oh, that ship sailed awhile ago."

Messy laughed and walked over to the couch and had a seat. Derek followed. Messy stretched out his 6'4" frame and took a sip of a beer. He is lighter these days than he once was. A cocaine diet will shed the pounds faster than anything JC can sell you. He waited his turn with the tooter as sweat rained down from beneath his hat. He grinned at Derek; he was high. "What do you mean that ship sailed awhile ago?" asked Messy.

"I dunno, bro, I think I was trying to make a joke or something," replied Derek.

Messy smirked and pointed at Derek. "I think you've done enough." He stood up, walked over to Derek and playfully pushed him out of his way.

Derek stood up and turned the makeshift tooter over to Messy. He tried to walk to the cooler located on the other side of the room. Everything moved quickly for him. The faster he moved, the more he felt like a sprinter closing in on the last few meters of a race. His finish line was an MGD. With fingers gripped onto the lid of the cooler he wrestled it open, dunked his hand into the ice water and grabbed onto a beer. The cold struck his skin and sent a shiver down his spine, his heart accelerated. Grabbing his chest in pain, he pulled his hand out from the cold and paused. After composing himself he stood to his feet and took a seat on the couch in the living room.

Derek took a sip of beer. Flavourless. His senses were shutting down; he tasted and felt nothing. It had been far too long that he'd felt nothing. Numbness had become one of the few feelings he could remember. It had consumed him and made him a zombie, and much like the walking dead he wanders aimlessly about, always numb, feeling nothing. Nothing is what he has amounted to. Nothing is what he is worth. Nothing feels real and for Derek everything needs to change.

Mistakes have been made – the kind he can't turn his back on – the haunting kind of mistakes. These two men have left a path of destruction the last two years. Choices were made, and they usually made the wrong one.

Derek's friends call him Sarge because of his last name, which means Sergeant in Polish. The irony is not lost on him. He and Messy are on the run and every cop in Canada is on the lookout for his six-foot, 208-pound frame. They just don't know who he is or where to find him.

In the last 18 months Derek has gained over 35 pounds. His once oversized hoodies now cling tightly to his shredded biceps. His family wouldn't recognize him if they had to pick him out of a lineup, or the morgue – neither of which are out of the realm of possibility.

Derek's parents came to Renfrew, Ontario from Warsaw, Poland. His Father, Peter owned a large electrical business and the family were firmly entrenched in the middle class. His Mother, Lena, was a stay-at-home mom.

His relationship with his parents was typical for a small-town family: dinner at 5:30 p.m., camping in the summer and mass every Sunday.

In his early teens Derek rebelled. Church became repulsive, camping was annoying and dinner at 5:30 turned into him and his buddies going to McDonald's after hot boxing his car.

His Father Peter used to tell him stories about a Polish thief named Zagadka. Zagadka was a legendary second story man, car thief and bank robber who was never caught or identified. Peter used to say that the joke in Germany was to visit Poland because your car was already there. As Derek grew older, he became tired of Peter's tall tales.

At 12 years old he began dating Kristy. They met in school and fell in love. She was a beautiful young woman with glossy tanned skin, and auburn hair that crashed over her shoulders. Her bouncy personality always had Derek's attention. They were their school's Romeo and Juliet.

At 16 Derek moved out of his parents' home to play hockey and live with his billet family.

After his hockey career ended, he moved into a run-down apartment in Ottawa with Kristy. For the next two years he bounced from job to job and place to place following her until they ended up in Thunder Bay.

Thunder Bay was a blue-collar town in Northern Ontario, located hours from any other major city. Derek loved it. Kristy went to Lakehead University and he enrolled in film school. They continued to date well into college.

Derek thought back to all the time he has spent regretting women he's been with and pining for a woman he's never met. Women have always appreciated his sensitive side and willingness to be open. He isn't a bad person; he just does bad things.

Messy and Derek didn't meet until college, despite growing up in nearby towns. They met when they were paired up on the same team in their recreational hockey league.

Messy went to school for journalism after his military stint. He was a guy that could entertain a table at the bar. He and Derek understood one another. They rejected small town life to chase crazy dreams, they were discovering the way they saw the world. They knew they had a different point of view than everyone else. They were both staunchly opposed to war and the drug war. They liked freedom and hated the idea of tyranny.

Derek had many detractors when he chose to enroll in film school. Everyone doubted his decision and he intended to make the doubters eat crow. His goal was to score films; he was a very talented guitarist and singer and he knew his future lay in music. That was Derek's end game. He didn't care what he did on a film set, he just wanted to be part of the process and get paid to do it.

December 2007

Derek walked into ScuttleButts Bar for his final night as a college student. He'd graduated and he was gone. He sat at a table with the two men to whom he'd become attached at the hip.

The first boy was Ryan Ludhani from Winnipeg. Ryan and Derek became buddies instantly. Ryan, or R-Luv as he liked to be called, was one of the most unique people Derek had ever met. He was the conscience of their group, the stabilizing force that kept them all together. He was 5'11, husky and of Native descent. He kept his scraggly hair long and wore a thick caveman beard. He wasn't interested in women, which helped him get women. He aspired to work as a director of photography. He'd hoped to, one day, film a documentary about his parent's struggles growing up in Northern Manitoba on a reserve.

The other gent at the table was Riley Heckman, often referred to as Hecky. He was the shortest member of the group, standing at about 5'9. He had short red hair that was nearly shaved off, and skin as white as a bed sheet. He always kept himself tidy and well groomed. He was the anti-R-Luv, in both personality and appearance. Like Messy, he was the son of a cop. He was the brains of the group, the most driven and the best communicator. Hecky was the only one of the boys who grew up in Northern Ontario. He hoped to be a film director.

R-Luv, Hecky and Derek had spent two years cutting their teeth in every aspect of the film industry. They had big dreams and big plans.

Messy joined the three boys later in the evening. His hands were cut and he had a black eye. "What the hell happened to you?" asked R-Luv.

"I found the wife fucking some clown," replied Messy.

The three boys looked at each other, confused. "Did you hit her?" asked Derek.

"No, you dummies. I hit the guy she was banging. Pour me a pint."

Messy sat down with the boys in a corner booth. They spoke loudly above the Sean Paul mixes that echoed throughout the poorly lit bar.

"Where you going next week, Sarge?" asked Messy.

"Shouldn't you be talking about your feelings?" asked Derek.

"I let my fists talk out my feelings with that dudes face." Messy sipped his beer and turned back to Derek. "Where you going next week?"

"Not really sure, home I guess," said Derek without conviction. Home was his only option; it meant making tape in a plant until he figured it out.

"Nothing there for either of us," remarked Messy.

Derek knew that, but money was tight and he dreaded asking his parents for more after they'd helped him through school. His only other option was to go further in debt, but he didn't want to do that just to fulfill his dream of moving to Vancouver.

Derek studied R-Luv's rainbow-coloured drink. "R-Luv, you have to stop drinking joke liquor."

"That's your opinion, Sarge," replied R-Luv.

"My opinion carries weight."

"You know what my Dad used to say about opinions?" asked Hecky.

"I'll bet it was racist," shouted Messy.

"Opinions are like dicks, only men should have them, and women should shut up and admire them."

"Jesus!" shouted Derek. "Your Dad is the worst."

"He's a nice guy, you just have to look at him as a whole," said Hecky in defense of his Father.

"Yeah, an asshole!" shouted Derek.

Hecky laughed off the ribs and took a sip of beer. "I guess this is as good of time as any to say I'm moving to Whistler".

"Really?" asked Derek.

"Yeah, man." he answered. "Dad got hired to work security for the Olympics so we're moving to Squamish when I wrap up."

Lucky bastard, thought Derek. Here he was packing up to move back to Renfrew with Kristy. All of his job applications were to factories while Hecky talked about joining the film union and starting his career.

After the bar Messy walked to Derek's apartment and they cracked open two beers in his living room.

"I spoke to my folks," said Messy. "I am going back home."

Derek took a sip of his fresh beer. "What did you say to them?"

"I said I'd go home. Maybe I'd go be a cop. What'd you say to yours?"

"I told my Dad if he forced me to go home, I was going to oversee the production and distribution of knees to his groin."

Messy laughed. "What about Kristy?" he asked.

"Kristy wants me to postpone going West so she can start work."

"Brutal."

"Yeah, it's not ideal."

"Do you ever worry about her breaking it off again?" asked Messy.

"I mean, yeah, but things were different then."

"True," replied Messy as he reached into his pocket and pulled out an eight ball of cocaine. He soft tossed it on the coffee table in the middle of the room. "You want to blast off?"

"What the fuck?" asked Derek. "Six seconds ago you were saying you might go be a cop."

"No. That was a lie."

"Jesus, dude. You can't be getting into that shit," said Derek as he walked over to the kitchen and poured a drink. He pulled up a folding chair beside the couch, "You have the most addictive personality I've ever seen. Didn't you get bounced from the force for having a pill problem?"

"I didn't have a problem. They had the problem."

Derek took his shot and grinned. "Yeah, with you doing too many fucking pills."

At sunrise they stumbled down the street to Subway. Messy was beaten, but he remained hopeful as he sat in a booth eating a breakfast sandwich. "I'm going West, Sarge."

Derek looked up from his meal. "Did you just decide that now?

"What's holding me back? I might as well join Hecky out there. Maybe I'll get some security work with his Dad or some news stuff."

*   *   *   *   *

The following day Derek met up with Kristy at The Prospector. The restaurant looked like an old-fashioned New York steakhouse. Derek admired the craftsmanship of the interior as he and Kristy were led to a back booth.

Kristy was happy and excited to be moving home.

Shortly after dinner they were enjoying cheesecake when Kristy talked about Messy. "You know, I'm not surprised Jess did that to him."

"What makes you say that?"

"She was very insecure. Selfish."

"I never noticed that, short of her being rude and inconsiderate."

After the meal they left the restaurant and began walking to Derek's car. Kristy became silent and withdrawn. She had yet to speak since they talked about Jess and Messy. Derek knew something was up. "Are you okay?"

Kristy looked at him and stopped walking. He stopped alongside her. Tears began to fall from her face onto the sidewalk below. "Derek, I have been thinking about this for a long time." Derek looked at her, confused. She continued, "The accumulation of school ending and the past few events in our life have made me realize that this isn't going to work out forever."

Derek squinted and stepped back from Kristy. "You mean us?"

Kristy wiped the tears from her eyes with the back of her hands. "I want things from life, you want things from life and our futures don't match."

"Yes, they do."

"Derek, stop." Kristy took a breath, he turned away from her and rubbed his head. She continued, "I didn't want to come here, but it was the only place for both of us." Derek turned back to face her, she continued, "I don't want to force you to move home because it suits me."

A young couple walking hand-in-hand walked past Derek and Kristy, interrupting their conversation. Derek watched for them to step out of earshot. "What about what I want?"

"What do you want, Derek?"

"You," replied Derek, pointing to Kristy with his right hand.

"We are never going to keep each other happy. No matter what we do, we will never be fulfilled."

"We'll make it work," replied Derek in a certain tone.

"Derek, I don't want to make it work." Kristy paused and wiped more tears from her face with her sleeves. "You shouldn't want that either."

"My career and all that shit will always come second and that's fine."

"Derek, we only get one shot at this life, and I don't want you to spend it wondering what might have been."

Derek began to cry. He hid the tears by putting his hands on his forehead. "Kristy, I don't care. I'll shoot weddings if I have to."

Kristy gestured wildly with her hands. "You say that now but I'm saving us a lot of wasted years."

"You are throwing us away."

"Derek, I did this to you before, and I'm doing it again. It would really be better if you never got tangled up with me ever again."

Derek paused and looked at Kristy. She had tears in her eyes. He began to crumble.

December, 2007
THREE

Derek arrived back at his place and lay down on the futon. The boys blew up his phone with texts that he had no interest in reading. He felt sorry for himself for a few minutes and tried to shake it off. He stood up, walked to the bathroom and felt a jolt of pain radiate up his back. He'd been suffering through sciatica since the summer prior when he injured it playing baseball. He popped some prescription Oxy and washed it down with water. Derek heard a knock at the door. Without waiting for it to be answered, Messy burst inside, "We're going out!"

"I'm not going out, dude."

Messy swarmed Derek and tackled him onto his couch. "What is wrong with you?"

"I just popped meds. I'm tired."

"Sarge," said Messy as he towered over Derek in a full mount, "do you have any more pills?"

"Not for you, fucker."

"Sarge," said Messy in a serious tone, "I know what happened."

"Fuck! Let me go!" Derek wrestled his wrist loose and stood up from under Messy. "How'd you hear?"

"She's out dancing."

"Jesus Christ, already?" Derek stepped away from Messy and shook his head. He walked toward another room, away from Messy.

"Are you still going home?"

"Driving home alone tomorrow."

"Fuck that, Sarge. Fuck Renfrew. Let's go West!" suggested Messy. "Let's get in your car and fucking go!"

"We can't," Derek turned to face Messy. "What about home?"

"Fuck it, Renfrew's full!"

"I don't know, I need time."

"No," replied Messy taking a few steps toward Derek, "you need to go out tonight!"

"I have to get Kristy back."

"Sarge," shouted Messy as he slapped Derek, "she's out there already. It's over. Time to do you."

"A decade, dude. I don't even know how to date."

"Dating is a waste of time. Drinking beer is not!"

"Did you learn that in your one day of being single, Mess?"

"No, I just think that you and I can finally move on to better things."

Messy wasn't going to leave Derek alone. They had a few drinks and hung out at Derek's apartment.

Derek felt lost and confused. He didn't know how to meet a girl; he'd only ever dated one. He popped a second Oxy to help with his back pain. He felt the pill begin to work as he watched Messy busting up his cocaine. Derek wanted in on that.

Derek hadn't done many drugs in his life. He bumped cocaine once when he was 19 and was prescribed OxyContin a year ago. He only took them when the pain was unbearable. Though, he liked them a lot.

Messy began to break up his coke with his credit card. He rolled up a twenty-dollar bill for his tooter and took a bump; he fell back into his couch and exhaled. Adrenaline and delight hit him and he grinned, "It's good! Have some!" He handed the tooter to Derek, who took a small bump. *Holy fuck,* he thought. It packed a punch. Messy took another bump and looked over at Derek, "You should e-mail your folks to tell them you won't be home."

"Dude, stop. I'm still going."

"Why go home? You're going to waste away there."

"Where else can I go?"

"Vancouver!" shouted Messy.

"And do what? Live in my car?"

"No, let's get a place together."

"I can't live with you. I love you, but we'd end up killing each other."

Derek leaned in to take another bump and there was a knock at the door. Messy tossed him a textbook and he placed it on top of the blow. "At least those worthless books are good for something," joked Messy as he walked to the door. He checked his face in the mirror before he answered.

Hecky walked in and slapped Messy in the head, "S'up cunts?" as he sat down next to Derek on the couch.

"Fuck all, drywall," said Messy.

"I couldn't get anyone to come home with me, so here I am."

"I'm not going to bang you, Hecky," joked Messy.

"Why didn't you and R-Luv find a girl to share again?" suggested Derek.

Hecky looked at Derek and laughed. "That happened one time."

"One pig roast is too many," said Messy.

"Hey, it takes two pieces of bread to make a sandwich," replied Hecky.

"Are you here for any reason, Hecky?" asked Messy.

"Yeah, I was wondering if you would want to stay at my folks place in Squamish for a bit and try to look for a place together in Vancouver."

Messy and Derek looked at each other and laughed. "Are you offering or asking?" asked Messy.

"Offering. My parents said that you guys are welcome to stay for a month or two. R-Luvs' coming."

"I'm in!" shouted Messy.

Messy and Hecky looked at Derek and grinned. Derek rolled his eyes. "When do we go?"

"Mid-January."

Derek thought about it for a few moments and realized that there was nothing for him at home. "Fuck it, let's go!"

January 15th, 2008

Messy and Derek took a red-eye from Ottawa International Airport to Vancouver.

Hecky had already landed a position in the special effects department on a small Canadian television show. It wasn't huge, but it allowed him to get his union hours. And it helped that he was being trained in explosives on set.

Within minutes of landing, Derek and Messy were waiting for their luggage by a baggage belt. Derek felt someone sneak up behind him and punch him in the back. "Fuck!" he exclaimed. He knew who it was.

Messy laughed as Derek turned around and gave Hecky and R-Luv a big hug. The boys were elated. It was happening. They were together on the other side of the country!

They retrieved their luggage and walked to Hecky's van in the parking lot. Hecky explained that they had a long drive ahead of them to his folks' place. His parents lived an hour outside of Vancouver, in Squamish.

Squamish had a population of just under 18,000 people and was sandwiched between Vancouver and Whistler. It was well known for tourism and adventure and offered picturesque views of water and mountains.

Derek took his first breath of fresh B.C. air; it was crisp and clean. He could taste the freshness on his tongue like he had just popped a stick of spearmint. They loaded their luggage into the van and piled inside.

Construction work was beginning on the highway's expansion for the Vancouver Olympics in 2010. Derek didn't care. He was optimistic about his fresh start. The film industry was booming, and he was getting in it at the right time.

Hecky pulled his van into his parents' garage at around 3:00 a.m. They unloaded their luggage and he led them into the house and downstairs to a large recreation room. The room had a modern décor and was equipped with two couches, a coffee table and a TV. Two smaller bedrooms and a bathroom sat adjacent to the room.

"Messy, you and Sarge can stay down here. R-Luv, you can have the room upstairs."

"Why does R-Luv get to be upstairs?" asked Messy.

"R-Luv isn't going to be getting muddy in my parents' bathroom," answered Hecky.

Derek nodded his head and looked over at Messy. Messy grinned and replied, "You're worried I'm going to juice in your Mom's caboose."

"Jesus Christ," exclaimed R-Luv as he shook his head.

Hecky laughed. "Don't even look at my Mom."

"I'll find another old lady to sleep with," said Messy.

"Anyone but my Mom."

October 4th, 2009
FOUR

Derek stood up to navigate his dumpy hotel room. He turned and bumped a piece of luggage. Tens of thousands of dollars scattered on the floor; just a few stacks of the many he and the boys have. This bag has at least sixty grand in it and there are more bags. And the boys have already paid their tax. They knew that they couldn't make a quick getaway with multiple bags of cash, so they each keep a suitcase close by, just in case they spot the heat around the corner. Like Neil McCauley.

The boys have fought, bled and fucking nearly died for the money on the floor. They might die for it yet.

January 16th, 2008

The first morning in Squamish, Derek used his flip phone to take video of the boys seeing the snow-topped mountains for the first time. They felt like kings in a castle, staring down at the rest of the world.

Derek and R-Luv walked into the living room and looked through the huge windows, gazing at the giant picturesque mountains in front of them. Derek walked over for a closer look, admiring the mountains and the beautiful view of the water.

"Jesus!" exclaimed Messy as he walked into the room. "That view."

Hecky walked in the front door and hollered at the boys, "We gotta roll to Van. Get dressed – we'll grab food."

The boys loaded into the van and drove into Vancouver to look at homes Hecky had found online. They toured all over the city but had no luck house hunting. They decided to hit pause and start fresh the next week.

* * * * *

On Saturday afternoon the boys boozed hard well into the evening. After working on a nice buzz they called for a taxi and took a ride out to a local bar that Hecky had raved about. They rolled in at around 11 p.m. It was empty, much to Hecky's chagrin.

They stood at a table near an empty dance floor, nursing beers. Messy looked around the empty bar and shook his head. "Is it always this busy?" asked Messy.

"Shut up," Hecky shot back.

"You know the crazy part is that I think Hecky fucked everybody here," joked Derek.

"Both of them?" asked Messy, sarcastically.

"I gotta have a smoke," said Hecky, "We should bounce."

"Make sure you hold the door open for those ladies when you take them out with you," said Messy.

"Yeah, Heck," said Derek, "show them chivalry's not dead.

"Oh, chivalry's dead," said Messy, "and feminism killed it."

The boys finished their beers and cabbed back across town to another bar. R-Luv sat in the front with the Cabbie while Hecky sat sandwiched between Messy and Derek in the backseat.

R-Luv turned around to face the boys. "I think we can all agree that Hecky never picks the bar again."

"Shut up, R-Luv. And why am I stuck riding bitch?" asked Hecky.

"Bitch sits bitch," joked Messy.

"Messy, stop crowding me." Hecky turned up his nose. "Jesus, you stink! You actually smell like you masturbated at the dump."

"Nope. I did, however, end my consecutive days with a shower streak at one."

"Gross," replied Hecky. "Boys, I promise you this place will be better!"

"It can't be worse," said Derek.

The taxi pulled up in front of The Bar. The boys exited the cab, walked inside and paid cover. The Bar was a large sports bar that had multiple pool tables and walls that were plastered with flat screen televisions.

The boys did a quick survey of their surroundings. The survey showed a 3/1 girl-to-guy ratio, which was good news for the boys. Messy led them through the crowd to an empty table along the wall where they sat down.

"Why didn't we come here first, Hecky?" asked Derek.

"Too far," replied Hecky.

The boys ordered shots. When their waitress came to the table Derek dropped a stack of money on her tray. They distributed their shots and caught the attention of a table of girls adjacent to them. Messy looked over to the table and cracked a smile. "You ladies want to do a shot?"

The ladies stood up to approach the boys. Everyone grabbed a shot, clinked glasses and slammed it. The girls returned to their table.

"Drink and run!" shouted Messy, to several smiles from the girls. The girls continued to flirt with Messy. Three of them were cute; one was not.

Messy turned back to the boys, "Someone has to tackle the D.U.F.F."

Messy, Riley and Derek shouted, "Not it".

"Goddammit," shouted R-Luv.

"Nice, R-Luv!" shouted Messy.

One girl approached the boy's table. She was a cute, confident, brunette. She had a bump in her step as she approached Derek and looked up at him with Bambi eyes. "Do you think ordering shots impresses people?"

Derek looked to the boys, "I'm not trying to put on a show, just playing catch up with my friends."

She grinned at Derek. "You could drink a whole lot cheaper at home."

"As could you."

She nodded and smiled.

"You know you shouldn't be pessimistic," said Derek.

"What do you mean?"

Derek took a sip of his Zywiec beer and set it down. "I mean that if you hold onto negativity it'll eventually destroy you."

"This world destroys everyone."

"See, that's what I mean," said Derek as he stepped away from her. "You're too negative."

"I'm really not."

"Prove it," said Derek as he smiled and stepped away from her.

She smiled, "I'm Cassie."

"That was better," he said as he walked away. He navigated his way through multiple smokers in the patio before he lit a cigarette. He sat down at an empty table near the edge of the room and looked out the window at the mountains and the moon.

A voice interrupted Derek's daydream. "Can I buy a cigarette?"

Derek turned to see a beautiful woman's smiling face. She was an older, elegant, brunette.

"Help yourself," replied Derek.

The lady held out a loonie and Derek shook his head, no thank you. She pulled out a chair, lit her cigarette and sat down across from Derek.

"I don't usually smoke – rough night tonight!"

"I'm sorry to hear that," replied Derek as he grabbed his phone and quickly texted Messy to get out to the smoking section ASAP.

Messy had fantasized for years about sleeping with a woman in her forties. Derek didn't like to sleep with vulnerable women. Messy did.

She and Derek were chatting quietly when Messy showed up at the table. He took one look at the lady and grinned at Derek. He knew the play. Messy sat down with them, took a cigarette from Derek's pack and lit it. Over the next few minutes they chitchatted before Derek excused himself. He walked into the bar and noticed that Hecky was sitting at their booth alone, playing on his cell phone and nursing a beer.

Derek stopped at the bar and bought two more Lech premium beers. He turned and bumped into Cassie again. "Are you guys staying here or are you going elsewhere? she asked.

"I don't know. What about you?"

"Not sure."

Cassie had written her cell number down and handed Derek the small sheet of paper.

"Text me later. We can hang?"

"For sure!" replied Derek. He took the piece of paper and kept walking to the booth without looking back. Hecky saw him and slid over to make room. Derek sat down.

Hecky grinned, "What was that?"

"4:00 a.m. booty call!" joked Derek.

"Not you too!" snapped Hecky.

"Why, what's up?"

"You aren't bringing a girl back to my parents; R-Luv already asked."

"R-Luv found a girl?"

"Yeah," replied Hecky, "he took her back to her place."

"Jesus!"

Derek was digesting that bit of news when Messy walked over and asked, "Can I bring one home?"

"God damn!" replied Hecky, "No!"

"Fuck, Hecky. Please? She's so hot, and old."

"Mess, no. It's weird for me!"

"It's weird that you can't get laid? You never get laid!" joked Derek.

"Shut up!" said Hecky, sternly.

"Want me to see if she'd let you in?" asked Messy.

"No!" yelled Hecky.

Messy held his hand in the air for a high five. "Tag team champions of the world!"

"Gross! No!"

"Fuck, fine!" Messy walked away dejected. Hecky stood up, walked over to the bar and ordered tequila shots. Derek watched Hecky fall apart in front of his very eyes. He slammed his four shots and ordered another four. The bartender shook his head no. Hecky slammed his hand on the bar and the bartender waived over the bouncer who grabbed him and escorted him to the door.

Derek and Messy waited in the bar for ten minutes and then left. They took a cab back to Hecky's parents house and found him at home in bed. Derek quietly closed Hecky's bedroom door and walked down to the kitchen to find Messy texting his girl. Derek followed suit. Messy poured two drinks in the kitchen and they waited.

A few minutes later they both received replies and passed along the address to the girls.

"Where are you taking her?" asked Derek.

"I don't know. You?"

"Hot tub?"

"Do you remember the last time we were in a hot tub?" asked Messy as a grin came across his face.

"Yeah fuck. You came in the hot tub and yelled tape'em up ladies."

Messy grinned. "Yeah, it was hilarious!"

Derek shook his head. "Not if you were in there." Derek took a drink. "I'm taking mine to my room. Make sure you double bag it so you don't end up with osteoporosis."

"Yeah," scoffed Messy. "As if I'm going to wear a condom."

Messy's girl arrived first and they went downstairs to the rec room. Messy told Derek that he would text him when they went into his bedroom so Derek would be in the clear to bring Cassie downstairs.

Derek waited patiently for her to arrive; he was nervous. He took an Oxy to help with his ailing back.

Cassie texted at 2:15 a.m., *here!*

Derek opened the door and she walked inside. He checked his phone; Messy gave him the all clear. He took Cassie's coat, "Can I get you a drink?"

"Sure, whatever you are having?"

"I'm going to have a Lodzkie."

"Okay. I'll have whatever that is."

Derek grabbed their drinks and led her to the basement. He took the last step at the bottom of the stairs and she spun him around and kissed him. They began making out and he picked her up and walked her over to the bed in his room. Derek began breathing through his nose; the smell of her skin and the scent from her hair drove him crazy. He laughed as she bit his lip and locked on. She began to unbutton his shirt. With every button undone she kissed his chest. Her soft lips made the peach fuzz on his chest stand straight up. Derek pulled his shirt off and threw it on the floor.

He could hear that Messy had soft rock playing in the background. Under the mask of the music he heard Messy smashing his headboard into the wall. S*ick fuck,* thought Derek.

Josh Cybulski

Cassie ripped her top off and pulled Derek on top of her as she lay back on the bed. Moments later they began having sex and Derek discovered quickly that she was loud. They had sex for ten, twenty, thirty, forty minutes. Changing positions three times until they took a water break.

Derek went to the bathroom and took another Oxy for his back before he took a piss. He opened the door to exit and Messy was standing in front of the door in nothing but his boxers. He grinned at Derek. "She showed!"

"She did."

"Mine's louder," smirked Messy.

"Your girl is a hundred."

"Yeah, she is!"

"How was it?" Asked Derek.

"It was everything I thought it'd be, that's why it lasted 36 seconds."

Derek walked to his room and walked inside. He could hear Messy banging the headboard against the wall again. Cassie heard it too. She looked over at the wall and back at him. "Is that your roommate?"

"Yup."

"Fuck, we can be louder," Cassie smiled at Derek and he smiled back. "Get on top," she demanded. Cassie lay on her back and Derek climbed on her and they began having sex. She started moaning before eventually starting to scream. She paused for a second and grabbed the headboard.

They started again, together as one smashing the headboard into the wall as she screamed and moaned. Derek could hear Messy and his girl getting louder. He knew he was hitting the headboard as hard as he could. For the next half-hour both couples went back and forth smashing the headboard as hard as they could.

Derek woke to the sun shining through the window into his eyes. His thoughts were water, piss, Tylenol, water, food, shower, water, sleep. He left his room and walked upstairs to the kitchen. He popped a few pills and drank some water. He got his bearings straight, walked back to the bedroom and went inside. Cassie was still naked in bed. He took a look at her and then took a longer look at a massive hole in the wall behind the bed. The entire frame of the headboard had penetrated the wall. *Fuck me!* He moved in for a closer look and upon further inspection noticed that it was a few inches into the drywall – not a simple patch job. Derek then realized that Messy's room could be worse!

Derek raced toward Messy's room and ran inside; Messy was banging his lady from behind. "Don't you fucking stop?" Derek exclaimed.

"Don't you fucking knock?"

"Oh, I'm sorry, but I just noticed the giant fucking holes in the walls!"

Messy's lady scrambled to cover herself with the bed sheets while he jumped off the bed and exposed himself. Derek put up his hands to shield Messy's unit from his view. "Messy, put some fucking pants on!"

"We are not fucked," he said in a calming tone. "We'll head to Horton's, take these girls home then hit the Depot and get some patch up shit."

"Do you know how to patch drywall Messy? Cause I haven't a fucking clue."

"Yeah, man. My Uncle worked in construction."

"Really, Messy, you think that shit is hereditary? Like how I know everything about electrical cause my Dad's an electrician."

"I learned a few things in the service. Look, why you mad, bro? You banged the wall as hard as me, maybe harder-!"

Messy finished his sentence and as he did Cassie opened the door. "Hey, Derek, can I get a ride?"

"Cassie?" asked Messy's lady.

"Oh my God, Mom!" Cassie exclaimed. Messy and Derek's eyes locked and they did everything in their power not to laugh. Cassie was furious. "Mom, this is fucking sick. These guys are half your age!"

"Cassie"—

"Eww, I could hear you doing it!"

Messy chimed in, "Everyone could hear us doing it". He stood with his chin held high. He was pretty proud of himself.

"And what about Dad? You guys aren't even separated!"

"Honey, calm down" said Cassie's Mom. "You know that we aren't together."

Cassie snapped back, "You still live together."

"Oh, Jesus," uttered Derek.

Cassie looked at Derek with a look of utter disgust. "I need to go!"

Messy chimed in, "We'll take you home."

In perhaps the most awkward morning after in the history of morning afters, Messy and Derek used Hecky's van to drive the girls' home, together. They then bought building materials and headed back to the house. They pulled their materials from the back of the van and carried them through the house into the basement. At the bottom of the stairs, R-Luv popped out of nowhere and scared the shit out of the boys.

"Jesus Christ, R-Luv!" screamed Derek. "Where did you come from?"

"Just got in. What's with this shit, you guys building an addition?"

"No, we made a tiny big mistake," said Messy.

R-Luv smiled. "Yeah, I saw the holes. You guys are dummies. Did you try to compete with each other?"

"No, no judgment," said Derek as he wiggled his finger in R-Luv's face.

"How are you going to repaint the wall?" asked R-Luv.

Derek and Messy looked at each other and shook their heads. "Fuck!"

October 4th, 2009
FIVE

For the first time in his life, Derek has more money than he would ever need. He and the boys have thrown their hat in the ring and climbed in to face something they may never understand. They've gone from poor to rich in a matter of months and now live in a world that will take some getting used to. Their anonymity is gone; their freedom to walk without fear is gone. They've brought a world down on them. Being rich has a cost.

They've hit the lottery, but not the lottery where you go to take a picture with the giant check. Not the one where your name and picture get splashed in the headlines. No one in Derek's family is calling him for a dollar. The people knocking on his door will swing an axe to come inside. None of the money can be touched; most of it is inaccessible. If he were to go after it, many alarms would go off. Too many people are out there looking for his stacks.

Derek is pining for his big stacks and his fresh start. In the meantime, he gets to sit in a shitty hotel on his little stack of cash and have no fun. Well, some fun. He can still buy drugs! No drug dealer on earth has ever asked where the money came from.

The Monday after their crazy weekend, the boys went to Vancouver to look at more potential rentals.

The first two homes they looked at were complete dumpster fires located in bad neighbourhoods. The third home was a four-bedroom, two full bath, two-storey home in an industrial area of Burnaby. It was renting for $2,250 a month, plus utilities: a bargain in Greater Vancouver. The home had three bedrooms upstairs and one on the main level. Two of the bedrooms had adjoining walls. Hecky joked that Messy and Derek could hear each other if one of them had a girl over...

After some discussion, the boys decided that the third house would be the best spot for them to live.

They signed a lease and got set to move!

*   *   *   *   *

The following evening, Hecky tried to rally the boys for a night at the rippers. R-Luv took the night off while Hecky dragged Messy and Derek to a dirty Squamish strip club. Hecky was hunting for more than just lap dances; he was on the hunt for blow. Messy and Derek knew it and didn't take issue with it. They had the same plan.

The waitress arrived at the boy's table and they each ordered a beer. After one look around the bar, Derek spotted three drug dealers. One of the dealers was a short, skinny, sketchy little man that was tweaked up on something. He'd be Derek's provider for the evening.

The beers arrived at the table and the boys settled up with their waitress; $9.50 each. They each gave her a ten-dollar bill.

Hecky grabbed his beer and stood up to take a lap. "You coming?"

"No, I'm good," replied Derek.

"C'est la vie," Hecky turned and took off to look for drugs and girls.

Messy and Derek sat quietly at the table, staring at the television in the corner of the bar showing an endless replay of hockey highlights.

Messy looked over at Derek and grinned, "What do you think they have in that office upstairs?"

"Not sure, an abortion clinic?"

"Tommy Stairs: abortionist," joked Messy in a thick Brooklyn accent.

Derek laughed and looked back at the television. The boys stared at the TV and nursed their beer for nearly an hour. Derek discretely popped his last Oxy.

Messy caught a glimpse and grinned. "What was that?"

"Tylenol, I've got a headache."

"It was not!"

"Fine fuck, it was an Oxy."

"You have any more?"

"No, I took them all."

"The whole bottle?"

"Yeah," answered Derek.

Messy wanted to score and leave, but he knew he couldn't walk up to a stranger and ask for cocaine. Derek wanted more as well. He watched the tweaker dealer walk to the bathroom and he knew he had a chance to score. "I've got to hit the head," said Derek.

"Yeah, dude. I'm going to circulate," replied Messy.

The boys stood up from their seats and walked through the crowd in different directions. Derek walked into the bathroom and checked under the stalls to see if the tweaker and him were alone. They were. The tweaker stood at a urinal. Derek walked up to the stall beside him and began pissing. "You holding?"

The tweaker looked Derek up and down and nodded his head.

"I think I'm going to get one rye and coke from the bar with the money in my back pocket."

The tweaker nodded his head, zipped up, threw a gram of blow on top of the urinal and reached his hand in the back pocket of Derek's jeans. He took his money, washed up and left. Derek tucked his gram away in his back jeans pocket.

He wasn't even one step out of the bathroom when he bumped into Messy and stopped. Messy was holding a glass of water and looked to be in a panic. "Are you drinking a water?" asked Derek.

"Yeah, I'm thirsty!"

"Dude, that's got to be the filthiest water on earth!"

Messy snapped back, "Dude, we got bigger problems. Hecky has been with a stripper for eight songs."

"He has money. He didn't have to pay to renovate his parent's house."

"Do we leave him in there?"

"Give him ten minutes. If he doesn't come out, we bounce."

Messy and Derek went back to their table and waited for thirty minutes before they left the bar and took a cab back to Hecky's parents.

Derek lay down and stared at the ceiling. He had little desire to start bumping lines by himself. He rolled over and went to sleep.

At 4:00 a.m. he woke up to the sound of Hecky and Messy laughing outside his door. He needed to go out and control them.

He opened his bedroom door and walked out into the rec room to find Messy and Hecky bumping lines off the coffee table. Hecky was speaking loudly, "She said she really likes me."

"Who's this?" asked Derek as he sat down on the couch.

Messy laughed. "The stripper."

"That's great, Hecky. How many twenties did you feed her to say that?"

Messy slid over and Derek sat beside him. Hecky wasn't pleased with Derek's stripper quip.

"This was after, dude. We were out having a smoke." Hecky began explaining how he got her number. Derek lost interest, rolled up a twenty and bumped a line of the boys' blow.

Messy looked at Derek and grinned.

Hecky paused mid-sentence and exclaimed, "After all the shit you gave me. You fucking hypocrite!"

Derek was caught red handed. "Fuck off, I was just breaking balls. I'm not busting you about the stripper thing though, that's fucked up."

Messy chimed in, "You were pretty hard on him and now you come in and do it with us like it's nothing."

"Would you rather I sit here not doing it? Maybe I could stare and make you uncomfortable?"

"Just sit here and shut up," said Messy.

"You can hang out here, you cokehead!" added Hecky.

"Are you and that stripper going to have kids?" joked Derek.

"If I ever have kids I'm going to feed them yeast so they raise themselves," said Messy.

"Call the number," said Derek.

Hecky pulled his phone and a piece of paper from his pocket and dialed the number. He put his phone on speakerphone. The phone rang twice and the call was picked up on the other end. A woman's voice spoke, "The number you have dialed is not in service, please try your call again".

Hecky hung up. "Fuck!"

"Try again," said Messy.

Hecky dialed the number again, slower this time. "The number you have dialed is not in--" Hecky shut the phone mid-sentence.

"Goddammit!"

"What'd you expect?" asked Derek.

"Well, my intention wasn't to marry her. I just wanted to bring a girl home. For once!"

Messy cut in, "Paying a girl to mash her tits in your face isn't a good way to pursue women."

"Lots of time for practice when we get to Van," said Derek. "Now mash up a line. I want to fire it up!"

October 4th, 2009
SIX

Messy sat on the couch eating Doritos and nursing a beer. He and Derek needed sun. They were stir-crazy; sitting in a hotel room for 72 hours straight will do that. The morning news played on TV and they've been all over it for days. Not the way they envisioned getting famous.

February 1st, 2008

     The boys moved to Vancouver on a Friday. They shopped for mattresses before Hecky dropped them at the new house with all of their belongings. He returned to Squamish for the weekend to go skiing. He would move in the following Monday.

     R-Luv, Messy and Derek spent their first hours in the house getting things in order. Derek cooked Shrimp Alfredo and garlic bread for supper and they watched a movie on Messy's laptop before turning in for the night.

     Derek went back to his room and lay in his bed staring at the ceiling. He began to wonder what he'd got himself into. Here he was 5,000 km away from home in a place totally foreign to him, chasing a crazy dream.

     He heard a commotion downstairs, followed by some laugher. He walked downstairs to the living room and found Messy and R-Luv drinking. Messy was lying on the bare floor and R-Luv was sitting on a paint bucket that the landlord left behind.

     "What's going on?" asked Derek.

     "We've got no money, no jobs, no furniture. I'm sick as fuck but I'm drinking anyways," said Messy.

"You're just a fucking treat eh, Mess?" Derek grabbed a glass and made himself a rye and coke. He lay on the floor on the other side of the living room, opposite Messy. R-Luv sat between them. "We moved 5,000 kilometers for this eh boys, fuck!"

"It's still better than what I would be doing in Pem," said Messy.

"Likewise," said R-Luv.

"Hey, thanks for dinner dude," said Messy, "It was great."

"Homemade shrimp, dude. What could be better?" said Derek with a straight face.

"Yeah, it was phenomenal," said R-Luv before doing a double take and looking back at Derek. "Wait, what?"

"No, it's not a thing," said Derek.

Derek laughed to himself, Messy and R-Luv looked at each other.

"What's so funny, dude?" asked Messy. "The shrimp thing? Not funny."

Derek continued, "No, dude. We don't have a goddamn thing, and we don't even have a chair to sit in."

"We've got that giant box my futon came in," said R-Luv.

"I've got a mat on the floor with one blanket," joked Messy. "I hope you are prepared for some just-friends spooning if I get cold."

"I'll never be prepared for that," replied Derek.

"I don't even have drawers to put my clothes in. The only thing I own is this goddamn drink, and it's a rental," said Messy.

"I don't even know if I can afford deodorant," said R-Luv.

"That's fine," said Derek. "You deserve to smell as bad as you look."

*   *   *   *   *

The next day the boys woke up around noon. Derek made breakfast and afterward they boarded a train and did a lap of the entire city. They saw some of Vancouver's beauty and some of its filthy underbelly.

They returned to the house, showered and dressed for the evening ahead. Messy threw on something pink, R-Luv threw on something denim and Derek put on jeans, a button-down shirt and a sports jacket.

They sat on the living room floor playing cards and talking about what lay ahead. Monday morning meant job hunting, reality, stress, bills and bullshit.

The boys called a cab to go to a nightclub near the mall in Coquitlam.

There were a few people in line when the boys arrived. At 10:05 p.m., Derek looked at his watch, "Goddamn, it is so early to be at a bar." He lit a cigarette and took a deep drag. A group of five girls lined up behind him. The girls were all pretty cute, and one in particular caught Derek's eye. She had sunrise-gold hair and blossom soft lips. She was a rebellious dresser, dressed in heels, jeans, a tank top, and a leather jacket that covered her tattoos.

Derek turned to her and grinned. "You wanna get out of here?"

She looked at Derek. "That's kinda forward."

"Nah," Derek scoffed, "I meant to a different bar. One with no line. Besides, you aren't my type."

"I'm everyone's type," she replied.

"Why's that?" asked Derek.

"Cause I'm hot," she replied.

Derek laughed, "I'm Derek."

"Tiffany."

*　*　*　*　*

The next morning Derek woke up naked on the floor of a movie theatre in a house he'd never been in before. The room was pitch black except for a small sliver of light coming in below the door. "Tiffany?" He called out looking for her to turn on a light. No answer. Derek stood up and felt the wall for a light switch. He shuffled carefully toward the light, located the door handle and opened it.

Outside the theatre in the open space, five girls from the night before were sipping on coffee and staring at Derek's naked body. He closed the door as quick as he had opened it and went back inside. He left it open just enough to locate his clothes and get dressed. He walked out to greet the girls. "Good morning ladies."

"Good morning" they replied.
"What are you up to?"
Tiffany answered, "Just talking."
"Oh yeah? Where are the boys?"
"You tell us," answered one of Tiffany's friends.
Derek pulled out his phone. Three text messages.
R-Luv and Messy texted at 5:00 a.m. R-Luvs' text read:

Sorry Sarge, I had to get out of there. I banged those two girls. Never had a threesome before. I felt weird after, they will definitely need to change their sheets. Anyway, I didn't really want to see them in the morning. Sorry to abandon you. Hope it's okay.

Derek couldn't blame him. R-Luv hadn't slept with many girls so two in one night and three in a week was a whirlwind for him. Messy's text read:

Hey Fuckface,
After I steamed their lenses, I didn't want to share a bed with them so I bailed. Any girls that double up on me aren't worth my time. Sorry to leave you. Hopefully you bail too before you have to do the walk of shame!

"Nothing from them," said Derek. Tiffany smiled at Derek as he started to walk toward the staircase; he turned to the girls and smiled.
"Take care, ladies!"
Derek ran upstairs and left the house. He sprinted all the way home.
He walked into the house, kicked his shoes off, and locked the door. He could hear Messy and R-Luv talking, their voices became louder as Derek walked in the kitchen. The boys were having a morning coffee on the floor.
"Pot is full, bud," said Messy.
"Pot is full?" Derek asked in a sarcastic tone. "You guys totally fucked me back there!"
"What?" replied R-Luv. "I'm no expert but I'm pretty sure you're the only person I didn't fuck last night!"
"Bingo," said Messy.
Messy and R-Luv laughed as Derek walked into the kitchen and poured himself a cup of coffee. "You guys finally fucked each other, eh? Who was the bottom?"

R-Luv and Messy looked at each other and smirked. R-Luv turned back to Derek. "Did it take the whole morning to find your dignity?"

"I just kept circling over and over asking myself, if I was dignity where would I be?"

"Somewhere back in Coquitlam, I think." joked Messy.

The boys continued to chirp Derek about how right they were to leave. He wasn't having it. "Messy, you just revel in amorality."

"What that mean?" asked Messy.

Derek shook his head and smirked. "Ugh, I hated that girl."

"Yo," said Messy, "she told R-Luv she was in school. What school would have her?"

"I don't know, dude. The Georgian Institute of Culinary Hairdressing."

October 4ᵗʰ, 2009
SEVEN

Derek's pulse raced more than usual. It's not coming down and he needs to stop. That'd be just what his parents need; to find out that he overdosed on coke, next to a huge bag of cash. His biggest fear was his family finding out what he's been doing.

But no one knows it was Derek, no one knows it was Messy. Their faces aren't splattered on the news or in the papers yet, though they might be soon.

February 2008

Monday morning, the boys woke up hung-over and in need of jobs.

Hecky had an explosives tech job lined for April 1st on the show he'd worked on previously. The boys pressed him hard to see if there was any shot that they could get on too. They weren't in Vancouver to stock shelves or wait tables. They wanted to be on set and to play music.

The boys' parents began to mail their belongings to them. Messy received his bass in the mail, R-Luv's drums arrived and Derek's parents sent out two guitars.

* * * * *

Later in the week, Derek started looking online for jobs that could take him to shooting season. He applied to twenty or so jobs. Every morning for the next ten days Derek went through this routine. Wake up, apply for jobs, nap, eat, and play music.

Finally, after a few weeks of searching he was given an interview with a liquor store on Hastings Street in Burnaby. The job was stocking coolers and shelves. Simple work.

East Hastings was a notorious area in Vancouver; notorious for all the wrong reasons. Derek had heard stories from locals about the area and had apprehensions about the job.

The store itself was called the Burnaby Liquor Warehouse. It was a giant retail liquor store. The outside was a deep purple and the inside had high-end finishes.

Derek killed the interview and received a job offer at ten dollars an hour. He was happy to have a job and he knew he'd make extra cash in tips.

On the drive home he gloated that he was the first one to lock down a job. Messy and R-Luv were jealous at first, however a few days later R-Luv got offered a job at a camera warehouse.

This left Messy the only jobless one left, which didn't sit well with him. He continued to search online and even started going out with resumes in person in an attempt to land a job.

*   *   *   *   *

Ten days after Derek was hired at the liquor store, his boss approached him and offered him a promotion to be supervisor. The job meant more responsibility with 32 hours a week and $11.25 an hour.

That same day the house phone rang at 6:00 p.m. The call was for Derek and on the other end was his buddy Greg from back home. Greg had moved to Edmonton months before Derek moved and worked on the oilrigs.

Derek answered, "Hello?"

"It's OC," OC meant O'Connor.

"OooooOC!" yelled Derek.

"How's Van?"

"Oh, it's pretty wild so far!"

"I've got next week off. I was going to fly into Van if you are free."

"Yeah, buddy. Do it! I've got a few days off. You can crash on our couch."

"Cool. I'm flying in on Friday."

Derek's excitement was obvious. OC was a good guy who was always up for a good time. Derek loved OC like a brother. They grew up together and their parents remained best friends.

*   *   *   *   *

On Saturday, Derek and the boys took him to Coquitlam for a night on the town. At 2:00 a.m. they left the bar and returned home, hammered drunk. OC climbed the neighbour's tree while Messy let his flag fly in the middle of the street.

The boys went inside the house and walked upstairs to Hecky's room. He started busting up lines for him and Messy, planning to split an eight. Derek also threw an eight in the mix and Hecky and Messy looked at him, "I don't do coke," joked Messy.

"Blow me," said Derek. "No really, give me some blow!"

Hecky busted up the rocks and lined it up with his credit card. He handed Derek a hundred. Derek took the tooter and bumped. "Fuck!" The rush went right to his head.

OC was uncomfortable as he watched them from the doorway.

"You can smoke a joint in here if you want," said Derek.

"Yeah, maybe I will," said OC. He left the room and came back a few seconds later with some weed.

Messy, Hecky and Derek made short work of the first eight ball. They chatted and poked fun at each other. OC poked fun at Derek for being a Voluntaryist.

"You know, OC, if my family all worked for the government, I'd be Liberal too," Derek snapped back before bumping again.

"You keep bumping that shit up your nose and you are going to be as bald as my Uncle."

"I'm fine with that," said Derek.

"Not when you're 30."

"You know, in a socialist utopia the haired would provide wigs for the bald," joked Derek.

"Don't start, Sarge. I get it, you hate government." OC turned to Messy and Hecky. "Has this guy ever given you his long-winded rants on how they lied about the Iraq War?"

"Yeah," said Messy, "he gets most of his shit from me."

"You?" asked OC.

"Yeah," replied Messy, "I was over in Afghanistan for a minute. Everyone would talk about what bullshit it was to go into Iraq."

"So, he's not just talking out his ass?" asked OC.

"Well," said Messy with a sly smile, "not about that."

Derek laughed. "You guys are just choked that my Marty Genetics are superior to your Marty Pathetics."

*   *   *   *   *

The next day Derek woke up at noon and he was in rough shape. Five hours of railers wears you out. He surveyed the damage; there were bottles and remnants of coke everywhere. R-Luv was the only one awake, he was quietly playing Rock Band next to OC who was passed out. He paused his game and fixed Derek a cup of coffee while Derek cleaned up some of the mess.

R-Luv handed Derek his coffee and he took it as he walked to the backyard. Derek sat in a lawn chair and lit a cigarette. He took a deep drag, shut his eyes and relaxed. As he opened his eyes the back door opened and OC walked out.

"What's up?" asked Derek.

"Tired as fuck."

OC sat in one of the lawn chairs and lit a cigarette. He took a drag and blew out the smoke. "Wild night, eh?"

"Yeah, pretty crazy. It's not usually like that. Normally we bang chicks, not railers."

"How often do you guys do that?"

"Not often."

"You must do it enough. You guys each did over two grams."

"That's the first time I've done it since I've been here.

"Alright," replied OC, "Just don't make a habit of it."

October 4ᵗʰ, 2009
EIGHT

Derek wondered if he could even leave the motel room. What if someone was watching? He knew he was more than a little paranoid. It had been days since they left their room and they were both going crazy. He took a shower, hoping it would calm him down. All it did was clean him up. He needed to see a face other than Messy's and have a drink other than beer. It was time for coffee and a real meal.

He looked through the peephole in the door before opening it. He peeked his head out slowly and looked around the parking lot. There were only three cars parked out front and one of them was theirs. He lit a cigarette, stepped outside and shut the door behind him. Smoke filled his lungs as he took a haul. It'd been days since his last smoke. He walked across the street to eat at a mom and pop style diner.

March 2008

On March 1st, the boys had another rent cheque to cut and Messy grew concerned about money. Derek arrived home from work at midnight. Messy was awake watching The Warriors.

Derek sat down on the couch beside him and opened a beer, "I dropped off your resume."

Messy replied, "Thanks, buddy. I got a job actually. It's with a production house down the street."

"Nice, that's awesome!"

"Yeah, I'm excited. It's ten an hour but could be a foot in the door."

Derek sat on the couch feeling jealous. Everyone had an opportunity to have a film job except him.

March 30th, 2008

Hecky received the call he'd been waiting for. Only it wasn't what he had hoped. His shoot was being pushed back a month to start on May 1st. He would get some explosives training before the shoot, but his work term had been cut drastically. He was barely scraping by.

Derek hoped to continue working part-time but even with his raise and tips he was barely breaking even. Messy and R-Luv were going in the hole a little deeper every week.

Messy began pushing hard for the boys to shoot something. They began shooting comedy skits around the neighbourhood and putting them on YouTube but they weren't something they could post on a resume and get work for.

Messy didn't have money to shoot anything, but he did have access to people and gear. It seemed feasible that they could make a film; they just needed capital to make it happen. They were fortunate to be getting paid every Thursday, but by Sunday the money was gone. Even with cutting out the coke money was still tight. They were stuck in a rut. All of that positive momentum from their move had subsided and the real world had crushed them in just two months.

April 25th, 2008

Hecky received the call to start work. The show had been cut from a 13-episode order down to just eight. That meant Hecky's three and a half months of work had become two. Money was already an issue for him and now he wouldn't get his hours to qualify for Employment Insurance when the work ran out.

Hecky was out of work by June 28th. He managed to save a few grand after paying off his debts. But the demand for explosive techs had dwindled.

Messy was getting the odd day call from a guy he'd met who was a Gaffer on B movies.

R-Luv was driving gear around and was unhappy about his job. He began talking about returning to Manitoba when their lease ended to work with his Father up North.

As for Derek, he was promoted to assistant manager in mid-June with a nice little bump in pay. Even with the pay increase he was still constantly broke. It had been a few months and he was no closer to any of his goals and not yet got a sniff of a film set. None of the boys were where they wanted to be.

* * * * *

By mid-July, Derek started to notice some serious security issues within his store. Every night at closing time, around 11:30 p.m., he and his staff would open the exit, lock a gate and set a security alarm. He would then lock the outside door.

The exit door was in a dimly lit alley away from the street with no windows facing it. It seemed easy for a thief to get to them before the alarm was set and force them back inside.

One night after a busy Saturday during the August long weekend he and two cashiers were counting money until midnight when the phone rang. "Hello?" answered Derek, thinking it was a customer inquiry.

On the other end of the line was a security company checking up on things. Their tardiness triggered an alarm. He calmly explained to them that they had a busy day at the store and were just finishing the counts.

That was good enough for them. No security officer showed up to check on things; nothing happened. Derek locked up and left. It seemed that the store was ripe for the picking if a thief were to know about their security issues.

October 4th, 2009
NINE

Derek walked into the diner to enjoy his first real meal in three days. At the front of the diner he was greeted by the hostess and led to a seat at the bar.

The diner had a long bar at the back, and it looked like a classic 60's diner, complete with a throwback theme. The waitresses dressed in 1960's themed dress and the men wore white slacks and shirt with a paper hat.

Derek sat down. The girl working the bar offered him coffee and poured it. The coffee was garbage – diner mud – but not to Derek, not then. Moments later she stopped in front of him and took his order: an extra large platter with three eggs, bacon, ham, sausage, hash browns, toast and brown beans.

Derek looked around the diner and laughed to himself. All his favourite movies had scenes in diners just like this. Robert De Niro meeting Amy Brennaman in Heat. Anthony Edwards discovering a nuclear bomb coming to L.A. in Miracle Mile. Michael J. Fox meeting his Dad in Back to the Future.

After a few minutes his food arrived and not much later he was done. He wiped his mouth and leaned back in his seat; satisfied.

He noticed a girl walk in unescorted, taking a seat at the bar two seats over. She was sharply dressed in a navy-blue pin stripe blazer and jeans. He could only see her back as she confidently walked past him. Her shapely figure caught his attention.

Derek knew it wasn't the best time to try courting a girl; he looked awful and he could taste the bitterness on the back of his tongue from his coke nasal drip. He tried to avoid eye contact. The more he thought about talking to her, the more he decided he shouldn't. His chaos didn't belong in her world.

"Could you pass the sugar?"

Derek felt her cool, soothing voice tingle his insides. Then it hit him. He had to reply. *Fuck!* "Huh?" He asked, startled by her voice. He looked up from his empty plate and locked eyes with her; his jaw nearly hit the floor. She was the most beautiful girl he had ever laid eyes on. Her long sable black hair hit the morning light as she brushed it from her face. It cascaded ever so perfectly over her shoulders and down her back.

He smiled and attempted to speak to her. *Nope.* He continued to stare into her rapture blue eyes that were partially hidden by long velvety eyelashes. Derek couldn't believe what he was looking at. Her eyes were as blue as the waters of St. Thomas. He couldn't find the words to speak. Rarely was he speechless, but looking at her, he was. Everything about her was bright and beautiful. She was the most gorgeous girl he'd laid eyes on.

"The sugar, please?" she asked again, politely with a smile. Almost as if she was used to this.

"Oh, yeah, no problem."

She reached out her hand and Derek handed her the sugar. Their hands touched briefly, and he felt the softness of her skin against his.

"Thanks."

She sat quietly sipping on her coffee. Derek watched her and thought hard about what to say. All he wanted to do was talk to her. What could he say? Every pickup line he knew was meant for trashy girls he would meet at the bar at night. *Do you want to come back to my hotel with my bags of money and drugs?* It seemed fate wasn't on Derek's side; she and he weren't meant to be. He watched her drink her coffee and text on her phone. It pained Derek to know he could never have a girl like her; he didn't deserve one.

August 2008

Tuesday night, after the August long weekend, the boys went out for a night at The Soho. They arrived at the bar and sat outside next to a large fire pit, where they discussed their struggles.

Their lease was up September 30th and Derek was tempted to abandon the whole BC move. The reality was that they couldn't pay their bills. August rent was a few days late and three of them were short.

Derek broached the subject, "Boys, I'm not going to live 5,000 km away from my family to work in retail and pay too much for everything!"

"Yeah, I'm with you," said R-Luv.

"Hecky, you are the only one making headway," said Derek.

"Yeah, I don't know," said Hecky. "With the economy tanking I might be out of work too. They are pulling productions every day, and no one wants to blow shit up no more."

"I've been talking to my boss," said Messy. "Our chances of getting in the union are slim. And without cash to shoot our shit, what's the point?

"It seems so early to throw in the towel," said R-Luv.

"It is, R-Luv," said Derek, "but how long are you willing to keep grinding out paycheques?"

"The rest of the world does it."

"Yeah, but did the rest of the world do what we did? We moved across the country to take a chance. No one is willing to take chances anymore. Shit, people can't even make a choice for themselves anymore."

"You're right," said Messy.

"I won't do it, I won't!" said Derek with conviction. "I won't call my parents either. I refuse. I'm either surviving here on my own or I'll go home and make tape."

"I can't go home," said Messy. "I can't let people there know that this didn't work."

"Neither can I, Messy," said Derek, "but I might have to soon."

That night the boys boozed at The Soho until it shut down. They spilled out drunk onto the street, hopped on a bus and headed home.

They arrived home, popped open more bottles of beer and sat around the living room. The mood was somber. There was only one thing that would lift this crowd, but no one had the money to make it happen and Derek didn't want to give up his stash. His mind had been racing for a few days. His mood and mindset were changing. He worried daily at work that someone was going to rob his store. He had anxiety during every closing shift that he worked.

"You okay?" asked Messy.

Derek paused for a moment. "I'm fine, dude. Just worried."

"About money?"

"Among other things."

"Like what?" R-Luv asked.

"Just work."

"You still like it?" asked Messy.

"I do, I just worry that some night someone is going to rob us."

"Why you think that?" wondered Hecky, jumping in.

"Well, I mean every night I count tons of cash. Last weekend alone we took in twenty-five thousand a day."

Messy chimed in, "You worry someone will come in during counts?"

"No," replied Derek. "After we count. When we are leaving, I mean. Like, our system for leaving is fucked."

"Have you guys ever been robbed?" asked R-Luv.

"No, the store used to be owned by a biker gang, so no one ever fucked with them. Now it's not."

"Crazy!" shouted Hecky.

"I worry about the day someone swings an axe through the door."

"That's surprising," said Messy. "You'd think they would tighten up."

"They are so cheap, dude. If you shoved a quarter down their throat, they'd shit out two dimes."

"Jesus," said Messy.

"Yeah, I have access to all the safes except for the daily drop box. And you could cut through that thing in ten seconds."

"With any luck, you'll be gone before that happens," said Hecky.

October 4th, 2009
TEN

Derek made a quick stop for two more coffees and walked back across the street to his hotel room. He strolled through the hotel parking lot and noticed a brown bloodhound dog wandering the parking lot alone. The dog had no leash or collar on him.

Derek lit a cigarette and approached the dog. The dog looked up at him and paused. Derek stood still and the bloodhound lay down on the ground. Derek slowly approached him and pet him on the head. The dog moaned and groaned as Derek began to rub his ears.

"Where is your owner, boy?"

Derek knelt to one knee and rubbed the dog on the back of his neck. The dog attempted to lick Derek, who withdrew. Standing back up, Derek looked around the parking lot and the dog began to pant heavily. Derek walked toward his hotel room and the dog followed him.

Messy was waiting for Derek at the door; he was a mess. "Is this me?" he asked pointing at the coffee.

"Well, it isn't the dog's," replied Derek sarcastically as he walked into their room. Messy shut the door behind them. Derek grabbed a bottle of water and poured it out into their ice bucket. He opened the hotel room door and set the bucket in the doorway. The dog began to drink it.

"What's with the fucking dog?" asked Messy.

"You need to breeze or fall out."

"I'm not sleeping and I'm not walking, Sarge."

"Dude, it's nice out. Go walk."

"I'm not getting clipped by 5-0."

"I was just out. There isn't a cop in sight," said Derek as he laughed.

"They are playing possum, Sarge. And if you keep going out there flossing, they are going to be in our lunch so fast."

"Messy, I spent eleven dollars. Don't jump the couch, alright. I was hardly suspicious."

"It can't be this easy, Sarge. We couldn't have gotten away that easy."

"We made a clean sneak – be happy. We are free!" Derek picked up his dirty laundry bag from his bed and slung it over his shoulder. He then grabbed his guitar case and walked toward the door.

"Are you going back out?"

"Jesus! Yes, Messy. Go out and get some sun, you hop-head." Messy had lost it. He jumped in his bed.

Derek walked across the street to the Laundromat. There were a few other people doing laundry inside the run down, dumpy building. He set down his laundry on one of the machines and began pulling out clothes and piling them into a washer. He started two machines and noticed a copy of a local Calgary paper on the table. He grabbed it and sat down to read it. The dog jumped up on the chair beside him.

A voice startled Derek from behind. "Didn't like the diner coffee?"

Derek turned around and looked up from his paper. Standing behind him was the girl from the diner; the most beautiful girl he had ever seen.

"Sorry?" Derek asked.

"You didn't like the diner coffee?"

"Oh, not really," laughed Derek.

"Me neither, it's awful."

"Why did you get it? Are you hoping they will get it right one day?"

"Something like that."

Derek looked back to his paper and pet the dog on his head. The girl walked over to a machine and loaded it with laundry. Derek watched her from the corner of his eye. *What could he say to her to seem interesting?*

She walked back toward him. "Do you play?" she asked as she tapped her foot on his guitar case.

"I do."

"Are you planning to serenade your dog in the Laundromat?"

"Maybe."

"You are certainly dressed to impress."

He looked at his clothes and laughed. He looked homeless.

"This outfit is revolutionary."

"You look like you just fought in a revolution," joked the girl.

Derek laughed; she was funny. She smiled at him and he smiled back. Over her left shoulder he noticed that there were the only two people left in the Laundromat.

"Mind if I sit?" she asked.

"Absolutely not."

"Where is your dog's collar?"

"He's not my dog, he was wandering this morning. I just gave him water and he's followed me since."

"Are you from town here?"

"I'm not, I'm from Ontario."

"Oh, you came all this way to do your laundry and pick up strays?"

"I actually live in Vancouver. My buddy and I are driving back there."

"So, why would you bring your guitar to the Laundromat?"

"To serenade the dog." Derek smiled and she laughed. Her laugh was perfect. He continued, "I had planned to play out-front to kill time."

"That's so cool! Are you going to play right now?"

"I think so!"

"I'll come watch," she said as she took a step back away from Derek to allow him to pick up his guitar case. He reached over and picked up his case and she smiled as he stood up. The dog followed him. Derek started thinking that the less he said the more impressed she would be. She watched as he walked to the door and grabbed a chair. He stepped outside, sat down and pulled out his guitar.

The door to the Laundromat swung open just as he began tuning his guitar. She walked outside and casually stood in front of him while he tuned. He glanced up and she was smiling at him and petting the dog.

"First customers," she joked.

"What do you want to hear?"

"Have you written anything?"

"I was asking the dog," joked Derek as he cracked a smile. She laughed and rolled her eyes. Derek picked at his guitar strings and began to play an original. He picked at the strings slowly and she smiled at him as he began to sing the words.

A single look, a single stare
And I can't look away
A single conversation stole my attention
And I can't look away
I've never known what I need
And now it's in front of me
And I can't look away
And you look at me and I smile
And I can't look away

The words poured effortlessly from Derek's lips. It was his first time playing that song for an audience.

She stood in front of him, swaying back and forth as he sang to her. She smiled the entire time he played, her halo-white teeth glowing in the rising sun of the morning.

Derek strummed the last few notes and for a moment the two of them stared at each other in silence.

"I'm Mandy."

"I'm Derek."

September 1st, 2008
ELEVEN

On Labour Day, Derek went to the Old Admiral pub at 4:30 p.m. for a beer. He had worked an 8-4 shift and was waiting for his bus to go home.

At 4:45 p.m. Derek's boss frantically walked in the door and walked over to him. "I'm glad you're still here. Can you close? Andrew called in sick."

He offered Derek two additional days off if he worked the close that night. Derek agreed. He left the bar and went back to work. He would be closing with three girls and a young man named Matty.

Matty was a Chinese kid that started at the store around the same time as Derek and they were starting to form a friendship. Matty dressed in bright flashy clothes, had magma-red hair and drove a matching convertible. He liked loud music, loud movies and loud everything.

At 8:00 p.m., Derek grabbed dinner from the Burger Shack down the street and ate in his office.

At 9:00 p.m. he entered the beer cooler and stocked it until 10:15 p.m., after which he began closing duties.

He instructed the three girls on the closing procedures he wanted to have in place that night. Sarah, a tiny, blonde college student was the first cashier Derek spoke to. Krissy was the second. She was a tiny, Asian college student. Lastly, there was a tiny, brunette college student named Michelle.

At 11:00 p.m. Derek locked the doors to the store. He and the girls carried the three tills and tip jars to the office where Matty joined them. They made their drops, grabbed their belongings and walked to the door where they waited for Derek to turn off the lights.

Derek unlocked the door and Matty and the girls exited while he followed. They watched as he began to lock the gate and set the alarm.

Derek felt someone grab his hair from behind and smash his face off the wall. He fell to a knee and heard, "Hands where I can see them!"

Someone was taking the store. Matty and the girls put their hands in the air and froze. "Fuck!" exclaimed Derek, his face now covered in blood.

The masked man whispered, "Keep your hands up. You're gonna go inside and do as we say. We won't hurt you if you're calm. Clear?"

"Clear," replied Derek.

The three girls and Matty stood against the wall with their hands up. They all muttered the word *clear*.

Another man appeared behind the first masked man. The men all wore black ski marks over their faces, black hoodies and jeans. They held large knives.

They allowed Derek to stand up. He re-opened the store and walked inside. The first masked man walked behind him, following his every move.

The girls and Matty followed, with the other two masked men in the rear.

The first masked man walked behind Derek as he walked down the hallway that led to the storage room. The office was in the same hallway. The first masked man stopped them in the hallway. He looked back at the girls and pointed to the floor. "Phones on the floor." They pulled out their phones and tossed them onto the floor. The two other men searched their hostages for additional phones.

The first man whispered, "Go into the stock room and wait. That's it. You won't see us again. Just sit down, shut up and it'll be ok."

The taller of the men opened the door to the stock room. Matty and the girls walked inside, and the door was locked behind them. The first masked man pointed to the office. Derek and the men walked inside. The first man turned on the lights, blinding Derek and blurring his vision. Derek shut his eyes; his head was pounding.

The men pulled out a duffel bag and set it on the floor. The first man pointed to the safe and the taller man dragged Derek over to it. Derek opened his eyes and opened the safe first try. The clock read 11:39 p.m. 21 minutes until the call came from the security company. The taller masked man cleaned out the safe.

The first man turned his attention to the drop safe – the safe with the real money. He bent down, studied it then reached into a bag and pulled out a modified plumbing snake. He maneuvered the snake and after about 30 seconds of struggling he pulled an envelope out. At 11:45 p.m. they pulled a second envelope. A minute later they pulled a third. The taller man began pulling cash from the envelopes and piling it in a bag. They pulled a fourth envelope.

After five more minutes of struggling, the men pulled the last two envelopes from the drop box. The first man stood up, wrote a note and shoved it in Derek's face. It read *Where is the last envelope?*

"I don't know!" yelled Derek.

He punched Derek in the face, dropping him to the floor. "Goddammit!" exclaimed Derek. "There are boxes under the registers, combo 6,31,39."

The taller man pulled out a rope and flipped Derek on his stomach, tied his hands behind his back and his hands to his feet. They put the last of the money in their bag and left.

Two minutes later the phone rang. Security calling. No answer. Five minutes later another call, and another call five minutes after that.

At 12:20 a.m., the RCMP arrived on the scene. Derek could hear voices and footsteps in the distance. He looked back over his shoulder and saw flashlights shining in the store. An officer entered the office, ran over to Derek and knelt down beside him.

"Is there anyone still here?"

"I don't know," replied Derek.

"Are you hurt?"

"I don't think so."

"Give me a sec, I'll cut these off." The officer helped free him, Derek shook the cobwebs off and tried to stand. "I think you have a concussion kid, you're pretty wobbly."

"How is everyone? They okay?"

"They are fine. You guys did the right thing here. They won't get far."

The officer walked him out of the store to the parking lot. There were four cop cars with lights flashing. The lights blinded Derek; he couldn't decipher who were police and who were paramedics. The robbery itself remained hazy. *Did this really happen?*

A paramedic walked him to the back of an ambulance to run a few tests. Sometime later, Derek was approached by a police officer – a larger man, at least 6'4 with a heavy build. He had thin graphite-grey hair, a weathered face and haunted deep-set eyes. He looked as though he had seen everything awful that this world could offer. He dressed in a suit and tie and held a file folder. He removed his badge from his jacket pocket and showed it to Derek. "Good evening, Mr. Sierzant? Am I saying that right? My name is James Robie."

"Sierzant," replied Derek, "my friends call me Sarge.

"That's what they call me too!"

"Sierzant is Sarge in Polish."

"Right on! Listen, son, I've got a few questions about what happened. Is it okay if we talk right now?"

"Yeah, it's fine."

Robie opened his folder. "Anything unusual happen tonight?"

After a moment of hesitation Derek answered, "Not really, no."

"No cars parked outside, any upset customers?"

Derek hesitated, "I had one customer upset because we wouldn't take back his empties. It's a holiday, company policy."

"How tall were the robbers?"

"I never saw them. The others may have had a better look. One guy seemed shorter I think."

"You think?" asked Robie.

"His voice came from lower than your voice would."

"Good catch," said the Sergeant. "Did they use any names? Codes? Have any smells or distinct voices?"

"I smoke so I don't smell so good."

"That's okay. Any names?"

"They only spoke twice, in a whisper." Derek winced. "Sorry I can't help more, they caught us off guard."

"It's okay, son. No one goes to work expecting this. If I have more questions I'll be in touch. You can grab your possessions tomorrow."

"Thank you, sir."

The paramedic finished the tests and cautioned Derek to stay in a dark, quiet room for the next three days. They allowed Derek to stand up and walk across the parking lot past the police officers. He walked toward the sidewalk when he heard a voice call out from behind him.

"Mr. Sierzant!" Derek turned around slowly to see Sgt. Robie running toward him. "Would you like a ride home son?" he asked.

"I was going to take the bus."

"We've blocked buses from coming down the block. Let me give you a ride, its no problem. I'm wrapped up here."

October 4ᵗʰ, 2009
TWELVE

Mandy Aruda: 4'11 of graceful beauty. The girl of Derek's dreams, the girl he could never talk to. She was classy and charming. Her eyes were captivating and her warmth inviting. She sat beside Derek, in a run-down Laundromat in Canmore.

"What's your story?" she asked.

"Well, I'm from Renfrew, Ontario."

She paused for a second. Derek knew she was working her geography.

"Peplinski! He's from there?"

"Yeah he is. How the hell did you know that?" asked Derek.

"My Dad is a huge Flames fan. Jim owns a dealership in Calgary."

"That's crazy!" said Derek, "Where are you from?"

"Here," she replied as she sipped from her coffee cup.

"What do you do for work?"

Mandy finished her sip. "My Dad and I actually own a few businesses, including the diner."

"Wow, that's really cool! Your Father must really trust you."

Mandy laughed. "I'm more of an adult than he is!"

"Why haven't you guys changed the damn coffee?" asked Derek.

Mandy laughed. "Ask my Dad."

"Don't think I won't!" yelled an animated Derek.

Mandy smiled, "Are you close with your family?"

"Umm, not really," replied Derek in downcast fashion. "I moved out at 16 to live with a billet family."

"What's that?" asked Mandy.

"I played hockey away from home and lived with a family there."

"That must have been so hard!" replied Mandy, sympathetic to Derek.

"It was. I lost a lot of years with them, but it was a good experience."

They went back and forth learning about each other. Before they knew it an hour had passed and Derek felt himself falling. He felt trusting and playful for the first time in years.

September 2nd, 2008

Sgt. Robie's car was what you would have expected from a hardened police detective. It was a Crown Victoria, and it looked lived in. Fast food bags on the floor and file folders on the seats.

Derek began to think about all his favourite cop characters from television and film. Murphy, Hanna, Mills, Somerset, Mackey, Vendrell, Gardocki, Lemonhead, even Shaft.

Robie started the car and put on his seatbelt. He took a look over at Derek to see if he was wearing his. He was. Robie then tossed Derek's cell phone onto his lap and put the car in drive.

"Here's your phone."

"Thanks," replied Derek, "you won't need it?"

"No, I checked the tapes. They toss your phones when they are still wearing gloves. Unless you have them in your contacts."

Derek laughed at the thought. "Yeah it's my parents. Go grab them!"

Robie laughed as he drove past Brentwood Mall. Derek's mind started to race. Did Robie have an ulterior motive for driving him?

"How long have you worked at the liquor store?" asked Robie.

Derek counted out the months in his head. "Seven months or so."

"You ever catch people loitering around the place? Any employees that may have had a grudge or anything?"

"People linger outside all the time. We have regulars that usually beg so they can buy singles. Up on the right," said Derek as he pointed.

Robie pulled his car over. He reached into his pocket and pulled out a business card. "If you have any questions or sleepless nights give me a call. Anything at all. Okay, son?"

Derek's jaw hit the floor. He was positive that Robie was implying his involvement. Derek was unnerved. He tried to keep it together. *Take the card and go,* he thought. *Take the card say thanks and get out of his car.*

"Thank you, sir. I appreciate it."

* * * * *

Derek awoke the next morning at 10:00 a.m. He walked downstairs and was surprised to find his three roommates in the living room sitting on the couch.

"Jesus, you guys scared the shit out of me!" shouted Derek. "Why aren't you at work?"

"Grab a coffee," said Hecky.

"What's up, boys? Are we finally sorting out our living arrangement?"

Derek poured a coffee and walked over to join them.

"You doing okay?" asked Messy.

"Not great. My store got robbed last night."

Derek saw the looks on their faces and he knew.

"You shouldn't sleep with a concussion, Sarge," said Hecky.

"You motherfuckers!" shouted Derek. "Jesus fucking Christ!"

"Calm down dude," said Hecky, "Keep your voice down!"

"How could you do that to me? Do you know how fucked up that is?"

"You weren't supposed to fucking be there!" shouted Messy.

"Yeah, why the fuck were you there?" asked R-Luv.

"I got asked to work a double shift, so I did. Wait, there was only two. Where was the third?"

"No, we were all there," said R-Luv.

"Look, we are sorry," said Hecky with sincerity. "But we did this for all of us, you included. We knew the police would question the employees, and you needed plausible deniability, which you definitely had."

"You fucking dummies!"

"What were we supposed to do, Derek?" asked Hecky. "Just sit tight and let an opportunity pass us by?"

"Yeah, I mean, I don't know. Maybe don't commit a felony."

Messy spoke up, "Sarge, you can sit on your high horse, but we did you a favour. We all needed that money, you included. Now we have bought ourselves some time here."

"It's true, I was a week away from leaving," said R-Luv.

"Yeah, me too!" said Derek.

"That's why we did it," continued Hecky. "We cashed in big."

"How much?"

"A hundred and four thousand!" shouted Messy.

"Jesus Christ!" screamed Derek.

"And you had nothing to do with it, Sarge," said Hecky. "And if anyone asks you don't say any different."

"What are we going to do with it?" asked Derek.

"Well," said R-Luv, "we need to get this out of the house ASAP."

"I thought that we could take out a little at a time, like a thousand a month, each," said Hecky. "That gives us 26 months to establish ourselves."

"We need to get a storage unit or something and get this out of here! We should sit on it for a bit before we spend it," said Derek.

"You sure have a lot of opinions on how to spend money you didn't steal," said Messy.

"Do you want to draw attention to us?" asked Derek.

"Not really," said Messy.

"Then shut your mouth and forget about it until Thanksgiving," said Derek.

The boys sat on the money for the next month. Robie would pop into Derek's work every couple of days to check on him, or to freak him out. Derek didn't really know. Robie never made any remarks to him regarding that night, nor did he ask him for an additional statement.

The boys were fortunate that another three-man crew was running around Vancouver ripping people off. Hecky's hope was that the robbery would get lumped in with the dozen that the other guys had committed.

*   *   *   *   *

By Thanksgiving, the heat seemed to be off. Derek hadn't seen a cop around the store for weeks.

October 4ᵗʰ, 2009
THIRTEEN

Their laundry was done. The hands on the clock were ticking down. Their time together was running out. Derek began folding his clothes on top of a table, as did Mandy. He knew it was pointless to fold the clothes. He was going to have to wash them again after his clammy, sweaty palms had touched them. He took off his sweater and set it on a chair. Mandy folded her last article of clothing, picked up her basket and walked over to him. She set her basket next to his.

"What are you doing later? Getting more tattoos?" asked Mandy, catching Derek completely off guard.

He looked at his tattooed arms. He should have waited to show her that. "I don't know," he answered.

She looked at him and smiled. "Would you like to do something?"

"My tats didn't scare you away?"

"Well," said Mandy, "I'd prefer you didn't have them, but you had a world before I came around." Derek smiled and Mandy continued, "Would you like me to pick you up?

"I would like," replied Derek

Mandy smiled, picked up her basket and walked toward the door.

"Great, I'll pick you up at 7!"

October 2008

On Thanksgiving weekend, Hecky drove down to the storage unit, took out four thousand dollars and put it in a duffel bag. He arrived back at the house and walked room-to-room dropping off a monthly allowance.

Hecky walked into Derek's room – he was lying in bed watching a movie on his laptop. He stood over Derek and grinned as he threw a stack of 20's onto his mattress.

The money sat on the bed for a few seconds before Derek picked it up and looked at it. A thousand bucks – more money than he'd ever had. He needed it to pay off a few charges owing on his credit card. Or he could go to the mall.

Derek opened his door and followed Hecky downstairs to the front foyer. R-Luv was standing there putting on his coat.

"What's up?" asked Derek.

"I'm going to Metrotown, I need some stuff. You want to come?"

The money in Derek's hand began to burn. "Yup!"

R-Luv and Derek left the house and jumped on a bus to Metrotown. Derek felt a level of discomfort. He wasn't used to having so much cash in his pocket. This was a first.

Derek had a quick lunch then made a quick stop at Pet Habitat before he set out to do some shopping. He dropped $150 on sunglasses, $50 on a Sidney Crosby hoodie, $45 on a Minnesota Twins New Era hat and $200 on a few pairs of jeans and new Pumas. That was it, he knew he had to stop spending.

R-Luv texted him and they met in front of the Real Canadian Superstore. He had more bags than Derek.

"Jesus Christ, R-Luv. What is the matter with you?"

"It's my fucking money," he replied. "You blow your money on Pumas and blow and I will blow mine on X-Box and Magic."

"Oh, you're a magician now?"

"Magic, it's a strategy game you fucking donkey," he replied sarcastically.

The boys walked into the Real Canadian Superstore where they purchased groceries for their Thanksgiving feast the next day.

Derek was walking through the produce department when Messy texted him *8?* Derek texted back *Y.*

After purchasing that, the groceries, his clothes and a cab home Derek had spent all but $200 in just a few hours.

On Sunday morning, Derek woke up and made himself a big breakfast. Afterwards, he sat in the backyard with a cup of coffee and a cigarette and began thinking about his money. The idea of Hecky having his money made him very uncomfortable. It hadn't crossed his mind before, but he really wanted to hang onto it himself.

He was finishing his cigarette when Messy and R-Luv walked outside and sat down.

"What's going on?" asked Derek.

"Not much," they both replied.

"You are putting on a feast tonight I hear?" said Messy.

"Yeah man. The works!"

"You can do that?" asked Messy.

"I can make anything," replied Derek, "You guys never asked."

"Speaking of," said R-Luv as he paused and looked over at Messy.

"Just say it, Ryan!" said Messy.

"Say what?" asked Derek.

"We need to ask Hecky for our money. We never agreed he could hold it, and neither did you."

"I was just thinking that," said Derek. "I don't like it either."

A few hours later Messy, R-Luv and Derek sat down in the living room and began stuffing their faces. Derek knew his meal was a hit. There was a lack of conversation.

After their meal the boys sat down with a coffee and a slice of pecan pie. As they started dessert Hecky walked into the house.

"Hello?"

"Hey, buddy. We're in here," replied Derek.

Hecky walked into the kitchen and grinned. "Jesus, that smells good. Who cooked?"

"I did. Grab a plate, there's lots."

Hecky reached into the cupboard and grabbed a wine glass and a plate. He made up a plate, poured some wine and sat down beside R-Luv.

"Sargey, where the fuck did you learn to cook like this?"

"I don't know, dude. I just picked it up over the years."

"Is this dill pickle soup?" asked Hecky with a mouthful of food.

Derek nodded his head and went into the kitchen and cut him a slice of pie and poured a cup of coffee. He walked it over to Hecky and placed it on the coffee table in front of him just as Hecky enjoyed his last few bites.

Messy stood up and cleared his dishes and dropped them off in the sink. He began to walk toward the stairs and Derek stepped in his path.

"Dishes?" asked Derek.

"Later," replied Messy as he sidestepped Derek and darted up the stairs to his room.

Derek knew what Messy was doing; he didn't want to be in the room for the awkwardness. R-Luv had left the room as well.

Some friends, thought Derek.

Hecky continued to eat his meal as Derek walked over to the coffee maker, poured himself another cup and shut the machine off.

"I thought you were having dinner with your folks?"

"Mom's sick. She wasn't up to it."

"Sorry to hear that."

"Ah, it happens," replied Hecky. "What did you guys do this weekend?"

"R-Luv and I hit the mall and pretty much spent the whole thousand. What about you?"

"You guys spent it all? I thought we are supposed to conserve that so we can get ourselves ahead. You can't just blow money on clothes and shit."

"Dude, I was wearing jeans from fucking high school. No ones going to care if I stop looking homeless. Don't tell me how to spend my money!"

"Look, man, I'm sorry. I'm not trying to control you. I just want us to be smart." Hecky began backtracking.

"No! Fuck that, Hecky. Stop trying to run everything." He paused for a moment. He knew he needed to lay it on thick. "You guys took my angle and beat the fuck out of me. I don't like you doing things without consulting the rest of us. I want a key to the locker tomorrow and I want one for R-Luv and Messy."

"You think that's smart? What if one of us takes it? Then we have four suspects. If it disappears and I have the only key, then obviously I took it."

"It isn't that, Hecky," replied Derek. "We need money to go home for Christmas and to buy gifts. You get that? This whole 26 months thing isn't going to fly. You know?"

"Yeah, I know. I spent $860 this weekend."

"Then what the fuck are you giving me shit for?" asked Derek.

"I had to fix my van."

"And?"

"And I have to pay Messy for blow. And I spent some on girls."

"What? Girls? Are you fucking serious? Why would you do that?"

"A hooker?" asked R-Luv from his bedroom.

"Shut up," replied Hecky. "No. Look, I bought her some blow cause I needed to get laid!"

"Come on, you're a good looking guy. You can put the time in and get laid without paying for yeyo."

"No, Sarge. I can't"

"Look man," replied Derek. "I don't want to shit on you, just make the fucking keys and let's move past this."

Hecky muttered to himself and spoke up, "Fuck, whatever!" He walked past Derek to the stairs.

Derek felt bad, "Hey, hold up." Hecky turned to face Derek. "I can't have you paying for sex. Next weekend we will go out big! We'll meet some girls the old-fashioned way."

"Sounds good!" said Hecky.

Hecky walked up the stairs to his room and closed the door. As soon as his door closed Messy walked down the stairs into the kitchen. The dishwasher was half loaded when R-Luv popped out of his room.

"We getting keys?" asked Messy.

"Yeah, and I'm going to keep them all too, you fucks!"

*   *   *   *   *

The following Friday, Derek finished work and sky trained to the storage unit. He navigated through the building and bumped into a man carrying a large backpack that was busting at the seams. It was Messy.

"Yo, what are you doing?"

"I'm taking my share dude," said Messy as he adjusted his backpack.

"You're going to blow through that in like a month," said Derek.

"You should take your money too." Messy pointed to Derek's work backpack. Derek opened the door and walked inside their unit. There were three bags inside each containing $25,000. Derek took his moneybag and dumped it into his backpack. He closed it and locked the door behind him. They boarded a sky train and headed back home to Burnaby.

Derek's phone rang a few blocks away from home. He looked at the I.D. and showed it to Messy. It was Hecky. He knew what they'd done.

"Hello?" answered Derek.

"What the fuck, Sarge?"

"Well, good afternoon! What can I do for you today?"

"Why did you take it?"

"We are busing home, looking forward to a good weekend. Should be fun! When will you be home?"

"Soon!" replied Hecky, sternly.

"Great! We'll see you soon!"

Hecky and Derek both hung up.

"Fucking guy knows better than to talk on the phone," uttered Derek.

The boys arrived home and dropped the bags in their rooms. Messy yelled out, "We need a safe!"

"For sure!"

A few minutes later Hecky stormed in like a hurricane, doors slamming, feet stomping. He was making his presence known.

Messy yelled out from his room, "You can stop banging, we know that you're fucking home!"

The stomping got closer as Hecky made his way up the stairs.

"Hello, sir," said both Messy and Derek at the same time.

"Who convinced who?" asked Hecky.

"Who convinced who to do what?" asked Derek.

"To take the money out."

"You won't believe us, but we both did it separately," said Messy.

"Bullshit!"

"No, for real, Hecky," said Derek. "I went there after work and Messy had already grabbed his cash."

Messy chimed in, trying to diffuse the situation, "You can't make it rain without the funds, and if we are planning on getting you laid, we're going to need to make it rain something fierce. No offense."

"Umm, offense, all kinds of offense. I don't know what's more offensive, that you guys don't trust me or that you think I can't get laid."

"It's the trust thing, 'cause we know you can't get laid." joked Messy.

"Why do I hang out with you two?" asked Hecky.

"Cause we're the shit." answered Messy. "Now let's drive the liquor into you and hit the town."

Hecky settled down after some sweet-talking as they pre-drank in the backyard. Hecky was able to move past the fact that Messy and Derek had taken out their money.

Moments later the front door alarm beeped twice and R-Luv opened the door to the backyard.

"R-Luv! Join us!" yelled Derek.

"In a few minutes, boys. I just have to say, I took out my money."

"Oh, goddamn!" yelled Hecky.

Derek laughed, "We did too."

"Yeah, so get dressed," said Messy, "we are going out tonight."

"I'm good," replied R-Luv as he looked down at his stained clothes.

"Dude," yelled Derek, "you look like you should be Kid Rock's drummer."

Messy laughed and spit up his drink, "Holy fuck, that is so mean."

October 25th, 2008
FOURTEEN

The following weekend came around and Hecky wanted to get at it again. The boys decided to host a small party on Saturday night with some of their co-workers.

Derek knew his work mates weren't welcome since some of them could be considered privy to the robbery his roommates had pulled.

On Saturday afternoon, Messy and Derek took a trip to Derek's work to stock up on alcohol. Messy was paying for their order when Derek's co-worker Matty walked up to him to say hello, clearly still shook from the robbery. An immigrant from overseas, living in Canada now for ten years, Matty was a good kid who'd always done the right thing.

"Hey, buddy," said Matty.

"Hey, Matty. How's work?"

"Not bad. What are you doing?"

"Just picking up some drinks."

"Is that all you?" asked Matty, in broken English.

"Nah," replied Derek, "for my boys and I. We are having a party."

"Why we never hang?"

"I don't know," answered Derek as he shrugged his shoulders. "We should sometime. Come by tonight, 6040 Woodsworth."

"Nice, buddy. I think I will!"

"Do it up!" Derek high-fived Matty and walked over to Messy to help him with their order.

"Is that the kid?" asked Messy.

"Yup – Matty. He's coming."

Messy nodded his head. "Hecky's going to be pissed."

"Yup," replied Derek, smirking.

At home, the boys put the booze where it needed to go and crashed for an afternoon nap. As he was settling in and getting comfortable Hecky came crashing into Derek's room and quickly shut the door behind him. He reached into his jacket pocket and pulled out what appeared to be an ounce of cocaine.

"Is that?-" asked Derek.

"An ounce of blow? Yes, it is!"

"What'd that cost?"

"$1,800."

"Jesus Christ," said Derek, as he shook his head.

"You owe me six hundred."

"What?" asked Derek.

"For the blow, what. You don't want in on this?"

"Why did you buy so much?"

"I figured that we've been partying lots so we could just buy in bulk. Save some money."

"You do realize that Messy will bump his six hundred in one night," Derek cautioned.

"Come on, give him some credit."

"Alright, we'll see."

At 6:30 p.m. the doorbell rang and the first party guests to arrive were a few of Hecky's co-workers. A short time later some of Messy's work mates arrived. He'd been talking about these people for so long that Derek felt like he knew them.

Messy was fitting in well at his new job and was particularly fond of one work mate, Mark. He had chestnut hair and brown eyes with orange tones. Dressed in a band t-shirt and baggy jeans, he was average height and rake thin.

Mark brought his best friend Cillian. He was well built, tall, had copper-coloured hair and spoke in a heavy Irish accent. Also, he had skin as pale as a jar of white out.

Mark made the introductions while Derek ducked out of the party to enjoy a cigarette out back. He was uncomfortable being the guy at the party that didn't know anyone. It was a first for him. He looked through his cigarette pack and realized he only had two left. He finished his cigarette and walked to Hill Top Grocer.

Inside the store he was greeted by name by the owner's son. They knew him well since he was there everyday. He walked through the store and stocked up on candy. He walked up to the front to pay for his items. As he approached the cash, he noticed a beautiful girl walk toward him carrying only a bottle of water. He timed his steps so they arrived at the cash at the same time.

"Go ahead," said Derek as he smiled, "I have more stuff."

She smiled back and put her water on the counter. Her eyes were golden brown with a yellow hue and her hair was tawny blonde. It shimmered in the light. She was casually clothed in a plain red tank top and skin-tight jeans that showed off her sturdy legs.

"I guess chivalry isn't dead."

"If that were true, I would pay," said Derek. "You must be planning a wild night. Are you planning to get really hydrated?"

"Are you planning on getting diabetes?" she asked as she pointed at Derek's armful of candy.

She paid for her water in perfect change, picked it up off the counter, smiled at Derek and started walking to the door.

"See you around," said Derek, feeling like an idiot as soon as the words left his lips. She exited the store and Derek put his candy on the counter. He bought two packs of cigarettes, paid and walked out of the store. As he stepped outside, he was startled by a voice behind him.

"Hey, Willy Wonka," Derek turned around. She was standing outside having a cigarette.

"Hey, what's up?"

"Not much," she replied, "I'm Beth."

"I'm Derek."

"Nice to meet you, Derek."

"Likewise," said Derek as he lit a cigarette.

"Do you live around here?"

"Right down the street, you?"

"Up the street," she snickered.

Derek spoke confidently, "Listen, my roomies are having a party tonight. You should come. Bring some friends.

"Are you trying to get laid?"

"No, if I was trying to get laid, I'd go on Craigslist."

Beth looked puzzled; Derek quickly realized his misstep. "Oh, that was a joke."

"How long have you been marinating that one?"

"Not long enough, I guess."

"Guess not! Where do you live?"

"We live down here at 6040."

"Yeah? I'll see what my girls are doing. Is there a candy buffet?"

"No, these are all for me," said Derek as he began to walk away. "It was nice to meet you." He continued to step away. *There is no way she is coming* he thought. He walked back to the house.

The party had filled up with people he had never met before. Messy opened the gate for him from the inside. He was there to greet Derek with a shot of tequila and a lime.

"Do a tough guy shot!" yelled Messy. "You should see this kid do it!" Messy held out his forearm and Derek snorted salt up his nose then took the shot and squirted lime in his eye. Messy then booted him in the shin. The crowd cheered and for some twisted reason everyone loved Derek.

He had a seat in one of the plastic lawn chairs and wiped his eye clean. He lit a cigarette and the loneliness began to set in. He contemplated leaving the party.

Before he had the chance to leave a group of seven beautiful girls walked into the backyard, led by Beth.

"Beth!" shouted Derek.

"Derek, hey!"

"You made it, and you brought a shitload of friends."

"I hope that's okay!"

The boys looked at Derek and smiled, "I don't think anyone here will have a problem. Drink?"

A few hours later, Derek was talking to Hecky in the kitchen when Messy approached them.

"Where did you find these girls?"

"Craigslist," joked Derek.

Messy snickered, "You saved this party."

"Yeah, well, you know. We all bring something to the table."

"Speaking of, do you guys want to table some rackit?" asked Messy.

"Yes, please!" said Hecky.

"Let's go!" announced Messy. Hecky and Messy started to walk toward the staircase. "You coming?" asked Messy, looking back at Derek.

"I don't know."

"Yeah you do, and yeah you are."

Forty-five minutes later the three boys were still in Hecky's room when there was a knock at the door. Hecky walked over to the door and opened it a crack. It was R-Luv.

"Is Sarge here?"

Hecky opened the door for R-Luv and quickly closed it behind him.

"Jesus Christ!" exclaimed R-Luv. "How much coke did you buy?" Hecky, Messy and Derek stood there quietly. "You three idiots are going to run out of money in a matter of weeks. Can you please explain to me why you would rather lock yourselves in a room and do that shit than hang out with the guests you invited? I mean, Jesus Christ, Sarge, there is a girl down there that I would give anything to be with and she's down there wandering around looking for you. You three need to smarten the fuck up. Goddamnit!" R-Luv stormed out of the room.

"Guess I'll go back downstairs," said Derek. "One for the road."

He walked over to the desk, bumped one more line and cleaned up.

R-Luv greeted Derek at the bottom of the stairs as he attempted to re-join the party.

"What is going on with you, dude?" he asked.

"Nothing, man."

"You've gone fucking mental."

"You're overreacting. I'm fine, fuck, just having fun."

R-Luv stepped out of the way as Derek brushed past him and walked into the kitchen. He poured Knob Creek to wash the bitterness out of his throat and walked outside.

In the backyard, the girls were keeping to themselves, talking in a group. Beth watched Derek grab his cigarettes from his pocket and pull one out. She walked over to him.

"Hey, Derek!" Beth said, excited to see him. "I was looking for you. Your roommate said you were talking to your friend."

"I was. What's up?"

As Derek spoke, he could feel himself racing, *slow it down Sarge, breathe*. His heart bounced in his chest like a basketball.

"One of my friends thinks your buddy is cute."

"Which buddy?" Derek asked.

"The tall one, what's his name?"

"Jyoshi Masih – we call him Messy, cause he's messy."

Still rushing Sarge. He cleared his throat and again tasted the bitterness of the blow. He sniffled and more drip went down his throat.

Beth grinned and looked at Derek a little strange. "Are you okay?"

"Yup, I'm good. Just tipsy."

"Nice. Well, we are going to head out in a few minutes. Thank you so much for having us!"

"Oh, it was my pleasure. You guys really classed up this place."

"Stop," said Beth as she grinned.

Derek saw her grin and knew he should be forward and ask her out.

"I should grab your number, maybe we could grab a drink sometime?"

"Yeah, I'd like that! Give me your phone, I'll put it in for you."

Beth took Derek's cell phone and entered her number in his contacts.

"Call me this week," she said. Beth waved bye to R-Luv and left.

Messy's buddy Mark stood up after the girls were out of ear shot and walked over to Derek.

"Messy told me you were good with women, but man!"

"What?" asked Derek.

"I fantasized the whole time about her inviting me over to her house to watch sports."

"That's a weird fantasy."

"I usually creep women out. I tell a lot of stories about my Mom that are laced with subtle racist undertones."

At that moment, Derek realized that most of the party had cleared out and it was 11:00 p.m.

"You didn't invite any work friends?" asked Mark.

"No, cause Messy told me your racist ass was going to be here."

"I feel like I could provide a useful buffer between the whites and others since most of my racist beliefs are for LOL's."

"Do you do any drugs, Mark?" asked Derek.

"Why? What do you have?" asked Mark. He continued as Derek laughed and shook his head, "I know what you do upstairs, I do it too."

"Oh," replied Derek, "then let's hit it."

Hours later, they were still up in Hecky's room. "What now boys?" asked Mark.

"Any ideas?" asked Messy.

"Well," replied Mark, "I was kind of hoping that we could combine all of our juicy b-holes together to make some kind of super sphincter."

"You're fucked," said Derek.

"He's a weird dude," said Messy.

"24/7, three hundred and sixty days a year."

"Dude, there are 365 days a year," said Derek, correcting Mark.

"Not if you take out the black holidays."

"Jesus Christ!" exclaimed Derek and Messy at the same time.

"What?" asked Mark. "I'm a mix – I can't make black jokes? Messy you said your Dad always talks about how brown people shouldn't celebrate Christmas."

"He's fucking brown!" yelled Messy.

October 4ᵗʰ, 2009
FIFTEEN

The hotel door was open a crack, no sound coming from inside. *Did somebody get to Messy? Were the police here?* wondered Derek. He began looking frantically around the parking lot. He put one hand on his gun and opened the door to look inside.

Messy was passed out in bed. He had one shoe on and looked dead. He might be, given the amount of coke he'd done.

Derek crept over to him and with the back of his fingers he checked Messy's pulse; he was still kicking. Derek stood up and noticed a phone in Messy's hand. It was their burner. Derek picked up the phone and opened it. There were two names in it, R and H for R-Luv and Hecky.

Hecky had sent a text to Derek and Messy. He was alive and well in Squamish. There were no messages yet from R-Luv.

Derek typed a message *At the hotel, all good, home in a few*. He then took a few minutes and tried to tidy up their disgusting hotel room for a third time. Each time he cleaned, Messy tried twice as hard to destroy it.

November 3ʳᵈ, 2008

The rainy season in Vancouver had begun. Normally this would be a dull, depressing time of year. But things were going well for Derek. He had money, free time and was meeting lots of girls. He was finally enjoying his time on the West coast.

One Monday evening, he had his first date with Beth. He wanted to throw some money around, so he rented a BMW and made a reservation at Yew Seafood and Bar.

He left the house at around 5:00 p.m. and parked his rental in front of Beth's. He waited for her for a few minutes until she opened the front door and walked outside. She approached the car dressed in a short dark skirt and a cute black and white argyle sweater. Derek jumped up and ran around the car to the passenger's side to open the door for her.

"This is a nice car! Is it yours?"

"No, I'm just trying to impress you!"

"Right! Where are we going?"

"Yew, downtown."

"Really? Wow!" Beth climbed into the car and Derek shut the door.

An hour and a half later they arrived at the Yew just in time for their reservation to be called.

Yew Seafood and Bar was a classy joint, similar to a modern New York City loft. It had large windows, booths, and an oversized bar.

The hostess seated them in the most awkward spot for a couple on a first date – the middle of the room.

Derek hated first dates. He hadn't been on many and they made him nervous. He began making small talk as they looked at the menu.

"I don't know what any of this stuff is," said Beth.

The waitress walked over to the table to take a drink order. Derek browsed the menu and made his choice.

"Let's have Laughing Stock Pinot and the seafood tower for four."

Beth looked at Derek and grinned, "Are you hungry?"

"Did you see what came on that thing? Oysters, crab salad, humpback shrimp, albacore tuna, scallops, lobster, spot prawns. I'm sure we'll find something in there we'll like."

"Do you always order for dates?"

"Not usually," replied Derek.

"That's a gutsy move."

Derek tried to change the subject.

"Where are you from, Beth?

"Here. You?"

"Not here," said Derek jokingly.

"Do you always bring your dates here?" asked Beth.

"Ha, I'm happy to report that you are my first date since my ex and I broke up in December."

"You've been single for a year?"

"Almost! What about you?"

"I've been single for awhile too, almost two years."

"What happened, if you don't mind my asking?"

"He was big into raves and all that. So anyways one night he went out with friends and OD'd on MDMA."

"Jesus Christ, that's a thing? That's so awful."

"Yeah, it is. They don't know what happened exactly. He just went to sleep and never woke up."

"Holy fuck." Derek sat there stunned. He didn't know how to react. "Did he have a drug problem or like any history with drugs?"

"No, just partying off and on. And then one night he went until he couldn't go anymore."

"That was it?" asked Derek.

Beth paused for a moment and caught herself drifting, "That was it." She took a drink, "So, I don't do drugs, nor do I like them. Do you do any?"

"No," answered Derek. "Well, I used to smoke weed, but I've sort of grown out of it. I do like to drink."

"Well, that's okay. Sorry I asked, it's just that for me to date anyone I have to know they are clean. I have no place in my life for any of that stuff."

The remainder of the dinner was a series of bad jokes, laughs, great food, great wine and an expensive bill that Derek happily paid for.

On his way out of the restaurant he noticed that it had started to rain. He stopped walking.

"You can wait here; I'm going to get the car and I'll pull it up front."

"That's okay, I can walk."

"It's fine, I don't want you to get drenched or slip. I'll be two minutes."

Derek regretted his offer as soon as the rain hit him. He quickly crossed the street, paid $35 for parking and walked to the rental car. He was soaked head to toe. He pulled the car in front of the restaurant and jumped outside to open the door for Beth. She exited the restaurant and ran to the car. Derek shut her door behind her and stood up straight when he heard a male voice call out his name.

"Derek Sierzant."

Sgt. Robie caught Derek's eye as he turned around. Robie was standing beside a young attractive female who was holding an umbrella in her hand.

"Sergeant! How are you?" Derek said as Robie extended his hand and Derek shook it, all the while trying to play it off as though he was happy to see him.

"I'm good, son. How are you?"

"I'm great! Hey, I never heard anything. Did you guys ever catch the dicks that robbed my store?"

Robie looked at his female companion and back at Derek.

"No, unfortunately the trail is cold on that one – no similar robberies either."

"Ah, that's too bad."

Robie looked past Derek and noticed the car.

"That's a pretty fancy ride you got there."

Derek smiled, "Yeah, it's a rental. First date you know."

"No, yeah I get it. That's why you bring her here too, right? Nice choice."

"Thanks," said Derek, keeping the smile on his face. His eyes darted to Robie's female partner. "Is it bring your daughter to work day?"

"This is Sgt. Anna Johnson."

Anna rocked the Sergeant look – she had shoulder length jet-black hair, forest green eyes and wore a red power blazer with jeans that accentuated her strong, curvy build. She studied every move Derek made.

"Hey, Anna. I'm Derek."

"Hi, Derek."

Robie interrupted, "Well since I never heard from you can I assume you recovered after the robbery."

"Yeah, I was okay. It took a few days, you know, but I'm a little more careful when I lock up at night."

"Perfect. Well, if you ever have anything to talk about, I'm here."

"Thanks, Sergeant," Robie shook Derek's hand, as well as Anna's.

"Be well, guys!" shouted Derek.

"Who was that?" asked Beth as Derek jumped back into the car.

"Police. My store was robbed a while ago. He had the case."

"Oh wow! Was that scary?"

"Terrifying."

Anna and Robie walked down the street to their restaurant and walked inside.

"What was that?" asked Anna.

"That's the assistant manager at the Hastings Liquor that was hit."

"Kinda odd – a kid working retail is eating here and driving a Beamer."

"Yeah, I'd say so."

At around 9:30 p.m., Derek and Beth found themselves parked in front of her house. He jumped out of the car and ran around to the passenger side and opened the door.

"Such a gentleman," said Beth as she held his hand and he pulled her out of the car.

Derek closed the door with his free hand and she pulled him in close and kissed him. She softly massaged his lips with hers. Slowly and softly, softly and slowly. She smiled and gently let go of Derek's hand. "Night!"

"Good night!"

Derek climbed in the car and took a deep breath; he felt like he was suffocating. She had his heart racing. Or was it Robie? Robie was curious. *Fuck, what have I done?* Derek guessed that Robie knew, or at the very least he had his suspicions. Moments later, he received an e-mail to his phone. It was from his Mother. It read:

Hi Derek,

I just thought I would send you that email I got about Meth. That is pretty scary stuff, so I thought you might want to share it with some of your friends. The drugs that are out there now that you aren't even aware that people can slip in your drink etc and get you hooked are REALLY scary. Please be careful when you are out at parties and bars etc. I know you are a big boy, but things can happen even to guys, not just girls.

Love you,
Mom

Oh, Mom. If only you knew what I was into.

Derek arrived home to find Hecky sitting in the living room watching television and drinking a pint. He walked over to the fridge and grabbed a beer for himself.

"How's the date?" asked Hecky.

"It was pretty good. The car and restaurant were a hit."

"That's good."

Derek sat down at the end of the couch and took a sip of his beer. He stared blankly for a moment.

"What's wrong?" asked Hecky.

"I ran into that cop tonight. The one that I said was weird."

"Did he see you with the car coming out of Yew?"

"Yeah, and it bugs me."

"What did you say to him?"

"I told him I rented the car to impress my date."

"Did he buy it?"

"Not sure; I'm not him. I don't know how strong his intuition is."

"Fuck, fuck, fuck!"

"Let's be real, Hecky. What – are they going to bug our house based on a hunch?"

"Maybe! I don't know how police work works, do you?"

"You know that I don't, but I would assume they need warrants, evidence, probable cause. You know, police shit."

"I knew we should have kept that money stashed away," said Hecky. "But no, you had to go flashing it all over town."

R-Luv's door opened. "What's going on?" he asked.

Messy came running down the stairs and he was pissed. "Would you two shut the hell up, I'm trying to sleep!"

Hecky pointed at Derek. "Tell them what you told me."

Derek took a deep breath. "A cop saw me coming out of Yew, driving the Beamer."

"So what?" asked Messy.

"It's the cop investigating the Hastings robbery."

"Oh fuck!" said R-Luv.

"Oh, we're fucked," said Messy.

"Boys," yelled Derek, "we aren't fucked! All he knows is that I rented a car for a date and took her to a nice restaurant. That's it!"

"You make 28 g's a year. How do you explain that?" asked Hecky.

"Tips. I get tips at work also."

"Oh, my mistake. $30 g's."

"I had some money saved. I don't live lavishly, that's how. What proof would this guy have of anything?"

Messy spoke up, "Sarge, you said this guy drove you home and grilled you. Did he have suspicions then? Will he have more now?"

"Look, guys, all we do is tighten up on the spending. No one spends a dime of that money. If they plan to watch us, they will do it soon. If we do nothing, then nothing happens."

*   *   *   *   *

The next morning, Derek woke up, dressed for work and headed out. He walked out to the street and from the corner of his eye he spotted a blue van he didn't recognize. It had tinted windows and it appeared like someone was inside. *Was it Robie?* He ignored the van and tried to appear aloof. He didn't want them to know that he'd made them, if it was them.

He climbed the hill and, once he was out of sight, called Hecky. He answered on the second ring.

"Eyes on the house!" shouted Derek as he quickly hung up.

The 123 pulled up to the bus stop, which Derek boarded and rode to work. He knew that he had Robie's attention. This was bad.

After work, he rode the bus home and arrived shortly after 5:00 p.m. The van from the morning was gone. He walked inside and found the boys sitting on the couch waiting.

"What's up, fellas?" asked Derek.

Hecky gestured for Derek to be quiet and held up a whiteboard that read *go outside for a smoke*.

"Not much," said Messy.

"I need a smoke," said Derek. "Tough day."

R-Luv opened the back door. Derek walked outside, leaving the door open for the rest of them. The boys sat down in their usual spots.

"What the fuck?" asked Derek.

"I don't want to talk in the house in case it's bugged." replied Hecky.

"How did they bug the house? Did you leave at all today?"

"No," replied Hecky. "I'm just paranoid, but still. These guys got followed to work too."

"For real?" asked Derek.

Hecky and R-Luv nodded.

"Jesus Christ. Okay, well, simple solution. Don't spend the money. Live poor, just like we were. How long can these guys sit on all of us? Like, a week? Maybe two weeks?"

"We can't leave the house empty," said Messy.

"No, definitely," said Hecky. "We should always have someone home."

"I'll do more evenings so I can be here during the day," said Derek.

Hecky shook his head, "No need – I won't be working for at least a few more weeks. Hopefully they are onto something bigger by then."

"Okay," replied Derek.

"I don't get it," said Messy. "Why have so many people on us?"

"Maybe they think we are into something heavier? Either way, let's put doubt in their minds."

November 2008
SIXTEEN

Over the next four weeks, every cent Derek spent came from his wages at the liquor store. It was a tough stretch; he needed cash to go home for Christmas. All he had left after paying bills was his ill-gotten money.

Everyday the cops tried new, shifty tactics to spy on the boys. They would change up the cars, change up the times and places they would stay. The boys played aloof and never gave the cars a second look. They just went about their lives like normal young men trying to get by in this world.

By mid-November, Derek would walk out of the house and the heat on the corner was gone. Either the police were upping their game or they had stopped looking at the boys.

As the days went on the boys continued to be cautious. After a week with no one looking at them they felt that they could slowly go back to spending their money, little by little.

December 5th, 2008

Derek arrived home around 8:00 p.m. after shopping for Christmas gifts. He walked into the living room to find Hecky and Messy sipping drinks and watching a hockey game.

Messy asked, "You want a beer?"

"I'm good," said Derek as he poured some Makers. "What's up?"

Messy slid over on the couch as Derek sat down and set his drink on the coffee table.

"Not much," said Messy.

"What do you mean 'not much'? A fucking lot is going on," said Hecky.

"What's up?" asked Derek.

"Messy is broke!" yelled Hecky.

"No fucking way," said Derek in disbelief. "How can that be?"

"I spent my cash," said Messy, "partying, and gambling."

"Jesus Christ," said Derek in shock wondering how someone could blow through money that quickly.

"I don't even have money to get home for Christmas," said Messy.

Derek knew that Messy was hurting; he was ashamed and embarrassed.

"I'll cover your ticket, dude. Don't worry about that," said Derek trying to brighten his day. "I thought you were saving cash to make your short film."

"I thought I was going to get on set, so I figured I'd have money to make it. But with the economy, no one new is getting on set."

Hecky nodded his head.

"It's true, I can't even get a sniff of a set and I'm in the union."

"You make bombs on set," replied Derek.

"Still man," replied Hecky, "I can do other things on set."

"Yeah, true. We have no hope in hell to get on set," said Derek in agreement. "How much did you blow?"

"22,000," replied Messy.

"Tell him the best part," said Hecky.

"I did it two weeks ago," confessed Messy.

"Jesus," exclaimed Derek, "when the cops were watching us?"

"Yeah," Messy said as he started to tear up. "I'm really sorry dude, you know me. I can't walk away down."

"He still owes," said Hecky.

"Fuck, how much?" The thought of his debt made Derek cringe.

"Fourteen hundred," said Messy as he fought back tears.

"We'll help you," Derek said as he stood up and walked over to Messy, giving him a hug. It hurt Derek to see his friend in pain. The boys agreed to give Messy $500 each to pay his debt.

The following evening, the boys had a few people over to the house for a party. Hecky made sure Derek invited Beth and her friends over. Beth and Derek had gone on a total of four dates and things were going very well. He liked her; she was funny and intelligent. She really liked Derek and that was troubling because Derek didn't much like himself.

Messy invited the usual suspects to the party – Mark and his girlfriend as well as Cillian. Hecky invited some friends from his work as well.

The drinking began in the mid-afternoon and people were hitting the bottle hard. With all the heat on the boys it had been weeks since they'd let loose. The environment of the party was a ticking time bomb; it was just a matter of time before minds started to wander from alcohol to drugs.

Hecky sat on the living room couch sipping on bourbon. His legs were shaking; he hadn't done blow in nearly a month. He wanted it bad!

Derek didn't want Beth to see him like that. He knew that if he was going to do that, he had to be careful.

There was still quite a bit of cocaine left from their bulk buy. Supply was sure to meet demand.

Hecky walked through the house past Derek and ran up the stairs to his room. It was time.

Derek walked up the stairs and knocked on the door. Hecky let Derek in and shut the door behind him. Messy was already sitting on the bed; he'd brought his blow with him.

"We'll just do it all here, boys," said Hecky. "I'll keep my door locked."

"Sounds good," said Derek. "I want to keep it quiet from Beth."

"How is that?" Asked Messy.

"It's good, she's cool. Funny too!"

"That's good, man," said Messy, as he struggled to put a smile on his face. "I'm happy for you. You deserve it after that last one."

"Thanks, Messy!"

The three amigos began banging out lines of sniff. A bump or two, and they would run back to the party, then back up to Hecky's, bump.

Beth began asking where Derek was going, to which he answered that his stomach was bugging him. It wasn't an attractive answer, but he knew it would squash the questions.

Another sniff, back to the party, back up to Hecky's, another sniff. The party was on until Derek walked out of Hecky's room with the boys and there stood Beth, holding Derek's bag of coke – the one that was hidden in his closet. Not hard to find if you snooped a little.

Hecky and Messy slinked past Derek down the stairs to avoid being privy to the awkward conversation he was about to have.

"You want to explain why you have a giant bag of cocaine?"

"Look, it's not mine."

"Fuck, Derek, I'm not an idiot."

Party was over. Derek swallowed his pride and went into damage control. *Fuck.* "Fuck!"

"Jesus Christ, why do you have it? Are you a fucking dealer? Is that why you have money?"

"A coke dealer? No, I don't deal."

"So, what it this? Personal stuff?"

"Yeah, I mean I guess so," said Derek, knowing that his answer would certainly end things.

"Why would one person need this much cocaine?"

"I don't know," answered Derek.

"I can't be around this kind of thing. I'm this hurt and we've only been on a few dates. I can't imagine if we had been together for a long time."

"I'm really sorry, Beth."

"Yeah, well, so am I. I see too many red flags with you. I can't have someone like you in my life."

Beth set the bag of cocaine in Derek's hands and walked away. Derek's face went red. Messy and Hecky watched from the bottom of the stairs as he walked over to his room and sat on his bed.

Derek dumped some of the cocaine on his side table and took a sniff. Hecky and Messy came running in. Messy grabbed Derek and pulled him back on the bed.

"Let me go, I want it!"

"Calm down!" yelled Hecky.

Josh Cybulski

Messy held on tight as Derek tried to worm out of his hold, but Messy was much stronger than him. After a few moments of fighting, Derek gave up, exhausted. Messy let him go.

Messy sat on the bed next to him. *What is wrong with me?* thought Derek.

"Are you okay?" asked Hecky.

"Ugh, Jesus," yelled Derek, "I ruin everything, man."

"This one is on me, Sarge," said Hecky. "I'm really sorry. I brought that into this house. I forced it on you."

"You didn't force that shit. I'm a big boy, I knew what I was doing."

"That sucks, dude," said Messy. "I know you liked her."

"Story of our lives eh, boys?" said Derek as he started to calm down, "We fuck shit up."

The boys sat in silence for a few moments. Hecky sat down on the floor against the wall across from Derek and Messy, who sat on the bed.

Messy crawled over to the side table and bumped a line. He sat back on the bed and broke the silence. "Do you ever think about the carnage that is behind the lines we do?"

"What?" asked Hecky.

"I mean that every line we rifle up our nose had a path to get to us. Do you ever think about it?"

"Do you mean what they cut it with? Like Drano?" asked Hecky.

"No man, I mean like what is the timeline of that drug's existence. Who grew it? Who packaged it? Who smuggled it here?"

"Messy, I think you think too much," said Derek.

"Oh, the rabbit hole I go down goes well beyond that, dude. I wonder who killed for it? Who used the proceeds from it to buy a gun? Or to have somebody kidnapped, or worse."

"Who sent it somewhere to fund a war," said Derek.

"I don't think about that kind of stuff," said Hecky.

Derek interrupted, "Messy, you might be a Voluntaryist yet."

"I think we need to think about that next time we bump," said Messy.

"I don't know, Messy. I think about war and shit enough. If I start thinking about that shit, I'm going to get real depressed," said Derek.

"I'm just saying it wouldn't hurt us to be more conscience of what we are doing and where it comes from."

"Fuck, Messy, I just got dumped. I don't need to be dumped on."

Derek bumped another line and Hecky stood up for Derek, "Yeah, serious, Messy. Leave him be."

Derek turned to Messy. "I get it. You think I'm putting up blinders and maybe I am. But I know what you are referring to. I know all about feminicidio in Juarez and shit."

"I think about that shit a lot."

"Do you think about that kind of thing when you wear a shirt that was made by a kid in a sweatshop in Taipei?" asked Hecky.

"Not really," replied Messy.

"Look," said Derek, "Juarez cartels, drug running, all that shit is part of a North American problem. Throw in the justice systems and the lack of freedom and the war on drugs. All that shit is why I'm a Voluntaryist."

"Now we're on a thing. Is our justice system so bad?" asked Hecky.

"Not if you are a criminal, under the hug-a-thug Canadian way." Derek paused and wiped his face. "Well, Messy, you tell me. You're a brown kid. Do you feel safe around cops?"

"Oh, hell no."

"So, would you feel safe in a police state?" asked Derek.

"Fuck no."

"Look man, I'm plenty aware. Maybe too aware," said Derek. "I think people who play the game by the rules don't want to believe that the game is rigged. They follow the progression as they are supposed to: go to school; regurgitate answers; get a shit job; pay for a shit house and a shit car. Pick right or left and parrot out those opinions. No one does all that and then wants to believe it's all a lie. But it is, and I know that. I don't want that life."

"It doesn't pay to be moral or good," said Messy.

Derek spoke up, "Two things happen to good people in this world. One is that the good goes and the bad comes, or the rest of the world's bad squashes the little bit of goodness that they have."

"Jesus, this is bleak," said Hecky.

"Fuck, look at us," said Derek. "We bust our ass to be broke all the time. We break the law once and now we are getting by just fine. There's a reason good people do bad things."

December 19th, 2008
SEVENTEEN

Two weeks later, Messy and Derek arrived via taxi at the Vancouver International Airport. It was the Friday morning before Christmas and the airport was packed. The boys' flight was set to depart at 8:30 a.m. and they arrived with time to spare.

Derek could feel his wallet busting at the seams. He had stuffed it with the nearly five grand that he planned to use for the trip. He waited with the luggage while Messy went to the bathroom. As soon as Messy was out of sight, Derek dropped an envelope with $500 in Messy's luggage and zipped it up. He felt good to actually help someone, even if that someone was a fellow criminal.

His parents were going to be shocked when he arrived home. He hadn't cut his hair since the previous January and he had grown a full beard. His tattoo count had tripled from two tattoos up to six with more on the way in the New Year.

Messy walked back from the bathroom and stepped in line. Derek spotted white powder under his nose.

"Did you bump in there?"

"Yeah," replied Messy, "don't worry, I brought some for you too."

"That wasn't my concern."

"I'm not bringing it on the plane. You think I'm that stupid?"

"Sometimes I wonder."

The boys checked in for their flight and dropped off their luggage. Messy brought enough cocaine for the boys to do a few more lines in the bathroom before getting a coffee and boarding their plane. By the time they boarded their flight the buzz was gone, and they slept.

Derek woke up hours later to find the passengers de-boarding. It was minus seventeen in Ottawa – a far cry from the five degrees in they left behind in Vancouver.

Derek's Father Peter picked them up and drove the boys to Renfrew. He shared stories about Zagadka that fascinated Messy.

They arrived at Derek's parents' home where Messy's Dad met him.

Derek walked into his childhood home and set down his luggage. His Mom and Brother Dannick ran downstairs to the front foyer and hugged him.

The house was a modest, raised bungalow. As soon as Derek walked in the house, he could smell his Mom's cooking. She had her roast chicken, homemade French fries and gravy on the menu with an apple pie for dessert. Derek enjoyed dinner with his family and had three slices of apple pie.

"What is the city like, Derek?" asked Peter.

"Crime-ridden," joked Derek.

"Maybe Zagadka lives there," added Dannick.

"Could be, they never found him," said Peter.

"D.B. Cooper lives there too," said Dannick.

"They never found him either," joked Peter again.

Derek smiled at his Mom, Lena, and she rolled her eyes at Peter. He was obsessed with Zagadka and the mystery and it annoyed her.

After dinner, Derek's friends arrived, and they headed to Ottawa. Derek and his friends met up at OC's house in the city and worked on a good buzz before cabbing to a pub on York Street. They checked their coats and were standing at the bar by 11:15 p.m.

Derek ordered Makers and stood at the bar next to OC, waiting for his drink. Derek's drink was placed in front of him – he grabbed it and took one step back from the bar. He bumped into a fellow patron of the bar: it was none other than Jyoshi Masih.

They high fived in celebration. "No fucking way! What's up?" yelled Derek.

"Nothing man, I'm high as fuck!"

"Nice."

"I jammed pissers with this sweet little nine iron last night," joked Messy.

"What the fuck is a nine iron?"

"I wanted to thank you for the money," said Messy as he placed his hand on Derek's shoulder. "I bought the family gifts."

Derek laughed and took a sip of his drink. "I'm sure you didn't."

"I won't forget it. I owe you."

"You don't owe me, dude."

"I do. Here is a down payment."

Messy held his hand for a handshake. Derek extended his hand and felt him slap a baggie into it. Derek looked down at his hand. It was blow.

"Have fun!" said Messy, as he walked away. He was messing up Derek's plans. Derek had wanted to stay clean; it had become a problem. *Maybe just one bump,* he thought. He didn't even have enough to get high. It was a gram, maybe a gram and a half. And it wasn't the quality Derek had become accustomed to.

As he was mulling it over, he received a text message. It was from Messy. It read: *if you want more the guy is at my table.* Derek went to Messy's table.

A few hours later the boys returned to OC's place with a group of girls. It seemed like simple math, four girls, four boys and four bedrooms in the house. The party went late into the evening, but Derek had a hard time having fun. Beth was still choking him up. He was upset that he'd hurt her. He hated hurting people.

Derek tried to be happy, but he wasn't feeling it. He walked outside to OC's front porch to have a cigarette. He stood on the porch smoking and watching the snow fall ever so gently onto the ground. The city lights illuminated the sky on what was a beautiful Ottawa night.

Derek pulled out his keys and coke tin. He quickly bumped a line off one of his keys. He closed the tin, tucked it away and continued smoking. His "tin" was given to him by a liquor rep. It was designed for mints, but Derek used it to keep coke.

The front door swung open and OC walked outside to join Derek for a smoke. He pulled out his pack, took out a single cigarette, placed it between his lips and lit it. They stood there awkwardly on OC's front porch for what to Derek felt like an eternity.

"You are getting good at meeting girls, eh?" said OC.

"Yeah you know, maybe I'll write a book one day,"

"You might need to, just to support your massive coke habit."

Derek's jaw hit the deck.

OC continued, "I can see it in your face and your behaviour. You are high as fuck. Is this ongoing?"

"No, dude," said Derek as he attempted to wrap his head around what OC was saying to him, "its just a once in a while kind of thing."

"I love you, man, but I don't believe you." OC paused for a second to regain his train of thought. Tears streamed down his face. "If you are doing it a lot, or you have a problem, I would hope you could be honest with me. I will listen and be there for you."

October 4th, 2009
EIGHTEEN

Mandy's car – a brand new 5 series BMW – pulled into the motel parking lot at 7:00 p.m. Mandy waved to Derek as he exited his room and walked over. He opened the passenger's side door and climbed in. "Nice car!"

"My Dad's friend owns the dealership here. I'd drive something less arrogant otherwise."

"Lucky you! Where we going?"

She smiled. "Do you like Thai?"

"I love it," replied Derek.

Mandy put the car in drive and drove out of the hotel parking lot. "What do you do for a living, Derek?"

"I actually own a food truck with three of my friends," he answered, knowing full well that he would have to tell a lot of half-truths.

"What do you do?"

"I'm the chef."

Mandy was surprised. "Oh, this place is yummy, but it's not real fancy."

"That's okay, I cook mostly Polish food anyway."

She turned her car onto Bow Valley and drove into a parking lot to a Thai restaurant called Thai Pagoda. She turned to Derek and grinned. "Is Polish food bad?"

They exited her car and Derek laughed. "No, it's awesome."

Mandy and Derek walked inside the restaurant and were seated.

Mandy picked up a menu. "I have to confess something."

"What's that?" asked Derek.

"I Googled you today."

Derek grew concerned. "What came up?"

"You set an OHL record for penalty minutes by a goalie."

Derek laughed and it caught the attention of other patrons of the restaurant "Yeah, now you know why I don't play hockey for a living."

The waiter approached the table and Mandy ordered a pad thai; Derek had spicy seafood yam talay.

"Who was the best hockey player you played against?" asked Mandy.

"Patrick O'Sullivan."

"Oh yeah?" asked Mandy as she sipped her water from a straw.

"I could never stop the guy."

"Crazy, do you know him?"

"No, not really. Spoke to him one time at the rink. Nice dude."

"Do you make a good living doing the food truck thing?"

"Wow, getting right to it eh?" said Derek, smiling.

"I'm to the point, Derek. Life's too short to dance around things. Let's start small. What's the food truck called?"

"Eat It and Beat It," answered Derek, with a smirk on his face.

"No, it isn't," said Mandy, tilting her head in disbelief.

"I swear," said Derek, putting one hand over his heart and the other in the air. "See, here's the thing: we have no room for these people to sit. So, get your food, eat it and beat it."

The food arrived at their table and they began to eat.

"Did you name the pooch?"

"I did," replied Derek. "I called him Moose because he barrels around like one."

"That's a terrible name! What about Milo?" asked Mandy.

"He's a big, manly dog, he needs a manly name!"

"What about Wyatt?"

"Oh, I like that!"

Messy and Derek cabbed home from the airport after their flight back to Vancouver. They would have some time at the house before Hecky and R-Luv returned.

Derek walked up the steps to the house and noticed footprints on the door, like someone had been trying to kick it in. Messy approached the door, touched one of the prints and it swung open. They both jumped back.

"Why is the door open?" asked Messy. "I thought they were gone."

"Shh," said Derek, giving Messy the sign to shut up. Derek reached for a Louisville Slugger in the front closet and walked around the corner. There was nothing. He paused and slowly walked down the hall to the kitchen. Out of the corner of his eye he could see the kitchen had been ransacked; someone had broken into the house and destroyed everything!

Messy followed Derek around the corner to the living room, which was a disaster. Derek and Messy walked through the living room and checked R-Luv's room. No one there. They walked back to the staircase and Derek whispered to Messy. "Call 911."

Messy dialed 911 while Derek walked up the stairs and checked the three bedrooms. His room was tossed. The thieves, who appeared long gone, had stolen the few valuable things he owned.

He did a quick inventory of the other rooms and noticed the thieves took Hecky's PS3, R-Luv's X-Box, the TV, a blu-ray player and then it hit him: they took what was left of their money! He called R-Luv. No answer. He dialed Hecky, who picked up on the first ring. "Hecky, it's Sarge. Listen for a minute, where is it?"

"Where is what?" Hecky asked.

"It. The house got jacked."

"Oh, fuck. It's under my bed."

Derek ran into Hecky's room and checked. The safety deposit box was there – the money was not. "It's gone." On the other end of the phone line there was nothing but breathing. "Cops are on their way," said Derek as he hung up the phone.

Messy hollered at Derek as he ran downstairs to R-Luv's room. Messy was standing near the closet, holding an empty deposit box. The boys walked out the front door and sat down on the front step.

"They got everything," said Derek. Messy nodded. They sat on the front step and Derek had a smoke.

A few minutes later the officers arrived. They began looking around to assess the situation. Messy and Derek took lawn chairs out of the backyard and sat out front waiting for the police to do their work.

Derek was about to light a cigarette when his phone rang. "Hey."

"Hey, its R-Luv. Sup?"

"The house got robbed!"

"Fuck off!" scoffed R-Luv.

"I'm dead serious, dude."

"Fuck, really?"

"Really," said a subdued Derek.

"Goddammit!"

While R-Luv was still coming to terms with the robbery, Derek spotted Robie and Anna walking toward the house. "The cops are here, I gotta run," said Derek as he ended the call. He greeted Anna and Robie. "I can't believe this happened again!"

"Looks that way," replied Robie. "Do you mind if we look around?"

"Hey, we called you," replied Derek. Messy and Derek stepped aside and let them pass. As Anna walked by, Derek caught Messy checking her out.

"Who is that?" asked Messy.

"That's his partner."

"Smoke show."

"Yup."

Robie and Anna emerged from the house an hour later and removed their gloves. "I'm sorry this happened to you, boys. Your insurance will walk you guys through what to do next."

"Uh, we don't have insurance," said Derek, dumbfounded. "I didn't know we needed insurance – I always thought landlords had insurance."

"They do, but not for your stuff."

"Fuck," said Messy as he turned and looked at Derek.

"What's your concern? All you lost was a half bottle of Calvin Klein-."

Robie cut in, "Look, boys, I'll do all I can to nail whoever did this."

"Thank you, sir," said Derek as he shook Robie's hand, then Anna's. The police left and the boys were free to return inside and pick up the pieces. Derek and Messy cleaned their rooms along with the living room.

With the place tidied, they sat down beside each other on the couch. They had no TV to watch, no stereo to listen to and no liquor to drink. They just sat there waiting for the shit storm to occur when Hecky came home.

After an hour of waiting, Derek could hear Hecky stomping up to the front door. The door opened quickly and slammed shut. Hecky kicked off his boots and stomped into the living room. "Do the police know who did it?"

"I don't know," replied Derek. "They were in here for like three hours doing their thing. They'll find them."

"Really? Did they find the guys that robbed the liquor store, even after they were in their fucking house."

"Would you just shut the fuck up?" yelled Messy.

"Really? How much money did you lose? None! You fucking junkie piece of shit!" Hecky yelled back.

"Hey, calm down" interjected Derek. "We're in this shit together. Messy is pissed off too. We all feel violated, alright?" Derek took a deep breath and let the boys breathe. "How much did you lose, Hecky?"

"I don't know, around $8,500. What about you?"

"Four K."

"R-Luv?" asked Hecky.

"I'm not sure but I would bet it was close to twenty."

"Jesus Christ! We really should have left that money in the locker," said Hecky as he walked over to the fridge and grabbed the last beer.

"Yeah, well hindsight is 20/20."

"I guess we should get a lock and maybe some food, eh?" said Hecky.

"And a TV," said Messy.

Derek was a little relieved that he no longer had the distraction of all that money. Paying his bills was going to suck, but he knew that, as long as he had all that extra cash lying around with nothing good to spend it on, he would just blow it on drugs.

Josh Cybulski

But the robbery was tough on R-Luv, who had plans to buy a Red camera and a lighting kit. Derek felt bad that the only guy with honest plans had lost all his money while the other boys blew through theirs.

*   *   *   *   *

A few days later, Derek was watching television and killing time before his afternoon shift. At 1:00 p.m. the doorbell rang. Derek walked to the door and answered it. It was Anna.

"Hey, Anna. How can I help you?"

"I have pictures of some potential suspects. I just wanted to see if maybe you had seen any of them at the store or in the neighbourhood."

"Sure, come on in." Anna stepped inside and Derek closed the door behind her. She kicked off her work boots and followed Derek into the kitchen. "Can I get you a drink? I just made some coffee."

"Sure, black would be nice. Should I put the file on the table?"

"Yeah, go ahead and have a seat. Sorry we don't have a real table yet."

Anna sat on the couch and waited while Derek poured their coffees. He carried both cups over to the living room and set Anna's down in front of her. She opened the dossier and smiled as she felt Derek's eyes look at her. He sat across from her and noticed how incredibly put together she was. "So, what am I looking at here?" asked Derek.

"This is kind of a long shot, but I wanted to see if any of these guys look familiar to you."

Anna pushed the file toward Derek. He sat down and began to look through the headshots. "All of these guys are thieves?" asked Derek.

Anna laughed. "Not exactly. These are persons of interest in cases."

"Jesus," Derek looked up. "I should move to a new area, eh?"

Anna laughed. "Maybe."

It took until the 30th page until Derek finally recognized somebody. He had seen him in the corner store buying rollies and cigarettes. The man was slight, had scraggly receding hair and piercing gun metal blue eyes. He walked with a slouch and talked like trouble, always giving Derek a bad vibe. Derek felt it in the pit of his stomach: this kid had robbed them.

Anna sat up in her seat as he studied the photo. "Him," Derek stated confidently.

Anna took a look and nodded. "Him what?" she asked.

"I've seen him around before. Short, little dude. Maybe he could be the short one from the robbery?"

"Really?"

"Definitely. Those blue eyes – icy blue eyes. Who is he?"

Anna looked closer at the picture and read notes on the file. "Kent Sanderson. He's been in and out a few times. B & E's mostly. I don't know, Derek. It seems like a stretch for this guy to knock off a liquor store."

"Yeah, maybe."

"Keep looking. Maybe someone else in there looks familiar."

He continued to look through the pages, but none of the faces stuck out to him. "No one else," said Derek.

"Okay. That's really helpful though, Derek. We will look into him."

"Let me ask, what are the odds of solving either of these?"

"Pretty good."

"Is it? Messy and Hecky aren't optimistic."

"Why's that, Derek?"

"I don't know – their Dad's are both retired cops. They just said these are tough cases to solve."

"Ah, don't worry. We'll solve it."

"Okay," replied Derek.

"How long have you guys lived here?" asked Anna.

"Since February."

"Do you like Vancouver?"

"I love the food. I'm a bit of a chef myself, so I do enjoy the cuisine."

"You cook?" asked Anna, surprised.

"I do, mostly Polish food." Derek pointed to the kitchen. "Would you like to stay for dinner?"

Anna tripped on her words for a moment. "Oh, um, I don't think I can. I have to run, you know, with the info you gave me. Rain check?"

"Ya, sure? You name the time and place."

"Okay. Well, I guess I'd better go."

Derek caught Anna checking him out as she stood up and followed him to the front door. She opened the door to let herself out to see Hecky walking up to the house. "Hi," said Hecky as he extended out his hand, "I'm Riley, I live with Derek."

Anna shook Hecky's hand, "Hello, Riley. I'm Sergeant Johnson. I'm investigating the break and enter."

"Thank you so much for that!" said Hecky, as he faked an exuberant smile. "I won't hold you up."

Derek and Hecky waved to Anna as she was leaving. They kicked off their shoes and walked to the kitchen. Hecky grabbed two ice-cold Dos Equis, popped the tops and handed one to Derek. "So, what was that about?"

"She brought a face book full of potential suspects. I actually recognized one of the guys walking around here."

"Oh yeah? You think he ripped us off?" asked Hecky.

"I do, yeah. Fucking guy is wired! I just pointed the finger at him for the liquor store."

"Why did you do that? Now we can't get to him if the police are watching him."

"Get to him? Are we CIA now? Making shifts and moves?"

"Probably not, but we could keep an eye on him and if something opened up, we'd have options."

"Let's let police. . .police," said Derek, as he made a stop sign gesture with both of his hands.

"We should have a look at him."

"If you say so," replied Derek.

"You got a name?" asked Hecky.

"Kent Sanderson."

Hecky reached for his laptop on the side table.

"What are you doing?" asked Derek.

"Looking him up."

"You won't find anything," said Derek as he scoffed.

"Got him. He lives on Hardy."

"Jesus Christ," said Derek shaking his head in disbelief. "Is there any anonymity left in this world?"

"Hardy, that's over by the ball diamond. And judging by his pics he hangs out at Shark Club a lot."

"Which one?" asked Derek.

Hecky smiled, "Burnaby."

"What's say we go have a drink?"

Hecky nodded in agreement. "Maybe we spin by Hardy first."

"Okay." replied Derek.

"An added bonus: "his status is *rents are out of town for a week!*" Hecky paused for a second. "If we do this, it's gotta be tonight."

"Wait," said Derek, "what exactly are we doing?"

"We follow him and try to find out if he ripped us off," replied Hecky.

"How will we know?"

"We'll see what he does. If he is blowing tons of money, it's a good bet he ripped us off."

January 2009
NINETEEN

Hecky and Derek waited a few hours for Messy and R-Luv to get home from work. Once home, they all loaded into the Windstar and made the short drive to Hardy Court. The homes on the street were large and beautiful – a way more affluent neighbourhood than Woodsworth Avenue.

Hecky parked his van roughly one hundred yards away from Kent's house and studied the other cars on the street. There were a few Honda Civics and Pontiac Sunfires and one other Ford Windstar with tinted windows and no stickers. The vehicle didn't have anything you'd expect to see from a vehicle driven almost exclusively by soccer moms.

Hecky pointed to it. "There's Anna's undercover."

"Are these guys even trying?" asked Messy.

"It doesn't look like it," replied Hecky.

"This doesn't bode well for us, though. We can't do anything in his house," said Derek.

"We could always go through the park and around back," said Hecky. "I'd be surprised if these guys are watching both sides of the house."

"We're not cut out for this shit," said R-Luv. "We aren't gangsters."

"That might work – snatch him while he's out and bring him in through Harwood Park," said Messy.

"Am I on mute? Are you guys seriously talking about adding kidnapping to our list of done deeds? Let's just leave it alone. I don't even care about the money!" said R-Luv.

"We have to get him first," said Hecky, further ignoring R-Luv. "How do we do that?"

The boys rolled over to the Shark Club and convened at a booth for a drink. Shark Club was a spacious, dimly lit nightclub. There was a large bar, a dance floor and multiple tables scattered throughout.

A waitress approached Derek just as he sat down. "Can I get some drinks for you boys?"

"Four caesars. Extra spicy."

Messy and Derek sat in a booth facing the dance floor while Hecky and R-Luv did a lap of the bar to look for Kent Sanderson. Derek took a long, slow look around and didn't recognize anyone. Hecky and R-Luv returned from the rooftop, walked over to the table and sat down.

"Anything?" asked Derek.

"Yeah, he's up there," said Hecky. "He's surrounded by a bunch of wannabe gangsters."

"Any chance of getting to him?" asked Derek.

"Not unless he goes to his car."

"Why don't we just go to his house?" asked Messy.

"Oh sure, let's just pop on over and ransack the place," said R-Luv, sarcastically.

"No, you meathead," replied Messy with vitriol. "We go in through the park and wait for him in the backyard. The kid smokes, right? You think he's going to smoke in his parent's house? He probably smokes weed out back. We grab him there."

"That's a lot of probably's," said Hecky.

An hour later the boys were creeping in the dark through Harwood Park. They took cover under a set of shrubs in the Sanderson backyard and, for the next two hours, they hid in silence. In that time very little happened: one neighbour let his Pug out to piss; another neighbour had a cigarette and a drink on his deck.

The boys were betting that Kent would come home alone. If he brought even one person home it meant they had wasted their time and risked the police catching them. Moments later the back gate opened and then quietly closed. Footsteps on the wet grass followed soon after. Derek could see the shadow of a large man walking toward him. The man lurked outside the windows, shining a flashlight into the house. *Was this the thief?* Derek started going over things in his head, *Would the boys need to jump this guy if they were caught?* He watched the large man reach for a cell phone and speed dial a third party.

"Yo, Robie," said The Man. "All is quiet, am I good to go home?" A few seconds went by. "Ten-four." The cops were packing it in for the night. If Kent did come home alone they could make their move. The Man walked across the grass, opened the gate and left.

"What do we do?" asked Messy.

"We should move on the house," said Hecky, "We move in five minutes and see if this guy ripped us off." The boys looked at each other and nodded in agreement.

Five minutes later the house lit up like a Christmas tree when someone walked out back and turned the lights on. The boys ducked back down and rolled down their ski masks.

Kent stumbled drunkenly into the kitchen. He walked into a table, grabbed a television remote and turned on the TV. He then stumbled back over to the kitchen and pulled a few items out of the fridge and placed them on the large kitchen island.

Derek peaked out through the shrubs and could see Kent picking at a plate and eating like a pig. Kent then grabbed a beer and took a gulp of it as he walked toward the back door.

"What's the plan now?" asked Derek. Messy shrugged his shoulders as Hecky fidgeted. Derek couldn't see what Hecky was doing; a second later he couldn't see Hecky at all. *Where the fuck did he go?* thought Derek.

Kent walked out the patio door and sat down in a lawn chair. He lit a cigarette and took a long deep drag. It had been hours since Derek had a cigarette – his cravings were so strong his hands were shaking.

"What are we going to do?" asked R-Luv.

Messy and Derek didn't know what to do and Hecky was nowhere to be found.

Kent finished his cigarette and discarded it in an ashtray. He stood up and opened the patio door to go inside. As he did R-Luv coughed. Kent stopped in the doorway and slowly turned around. The boys did their best to stay low and out of sight.

Derek peaked through the shrubs and spotted Hecky. He was inside the house, approaching Kent slowly from behind.

Kent turned on the porch light and continued to look around the backyard from the patio doorway. Derek locked eyes with him and froze. He pointed at Derek and as he did Hecky wrapped a belt around his neck from behind and began to choke him.

Kent struggled and pushed back into Hecky, who held on, but couldn't match Kent's brute strength. He held his own as he took elbows in the head and waited for help from the boys. Kent's elbows threw both of them back into the kitchen.

The boys bum rushed Kent. Messy was the first to run inside and his military training kicked in. He hit Kent twice as Messy swept Kent's legs out from under him. Kent fell and whacked the side of his head against the edge of the granite countertops. On his way to the ground his face slammed into the slate floor.

"Jesus Christ!" yelled Derek.

"I thought I could take him," said Hecky.

Derek rolled Kent onto his back. His face was a mangled, bloody mess and his teeth were scattered on the floor. Derek checked his vitals; Hecky had punched his ticket.

"Is he breathing?" asked Hecky.

"No, he isn't breathing. He just slammed his head off a rock slab!"

Messy and R-Luv both began yelling, "Fuck, fuck, fuck, fuck!"

"Close that fucking door," yelled Derek, "and turn the lights off!"

R-Luv shut the patio door and Messy looked to dim the lights.

"You just killed this guy for no fucking reason!" said Messy.

Hecky held up Kent's wrist. He was wearing Hecky's watch. "For good reason. This cunt ripped us off!"

"We need to find our other shit!"

"Check upstairs," shouted Hecky. "I came in the second story window. He's got shit everywhere."

"What do we do with him?" asked R-Luv. "Can we save him?"

"This isn't on you, R-Luv," said Hecky. "I got in here. I started and ended this whole thing. Put that shit out of your head; there is no saving him. It's done."

"What are we going to do with him, Hecky?" asked Derek.

The boys stood in the dark with the dead body of an enemy. Hecky had gotten them in way over their heads.

A half-hour went by and no one said a word. They were clueless. Derek went through a wide range of emotion. Rage, empathy – he didn't know how to feel. That's when it hit him; the police would be back in the morning. "Fuck me!" yelled Derek. "The cops are probably coming back tomorrow!"

"Jesus Christ," said Messy, "You're right."

"You know what?" said Derek, as he grabbed the boys' attention. "I'd rather think about this at home. We need to get him out of here, get this cleaned and fucking hit the road. Can we do that? Quickly? Neatly?"

"I think we can," said Messy.

Hecky nodded his head. "Yeah, but we can't exactly roll up in the Windstar and stroll out with a corpse."

Derek knew he needed to take control. He took a deep breath and took things over. "Okay, let's do this. Hecky, toss me your keys. Messy and I will drag him out of here to the car. You clean up this goddamn mess and R-Luv, you go gather all our shit from his room, and while you're at it grab some other shit too. First things first, everyone needs gloves!"

Messy and Derek exited Kent's home through the patio door into the backyard and walked out into Harwood Park. They walked in the dark, through the field, to the van parked a few blocks away. As they walked Derek vomited all over the ground. He stood back up and took a deep breath, then threw up again. After another deep breath he finally composed himself. "I'm thinking we should back the van to the end of the court to use the shrubs as cover. I've got no problem dragging him in the dark, its just getting him out of the house unnoticed."

"Yeah, dude, not a bad idea. I'll drive over there in like ten minutes."

Messy and Derek approached Hecky's van and unlocked the door. Messy pulled out a bag and grabbed gloves, handing one set to Derek and keeping the other three. He jumped in the van as Derek began to sprint back across the park to Kent's house.

Derek walked back into the kitchen and noticed that Hecky had made a makeshift bandage for Kent's head to slow down the bleeding. He knelt down and folded Kent's arms across his chest and placed a blanket next to his body. Derek rolled Kent's body onto the blanket and wrapped it around him. He and R-Luv then dragged Kent's lifeless body across the kitchen and outside to the backyard.

In the backyard Derek continued to drag Kent toward Harwood Park. They dragged his body alongside Kent's home toward Hardy Court where Messy would meet them.

Messy hadn't yet arrived with the van. Derek crouched down and waited for him to pull around. Thirty seconds later the Windstar turned the corner and drove toward him.

Kent's body was already in position when Messy turned the van around and backed it up. He popped the trunk and Derek yanked it open. They lifted Kent into the van and Messy shut the trunk. "Drive like a block from here and we'll meet you," said Derek. Messy jumped into the van and drove off slowly into the darkness. Derek ran back through Harwood Park and the Sanderson backyard into the house.

"How's it going?" asked Derek.

"Fuck, I could use a hand! Can you clean the counters?"

Derek grabbed some of Kent's clothing and began soaking up blood from the countertops. After soaking up all the blood, he tossed Kent's clothes in a nearby garbage bag. He looked around the kitchen; it was clean – no traces of a struggle.

Hecky and Derek stuffed the garbage bag full of evidence to take with them. Derek threw the garbage bag on the patio stones in the backyard and waited for R-Luv to come down from upstairs.

A minute later, Derek heard R-Luv running down the stairs. He had a suitcase in each hand and a duffel bag on each shoulder.

"Let's go, boys," said Derek.

The boys hustled through the kitchen, shutting every light off and closing every curtain. They exited the home through the back doors. On the way out, Derek picked up the garbage bag and carried it with him.

Messy met the boys one street over on Hardwick. They piled into the van and drove home, Messy did his best not to arouse any suspicion.

"Should we really have the brown guy driving?" asked R-Luv.

"Fuck off, R-Luv," Messy shot back as he pulled the Windstar into the garage. R-Luv jumped out of the van and quickly closed the garage door behind them. The boys scattered out of the van and began to pull everything out except Kent's body and the garbage bag. The boys lugged the bags of stolen goods into the house and piled them in the living room.

"Jesus Christ. How did this guy carry this much shit out of our house?" asked Messy. "Even with four of us it is impossible."

"This isn't just what he stole from us," said R-Luv. "I grabbed other shit too." R-Luv walked into the room and opened one of the suitcases. It was full of hundred and fifty-dollar bills.

"Jesus," exclaimed Messy.

"Fucking eh!" screamed Hecky.

Derek shook his head in disbelief. "Guys, what are we going to do about the dead kid in the garage?"

"Well, you're the smart one," yelled Messy. "Think of something!"

"Oh, okay, Messy. Let me see, what do I usually do with a rotting carcass in my garage?" Derek snapped his fingers. "Oh, that's right. I toss him in the back of my pickup and take him to the local dump. 'cause I dispose of bodies every goddamn fucking day!"

"Lower your voices," said R-Luv. "And fuck you, Messy. Why don't you figure it out? Your Dad was a cop."

"Look, boys, we're in this shit together," said Hecky in a calming voice.

Derek took a deep breath to try and calm down. "Okay. Well, he can't stay here and we're losing darkness."

October 4th, 2009
TWENTY

After the meal, Derek tried to pay the bill. Mandy insisted that they split it, which they did. They left the restaurant and began walking to her car. "Would you like to go for a walk?" she asked. "There is this great bakery a few blocks from here. You will love it!"

"Okay," answered Derek as he smiled and looked ahead.

"Tell me about your family."

"My parents are good people –very religious, church every Sunday, strict, that kind of thing," Derek replied.

"Are you close with them?"

"Yeah, I mean, I guess. We try and talk every day."

"What's your Dad like?"

"He's the best man I know. He always does right, prays, has loved one woman his whole life. He does carpentry for fun and always makes people things for free."

"Oh, that's neat!" said Mandy, "What about music?"

"What about it?" asked Derek.

"Do you have a favourite band?"

"Hail the Villain," replied Derek.

"Never heard of them," replied Mandy. "Why do you like them?"

"Envy mostly," replied Derek as he laughed. "Their front man, Bryan Crouch, is a maniac. Hell of a nice guy too, but onstage he does not care. They opened for my buddies back home and signed a record deal in the spring."

"Very cool. Do you have any hobbies other than jealousy?"

Derek smiled. "Not really. You?"

"I do pottery," answered Mandy.

"Really? That's so cool!"

"Yeah, it's pretty neat!"

"What's the first thing you ever pottered?" asked Derek.

"It was a tea pot for my Sister."

"Did she like it?"

Mandy grinned and looked down like she was guilty of something. "I don't know. I never gave it to her."

"No?"

"I kept it. I decided I wanted to keep the first thing I ever made."

"That's okay, I get that. Do you have any other siblings?"

"Nope, just a younger Sister."

"What about your folks? What are they like?" asked Derek.

Mandy paused. She was unsure of how to answer the question. Finally she did, "I lost my Mom I was 10."

"Oh shit. I'm sorry to hear that."

Mandy sighed. "It was hard – she was my best friend in the world."

"Jesus, I can't even imagine."

Mandy took a deep breath and looked down at the table. "I never had a chance to be a teenager – never partied or did drugs or any teenager stuff."

"I'm sure your Father probably appreciated that. What is he like?"

"He's the most loyal person I know. He'd do anything for his friends and family. He's a lot of fun too, always smiling, always dancing. You'd like him."

"Like him? He sounds like me!"

Mandy and Derek smiled at each other as they continued walking to the bakery. Mandy gently took his hand and caressed it in hers. Derek felt all emotion fall over him. She looked up and over at him. The feeling of those eyes looking at him was more than he could handle.

January 2009

Hecky opened the garage door and pulled outside in the Windstar. He drove the van back to Woodsworth and parked it on the side of the road.

Messy, R-Luv and Derek stayed in the garage, staring down a dead body. It would be a matter of days before people noticed that Kent was missing, and they needed to make their moves by the time that happened.

"What do you guys think?" asked Derek.

"I think there's a fucking dead body in our garage," replied R-Luv.

"Very perceptive," replied Derek.

"How did they get rid of bodies on The Wire?" asked Messy.

"Which time?" asked R-Luv. "They got rid of a lot of bodies."

"The last time – Marlo."

"You want to start piling bodies in the vacants?" asked R-Luv.

"Yes," replied Messy.

"Jesus Christ," exclaimed R-Luv. "Where do you know of vacants in this city? We aren't living in Baltimore."

"I'm going to put them in your empty head," joked Derek.

"I've never even seen The Wire," said Messy.

"We could put them in some of the empty houses in the city. They are all in rich areas, though," said Derek.

"It's not a bad idea," said Messy.

"Boys, what can we actually do here?" asked R-Luv. "For real."

"Well, we do live on the coast," said Messy suggestively.

"You want to toss him in the ocean?" asked R-Luv.

"No good?"

"We could. We'd have to hustle."

Messy cut in excited, "Ohh, lets fake his death."

"How do we fake his death?" asked Derek. "He is already real dead."

"We used to do it when guys would pass out. We'd put them in the driver seat of the humvee and push it. Then yell to wake them up as a goof."

"He ain't waking up, Messy."

"Sarge, I know that. Look, we get his car, put him in it and push it into the ocean."

Hecky walked back into the garage in mid-conversation. "What are you guys talking about?"

R-Luv answered, "Messy thinks we should push his car into the ocean to fake his death."

"That's fucking great, Messy."

"What?" exclaimed R-Luv.

"Hear me out," said Hecky. "We keep him here for today, and Sarge and I can run over and grab his car now. We park it here with him – tomorrow night we spin out of the city with my van and his car. His car goes over the edge on the Sea to Sky highway."

"I don't know, dude," said Derek. "That's a lot of plates to spin for an entire day. It could go sideways."

"Dude, no one is out on those roads at night. We speed through there in his car like jackasses. Five minutes later his car is submerged. If the cops ever find it, they will question road crews about what they saw and that's that. That's if they find him. Best case is no one does, or they find him weeks later. Evidence destroyed.

"You really think its that easy?" asked R-Luv.

"It could be. If we do this, we have to get over to his house quick."

"Ah, fuck," yelled Derek. "Ok, I'm in unless someone has a better idea."

R-Luv and Messy looked at each other and nodded in Hecky's direction. Hecky and Derek took off to Kent's parents, hoping and praying that the police weren't back doing surveillance.

At around 2:00 a.m., the boys left the house. R-Luv drove Hecky's van with Messy and Derek in the passenger's seats. Hecky drove Kent's 2006 Pontiac G6 with Kent's body in the trunk.

The caravan headed out of the city before merging onto the Sea to Sky highway. They didn't speed, they didn't drive slowly, they didn't draw any attention, they just drove.

They were gambling on there being no drivers on the road and no rubberneckers. They were also betting on Hecky being able to drive through a construction zone without being stopped. He'd driven the road every night for months and claimed to have never seen a cop and the boys were taking his word for it.

None of the boys had slept since Kent's death. Still, Hecky seemed to be dealing with it best, even though he had been the one to put the dog down.

After forty minutes of driving Hecky called Derek. "Hello?"

"Yo, pull in front and drive for about ten minutes. When you see the rest stop, pull off to the side."

Derek hung up his phone, relayed the message to the boys and did as he was told. They checked their rear-view mirrors to see Hecky pull over and shut off the lights.

A few minutes later they passed through a construction zone until they were met by a man with a stop sign. They waited while traffic zipped past them in the other direction.

Derek called Hecky a few minutes later from the other side of the construction zone and told him about their holdup. Hecky instructed him to pull off about five kilometers up the road. Derek relayed the message to R-Luv and they drove to the spot. He killed the lights and they waited.

Ten minutes of waiting felt like an eternity: Derek knew that they weren't cut out to be criminals. He kept picturing Hecky in the G6 being chased by the police. There wasn't a plan B – this was it. If Hecky succeeded they would have seconds to glove up, move Kent into the driver's seat and push the car into Lion's Bay.

Derek spotted the G6 headlights in the distance; Hecky was moving, quick. The car approached the boys and began to slow down – the reflection of the brake lights could be seen on the wet highway surface. Hecky turned left and pulled up alongside the van close to the edge.

The boys were going to push the car through a six-foot gap in the steel barrier. But it seemed unlikely that a car would drive through the opening without smearing paint or applying the brakes. So to counter that, Messy planned to sabotage the brakes and went to work on them. R-Luv ran out to the road and kept look out. "Go!"

Hecky popped the trunk of Kent's car and it was on. Hecky and Derek each grabbed one end of Kent and walked his body over to the driver's side of the car. Messy cut the brakes and jumped in the car from the passenger's side to help guide the body into the driver's seat.

With Kent's body in place, Derek passed the seatbelt to Messy. He clicked it in place and jumped out of the car. They shut the doors while Hecky called back to R-Luv. "How are we looking?"

"All clear," replied R-Luv.

Messy, Hecky and Derek walked around back of the car and began pushing it toward the water. They pushed with everything they had but could not get the car to move.

"Did you leave the parking brake on?" asked Derek. Hecky winced and corrected his mistake.

"Weak, dude."

"No one's perfect," replied Hecky. He shut the door and walked to the back of the car. They pushed the car again and this time they were able to move it toward the edge. It scraped the rail before falling over the edge and crashing below. A bubbling sound followed as the car slowly submerged into the icy water.

Hecky yelled out, "Let's get the fuck out of here."

*   *   *   *   *

Derek woke up the following morning at Hecky's parents and walked downstairs to the kitchen. He made himself a coffee and turned on the Vancouver morning news to see if anything had been discovered at Kent's home or on the 99. No news.

He walked out onto the patio and sat down on a patio chair. His hands shook as he grabbed a fresh cigarette. He placed it between his teeth and lit it with a deep haul. His hands kept shaking. The patio door opened behind him and Messy walked out holding a cup of coffee.

"Remember our first morning here?" asked Messy.

"Best day of my life."

"Same," replied Messy. "I never thought we'd be doing this."

"Yeah, it's fucked up."

"You know what is really fucked up? Hecky did this, and you and I are the ones losing sleep. He isn't broken up at all – kid's out like a light."

"Well, to be fair, he was up until 6:00 a.m. torching clothes."

"Don't matter," replied Messy. "If that's me I'm not snoring on my folks' futon. . . and I've killed people before."

Hecky's behaviour had changed since the liquor store robbery. His confidence had grown; he had swagger. It scared Derek and shook Messy too. However, part of Derek was convinced that Hecky attacked Kent Sanderson for all the right reasons.

Over the next few days, the boys took time off from work and enjoyed Squamish. After every sleepless night, Derek had the same routine: wake up; make a pot of coffee; watch the news; chain smoke; talk to Messy.

*   *   *   *   *

The boys returned to Burnaby the following week and Derek was able to start sleeping again. Hecky spent the next week convincing the boys that they had done the right thing. Sanderson stole from them, stole from others, made peoples lives miserable, and was a drug addict. He preyed on people and didn't serve a purpose in this world. But every time Hecky reminded Derek of all these things, Derek thought to himself, *how are we any different?*

*   *   *   *   *

A week after the body dump Derek came home from work and found the boys sitting around the living room. There were two duffel bags on the coffee table and two suitcases on the floor. The boys invited Derek over to see what they had taken from Kent.

Hecky opened the first suitcase and placed it on the floor. He began pulling out stacks of money and piled them on the table. The bigger the pile, the wider his smile.

After the money was all stacked up, Hecky began pulling out bricks and bags of drugs: weed; cocaine; heroin; speed; MDMA; and Oxy. He paused for a moment to admire their haul before opening the second suitcase. He pulled out even more dope and money.

After adding to the piles, Hecky finally opened the first of two duffel bags and set it on the floor. In the duffel bag were three Rolex's, as well as a few TagHauer watches, some diamond rings, earrings, gold chains, a blu-ray player, their PS3 and X-Box, and an additional PS3 and X-Box.

In the second duffel bag were some expensive bottles of liquor and a few articles of Armani clothing.

The boys stood in silence, staring at their haul. They were in disbelief. Hecky counted off the money that was originally stolen from them and evened things out with R-Luv, Derek and himself. He then began dividing up the new money into four piles. Messy looked at the drugs on the table. "What are we doing with this shit?"

R-Luv shook his head and Derek shrugged his shoulders. They had no idea where to sell drugs – outside of the cocaine they could have happily flushed the rest of it.

"I know a guy that would buy all of this," said Hecky.

"Who?" Derek then abruptly threw his hands in the air. "No, you know what? I don't want to know."

"It's a guy from work, my usual coke go-to," said Hecky. "You don't need a name. I could probably get us, like, twenty grand for all of this."

"If it's worth it to you then go ahead," said Messy.

R-Luv and Derek both shook their heads in agreement.

"How much money is that?" asked R-LUV.

"I've counted 184."

"Thousand?" asked Messy.

"Thousand!" yelled Hecky.

"Holy fuck!" exclaimed Derek.

"Forty-six thousand a piece!" yelled Hecky.

"Holy shit," said R-LUV. "How the fuck do we hide this?"

"R-Luv is right," said Derek. "This is excessive. He's got seventy g's to deal with and you and I have fifty."

"This time we do the storage locker," said Hecky, "and we sit on it until we can do something safe and smart. We've got all this other shit to deal with too – we can't exactly wear this guy's diamonds out on the town."

"Sounds good," said Derek. "We'll go out tomorrow and get a locker. You deal with this other shit."

Messy and R-Luv nodded in agreement.

"Okay, I will," said Hecky as he scooped up the dope off the table and threw it into the duffel bags. Hecky walked out of the living room and up the stairs to his room.

The boys began putting away the money, diamonds and clothes. "What are we going to do with these diamonds?" asked Messy.

"I don't know, dude," replied Derek. "Sell them on Craigslist."

"That's a good way to get robbed again," said R-Luv. "Besides, I thought you only used Craigslist to get laid."

"Usually," joked Derek.

"What are the odds that you finger the guy who robbed us and we find him right away?" asked Messy.

"Huge coincidence," said R-Luv.

"You believe that?" asked Messy.

"In coincidences, of course I do," replied R-Luv. "Do you?"

"Maybe. Do you, Sarge?"

"No," said Derek, matter of factly.

"You don't believe in coincidences?" asked R-Luv.

"I believe that there are consequences for actions, like this for example. We'll pay for this somehow. Coincidences happen in the movies. They are a plot device, not a reality."

"You play with fire you get burned, right?" asked R-Luv.

"Yup," replied Derek. "Fire doesn't care who it burns."

January 2009
TWENTY-ONE

The next day Derek met Messy at a Self Storage Depot on the Lougheed Highway. They rented a 5 x 8 storage unit, paid in full and left.

They arrived back at the house and found Hecky sitting on the couch sipping on Knob Creek and watching First Blood.

"Did you get the unit?"

"Ya," said Derek. "Paid in full."

"We might need a bigger unit," Hecky pointed to a duffel bag sitting next to the couch. The bag was overflowing with stacks of money.

"Holy shit, Hecky. How much is this?" asked Derek.

"Thirty-eight thousand."

"Jesus Christ," exclaimed Messy.

"How are we going to spend this without alarm bells?" asked Derek as his shoulders slumped in disbelief.

"We'll figure something out," Hecky said confidently. "For now, we each pull out one thousand a month and no one will suspect a thing."

"We've already had police snooping," said Messy. "How long until they start piecing shit together?"

*   *   *   *   *

Hecky and Derek woke up the next morning and boxed up the money, clothes and jewelry before driving to the storage unit.

On the way back to the house Hecky pulled onto Woodsworth. In the distance Derek could see Robie's car parked in front of their house. There were two people sitting inside.

"Goddamn, what do they want?"

"Maybe they want more info about Kent." suggested Derek.

"I fucking hope so, man. Just make like you don't even see them." Hecky pulled his van into a parking spot a few cars back from Robie's Crown Vic. The boys got out of van and walked toward Robie's car. As they inched closer to the car Derek could see Anna sitting in the passenger seat. They breezed past the car as if they didn't notice them.

"Derek!" It was Anna's voice.

He turned casually and smiled. "Hey! What are you guys up to?"

"We were looking to talk to you about Kent Sanderson," said Anna.

"Who?" asked Derek, pretending to be puzzled as he walked toward the car and crouched down.

"The boy you fingered."

Hecky snickered and began to laugh. Derek gave him a playful push and smiled. "You're fingering boys now, Sargey!" Hecky shouted jokingly as Derek gave him another push.

Robie tried to reel the boys back in. "You said you'd seen him around your store."

"Yeah, all the time. I'd see him out at the bar too once in awhile."

Robie looked at Hecky then over at Derek. "Your roommate is free to go inside. This won't take long."

Hecky smiled. "Take care, guys."

He turned and began walking inside. Derek knew the wheels were going to be turning inside his head.

"Where were you on the 17th?" asked Robie.

The 17th was the night Hecky killed Kent. "The 17th," said Derek, in an uncertain tone. "I think I was out with the boys. We went drinking."

"Where'd you go?" asked Robie.

"Shark Club." Derek pondered for a moment. "Actually, if I remember right, that kid was there too."

"He was," said Anna.

"Why do you guys ask?" asked Derek as he smiled at Anna.

Robie immediately interjected, "His parents reported him missing."

"Oh, shit," said Derek as he snapped his head in Robie's direction. "Really?"

"Derek, did you see him talking with anyone?" asked Anna.

"Well, it's a club, so yeah, he was talking to people. He was at a big table."

"Anyone stand out to you?" asked Robie.

"Not really. To be honest with you it was a table of people I didn't really want to associate with."

"Not your crowd?" asked Robie.

"Nah, I like older women."

Anna laughed nervously as he smiled at her. Derek knew that he was getting to Anna, and Robie didn't like it. "Alright, we'll be in touch."

Derek began to walk toward the house. "I hope so! Bye, Anna."

Anna waved as Derek walked up to his front door and walked inside. Anna and Robie turned and walked to their car. "You know that kid is bad news," said Robie.

"You think so?"

"He isn't looking to fall in love."

Anna replied, "Neither am I."

Before Derek had even shut the door, Hecky was in his face. He grabbed his shirt and pushed Derek into the back of the front door.

"You fucking idiot. You told them we were there!" yelled Hecky.

Derek pushed Hecky off of him and yelled back, "They knew before I told them. You don't think the first fucking thing they did was check who had seen him last? He's missing – they ask questions."

"They ask and you lie. That's how we stay out of this shit."

"No. I lie, they call me on it and then I'm fucked!" yelled Derek. "I didn't draw any suspicions, I'm just some kid who parties too much and saw this kid a few times. Calm down!"

"If you go down, I'm not going with you."

The RCMP ramped up their search for Kent. His face was plastered in the papers, on the news, and his name was everywhere. No one knew where he was.

Then a bombshell: the police announced that Kent Sanderson was a member of a Vancouver gang called the R.O.P., who were commonly referred to as The Jankers. They were a gang made up primarily of young, white, ex-convicts.

After the announcement, the boys met for dinner at The Soho. They arrived as a group and walked inside, choosing a booth near the back corner. They took their seats, ordered six pounds of chicken wings and four pints of Russell Cream Ale. The waitress left and R-Luv was the first to state the obvious. "The fucking R.O.P.! What are we going to do?"

"Slow your roll, R-Luv," said Hecky. "What do they know? What do they really fucking know?"

"What if someone saw something" suggested R-Luv. "Now we got a gang and the cops after us."

"Look," said Hecky, trying to reason with R-Luv, "if it comes down to it, I'll fall on the sword for you."

"I doubt that," said Messy.

"I love you, guys," continued Hecky. "I'd do anything for you, even if it means a painful existence for me."

Derek knew that R-Luv was buying Hecky's sincerity. He raised his eyebrow to Messy. There wasn't a bone in Derek's body that believed Hecky wouldn't sell them out for his own protection. "Guys, look," said Derek, "they don't have shit. There is nothing in the car. Stop worrying; that's what will sink us, no pun intended. Just stick together, and don't bring it up again."

The boys agreed.

*   *   *   *   *

A few days after the R.O.P. press conference, Hecky and Derek were at home when there was a knock at the door. Hecky answered the door and found Robie and Anna holding a book lined with profiles of R.O.P. members.

Hecky let them into the house and showed them into the living room. They paused their game of NHL 09. Anna sat down beside Derek and Robie sat across from him. Derek sat up straight and greeted them.

"Hey, guys. How are you?"

"I'm okay, kid," said Robie.

"I'm good," replied Anna.

"What can I do for you?" asked Derek as he looked over at Hecky.

Hecky started to sweat, his face clammy and ruddy. He quickly excused himself and walked upstairs. Derek knew that he was going to listen from the top of the stairs. His biggest fears were coming true: the cops were investigating Derek.

Derek planned on being honest. If he saw other gang members, he would let the Sergeants know.

Robie threw the book of R.O.P. pictures on the coffee table and opened to the first page. "Have a look and see if you recognize anyone."

"Okay," replied Derek. "Do you guys want a drink or anything?"

"All good, just look," said Robie as he pressed his hand on the book. Derek began scanning the pages. It wasn't like the book from before. There were only fourteen pages, each page displaying a member's picture as well as their criminal history.

Derek pointed at a picture. "Him, I've seen him before."

Robie pulled out his pen and notepad and began writing notes.

"Where?" asked Anna.

"My store, a few times, and I think he was at Shark Club."

"Good," said Robie. "I'm going to grab something from the car." He stood up and excused himself.

Anna looked at Derek and smiled. He smiled back and looked through the book. He didn't recognize any other men.

Anna closed the book and set it down. Robie walked inside carrying a laptop bag and sat back down on the couch. "You probably don't know this, but Kent lived a few blocks from here."

"Oh, really? I had no idea," said Derek as he feigned surprise.

"I grabbed this because I wanted to show you a larger database of gang members from other crews. Tell me if any of these guys look familiar."

"How many gangs are there?" asked Derek.

"Twelve that we categorize as gangs, if you count the R.O.P. But at any one time we guess there are probably 130 or so in Greater Vancouver. A lot of these gangs are what we call puppet crews."

"So, you want me to look at every gangster in Vancouver?" asked Derek.

"Every gangster that has a documented rivalry with the R.O.P."

"Okay, I get it."

For the next twenty minutes he looked at pictures of gangsters. Robie stepped outside for a cigarette. As he shut the door Derek turned to Anna.

"Isn't there like a gang unit or something that handles this stuff."

"He borrowed these files from the Vancouver Gang Task Force and a few things from Surrey PD. He's fairly certain that a rival gang has done something to this kid. These guys have been killing each other all over Van for the last year and half. We need it to stop because innocent people are getting killed."

"You mean like in Surrey?"

"Yes. Please keep looking, Derek. The inner workings of the police aren't the concern right now."

"Sorry, Anna."

Derek turned and smiled. He continued to look through the pictures. He recognized some men from the news.

Robie came back inside and sat across from Derek on the couch. They sat in silence as Derek stared at pictures. He finished and Robie pressed on with the questions.

"Did you recognize any of them?"

"Just The Brothers, but I only ever saw them on the news."

"You haven't seen any of these faces around here or your store?"

"Not that I can remember."

"Why did Kent stick out?"

Derek thought for a moment. "When he came through, he treated my cashier like shit. I always remember people like that."

"Okay, I don't know that I have any other questions. Do you, Anna?"

"I don't think so."

"Alright, Derek, I think we're done," said Robie.

"I'm really sorry I couldn't be more help. Good luck."

Derek walked Robie and Anna to the front door and they shook hands before Derek lead them outside. He walked back into the kitchen. Hecky opened his bedroom door and walked down the stairs. Derek grabbed two beer from the fridge just as Hecky walked into the kitchen, Derek popped open the beers, walked over to the couch and sat down. Hecky sat across from him and he handed him a beer. Hecky took one look at Derek and had a sip. He was out of breath and his jaw was clicking. "Did you bump?" asked Derek.

"A little," he replied.

"It's early, dude. Are you alright?"

"No, I'm not fucking alright!"

"Outside," said Derek.

Hecky and Derek walked out to the backyard and sat down. "Hecky you weren't down here, we aren't suspects. In their minds they just extracted everything they can from me. So, drink your beer, smoke cigs and stop doing coke at 10:00 a.m."

"Sarge, I don't like this."

Derek lit a cigarette. "What'd you expect? That we'd go unnoticed?"

"No, but I didn't plan on this happening. It's not like we knew he was a gangster. He was just some prick that ripped us off."

"You're right, it wasn't expected. But this interrogation was. I knew the second you told me about the robbery that this would happen."

*   *   *   *   *

A few days later, Hecky was offered a job in Whistler on a movie called Hot Tub Time Machine. He took it to get away from the craziness at the house.

The first night Hecky was away the boys met after work at a local bowling alley. They sat down at a table with a few pitchers while they waited for a lane to open up.

Bowling wasn't Derek's first priority. He was just looking to get smashed and forget about the constant stress Hecky was causing.

"When I can, I'm moving away from Stressy," said Messy.

"Yup," said R-Luv in agreement.

"Are you guys moving out together?" asked Derek.

They looked at each other and shook their heads no.

"We've got money to do it," said Derek. "Might be nice to have space."

"Don't paint this in any other light other than the one it is," said Messy. "It's Stressy, man. I can't fucking live with him anymore."

"Same," said R-Luv. "Speaking of, what is the police situation?"

"I was being looked at as a lead. They're done now. I've given all I can."

"So Stressy should be able to cool off soon?" asked Messy.

"Stressy should be stress free upon his return," said Derek.

"Thank God," said R-Luv. "I thought he'd turned a corner and was becoming fun, but Jesus, he turned three corners and he's back to where he was."

"Let's hold off on the moving out talk guys," said Derek. "Give Hecky a chance to cool off."

"Fine by me," said Messy.

For two weeks they kept things quiet and stayed out of harm's way as the city exploded into a gang war. There were two factions involved in the gang war and in February it escalated into a brutal shooting in broad daylight.

*   *   *   *   *

Derek worked the day before Hecky was set to come back from Squamish. It was Tuesday, February 10th and he had the night shift. He was stocking the beer cooler when he noticed Anna through the cooler door. Derek exited onto the store floor. Anna didn't see him until he walked toward his office, two aisles over from her.

"Derek?"

"Sgt. Johnson, how are you?" They smiled at each other.

"Call me Anna," she said as she smiled nervously. "I'm good, you?"

"I'm okay. Working hard, you know. Can I help you with anything?"

"Maybe you can give me a few wine recommendations?"

"I'd love to. Are you pairing these wines with anything?"

"I cook a lot of fish and pasta."

"Alright, follow me."

Anna followed Derek as he walked over to the Italian section. He studied a few wines, pulled a bottle from the shelf and handed it to Anna. "This is called Santa Christina Toscana. It's a mix of 60% Sangiovese, 40% Cabernet, Merlot and Syrah."

"Okay, what does that mean?"

"That's nerdy wine talk, but it pairs great with pasta with red sauce."

"Okay, great!" said Anna.

"Now, let's find you something to pair with fish." Derek looked back at Anna and smiled. "What kind of fish?"

"Salmon," she replied.

"Okay, salmon," Derek took another quick look around the store. "Road 13!" Derek led her to the BC wines and grabbed a bottle of Road 13. "You'll love this. It's got orange overtones of viognier with the acidity from the Sauv Blanc and the Riesling."

Anna took the bottle from Derek, studied it and smiled. "They are expensive, eh?"

"Alcohol in Canada is always overpriced. We are the country that fun forgot."

"Is this the stuff you buy regularly?" asked Anna.

"I wish," replied Derek.

"I appreciate all the help, Derek. You're very good at your job." Anna walked toward the cash. It was the first time Derek had seen her in street clothes: she had a beautiful pear-shaped body and legs for days. As he watched her, Hecky approached Derek from the side.

"What the fuck was that about?"

"Fuck! Where'd you come from?"

"I just got into town and was coming to grab beer. Why were you talking to that axe wound?"

"She's cool. We were flirting, calm down!"

As Derek finished his sentence Anna looked back toward him and he waved good-bye. She waved and smiled. Hecky glared at Derek as Anna left the store.

Hecky exited the store and went next door to the pub to have a few drinks. Derek finished his shift, locked up and walked next door.

"How goes it?" asked Hecky.

"Good, man. Everyone's doing their own thing. How was the shoot?"

"It was a blast. Hung out a bit with Craig Robinson. He's cool."

"That's awesome, dude. You got a line on your next job?"

"I do, but it's not a shoot."

"What is it? asked Derek as he motioned to the bartender to bring him a drink.

"I want to do the food truck thing. I think it could work and we could put our cash through it."

"Really?" asked Derek as he took a drink. "What about startup cash?"

"If we could each get 10k from our parents we could get close. I figured fifty thousand for a startup, and we've got the extra ten lying around. My parents already offered ten. I've got a whole presentation for you. You'll love it."

"Wow! I think mine would do a small loan," replied Derek. "Maybe more if I got it back to them quick."

"Even if we bleed money for a year, we just put our own cash through it until we turn a profit. With your skills we could make this work." Derek thought for a moment and Hecky continued, "Do you think you can get the boys on board?"

"If it means they can touch their cash they will get on board."

"Yeah, well, let's just put the idea on the table and see what they say."

The boys drove home. When they arrived at the house R-Luv and Messy were sitting on the couch watching Rocky Balboa. Hecky ran upstairs and threw his luggage in his bedroom. Messy greeted Derek. "How's Stressy?"

"He's good, seems relaxed," said Derek, knowing that he was lying.

Hecky walked into the room and sat down. "How's it going?" he asked.

The boys responded by nodding their heads and smiling.

"You want to go for a smoke?"

"No, the movie is almost over," responded R-Luv.

Derek walked over to the white board on the wall and wrote in dry erase marker *money talk, backyard.* "I really think you guys should." Derek pointed to the white board.

"Yeah, I'll go," said Messy. He stood up, along with Hecky and Derek. Messy grabbed R-Luv by the shirt and pulled him to his feet. The boys walked out to the backyard. Hecky and Derek lit cigarettes and sat down.

R-Luv closed the door and Hecky began, "Alright, guys. We all want nice, legal money. What I am proposing is that we start our own food truck. Now, before you shoot this down, hear me out. We probably need fifty grand to start and my parents have offered up ten."

"Holy shit," said Messy.

"I know, right," said Hecky. "Now what I purpose is that you guys try and get the same loan from your folks. Try getting ten and promise to re-pay it in six months. That would leave ten thousand outstanding. I just made six grand after taxes for two weeks work, so on paper this all looks legit. We each put in the extra startup costs and we are all 25% shareholders."

"Umm, if we do this, who runs it?" asked R-Luv.

"Well, I don't have a job, so I could work there everyday. Messy, you make minimum wage so it's not impossible to believe you'd quit that job to work the truck." Hecky paused and smiled. "Guys, we could do five days a week and R-Luv and Sarge do Saturdays. Or we could just be an office park truck and work Monday to Friday, pay Messy and I a wage plus our share."

"Don't we need permits and shit to run a food truck?" asked Derek.

"We do," replied Hecky. "I've already submitted our application for one. It's eleven hundred a year."

"Where are you planning to get a truck?" asked R-Luv.

"I looked at buying one. but its too much cash up front," said Hecky. "I think we would be best to lease with the option to buy."

"Who is going to make the food?" asked Messy.

"Sarge can prepare the meals in the evening and we just have to assemble them. It's easy to make a sandwich when the stuff is prepared."

"Would we do just sandwiches or other shit too?" asked Messy.

"Soup and sandwiches would be best I think," replied Hecky. "We only have one big issue. We have to rent kitchen space to prep the food. Van doesn't allow cooking on the truck."

"What's that cost?" asked R-Luv.

"$2,500 a month. But if we do this right? Maybe we grow it and sell it. Who knows? What do you think?"

"You got a name?" asked Derek.

The boys sat in silence for a minute before Messy spoke up. "Between the Buns."

"Meatbeaters," said R-Luv.

"Gross," replied Derek.

"Maybe this is something we need to sleep on. How do you guys feel otherwise? Are you in?" asked Hecky.

"I'm in," said Messy.

"Let me think on it," said R-Luv.

February 11th, 2009
TWENTY-TWO

The following day, Derek worked a 3-11 p.m. shift. He closed up shop at 11:15 p.m., walked out of the liquor store to the parking lot and heard a voice call his name. It was Sgt. Robie standing next to his car, smoking a cigarette. Derek didn't recognize his face, but he knew the voice. "Evening, Sergeant. You making sure we don't get robbed again?"

"No, nothing like that. I did notice a van parked here last night."

"That was my roommate. We had a drink next door after work."

"It's always a little curious to see a van parked next to a spot that had a box job pulled a few months ago."

"I could see that," replied Derek as he looked back at the store. "It's nice to know you keep an eye on us. I don't want to go through that again."

"It's no trouble, son."

"Anyways, sorry, but I have to cut this short to catch my bus."

"Nah, I'll give you a lift home."

"Are you sure?" asked Derek.

"Yeah, not a problem."

"That would be great! Thanks!"

Robie lead Derek over to his car and they climbed inside. Robie pulled out of the parking lot onto Hastings Street and began the ride to Derek's.

"Busy tonight?" asked Derek.

"No, a bit of a change."

"That's good. Yeah, the city has gone to hell lately."

"That's nothing new," said Robie. "These gangs will be killing each other for a while before it gets cooled."

"Do you ever get scared? Being a cop and all." asked Derek.

"Not really. I mean I've never been shot at or had to pull, but if I did, I'm sure there would be some fear."

"I couldn't do your job," said Derek. "You're braver than me."

"I think I hug my wife and kids a little harder than, say, a guy going to work at a factory, you know?"

"How many kids do you have?"

"Two girls – seven and three."

"I'm scared to have girls," said Derek. "With boys you worry about him, with girls you worry about everyone."

"Oh, I live that," said Robie.

"At least you can show those boys a badge and a gun," joked Derek.

"I won't hesitate to do so."

Robie pulled the car onto Woodsworth and drove toward the house. He turned around, drove back up the hill and parked. He turned to Derek as he was about to exit the car.

"My partner has a thing for you."

"Anna?"

"Yes, its nuts if you ask me. Just with her being fifteen years your senior and obviously it's a conflict of interest."

"Yeah, I'd say so."

"Did you know?"

"I had my suspicions," said Derek with a grin.

"Alright, you didn't hear it from me. Now go on, have a good night."

"You too, sir!"

Derek exited the car and looked both ways as he anticipated crossing the street. Halfway across the street he heard Robie say, "You're a good kid, Derek," and smiled as Derek turned back to face him.

"I appreciate that."

Robie began rolling up his window when the passenger door opened. Derek crouched down and could see movement in Robie's passenger seat. A gunshot echoed and blood splattered on the driver side window. *What just happened?*

A shadowy figure emerged from the passenger side of Robie's car and just stood next to the car. In the middle of the street Derek dropped his bag, frozen solid. The figure walked around the front of the car toward him, holding a knife. *Run, Derek, run!* Repeating it over and over in his head, *Run, you fucking moron, run!* The figure was dressed in black from head to toe.

Derek's brain said *go* and his body said *no.* He couldn't move. For the second time in the last month he had witnessed a murder. The figure approached him, letting a knife fall by his side. The figure used his left hand to remove his mask: it was Hecky!

"What the fuck did you just do?"

"Shut the fuck up!"

"Jesus Christ," screamed Derek.

Hecky placed his bloody hand across Derek's mouth and looked him in the eye. "Shut the fuck up! Relax, before someone sees us!" Derek nodded his head.

"If I move my hand are you going to be quiet?" asked Hecky.

Derek nodded his head and Hecky moved his hand. They walked to the front of the car.

Quietly, almost to himself, Derek asked, "Why, Jesus fuck, why did you do that?"

"He was on to u s, dude. You think a cop takes this much interest in you without having a reason why? Why else would he drive you home?"

"He wanted to tell me his partner has a thing for me," said Derek.

"You are so naïve."

"And you've lost your fucking mind. Like, fuck, why did you do that? He's got kids!"

"You've got your freedom, Derek. This guy was going to take us down." Hecky took a moment to breathe. "Look, we can't argue. We need to get him off the street before someone sees us. Go move my van."

"I'm not helping," said Derek.

"Get your fucking bag and go move my van!" said Hecky sternly, as he threw his car keys to Derek.

"We can't keep stacking bodies!"

"If I go down, we all do. You, R-Luv, Messy, all of us."

"You motherfucking cocksucker!" echoed Derek's voice in the street, as he grabbed his bag and walked into the house. He dropped his bag by the couch and walked through to the back, where he opened the garage door. He drove Hecky's van onto the street in the back alley and pulled over to the side. Hecky drove Robie's car, lights off. He pulled up beside the van with the driver's side window still bloodied. Derek watched Hecky pull the car into the garage and motion for Derek to park on the street.

He parked the van and walked back to the garage. He saw that Hecky had already moved Robie's body from the car and placed it on a tarp on the floor. There was blood all over the car's interior as well as Hecky and the tarp. Hecky put on old work pants, gloves, a mask and a toque. Derek took one look at his clothes and realized he needed to change. "Don't tell the boys," said Hecky. "It's you and me."

"I know fuck. I'll be right back."

Derek ran into the house and up to his bedroom to change. He put on plaid pajama pants, an old sweatshirt and an old pair of running shoes.

On his way back through the kitchen, Derek noticed the portable phone and contemplated calling the police. *Could he do that to his friend? Could he still call Hecky a friend?*

Hecky was crying on the floor when Derek walked into the garage. "You alright?" He felt stupid asking.

"I never wanted this. Look what we've become."

"I know, man. This has spiraled."

"I just want to do the truck thing and be normal, you know?"

"I know, buddy," said Derek. "We just have to do this and then we can get going on that."

"We can't keep dumping bodies."

No shit! thought Derek. This was the last thing he felt like doing. He took a minute to breathe and thought about Anna; she would be devastated. "Hecky, get up, we need to eradicate this, now."

"What are we going to do?"

"I don't know," replied Derek. "Could we make it look like a suicide?"

Hecky rose to his feet and looked at Robie's dead body. "I don't think so," Hecky crouched down and took a closer look at Robie's bloody face.

"I think we have two options: we send him fishing or we torch the car."

"Whatever you think is best," replied Derek as he stuck out his hand. "Give me your phone."

"Nice, good call. Take it."

Hecky handed Derek his phone and he walked the phones inside and left them in the kitchen. As he was setting them down he wondered what sort of device Robie had. *Oh fuck*!

Derek raced through the house and ran out to the garage. Hecky was standing over Robie

"What's wrong?" he asked.

"Does his car have a dash cam or GPS?" asked Derek.

"Relax – no dash cam or GPS. I put his cell phone on the seat.

"They can track his cell, right?"

"Yeah, which is why we have to drive his car around town for a while so that the last spot he was at, before he died, isn't our front fucking lawn."

"Okay, what are you thinking?"

"I don't know, Sarge. We're going to be exposed no matter what we do."

"Why did you have to kill this fucking guy, Heck?"

"You're like a chick, Sarge. You keep going all the way back to that."

"That? That happened a half an hour ago!"

"Don't get tough, Sarge. That's not what we need right now."

"No, what we need is this fucking body out of our garage."

"Okay, any ideas?" asked Hecky.

Taking a moment, Derek replied, "Honestly, I think one of us drives his car around for a few hours and the other takes your van with his body to make the switch. Then we torch the car somewhere."

"The other option is to rip out his radio and drive it around in the van along with the cell and drive him in the car up to the water."

Hecky's suggestion gave Derek an idea. "Why don't we torch the car here and dump him up the coast."

Hecky thought about it for a second. "I know the spot".

"Okay, let's get him out of here."

Hecky stripped Robie's clothes off and put them into a garbage bag. He then scrubbed him down with soap and wrapped him in the tarp.

Inside the car, Derek scrubbed the windows, the seats, the doors and the dashboard. He couldn't leave a trace of anything in case the fire was put out quickly.

"We'll have to burn these clothes and the tarp and that," said Hecky.

"We'll torch his clothes in the car. Everything else we torch after."

Hecky had a better idea. "Why don't we park the car somewhere, dump him, come back and torch everything in the car."

"Sure, Hecky. Whatever gets him and this car out of here."

"I'm starting to see how the chaos works," said Hecky.

"Jesus, Hecky. Do you think you're evolving or something?"

"How am I not, Sarge?"

"Dude, we've gone from people to animals in a matter of weeks."

Hecky shook his head and focused his attention on the cleanup. Derek turned and looked around the garage before looking at Robie's body. "What did you do with his gun?"

"It's with his clothes over there," pointing to Robie's clothing, his gun sitting on top. Derek studied it for a second and pulled it out of the holster. He placed it back and threw it back on the pile of clothing.

"Torch it too, eh?" Derek asked.

"We should keep it, no? In case we need it?"

"If you want to keep it make sure to keep it elsewhere."

"Did you look in the trunk?" asked Hecky. "I hope there isn't anything that can track us in there."

"Oh fuck, eh," Hecky grabbed Robie's keys out of his pants pocket and tossed them to Derek who walked over to the trunk and opened it. Inside was a bounty of booty.

The first item Derek noticed was a Remington Model 870P police issue shotgun. Next to it was a box of shotgun shells. There were various black blankets covering other items. "Jesus Christ," exclaimed Derek.

"What is it?"

"Shotgun," Derek said as he lifted one of the blankets. Under it was a stack of hard cases. Opening them up, Derek saw it was surveillance equipment.

"That's pricey gear," said Hecky as he walked over to the car.

"You know anything about this stuff?" asked Derek.

"Yeah, there is like an easy five or ten thousand here."

"New?"

"No, used," replied Hecky. "Just leave the cases on the floor."

"We can't keep this" said Derek.

"Ugh, fuck fine!" Hecky pulled up another blanket. He found more shotgun shells, a box of 9mm bullets and a small gun case. Inside the case was another 9mm. Under the last blanket was a duffel bag with spare clothes and a few hundred dollars in petty cash. Derek cleared a space on the shelf to store the money.

"Oh, so we can keep the cash," remarked Hecky.

"And the guns – anything that doesn't have a computer chip in it."

Derek set down the bullets and gun on Robie's clothes. He was about to shut the trunk when noticed the outline in the carpeting for the spare tire. He pulled up the carpeting out, seeing that there was nothing on top of the spare tire. He picked up the tire and set it on the ground. As it bounced on the cement, three stacks of cash and two bricks of a pressed white substance fell out.

"What the hell?" asked Hecky.

"Spare tire," replied Derek.

"Nice!" Hecky kneeled down and picked up the cash and the bricks.

"Jesus Christ," said Derek. "How much is that?"

"Ten grand," said Hecky as he smiled, "per stack."

"Fuck me. Why does a cop have money and drugs in his spare tire?" "Well, Sargey, I'm thinking your boy might have been a bit dirty."

"No fucking way!"

Hecky stood up and looked in the trunk. Derek could see Hecky bent over trying to reach something and then, as he stood up, he had his hands full and a shiteating grin on his face. Hecky had five more stacks of money and two more bricks of cocaine. "Oh my God!"

"Shh," said Hecky. "This is like ninety grand!"

"How much coke?" asked Derek.

"Four bricks, and two bricks of something else. Heroin, I think, and two more guns."

"How many grams is a brick? Is it a thousand?"

"I think so, that's why they call it a key," replied Hecky. "We just hit the Rampart, bring-down-the-LAPD, motherfucking motherload." Hecky nearly jumped off the ground he was so excited. "We need to get all this shit stashed somewhere and get the car and the body out of here."

"Okay," replied Derek as he stood up and went to work. Half an hour later, Hecky and Derek set off: Hecky drove the van and Derek drove Robie's car. Everything they wanted was left stashed in Hecky's locked tool chest. They drove to Kent Sanderson's house, parked Robie's car on the street and left it there.

"We need to go back home," said Derek as he climbed into Hecky's van.

"Why?"

"If our alibi is 'we were at your folks' place', then we should have our cell phones with us."

"Fuck, you're right. We could probably use some clothes too."

The boys drove back to the house, picked up their cell phones, packed clothes and took the highway to where they'd dumped Kent's body.

Unfortunately for them, the road construction crews had moved right next to their potential dumpsite. "Goddammit," said Hecky as he pondered their options moving forward. "I know another spot."

Hecky kept on driving toward Squamish. Fifteen minutes later he pulled onto a side road that led down toward the water. He parked the van in a dirt parking lot and shut it off.

"How do you know about this place?" asked Derek.

"We shot here."

From what Derek could see it looked like a nice spot. There were picnic tables, a boat launch and outdoor outhouses.

Hecky's plan eluded Derek, but he knew Hecky would clue him in. Hecky stepped out of the car and walked around looking for something.

Derek also stepped out of the car, walking to the outhouse to take a piss. Opening the door, he was hit with an unbearable stench. It was as if someone had dumped a body inside. It hit Derek – that was it! Derek studied the size of the opening in the toilet; it was larger than a regular toilet. He pissed, zipped up and ran outside.

"Hecky?"

"I'm over here," Hecky called out from down near the water. "Sup?"

"What are you doing?"

"I'm looking for an anchor."

"Fuck the water, I've got an idea."

"What's that?

Derek pointed to the outhouse and grinned.

"What?" asked Hecky.

"We dump his body in there."

Hecky seemed skeptical.

"Now – hear me out – any evidence will be contaminated, and the smell will be virtually unnoticeable."

"What about if he floats to the top?" asked Hecky.

"How many people actually look in the shitter when they're in an outhouse?"

"I do," replied Hecky, "doesn't everyone?"

"We anchor him then. We were going to anchor him anyways, right?"

"Will he even fit?" asked Hecky.

"I'm not sure."

"I mean, it's worth a shot. If he stays submerged, the bacteria will break him down I would think."

"That's what I was thinking. Just grab an anchor."

"Okay," replied Hecky, "can you grab a saw from my toolbox? We can cut a rock off the picnic table and use that to anchor him."

Together, Hecky and Derek dragged Robie's body over to the outhouse and opened the door. Hecky took a look at the width of the toilet.

"I hope this works."

Hecky chained Robie to a rock, pulled him into the outhouse and they positioned his legs in the toilet. With the body in place, Derek wiggled his corpse back and forth until he was waist deep in waste. Hecky picked up the rock.

"Can you do this?" asked Derek. "Hold it up and make sure to let go."

Hecky held the rock above Robie's corpse while Derek raised the body's limp arms above its head and then they both let go. Robie dropped straight into the shit below.

The awful stench filled Derek's lungs, leaving him gasping for air as he struggled to regain his breath. Hecky had his hands on his knees and was keeled over gasping for air.

The boys exited the outhouse, coughing. Hecky walked over to his van. He opened the toolbox, pulled out his flashlight, and walked back inside the outhouse. Derek could see him shine the light into the toilet. Robie's body was on top of all the shit.

"Fuck," exclaimed Hecky. "We need a stick to push him under."

Hecky exited the outhouse. As he did, the boys could hear a car driving down the hill.

"Fuck, car! Go back into the outhouse!" yelled Derek.

The boys both walked into the outhouse and stood in separate stalls.

"What do we do?" asked Hecky.

"Follow my lead. Come out in like two minutes."

"Thank fuck we changed," said Hecky. He stayed put as Derek exited the outhouse and noticed an RCMP squad car and two male RCMP officers in the parking lot. *FUCK! ME!* Derek closed the door and approached the car. One of the officers shined a light in Derek's face.

"What are you doing, son?"

"Using the can, my friend had to take a dump." Derek panicked; *did he or Hecky have any blood on them?*

"Where are you headed?"

"Squamish. We are going to my buddy's parents for the night."

"Are you coming from Van?"

"Yes, sir," replied Derek.

"Where is your friend?"

"Toilet," replied Derek as he pointed at the outhouse.

"Have either of you been drinking? Or doing anything else?"

"I just got off work. This was just a whim to head up there. We have tomorrow off so we were going to ski."

Hecky appeared outside of his stall and the door slammed behind him. He walked down the hill toward Derek.

"Evening, officers," said Hecky.

"Good evening. Can we see both of your ID's, and the registration and insurance for your vehicle?"

Hecky and Derek took out their wallets and handed over their licenses. Hecky did the same with his insurance and registration.

The older officer walked over to his squad car and checked the information.

"Did the Canucks win tonight?" asked the younger officer.

"Of course they didn't," replied Derek. The officer nodded his head and grinned.

"Why are you wearing pajama pants?" asked the younger officer.

Oh fuck, thought Derek. He needed an excuse. "I just threw them on before we left. Like I said, this was on a whim."

The younger officer looked back at his partner, who was walking back toward the boys. "Why didn't you piss on the side of the road?"

Derek replied, "I was worried the cops would catch us."

The older officer grinned and handed back their licenses. "You guys are good to go. Drive safe,"

"You too!" replied Derek.

The younger officer turned to his partner, "I should go while we are here," and walked up to the outhouse.

Derek's heart sank as the officer walked into the stall with Robie's corpse.

Hecky and Derek began walking quickly to his van. Derek heard the outhouse door slam shut and turned back to see the younger officer jogging down the hill toward them. *He found Robie!* he thought.

The officer raised his hand and waved good-bye. "Goodnight, fellas!"

The officers climbed into their squad car and drove up the hill into the night.

Hecky looked over at Derek and they both started to scream obscenities. Grabbing his flashlight, Hecky ran over to a nearby tree and grabbed a very large branch. He ran uphill to the outhouse and inside the stall containing Robie's body. A minute later Hecky ran behind the outhouse and tossed the branch into the woods.

"Let's get the fuck out of here!"

The boys piled into the van and drove to Hecky's parents to get gas cans and leave their phones behind.

Their next stop was a 7-Eleven for Belmont Mild's and gas. They chain smoked all the way to Vancouver.

At around 3:30 a.m. Hecky pulled off to the side of the road about eight blocks away from Robie's car. Derek jumped out and covered the van's license plates. It was there Derek realized the flaw in the plan. He climbed into the van and whispered to Hecky, "Fuck, they are going to trace Robie's cell phone back here and know this is the last spot he was before his car got torched."

"Then they check the security cameras! Fuck! What do we do?"

"I'm going to walk to the car and when we get out of suburbia, we switch the cell and radio to your van and the gas to Robie's. Then you ditch his cell and radio somewhere and meet me at the park."

"Fuck," said Hecky, "more plates to spin?" Hecky stopped the van; Derek jumped out and walked the short distance to Robie's car. He followed Hecky as they drove to the park. It was nearing sunrise and exhaustion was starting to set in for Derek. He'd worked a full day and came home to commit accessory after the fact. He was worn out. Adrenaline was the only thing keeping him going.

Hecky chose Mt. Seymour as the spot to torch the car. It was still dark enough to hide the smoke. The fire needed to burn hot and fast.

Hecky was behind when Derek arrived on the mountain in Robie's car and sat there waiting. It would be a half hour before Derek saw Hecky again and twenty minutes before he would torch the vehicle. It was the longest twenty minutes of Derek' life. It was just him and his thoughts, and they weren't pleasant. He was concerned with what he was becoming and what Hecky had turned into. The world was becoming his own personal hell – one that parents fear their kids will get wrapped up in. The boys were proving just how ugly the human condition could be, and Hecky's personality, in particular, was becoming an abhorrent thing.

Derek's time alone ended; Hecky was picking him up. He wiped down the car with a rag, popped the trunk open, pulled out two cans of gas and doused the car. He made a trail away from it so he could make his getaway. On the horizon, he could see an outline of Hecky's van driving toward him. Hecky pulled up about a hundred feet away from Derek and parked his van. He popped the side door open and Derek set the gas cans inside.

"We need to torch these clothes and return the cans to your parents ASAP," Derek exclaimed.

"Hurry up!" yelled Hecky.

Derek shut the door and walked back over to Robie's car. He pulled a book of matches from his pocket and lit it with a single match. The matches caught fire and Derek tossed them onto the ground, catching the gas on fire. Derek ran to Hecky's van, climbed inside and strapped in. He could see the entire car was ablaze. It was bigger than they could have imagined.

"Fuck!" yelled Derek, "it's huge!"

"Is it too big?" asked Hecky.

"Yes! Let's go!"

One hour later, Hecky and Derek torched their clothes along with all evidence at Hecky's parents in Squamish.

Derek showered; the warm water rained down on him as he leaned on the wall. He felt unusually calm for someone who had witnessed a murder, uncovered a police conspiracy, found hundreds of thousands of dollars in cash, dope and guns and covered all of it up.

After his shower he climbed into bed in the basement bedroom. He flipped on the TV and changed the channel to catch the start of the local BC news. Sure enough, a torched car in Burnaby was the top story. The opening shot was an aerial view from the news chopper. The newscasters described the scene as chaotic and disturbing. There were police, fire and paramedic on the scene.

Hecky came in the room and looked at the TV. He wore his sense of relief like some sort of body armour. The car was completely obliterated; it was a shell, a hole in the ground.

"Holy shit, that thing is fucking toast," said Hecky, almost gleeful about their handiwork.

"Good luck sorting that out."

"What's wrong?" asked Hecky. "We made it!"

"Made what? Made myself an accessory?"

"You're just tired. Go sleep."

"Yeah," Derek sighed, "maybe."

Hecky tapped Derek on the shoulder and walked out of the room and closed the door. Derek pulled the covers up and began to stew. Most people would be envious of him. He had more money than he ever imagined, but he also had a memory bank full of bad things he had done.

October 4th, 2009
TWENTY-THREE

Mandy pulled her car into the hotel parking lot. She looked over at Derek and smiled. "I can't believe you're leaving!"

"I'll come back," said Derek.

"You should," Mandy exited her car and walked toward Derek. "I'd like you to come back."

"I'll leave you my number. Call me and I'll answer. I'll drive here any time. I'll be spontaneous and free, for you."

Derek couldn't believe that a girl this smart, beautiful and perfect would be interested in him.

"I've never opened up to anyone like this, Derek," said Mandy. "I think it's funny that we are adults and I'm sneaking around with you like a teenager. It's exciting."

"It really is," replied Derek.

"Safe travels, Derek. There and back to me."

"Thank you," replied Derek. He exited the car and walked toward the door to his room.

Mandy exited her car and yelled, "Derek!"

She ran to Derek as he opened his arms, swept her up and they embraced. She pressed her face to his and planted her lips, kissing him as he kissed back. Her tiny feet lifted off the ground as Derek held her. Her kiss was as soft and tender as the skin on her cheek.

After a few moments, Derek set her feet on the ground. She wiped the hair out of her eyes and blushed.

"I was calling you to give you my number," she said, "but I'm really happy you misinterpreted it!"

Mandy placed a small piece of paper gently on Derek's fingertips and slid it into his hand. "Please call me, Derek." Mandy walked back to her car and drove off into the night.

In the distance, Derek could see Messy walking toward him with a big bag of McDonald's in his hand. He had a Messy grin on his face. He shook his head at Derek, continuing to grin.

"I thought I spotted a creep."

"That was the most romantic thing I've ever seen!" replied Messy. "Did you fall in love on a first date?"

"She is perfect, dude."

"No one is perfect, Sarge."

February 12th, 2009

At around 2:00 p.m., Derek woke to the sound of Hecky grinding coffee upstairs. He lay in bed for a few minutes, trying to shake the cobwebs loose. He got his wits about him and that's when the events from the night before came creeping back in.

He pulled on a pair of Puma jogging pants Hecky had left on the floor. They weren't pants, at least not on Derek; they were more like capris. The only shirt lying around was a t-shirt that had their college's name across the front of it. *Simpler times,* thought Derek.

He joined Hecky in the kitchen. Hecky was pressing the coffee and frying up eggs and bacon.

"Grab a seat," said Hecky in a chipper voice.

On the other side of the kitchen island Derek sat down on a stool.

"We on the news?" asked Derek.

"Top story. The car is torched. They may not even be able to identify who it belonged to."

"Makes evidence hard to find."

"No kidding," Hecky turned and tinkered at the stove, flipping the bacon and eggs. "Thank you, Sarge. I don't know what would have happened if you didn't help me."

"You'd be in a 5 by 8."

"I think so too!" Derek pulled out a cigarette and placed it between his teeth. Hecky continued, "We'll eat and we can head back home."

"Ok," said Derek as he stood up and walked toward the patio door, "what do we tell the boys?"

"Not a thing. This stays between us. Is that okay?" asked Hecky.

Derek shrugged his shoulders. "Yeah, I mean, I guess."

That evening, Derek and Hecky drove back home and met up with Messy and R-Luv at The Soho.

They arrived at the restaurant to find that their friends already had a pint in front of them and were talking. Hecky and Derek greeted R-Luv and Messy and sat across from them. "What's up?" asked Hecky.

"We got money!" yelled Messy.

Hecky was so happy he nearly fell out of his chair. "No way!"

The boys were ecstatic as the waitress approached the table. They ordered food and continued their discussion.

"Did you get the money, Sarge?" asked R-Luv.

"Paid in full!"

"Nice! So, where do we start?" asked Messy.

"We start by getting shitfaced tonight!" The boys cheered in unison. Hecky continued, "I'll lay out the plan and we can start next week. The permits are in; we are approved to begin setting up our truck. We just need a name."

The waitress dropped off wings and drinks, barely acknowledging the boys.

"She's friendly," joked R-Luv.

"Yeah, man, I hate the eat it and beat it attitude of this place."

"Jesus Christ," said R-Luv.

"That's the one," yelled Hecky.

"What is?"

"Eat it and Beat It. That's our name!" said Hecky.

"That's brutal," said Derek.

"I love it," said Messy.

"Me too," R-Luv agreed.

"Three to one. Eat It and Beat It!"

"Fucking democracy!" Derek was discouraged, He knew he was beat.

"So, we can pick up the truck Monday. I got a mechanic from set to help us for a decent price."

"How much?" asked Messy.

"$750 a week."

"Why so cheap?" asked Derek.

"He collects EI and its cash."

"I get it," replied Derek. "Avoid paying taxes. I like it."

* * * * *

Over the next week, Derek spent his time mixing up concoctions to test on the boys. On Thursday night, Derek, Messy and R-Luv went for dinner. As they returned home, Derek pulled onto Woodsworth Avenue and could see a Crown Victoria parked in front of their house. The car was similar to Robie's. Derek drove past the car and spotted Anna sitting in the driver's seat. Messy did a double take, turned to Derek and smiled. "Look's like the Cougar Cop isn't going to give up on you, Sarge."

Derek parked down the street and the boys exited the rental car and walked toward the house. Derek watched Anna exit her car and walk toward them. "Hello, Detective," said Derek with a smile on his face.

"Good evening, boys. Can I speak to Derek for a second?"

"What's up, Anna?

"No need to cast us off so quick," said R-Luv.

"Yeah, unless you guys are going to kiss," joked Messy.

"Messy!" said Derek sternly. He turned to Anna. "Is everything okay?"

"Did my partner come see you sometime last week?" she asked.

"Yeah, he came by my work. Shit, what night was that, Wednesday?"

"He hasn't been seen since he picked up a coffee near your store."

The boys looked at Derek and were blindsided by the news. "Really?" replied Derek.

"He dropped you off here, stayed in his car for quite some time, then drove around before parking over near Kent Sanderson's house. His car was then found torched a few hours after that. We are checking security cameras around the Sanderson's."

This news wasn't too concerning to Derek. They knew all of this would happen and they covered their tracks.

"We chatted for a few minutes about his kids. Then I went inside."

"Did you see where he went? Any of you?" asked Anna.

"I showered and packed a bag. We drove to Squamish for the night."

"I was asleep," answered R-Luv.

"Ditto," answered Messy.

"If you guys remember anything, call me, please," Anna handed them a card and began to walk away.

Derek followed Anna, then stepped in front of her to stop her. "Anna, what happened? He seemed fine. I can't believe he would up and leave."

"He didn't leave," replied Anna. "Did you see him on the street at all?"

"We left out the garage in the back. I never saw the street."

"Shit!"

Derek looked around at his neighbours' houses. "Don't our neighbours have cameras?" asked Derek, knowing that none of them did.

"No, we checked that already."

"I'm sorry I can't be of more help, Anna. I really am."

"It's not your problem. We'll sort through it." Anna pointed to Derek's rental. "What's with the Nissan?"

"Rental – we're going up to Squamish tomorrow."

"Kind of a downgrade, no?"

"I didn't want girls liking the car more than me again."

"Right," Anna smiled and walked back to her car. "Bye, Derek."

*　*　*　*　*

The next day, the boys drove to Hecky's parents place. In the driveway sat a fully painted food truck. The sign on the front read *Eat It and Beat It.* Messy laughed as they drove by. "Are you alright with that, Sarge?"

"As long as we make money, I don't care what he calls it." Derek parked the car and the boys dragged their belongings into the house.

They walked in the front foyer and were greeted by Hecky. He was drinking a scotch and holding an unlit cigar. "Welcome, fellas!"

"Truck looks good!" yelled Derek.

"Leave that. I'll give you a tour."

A few hours later, Hecky poured four glasses of Johnny Blue and handed out four Cohiba cigars. The boys stood on a patio that looked out over Squamish, lighting their cigars.

"So why did you bring us up here, Hecky?" R-Luv asked skeptically.

"There's good news and bad."

"Bad," shouted the boys.

"Alright," said Hecky, "so we went about twenty grand over budget on the truck."

"It cost seventy?" asked Derek.

"Yup, all cash" replied Hecky. "So on paper it will cost fifty."

"That's fine," said Derek.

"Yeah, it's okay," said Messy. "What's the good news?"

"I lined up five office parks we can hit. Monday to Friday, breakfast and lunch. No evenings or weekends. No way to track how many customers we get, so we can start putting our cash through on day one."

"That's awesome!" said Messy.

"Yeah, that's great dude! When do we start?" asked Derek.

"Two weeks. We need to get our menus out to be printed and all that. I started a Facebook group already too."

"Cool! I have my recipes; we can name them today. Are we running with the TV theme?"

"Yes," replied Hecky.

"I like that," said Messy.

For the next few hours, the boys bounced ideas around about what to name the menu items. One of the breakfast sandwiches was called the Bacon Bad. It had three strips of bacon, two fried eggs, two strips of fresh marble cheese, aioli, lettuce, tomato, all on a fresh everything bagel with a dill pickle on the side.

Their chipped beef was called Chips Beef. Their club sandwich was called the S Club 7. They even had a Lex Luthor burger that was a burger served on a glazed donut!

That night the boys headed out to a pub for drinks and dinner. They dropped the food truck off at a local garage to have the last of their work done. R-Luv and Messy followed in Hecky's van.

Derek took the opportunity to discuss the events that had occurred with Det. Robie. Hecky broke the ice. "R-Luv told me Robie's partner was by the house."

"Yeah, she came by, asked a few questions. I said exactly what we discussed, and the boys were clueless."

"Good," said Hecky, "that's good. What should we do with that cash?"

"Not sure."

"I sold the dope, eh."

"No way, for how much?"

"One twenty-five."

"Shut up!" exclaimed Derek. "Jesus! How do we hide that?"

"I don't know, dude. It's a good problem to have I guess."

*   *   *   *   *

The boys packed up and drove back to the city the next day. Halfway home, they were brought to a stop by a traffic jam. They waited patiently in the van while Messy complained about B.C. traffic. Closer and closer they inched toward the root of the problem. Derek could see countless police cars and fire trucks on the scene.

"Accident?" asked Hecky.

They inched forward between Lion's Bay and the Burrard Inlet. Hecky noticed a policeman directing traffic and, off to the side of the road, a huge crane on the back of a flatbed truck. He looked at Derek and panicked. "They found the car!"

"Check the radio," yelled R-Luv from the backseat.

Derek searched for a signal to a talk radio station. A news report came on, ". . . and if your heading up to Whistler today, you might want to give yourself an hour or two buffer as police and fire crews are pulling a car from the water near the Burrard Inlet.

"Jesus!" yelled Derek.

Hecky drove past the police presence and they were back driving at full speed.

"Holy fuck," said Hecky. "They found him."

Messy tried to be the voice of reason, "We knew it was possible boys, just calm down."

"How long until they trace that back to us?" yelled Hecky.

"How?" asked Messy.

"Evidence."

"We cleaned it up," said Messy.

"All it takes is one thing, Mess," said Hecky.

"We'll be fine," said Derek. "R-Luv, are you good? You're awful quiet."

"I'm fine, we're fine boys. Maybe it was another car. This is Vancouver. A lot of shady shit happens." R-Luv was able to calm the boys down with one simple statement.

An hour and a half later, the boys arrived home just in time to watch the six o'clock news. R-Luv was wrong; the car in the water was indeed owned by Kent Sanderson. And from what the news was able to reveal there was a body inside of it. The boys hoped that any evidence had been destroyed.

*　*　*　*　*

The following few days were filled with panic, anxiety and stress. The police were hunting for Sanderson's killer. The world knew that he was dead and that he was part of the R.O.P. – a gang involved in a turf war with the Crazy 8's.

Another story on the same newscast was the disappearance of Det. Robie. He had yet to be found and police were beginning to speculate that he had been caught in the middle of the gang war. Robie had a long list of enemies so, between that and Sanderson, the murders committed by the boys were lumped in as part of the Greater Vancouver Gang War.

*　*　*　*　*

The boys settled on opening Eat It and Beat It during the first week of April. March was especially warm, and they managed to get the truck operational for a soft open. On April 2nd, Hecky drove the truck on its maiden voyage. They set up at 7:00 a.m. in Burnaby, near warehouses, production houses and factories.

Derek took a day off work for the opening. They opened and their first clients were Messy's work buddies Mark and Cillian. "Do you feed the homeless?" joked Cillian as he stood in a suit and tie.

"You're dressed up," said Messy.

"Well, Mess, the headlights in my car are no longer operational, so I've been leaving the house dressed in what I would like to be buried in."

The boys laughed and both Cillian and Mark ordered a Bacon Bad. They both gave thumbs up: two satisfied customers!

Between 7:00 to 9:00 a.m. the boys had a total of seven customers, all who appreciated delicious homemade food at a reasonable price.

Around 11:00 a.m., the boys experienced their first lunch rush. Word had gotten out that a food truck was coming and the people working in the area were looking for a change from the few alternatives they had to get a hot lunch.

Between 11:00 a.m. to noon, the boys served 35 customers. Between noon to 1 p.m. they served 37, between 1 to 2 p.m. they fed 26 people and between 2 to 3 p.m. they served 19. Total take for the day was $1,720 – well above what the boys had ever dreamed of for a first day. Hecky threw some ill-gotten money into the envelope and deposited it at a local bank. A $2,550 day.

That sort of production called for a night out on the town. They packed the truck up and drove it home.

The boys put on their best suits, nice cologne and took a cab to The PearTree restaurant on Hastings.

After dinner they headed downtown and paid a bouncer to skip the line. Once inside the club they scoured for girls they could hit on.

Halfway around the bar, Derek could hear Hecky behind him screaming his name. Derek turned back to see Messy was pointing to a table of older women. It was Anna and her friends. Messy grinned. Hecky looked less than impressed.

Derek leaned in and spoke to Messy. "You know if we hang out with her, we have to behave, right?"

"I can go a night without it."

"Alright, pass the word to Hecky."

Messy leaned over to Hecky to explain the situation. Hecky looked none too pleased as he nodded his head in agreement. They approached Anna's table and she saw Derek out of the corner of her eye. She quickly stood up and screamed, "Oh my God," before running over to Derek and greeting him with a hug. Derek saw that Messy had a big grin on his face.

Derek introduced the boys to Anna's friends, and they sat down. The evening was like any other: drinks, dancing, yelling, dance floor make out sessions, a cab home, cocaine, broken phones, retching on the floor.

*   *   *   *   *

Derek woke up at around noon the next morning to the sound of the doorbell ringing. Being the only one up, he put on a pair of cargo shorts and walked downstairs.

He opened the front door and was greeted by a smiling Anna. She was carrying a couple of bagels and a tray of coffees for the boys. "Good morning," she said in a chipper tone.

"Good morning," replied Derek in a less than enthusiastic tone.

"Are your roomies still asleep?" asked Anna as she set everything on the kitchen counter and looked around at the mess of empty bottles.

Derek followed her into the kitchen. "Yeah, they won't be up for awhile."

Anna lunged at Derek and began kissing him. He pushed her against the fridge and began to kiss her back. They kissed passionately for a minute until he stopped. Anna walked over and picked up a coffee. Derek turned to her and smiled. "I wasn't sure about last night."

"I like you. You do something to me that I can't explain."

Derek blushed and leaned in to grab a coffee. "We should go on a date, like a real date. Not drinks at a club."

"Okay," she replied. "Tonight? I'll pick you up at 7. You pick the spot."

"Okay!"

Anna walked to him and planted another aggressive kiss on his lips.

"Bye, Derek," she said as she walked past him and left.

Messy walked into the kitchen to find Derek about to walk out the back door for a cigarette.

"Did she come over last night?"

"No, she came by this morning to bring us coffee."

"She gets my vote," joked Messy.

Derek stepped outside for a smoke and stood with the door open. "Yeah, I'm skeptical about this."

"What do you mean?"

"I feel like she could be working an angle, you know?"

Messy scoffed, "Yeah, 'cause she is smoking and you're a piece of shit."

"Yup," nodded Derek.

"Give yourself some credit, dude. You're a good-looking cat and on the surface you are successful and confident. Chicks like that shit."

"She wants me to take her out."

"Take her to The PearTree."

"That's the plan."

"If you bring her home, don't bring her here. Hotel or her place."

"Yeah, I know. I don't want to deal with the repercussions of that."

"No, you don't."

It was later that evening and Derek, dressed in suit and tie, stood smoking a cigarette on the front step. A brand new, blue Ford Edge pulled up in front of the house. He approached it and the passenger's side window rolled down. "Hey, handsome," said Anna, as she grinned.

She unlocked the car and Derek opened the door and climbed inside. "I think they are paying you too much!"

"I'll be paying for this long after I'm dead."

Anna rolled up Derek's window and Derek put on his seatbelt.

"Where to?" asked Anna.

"Hastings. The PearTree."

Anna drove to Hastings Street and parked her SUV in front of the restaurant. They exited and walked toward the restaurant. Derek could see Matty building a display through the window of his store across the street. He recognized Derek and grinned when he saw Anna. Derek smiled back and shrugged his shoulders. They walked into The PearTree and the hostess immediately recognized Derek from the evening prior.

"Welcome back!" said the hostess as she smiled.

She seated them at a table in the middle of the restaurant. Derek thought to himself *these hostesses will never learn that I tip better when I'm sitting in a booth.*

Anna and Derek began discussing Anna's lack of experience in fine dining. The conversation eventually shifted to Eat It and Beat It. Anna had a lot of questions regarding the menu and how Derek became a sandwich connoisseur.

Derek began to question Anna's motivation for these questions, but as quick as she brought it up, he was just as quick to change the subject again.

Anna answered Derek's questions about how she became a cop. It was in her blood: her Father, Grandfather and Brothers were all cops. It was a rite of passage. That meant that should a relationship progress Derek was going to always run the risk of being exposed.

They finished dinner and Derek paid the bill. They walked back to the SUV. As they crossed the street Anna's phone rang. She unlocked the car and answered the call. She spoke on the phone while Derek climbed into the passenger seat. She became very animated, but Derek couldn't catch what she was saying. It was about a case she was working – her number one suspect was likely sitting in her passenger seat. Derek kept the door ajar to catch some of what she was saying. Her tone was stern as she dropped Robie's name a few times.

"Nothing in the cell records?" asked Anna. She paused as for a moment. "What can we do, Mike? Until something breaks, we treat it as a missing person." There was significant desperation in Anna's voice. "I know, he's laying in a hole."

Oh Anna, you are so right.

Anna ended the call, opened the door and climbed into the SUV.

"Who was that?" asked Derek.

"Just another detective."

"Oh?"

"I don't want to talk about it. No offence, it's a fluid situation."

"Hey, none taken. If you wanted to talk, you'd talk."

Anna started her vehicle and drove down Hastings Street into North Vancouver. She arrived at Deep Cove and parked in a parking lot next to the water.

"What's up?" asked Derek.

"I come here to think sometimes; it's a good place to just walk around."

Anna jumped out of the car, as did Derek, and followed her as she walked down to the water.

She stared blankly at the water for a few minutes before she took a step back and looked at the beach. "I came here for the first time like three years ago. The first case I ever pulled was here." Anna continued as she looked out to the water, "I show up, and the first thing I saw was this kid, 17, dressed in baggy clothes, just like any other kid. Except somebody had put five bullets in him." Anna tried to compose herself. "They killed him like an animal because one of his friends was an R.O.P. puppet and someone saw him buy some pot."

Derek froze. *Is she pouring her heart out or warning me?*

"That is fucking awful."

"It was. The really awful part was telling his parents that his six-year-old Brother watched it happen."

"Jesus!" Derek bit his lip and looked out to the water. He didn't know what to say to her.

Anna looked back at Derek. "Vancouver's a funny place. The gangs come in waves, and each one is more ruthless than the last."

All these cautionary tales made gangster life sound unappealing. Derek's mind raced. *What was Anna's motivation for bringing him here? Was it personal or was it about him?*

Anna let Derek take her hand and stroke it slowly. She put her left hand on Derek's right shoulder and leaned forward and rested her head. Derek wrapped his arms around her and consoled her while he studied the area. Derek knew the case Anna was talking about.

Matty used to tell Derek Vancouver gang stories while they were unloading beer at the store. He had grown up in Abbottsford and went to school with members of several gangs. In his time in Abbottsford he'd heard stories about other gangs such as the UN, Independent Soldiers and the Hells Angels. These four factions basically ran the drug trade in the suburbs of Vancouver, at least according to Matty. He had talked constantly about the temptation to join a gang and run with a crew. Five minutes with Anna and Matty might think twice about that.

Anna and Derek climbed back into her SUV and they drove back through North Vancouver. Derek wasn't sure what just happened or what Anna's intentions were. For all the time he had spent causing Anna to be flustered, she had turned the tables and was returning the favour.

"Where are we going?"

"I figured we could go to my place," said Anna. "I live right here."

"Okay."

Anna pulled into her condo parking spot and cut the engine.

They rode the elevator to her floor and entered her apartment.

Derek took a look around to study the unit. The home was well decorated with a white and black contemporary theme. The kitchen had grey wood cabinets, with white quartz countertops and a stone backsplash. It was a beautiful open layout, but still managed to feel cozy.

Anna walked into her bedroom and dropped off her purse. She walked back out and turned on her sound system. Derek breezed past her and sat down on the couch. A few seconds later, he saw her pour him a glass of Belvedere and a glass of red wine for herself. She walked toward him and sat next to him without touching him. She handed Derek his drink.

The music was unrecognizable to Derek; it was classical. Whatever it was, it was setting the mood, for her at least. Derek was used to 90's alt rock.

Before he could comment on the music, Anna made her move.

March 2009
TWENTY-FOUR

The next morning, Anna dropped Derek off at the house and he walked into a roommate ambush.

Hecky was making eggs in the kitchen. Derek walked past him and poured himself a cup of coffee. Hecky began mumbling to him, "Keep her at a safe distance, Sarge. We've got a lot of plates spinning and we don't need her to bring them all crashing down."

"Slow your roll, Hecky. I know what I'm doing."

Derek went to the liquor store to collect his tips that afternoon. As he was walking in, Matty was walking out. He had just completed a day shift and was walking to his car.

"Sup?"

"Hey, Derek – just finished work. Heading to my folks place."

"Nice."

"Who was the girl last night?" asked Matty, "She looked familiar."

"She's a cop."

Matty nodded his head. "I think I've seen her before."

"Yeah."

"What are you saying right now?" asked Matty. "You want to hang out or something?"

Derek looked at his watch. "We can, yeah. I just came to get my tips."

"How about you get your trunks from your place and you can come out to my parents' for a dip?"

"Sure, sounds good!"

Derek picked up his tips and he and Matty drove to Matty's parents, stopping at Woodsworth on the way.

The home was a 4000 square foot mansion. It couldn't have been more than five years old. Derek stared at it in awe. Matty opened his parents' garage door using a code. He didn't hide it – 7954 – and the door opened.

Derek and Matty walked through the house. Everywhere Derek looked he saw an item that was more expensive than all the items in his home put together. The house was ultra modern, heavy on the use of whites, blacks and greys.

As they walked to the back of the house, Matty pointed to the change room. "You can change in there."

"No way, it's an indoor pool?!" Derek walked into the change room and changed into his trunks. He exited and spotted Matty bringing over a couple of Stellas.

Derek jumped into the pool and swam a few laps while Matty played on his phone and drank. Derek surfaced and climbed out of the pool. Matty handed him a beer as he lay down on a lounge chair.

"This is living, eh," said Matty.

"Yeah, thanks for having me."

"I'll be honest, I wanted to talk."

"The robbery?" asked Derek.

"Does it bother you at all?"

"Well, yeah. I mean I hated feeling hopeless while it was going on."

"Does that feeling linger?"

"Not really," replied Derek as he shrugged his shoulders, "I just try not to think about it."

"I can't stop; it haunts me, dude. I cannot stop thinking about that."

"How come?"

"It just felt like high school all over again. I got that helpless feeling like I was being bullied."

"That's fine, Matty."

"No, I can't feel that helplessness again. I won't feel it."

Derek paused for a moment. "It's fine. We'll learn from it."

"I'll tell you one thing, dude. If I ever come across those guys, I'll get my cousin George's crew after them."

"Who is George?"

"My cousin. He is thug as hell!"

"Like for real?" asked Derek.

"Like full on tatted up, slinging dope, carrying a piece, thug."

*   *   *   *   *

The following week, business began to slow down at *Eat It and Beat It*. After paying their bills they were down $2,000. Two weeks after that, they were down $3,000, each week. The truck was beginning to bleed money, but after cleaning their cash they were profitable on paper.

Hecky was starting to get antsy. His baby – their ticket to legitimizing their dirty money – was failing. Their initial guess was that they wouldn't turn a profit for about six months. That was a worst-case scenario. They hoped they would lose a grand a week.

It only took them three weeks to lose what they estimated they would lose in two months. They needed a solution, or they would be pissing away their hard-earned dirty money.

On top of their money woes, R-Luv had started chipping and Hecky, Messy and Derek were joy popping. Hecky was the biggest culprit. If Messy and Derek had a two hundred dollar a week drug habit, Hecky had a thousand dollar a week habit. They were draining their resources quicker than five food trucks ever could.

*   *   *   *   *

After a third unsuccessful and heavily deflating week, Hecky sat the boys down in the backyard for a chat. He'd drawn up a marketing plan to bring in new clientele. Hecky's plan was a month-long blitz that involved television, radio and newspaper ads, as well as billboards around the city. He had done his homework and even consulted with a local marketing firm. It would cost the boys $50,000 to flood Vancouver with their marketing. It was a gamble, but the reward was worth it. The boys voted unanimously in favour of Hecky's plan.

The first week with the new ads the boys lost a grand. The following week they cut their losses to $800. The ads were working, slowly. The boys closed the month $3,500 in the red and Hecky felt like it was a success. He wanted to invest another $25,000 into marketing.

The boys obliged, although, after the first month, their faith in him had waned. They'd had a minor increase in business, but were spending a lot on advertising. They'd spent almost $150,000 on an unprofitable food truck and laundered just $50,000.

The boys lost $3,000 the next month. The business was slowly trending in the right direction and getting positive reviews online.

After month two, the boys scaled back their marketing to $5,000 a month; but even then, they were losing $8,000 a month in dirty money. After laundering $12,000 a month, the boys were turning a profit of $1,000 a week, on paper.

*   *   *   *   *

A week passed and the boys were at The Soho. With their money disappearing, Messy, Derek and R-Luv were panicking. Their laundering machine was becoming a money pit. After a few beers, Messy suggested that they look to sell the truck while it looked profitable. Hecky lost his shit.

"I put everything into this goddamn thing and this is the thanks I get?"

"Calm down!" exclaimed Derek.

"Yeah, man, relax. It was just a suggestion!" yelled Messy.

"We do need a plan; we are bleeding cash." said Hecky, more calmly. "I'm open to ideas that don't involve selling."

"How does anyone run a legitimate business in this country?"

"Seems impossible," said R-Luv.

"It pisses me off," said Derek. "I have all of these people working in my store taking fancy vacations with their parents, posting pictures online."

"How's that possible?" asked Messy.

"Oh, their parents are loaded! You should see the shit they have. Jewelry, electronics, cash."

"Home alarms?" asked Hecky.

"Yup and I know the codes, ha-ha!"

"You do not!" shouted Hecky.

"I do!"

"What do they do?" asked R-Luv.

"They own restaurants. I thought about bringing it up before, but we went legit. It would be an easy take."

"When they back?" asked Hecky.

"Two weeks," replied Derek.

Hecky smiled wide and Derek became uptight; he knew what Hecky was thinking.

"We need to do that place, like yesterday." said Hecky.

"Come on, man," replied Derek. "We already did my work, now we're knocking off my friends."

"They have insurance!"

"It ain't right, man."

"It's necessary." replied Hecky. "Unless you guys are okay with us continuing to bleed money."

R-Luv and Messy nodded and looked over at Derek. Messy gave Derek a look as if to say fuck it.

They finished their beer and drove back to the house. They needed to start planning right away if they were going to do things right. The boys sat down in the living room and Hecky began to make lists – responsibilities, supplies, contingency plans, alibis, hideouts. After three hours, and going over every scenario possible, they had a plan. R-Luv and Messy would scout the house for four days to look for security features or looky loos. Hecky would gather supplies from around town; the boys needed outfits, masks, gloves, and tools, not to mention a huge moving truck for transport.

Derek's job was to keep tabs on Matty and make sure there weren't any surprises. He also needed to steal a license plate and figure out how to fence the items they were stealing. He had heard a recent news story from Washington State where a man had successfully robbed a bank but didn't plan what he would do with the money afterward. He put it in a friend's crawlspace and eventually lost a huge chunk of it to mold and the elements. Derek knew that they couldn't have that happen.

After four days of scouting the house, gathering supplies and drawing up the plans, the boys met back at the house. Messy and R-Luv looked beat – 96 straight hours in a car did them in. They had taken turns sleeping, but it wasn't the same as sleeping at home. It was all worth it, however; they determined that Matty's family didn't have anyone checking in on the house.

Hecky did well too. He located a white cargo van within four blocks of the house that was perfect for unloading the stolen goods after the robbery. They would then transfer the goods to Hecky's Windstar and rent an SUV, drive to Alberta and sell the stolen property.

* * * * *

The night before the robbery, Hecky sent R-Luv and Messy to bed early to catch up on their rest. At around 11:00 p.m., Hecky and Derek left the house and swiped the van and a license plate. They returned home shortly after midnight. Hecky woke the boys and grabbed the supplies while Derek re-plated the van.

20 minutes later, they made the 15-minute drive to Matty's parents' and Hecky parked across the street from the house. Derek jumped out of the van and crossed the street onto the property. He kept repeating to himself 7954 and 9812, codes to the garage and house. He pressed 7956, *fuck!* 7954, *bingo!* The garage door opened and Hecky pulled the van inside. As soon as the hood cleared, Derek closed the door. They were in!

The boys jumped out of the van and walked toward the door into the house. Hecky had a crowbar in hand as he approached the door. Derek signaled stop, brushed by Hecky and opened the door. He stepped inside and heard the alarm beeping. He keyed in the code 9812...silence.

"Keep your masks on, there could be cameras."

The boys nodded their heads.

Derek was first man into the kitchen; it was something out of a home improvement magazine.

"This is a nice fucking kitchen," said Hecky.

Messy had already walked past Derek into the living room.

"Holy fuck!" he exclaimed.

On the living room wall was the biggest television the boys had ever seen. Along with it was a PS3, an X-Box 360, a Bose home theatre system, along with a few hundred Blu-ray movies and games. On top of that was two Macbook laptops and a desktop computer, also a Mac.

Hecky pointed at R-Luv, who nodded. He dismantled their setup in five minutes. Hecky would re-program the computers in a night.

The boys followed Derek as he walked down the hall to the bedrooms. They walked into a guest room with a Macbook Pro in it. Guest bedroom number two – the same.

Hecky grew impatient and charged down the hall to the master bedroom. "Oh my God, you guys."

The boys walked in behind him and took a look around the room. Another 80" television, a dozen high-end guitars, and the biggest jewelry collection anyone had ever seen.

"Holy shit! Look at all these guitars!" Exclaimed Derek. "Careful with that Blackie Strat, Messy!"

The jewelry box had a small lock on it, which Hecky quickly mashed with a crowbar. Inside the box were gold, silver, diamonds and pearls. Hecky grabbed a duffel bag and began emptying the jewelry into it.

"Case up those guitars!" he snapped at Messy.

Derek entered the walk-in closet to find at least 30 designer men's watches, 30 designer suits, a dozen pairs of sunglasses, high-end shoes and expensive clothing, not to mention all of the expensive women's clothing and shoes that he knew nothing about.

Hecky followed Derek into the closet.

"Holy shit, dude," said Hecky as he smiled at Derek through his mask.

"We need a bigger bag!"

"We're going to need ten bigger bags." yelled Hecky.

Derek began pulling suits out when he stumbled upon a small hidden safe.

"Yo, check this out."

Hecky walked over and took down the model number. Derek didn't think anything of it as he packed the last suit into a luggage bag and stood to his feet. Hecky strolled back in with one of the Macbook Pro's and a toolbox.

"What the fuck are you doing, Hecky?"

"We built one of these fuckers as a prop last year. I'm going to see if I can break it," replied Hecky. "You keep going, dude. Grab everything that's worth anything."

"How do you know what to do?"

"A bunch of the guys we brought in were safe crackers. They showed us how to build one and how to break one."

Hecky stayed in the room to try and crack the safe while Derek took the luggage to the van. R-Luv and Messy loaded the electronics and guitars into the van.

Derek turned back to walk into the house when a set of headlights shone through the garage door lighting up the room. They ducked for cover and quietly closed the van door. He heard a car door open, followed by footsteps getting louder and louder. Someone was walking toward the house! Derek stayed low as he listened attentively for the garage door to open. In the shadow of the headlights, he could see the shape of someone's head on the right side of the van. It looked as if they were peering in through the window. Derek looked up on the left side of the van and noticed the car was a security vehicle. *How the fuck did Messy and R-Luv miss this?*

He ducked back down and crawled toward the door into the house. The figure outside was still peering in through the window on the right side of the van. Derek crawled to the door, opened it and crawled inside. Messy and R-Luv were walking toward the door with their arms full when they saw Derek, who quietly closed the door behind him.

"What the fuck are you doing?" asked Messy.

"Get down! Security is outside!"

Messy and R-Luv ducked out of the way. Derek crawled past them to the master closet.

"What's up?" asked Hecky.

"Get down, security is outside!"

"Oh fuck," said Hecky as he dropped to his chest.

Derek could see a flashlight through the window.

"How many guys?" asked Hecky.

"Just one I think."

Hecky and Derek stayed low for a few minutes until security left. Messy and R-Luv came in the room.

"How did you guys miss that?" asked Hecky.

"We didn't. He never came before," answered R-Luv.

"Fucking Jesus, that was close,"

The boys caught their breath.

"You guys want to see something?" asked Hecky.

"Did you get it open?"

Hecky turned and smiled. "Yup!"

He walked the boys into the bedroom closet and opened the safe to reveal massive stacks of money.

"Holy shit!" yelled Messy.

"How much fucking money is that?" asked Derek.

"I haven't counted it," said Hecky, as he began to pull out stacks.

"Check to make sure there are no dye packs," said R-Luv.

"Why would there be a dye pack?" asked Hecky.

"You never know," replied R-Luv, "banks do it!"

Hecky began pulling out stacks of money and checking them. Each stack was ten thousand dollars. He went through the stacks checking for a dye pack. He counted the last stack, turned to the boys and smiled.

"43 stacks. $430,000!"

The boys stood in silence. They had hit the big time. This wasn't ripping off a store or some small-time thug, they were ripping off a big time player, connected to something.

"Do we do this?" asked Derek.

"Fuck yeah!" replied Hecky.

Derek cautioned the boys, "If we do this, we are all the way in."

"We are already all the way in," replied Hecky. "We've already busted in here and loaded the van. No reason to turn back now."

"This money means that people are after us," Derek continued.

"People are already after us," said Messy. "What does this change?"

Derek looked at Messy and grimaced. "Its up to you guys. I just worry that if we jump into this life with both feet, we are going to end up with toe tags."

"I'll roll the dice," said Hecky.

"Me too," said Messy.

Derek looked over at R-Luv, thinking he'd have R-Luv's support.

"I'm okay with it," said R-Luv.

Derek locked eyes with R-Luv and shook his head. "Are you sure? We are already vulnerable in this world. Do you really want to intertwine yourself in another one?"

"What's one more?"

"Guys, we are bringing on a whirlwind of shit. These stories we hear of in the news – we are going to become one of those cautionary tales."

"We should go," said R-Luv.

"Yeah, let's go," said Hecky.

The boys loaded the van, opened the garage door and left. The drive back to the house was silent; the boys were excited, and Derek was nervous. They hadn't tipped off the police or anyone, for that matter. They were in and out, quiet and professional. But Derek knew they had poked the bear.

Hecky circled a few blocks and doubled back several times to ensure they weren't being followed.

They pulled into the garage and unloaded their ill-gotten goods. Derek removed the plates from the van; he and Hecky returned them and the van back where they belonged. They worked for an hour without saying a word to one another.

Derek followed Hecky back to the house. Inside they found R-Luv and Messy drinking Johnny Walker Blue and celebrating. They had lined up forty stolen bottles of high-end liquor on the countertop.

"You swiped this?" asked Derek.

"Yup," replied R-Luv.

Hecky and Derek walked over and poured some Johnny Blue.

"You guys are nuts," said Derek as he raised a glass. "Cheers, boys. I hope you know what we are doing"

Hecky poured himself a glass and took a sip, "What's the final haul?"

R-Luv had taken an inventory. He threw the white dry erase board on the table, which read:

- Four hundred and thirty thousand dollars cash
- Four bottles of Johnny Walker Blue; four bottles of Belvedere; three bottles of Grey Goose; a Glenfiddich 1937; a Highland Park, 50 years old; Royal Salute by Chivas Regal; The Macallan 1939; four bottles of Dom and a mix of twenty high end liquors

- Fifteen Armani suits, and fifteen other suits ranging from Versace to Dolce & Gabbana
- Forty-four dresses ranging from Versace to Louis Vuitton
- Seven Louis Vuitton handbags
- Twenty-seven pairs of women's shoes, twenty-five men's pairs ranging in brands from Gucci to Louis Vuitton
- Seven men's Rolexes, five women's Rolexes, and eighteen other watches ranging from TagHauer to Richard Mile
- Thirty-five pairs of sunglasses, ranging from Oakley and Ray Bans to Dolce & Gabbana and Cartier
- Eight Macbook Pro laptops and four IMac desktops
- Seven flat screen televisions, including an 80"
- Nine iPod's
- Seven Blu-ray players
- Four Bose home theatre systems
- Four sets of Bose headphones
- Four full sets of Titleist golf clubs
- Twelve guitars, including four Paul Reed Smiths, two Ibanez and two Gibson Les Paul's.
- Three X-Box 360s and three PS3s
- Forty PS3 and X-Box 360 Games

The list went on and on: clothes, jewelry, electronics, and even food. R-Luv had raided their fridge and freezer, taking steaks, roasts and seafood.

"Fuck, boys, what are we going to do with all of this?" asked Derek.

"Road trip," replied Hecky. "I'm going to Alberta with Messy."

"I can stop working," said Derek.

"Yeah, I think the time has come," said Messy. "We all need to focus on the truck now. We can finally rest easy and make this thing work."

*   *   *   *   *

The next day, Hecky and Messy loaded the van and drove to Alberta.

Derek gave his two weeks notice to his boss. After work that night, Matty asked Derek to go for a beer next door.

The hostess sat them down in front of one of the big TVs. As they were drinking, Derek struggled to keep his secret. He had robbed Matty's parents, and he figured Matty must not yet know. He made small talk, "You good, buddy?"

"I was, until this week."

"Why, what happened?"

"My folks place got robbed."

Fuck! thought Derek. "Fuck, eh!"

"Yeah, man, it's fucking terrible."

"Do the police know who did it?"

"Come on," said Matty as he snickered. Derek panicked as Matty continued. "The cops don't know who robbed this place."

"Fair point," replied Derek, breathing a sigh of relief.

"I feel," Matty rubbed his head, "violated, I guess. Guys like us work so hard, and where does it get us?"

"Nowhere," replied Derek

"My folks, too. Like, they bust their ass to get where they are and then some lowlife robs them. It's fucked."

"I know, dude. I get it."

"You know my cousin slings, right? Anyways, he always tries to reel me in, but I always tell him no. I never wanted to enlist in that war and step in to battle something I'm not prepared to fight."

"Yeah, most of those guys end up dead or in jail."

"But looking at it now, if my family and I are going to have our lives interrupted by them anyway, then why the fuck not?"

"Are you thinking of going into his business?" asked Derek.

"I seriously am."

"Bad idea, Matty. You are a good kid. Good things will happen to you. Your parents do well – they must have something tucked away for you."

Derek felt guilty, thinking he and his buddies had pushed Matty to this.

"That's naïve. Good things don't just happen."

"Yeah, well," Derek glanced away, "you do this, and bad things will happen. You aren't above the trouble you are sure to bring on."

"Sarge, we make what, like, $1,800 a month after tax and tips?"

"Yeah, if we have a good month."

"My cousin will start me," Matty paused and repeated himself, "start me at $500 a day, for a few hours of work. Cash – in my hand end of day."

"Doing what?" asked Derek.

"Packaging and weighing."

"I know what that means."

"It would take me less than eight weeks to earn what I would make in one year at the liquor store."

"At what cost though?"

Matty shrugged his shoulders. "It's something to consider."

"Consider the flip side to that," said Derek, cautioning Matty. "I don't think you understand the paradigm you will put yourself in."

Derek patted Matty on the shoulder and stood up and walked over to the bathroom.

"Why not go to your parents for more money. They seem well off."

"I burned that bridge, man. When I dropped out, my Dad cut me off."

"I gotta hit the head," Derek said, walking to the bathroom.

A few minutes later he returned to see Matty with a strange look on his face.

"Smoke?" he asked.

Derek nodded as Matty stood up and put on his jacket. Once outside, they lit smokes and Matty stepped to Derek real close. He opened his hand to reveal a baggie of cocaine.

"I went looking for your lighter and I found this."

"What the fuck? Give it back!"

Matty put the coke back in Derek's coat pocket and turned away. "I can get you better shit than that," Matty said with an excited look.

"Right, your cousin?"

"Yeah, man. It's like I told you – one phone call is all it would take."

"Matty, be serious. You are too nice of a guy for that life."

"I think I'd be alright."

"You really want to risk your freedom like that, or your life. Half those guys end up dead in their 20's."

"Aren't we all just killing time until time kills us?"

"I guess." replied Derek.

"It's a moot point for you. You've got your truck, you're good. I'll figure out my own shit."

"To each his own."

"I will bring an eight to you tomorrow and it will blow your mind. Two hundred."

"Done." replied Derek.

And like that, Matty had become a dealer. If only Matty knew what Derek was into.

* * * * *

Hecky and Messy returned from Alberta six days later. Their total haul for the trip, minus expenses, was just under $40,000. Total cash haul for the job was $470,000, plus what they kept. They needed to start putting cash through the truck with more urgency.

* * * * *

Two weeks after Derek left the liquor store, the boys made two grand profit and three grand the week after. They held steady at three grand for a few weeks, but on paper they were showing eight grand profit. Word was out that they had the best sandwich in the city and people began to flock to the truck to try Derek's concoctions.

In May, the boys extended their hours into the night to attract bar goers and their profits ballooned to five thousand dollars a week, in honest hard-earned cash. All the while, they were washing ten thousand. Derek deposited $15,000 into his account and paid $650 for his bills.

He paid off his student debt in the first week of June. There was no need to buy food, booze or any toys because he had everything. He did need a car, though, and with all that he and the boys had been doing, they were starting to outgrow their house.

For his birthday, he bought himself a fully loaded Ford Edge SUV, just like Anna's. The boys thought Derek was crazy, but he knew that within a few months he'd have the car paid off. The neighbours began to grow suspicious about all the money they suddenly had.

They began bringing the truck around the house as a way to take eyes off of them. They needed to show the neighbours that they were legitimate business owners who were just trying to make a go of it.

Derek went back to Matty to buy more sniff and, once again, Matty asked Derek if he was interested in slinging. He wasn't. Matty told Derek that he was making $30,000 a month and had bought a brand new RX-8.

October 4th, 2009
TWENTY-FIVE

Messy ate burgers on the couch while Derek lay in bed, still floating from the high of falling for Mandy.

Messy prattled on about what makes certain burgers better than others and how the motel room sucked cause there weren't enough burger joints within walking distance. He began to delve deep into the subject when Derek's cell phone rang. Derek sprung to his feet, jogged over and answered it. On the other end of the line was Hecky. He had bad news.

June 2009

Derek drove his new Ford Edge back to the house to meet the boys for dinner. He pulled onto Woodsworth Avenue with his music cranked and as he approached the house, he noticed Anna sitting in her Edge. He honked and parked the car. Anna approached the car as Derek jumped out.

"You couldn't resist copying me," said Anna as she cracked a smile.

"I had to!" said Derek, smiling back as they embraced in the street.

"So, birthday boy, would you like to have dinner with me?"

"I'd love to," replied Derek, "but I'm having dinner with the boys. You should come with. Call your girlfriends, we can go out after!"

"Yeah, okay. Sure!"

Anna called her friends and they met up with the boys at Secret Room on Alexander. The irony of going to the Secret Room made Derek snicker.

The evening started off with laughs over dinner. Derek knew that Hecky felt boxed in, especially since he was high on blow. Messy was too.

Derek was as well.

However, Derek and Messy were keeping it together a little better than Hecky. He was agitated that Derek had invited the girls; he felt as though Derek ruined the evening. *Fuck him*, thought Derek. *It's my birthday.*

After dinner they continued at The Bar. More drinking led to dancing, and dancing led to more drinking, and more drinking led to more rackit.

Hecky, Messy and Derek were snowbirds riding the wave. It was incredible to Derek that Anna was a cop, a detective no less, and she didn't seem to notice that three of the four guys she was partying with were banging enough blow to kill any normal human.

Hecky and Derek were baiting Anna to catch them bumping lines. Derek felt a weird sense of excitement and Hecky finally understood why he was getting off on it all.

*   *   *   *   *

Shortly after his birthday, Derek went home for his Grandparents 50th anniversary in Renfrew. He attended his family party and had a great time celebrating the occasion. His family was happy to see him; many hugs and tears were exchanged and wept.

He left the party half in the bag and began walking down beautiful main street Renfrew. The downtown had the old-fashioned, small town charm you'd see in movies. He strolled down the sidewalk like McAdams and Gosling in The Notebook.

Derek needed to think. He walked into his bank on the east side of Raglan Street and withdrew a hundred bucks. He pocketed the money, walked out the front door and stood on the corner of Raglan Street and Renfrew Avenue, listening to his iPod. He waited patiently for the light to turn, remembering that there was a trail down Renfrew Avenue that led out to the Mate-Way Activity Centre. That road ran perpendicular to Highway 132, a straight shot out of Renfrew.

Across the street to Derek's left was the post office, to the left of that was an alleyway to another street.

Derek's mind wandered; he began to think that if he ever had intentions of knocking off a bank, this would be the one. The police station was located on the other side of town and by the time the cops responded, Derek and his crew could be switching cars and heading to Highway 132.

He snickered to himself and put these silly thoughts out of his head. He walked to the bar and sat on the patio, drinking Chivas, still thinking about that escape route. It was the kind of route a bank robber would dream about. But he didn't need the money.

*   *   *   *   *

Two days later, Derek was craving sushi. Renfrew had one place to get it, located on the corner of Renfrew Avenue and Raglan Street, directly across the street from Derek's bank. Derek took his Brother out for lunch.

During their second course, he saw an armored truck pull in front of the bank and stop. The two men in the truck sat still for a moment before the passenger exited, walked around back and climbed inside.

The guard was inside for a minute before he re-emerged with a cart stacked with moneybags. The guard had to look down and lift his cart onto the sidewalk before wheeling it up to the front door. During that time, he could have been ambushed from any direction, Derek thought.

His mind began to race. How often did they do deliveries? How much money was in there? Is there another guy in the back of the truck? How are the driver's sightlines? Would the driver exit the vehicle if attacked?

A few minutes later, the guard returned and the truck left. Dannick caught Derek staring and called him out. "You listening?"

"Sorry, bud, just in a daze!"

*   *   *   *   *

The next day, Derek went back downtown and walked alongside the back of the bank. He then walked straight down Renfrew Avenue, continuing to the hiking trail and walked it. The trail was wide enough for a skilled driver to navigate it. The concrete blocks placed in front of the trail's entrances were another story.

Derek knew that all these obstacles stood in his way. As he played the scenarios through his head, he kept laughing to himself about how crazy this idea was. Why get greedy?

*   *   *   *   *

Derek flew back to Vancouver on Wednesday, where Hecky was waiting for him at the airport. As they drove to The Soho in the mid-afternoon, Derek eased into the passenger's seat of the van, kicked off his shoes and took a deep haul of his cigarette. A calm came over him. The breath of tobacco laced with fresh mountain air calmed his nerves. Now that he was far enough away from Renfrew, the lure of knocking off that truck would subside.

The boys arrived and sat in their usual booth in the back corner. Derek felt weird to be at The Soho so early in the day. Moments later, Messy and R-Luv rolled in and sat with them. They ordered dinner.

Derek noticed that something was off.

"What's going on boys?"

"Tell him, Hecky," said R-Luv.

"Tell me what?" asked Derek.

Hecky looked Derek in the eye and said, "I took a hundred g's from our last job and invested it in another job."

"Invested it? You bought coke with it," yelled R-Luv.

"Keep your voice down," said Messy. "He bought five kilos."

"For a hundred g?" asked Derek.

Hecky nodded and smiled.

"That's a good fucking price," said Derek as he nodded along.

"Jesus Christ," exclaimed R-Luv.

"I'm not condoning it, but that's a good price. Where'd you get it?"

"Guy up in Squamish," replied Hecky. "He had it and needed cash quick. I work with him at the ski hill."

"And what are we going to do with that much coke?" asked Messy.

Hecky looked over at Derek and smirked; Derek's immediate thought was Matty. *Fuck me,* thought Derek. *What were we getting into now?*

"Any ideas?" asked Hecky.

"What about your guy that you sold our other shit to?" asked Derek.

"No good, he's out."

"He's out? What, is he the only drug dealer to ever quit drug dealing?"

"I guess. Any other ideas?"

"One," replied Derek as he hesitated. Things were going well for the boys; Derek felt as though Hecky was getting greedy and reckless.

"One is good," replied Hecky. "Honestly, I don't know why I did this. I've been all fucked up lately."

"No excuses," replied R-Luv. "I'm sick of excuses. We pull a stealth job and then you do this."

"Fuck, R-Luv. You don't even know what I'm going through."

"Enlighten me, Hecky. Unburden yourself," said R-Luv.

"I've got depression. Like, clinically diagnosed depression."

A silence fell over the table as the waitress brought eight pounds of wings to the booth. She put the wings on the table and the boys digested the news.

Hecky continued, "And I'm bi-polar."

Messy and Derek looked at each other. Was he being truthful? If he was, Derek felt for him.

*   *   *   *   *

The next morning, Derek received a text just as he woke up. It was Matty welcoming him back to Vancouver. He had the day off and was checking to see if Derek wanted to go for a beer.

Matty drove over to the house, picked up Derek and drove them to Oscar's Pub on Hastings Street. They sat and shared an afternoon pitcher. Derek knew what he wanted to discuss, but he wasn't sure how to bring it up. Something was different with Matty. He had swagger and was starting to look the part and not like the innocent boy Derek first met.

After his second beer, Derek finally worked up the nerve to bring it up. "Matty, when you said you had connections, what did you mean?"

Matty grinned. "I meant that if you wanted things, I could get them."

"Are you deep in this shit now?"

"What do you care? You told me not to get into it."

"I'm still telling you that, Matty."

"You didn't come here for that. Did you want me to hook you up?"

"I'm not slinging 20's to get by."

"Neither am I. I got my guys doing that. I just bag and point them in which direction to go."

Matty looked at Derek who nodded his head with a look of skepticism on his face. "Don't judge me. You don't know my shit."

"I do know, Matty. I took the fucking beating at that store. I got robbed too."

"It wasn't just us!" shouted Matty. "My folks got ripped off too."

"And that sucks."

"Yeah, well, I'm sick of feeling this way."

"What way?" asked Derek.

"Dispensable. Powerless."

"So, you think that by slinging you won't feel used? These guys will chew you and toss you."

"I'll get out when I have enough to do what I want."

"And what's that?" asked Derek as his set his beer down.

"Leave this soulless fucking place. For good."

Derek paused for a second. "What if I wanted to hook you up?"

"Whatcha mean?" asked Matty.

"What if I brought something to your doorstep? Do you know people who would open the door?"

"Well, I'm into it now. My cousin moves," said Matty with a grin, "but his pipes are dry."

"I could bring gas to the pumps."

"How much?" asked Matty.

Derek took a sip of his beer and held up five fingers. Matty was stunned. "Five?" asked Matty.

Derek jingled his keys.

"Fuck off, Sarge," said Matty, as he laughed to himself.

"I'm dead fucking serious, and if he wants it, tell him its 35 per. You set it up. Just us three, no bullshit."

"Where you get it?" asked Matty.

"Don't worry. What matters is that I have it and that you can have it. Five by thirty-five. Set it up."

"Let me get in touch."

Matty walked outside and Derek stood up and walked to the bathroom. Matty was back at the table when Derek returned to his seat.

"It's on," said Matty, "tomorrow at noon. Liquor Store parking lot."

"That's fucked, dude. Right out in the open in broad fucking daylight."

"Do you prefer an alley at night?"

"No."

"Well, at least we know the cameras there don't work."

Derek drove to meet Matty and George the next day. He brought a gun in his shirt and taped an extra to the bottom of his seat; if shit went down, Derek was game.

He pulled into the Liquor Store parking lot and backed in next to Matty's car. He admired the cloudless blue sky as Matty entered the passenger side and dropped his heavy school bag in Derek's lap. Derek unzipped the bag and looked in it. He checked to make sure the cash was legitimate and not just a couple of hundreds and a bunch of fives. It was good. Derek grabbed the bag of bricks from under his seat and handed them to Matty.

He opened the bag and took a look. "Looks good!"

"You aren't going to try it?" asked Derek.

"Fuck, no. I don't do this shit. Besides, if you rip him off, he going to bend you, homey."

"Noted."

"See you, bud," said Matty as he jumped out of the car.

Derek felt under his shirt with his hand. He was drenched in sweat.

October 4th, 2009

Hecky was on the phone. He was supposed to meet up with R-Luv and head home, but R-Luv never showed.

"Have you heard from him, Sarge?" asked Hecky.

"I haven't heard shit. We've just been laying low."

"Sarge, fell in love again, dude!" yelled Messy.

"Shut up, this is serious! Did you text him?" asked Derek.

"I tried everything. I don't know where he is. This isn't like him."

"Okay, we're heading tomorrow."

"I'm going to wait a few more hours and then head home. I can't wait here forever."

"Do what you have to do, Hecky. Let me know if you hear from him."

"Likewise. Drive safe!"

"Later, Hecky," yelled Messy.

Derek hung up his phone and received a text from Mandy.

It read, *Breakfast at my place?*

That's forward! He texted back.

I meant my diner, you sicko!

Oh, ha-ha, okay I will meet you there! Is 8 a.m. okay? asked Derek.

Okay, guess I can sleep in! Night!

Goodnight!

"Is that your girlfriend?"

"Dude, stop!" joked Derek as he pushed Messy.

At 7:30 a.m., Derek woke up, crawled out of bed, showered, dressed and walked out of the motel.

"Hey you!" yelled Mandy as she jumped out from around the corner.

"Jesus Christ!" shouted Derek, nearly jumping out of his shoes.

"How'd you sleep?"

"I might never sleep again."

"Did I scare you?"

"Just a little," replied Derek, as he clutched his heart.

"Yeah, I got you good!"

"How long were you waiting?"

"Just a few minutes."

Messy walked outside and stood behind Derek. He looked tired and strung out. He and Mandy exchanged smiles and she tried to make nice. "Good morning, I'm Mandy."

"Hey, I'm Jyoshi," replied Messy. It was the first time Derek ever heard Messy introduce himself as Jyoshi. Messy walked to the car and opened the trunk. As he did Derek's phone rang.

"Must be Mommy," joked Messy.

Derek answered. It was Hecky. "Hey, what's up?"

"Are you near a TV?" asked Hecky. "Turn it to Vancouver news!"

Derek walked into the room and looked for the remote. Mandy and Messy followed him.

"What's up?" asked Derek, "Global BC, Messy."

"My Dad just texted me and said there was a murder on our street," replied Hecky, "I'm still driving home."

Messy found the remote and flipped to Global BC. They were displaying a shot of the boy's street with the caption: Murder in West Point Grey.

"He's right. That's our street." Derek studied the image and realized the murder house was their house!

July 2009

A week after Derek made the exchange with Matty, he and Messy were invited to a pool party. Messy's co-worker Mark was house-sitting his parents place.

The home had a pool inside and out, a fifteen thousand-dollar BBQ, a twenty-thousand-dollar sound system – high-end EVERYTHING.

Derek began to mingle but was bored within an hour. What interested him was the high-end items in the home that could easily be removed.

Messy and Derek sat on lawn chairs; Derek smoked and looked around as if he was looking at women.

"Don't even think it," said Messy.

"What?"

"We aren't knocking this place down – not going to happen."

"I was looking for girls."

"You were not. You were thinking this place looks like an easy target."

"Goddamn." Derek grinned at Messy. "How'd you know?"

"There isn't a looker in this whole goddamn place."

"You know you guys were all good hitting my places, but a score falls in our lap and you don't want it?"

"What was that you said last week about not being greedy?" asked Messy. "We're sitting on like six hundred grand in cash. Isn't that enough?"

"It is, until we get jammed up and need more. This is ripe for the picking, dude. I already unlatched the upstairs windows."

"How?" asked Messy.

"Dude, he let us into the house. It wasn't that hard to unlock some windows."

"Fuck, really?"

"Yeah."

"Goddamn," said Messy, "Fuck, yeah, we have to do it."

"When are his parents back?"

"Five weeks. And Mark is gone for a four-day weekend next weekend.

"Do you think Mark is smart enough to check the windows before his trip?" Asked Derek.

Cillian walked over to the boys, he was dressed in a pink belly shirt. "Hey, boys. How are you?" Messy high-five Cillian and he sat beside them.

"Hey Cillian, does that shirt come in boys?" asked Messy.

Cillian looked at Derek and Messy and grinned. "Messy, I think its pretty safe to say that you've come in enough boys for all of us."

Derek laughed uncontrollably.

"Fuck, I teed that one up," said Messy.

Cillian pointed at a girl. "I told that girl over there that if she smelled as bad as she looked, she'd clear out the place." joked Cillian.

"That's so fucking mean," said Derek as he laughed.

* * * * *

The following Friday, the boys rented two cargo vans and drove to Mark's parents in broad daylight. It was a three-man job; Messy, Hecky and Derek were on board. R-Luv had to man the food truck and preserve an alibi. He would join the boys on his three hour "lunch".

The boys pulled into Mark's parent's driveway. Derek jumped out of the car and made his way inside the house through a second story window. Moments later the garage door opened, Derek walked outside and opened a second garage door. Messy and Hecky backed the vans into the garage. As soon as the hood cleared the doorway, Derek shut the doors and made his way inside. He cleared the home before they began the hunt.

After two hours of tearing the house apart, they packed the vans, opened the garage doors and took off. Derek took R-Luv back to the truck and made his way back to the house.

Hecky and Messy were parked on the street when Derek arrived back at the house. He jumped into the van with Hecky and they began the nine-hour drive to Canmore.

* * * * *

The next day, Messy and R-Luv drove the other van to meet Derek and Hecky in Canmore and unload the rest of the goods.

After exhausting the pawn shops in Canmore, they drove the hour and a bit to Calgary and began unloading items there.

They returned to Vancouver, having lined their pockets with sixty-three thousand dollars in cash.

* * * * *

Early the next day, the boys approached the house having returned from Alberta. Anna's car pulled up on the street. She jumped out and ran up toward the boys who were standing at their front door.

"Hey, Anna," said Derek as he smiled at her.

"Where the hell have you been?" she asked, sternly.

"We went on a roadie."

"You didn't think to maybe give me a heads up?" she asked.

"I didn't know we were in that position right now."

"It's not a position, Derek. It's common courtesy to send a text saying, Hey, I'm taking off for a week."

Derek scoffed out loud, "It was three days, Anna."

"Whatever," Anna turned and stormed off. "Go on your secret trips and see if I care."

"Well, obviously you do care. You wouldn't be here otherwise."

"What are you hiding?" Anna stopped and turned to face Derek. "What's your big fucking secret?"

"What are you talking about?"

"When I met you, you were flat broke. Now you have all this money – trips out of town. What changed?"

"I own my own business, Anna."

"What business is that?"

"The truck," replied Derek.

"No one is making that kind of money selling soup and sandwiches in an office park."

A voice shouted from behind Derek, "We are!" It was Hecky. "We are making that kind of money. In fact, the reason we took this trip was to try and line up a new beef supplier in Alberta. We are trying to get better."

Anna stormed off to her car and drove away.

That evening, a member of the R.O.P. was shot and killed in his truck at close range by members of The Devil's Grip. Three nights later, a member of the R.O.P. was shot in his car in broad daylight, in the middle of an intersection three blocks from Woodsworth Avenue. Another shooting near The Soho two days later. Things in the city were blowing up and Hecky wanted to move. The boys had outgrown their four-bedroom home.

Hecky began searching for an alternative home for the boys to move to. He eventually settled on moving into a five-bedroom home on West 3rd Avenue in Point Grey. The house was mint. It had an incredible view of the ocean, as well as views of Stanley Park and the North Shore Mountain. Inside, it was an upgraded kitchen, complete with high–end stainless steel appliances. It also had three large upstairs bedrooms, and on the main floor was another bedroom, as well as a spacious living room, family room and dining room. The house even had a library in addition to a large open deck outside. On the bottom floor were three spacious multifunction rooms with a walkout that was level to the backyard. Utilities not included, and all for the low low price of $7,500 a month. The boys were stepping up their game.

*   *   *   *   *

It was a week before the move and Derek was packing up the living room when the doorbell rang. Matty was at the door. "What's going on, bro?"

"Hey, can I come in for a bit?"

"Yeah, come on in." Matty walked in and kicked off his flip-flops. Derek led him to the living room. "Do you want a beer?"

"Nah, I'm good, man," Matty pointed to the boxes. "You moving?"

"Yeah, man. We got a new pad in Point Grey. We're all moving there."

"Oh shit," replied Matty. "You guys are moving on up."

"Yeah, buddy. So, what's up?"

"Listen, man. I know you said what we did was a one-time thing."

Before Matty could finish his sentence, Derek cut him off. "It was, and it will stay that way."

"Listen, Sarge, my cousin wants more of that shit. He'll pay!"

Derek walked over to his whiteboard and wrote *outside* on it. Matty followed him into the backyard. Derek shut the back door.

"We don't talk in there."

"Sorry," Matty apologized, "but I'm serious. Big money, dude."

"Matty, you heard of a kid named Damon Wong?"

"No, who is he?"

"He was a track kid from Surrey. He went to Seattle to allegedly make a deal."

"Yeah yeah, shit, yeah, I remember hearing about that a long time ago. He never came back. They kept calling him Speed Damon?"

"That's right. And that right there is the reason I will never hook you up again. If I were you, I would stop associating with your cousin on that level."

Hecky walked outside through the back door and lit a cigarette.

"Hey, boys. What's up?"

"Matty was just leaving."

"Ah, too bad. I've got a bottle of bourbon and a few steaks to cook up. Stick around, bud."

"What kind?" asked Matty.

"Prichard's, double barrel."

"I'm in," replied Matty, as he looked at Derek and smiled.

Derek knew Matty's play; befriend Hecky and use him to get plugged into the pipeline.

Derek's only move was to get Matty away from Hecky. He went to the bathroom to collect himself.

After a few minutes, he knew he had to go back out. He exited the bathroom, where Messy was waiting for him.

"Dude, why the fuck is he here?"

"I know. We need him out!"

"Damn right. Go keep them at arm's length. I'll think of something."

"Oh, you'll think of something. You going to hatch a scheme, are you?"

"Just go, Sarge."

Derek returned to the backyard. Matty and Hecky were making small talk about Korean BBQ and Derek wondered if he missed all the talk about cocaine. An awkward silence fell over the yard. *What was Matty's play?* Derek wondered. *Why come to them for blow?*

Derek's first intuition was to ask him. "Matty, why are you here? We don't have any. We buy small, for personal use. Nothing more."

"Oh, Sarge. I think your boy is holding out on you."

"What is he talking about?"

Hecky swallowed hard. "I've got five more bricks upstairs – same price. If you want them, they are yours."

"You motherfucker!" yelled Derek as he got in Hecky's face.

"What the fuck?" yelled Messy, from inside the house.

Matty walked inside and Hecky looked at the boys and smiled.

"Wipe that fucking smile off of your face, Hecky. Where are you getting all the blow?" asked Messy.

"I traded for it."

"Traded for it – what the fuck did you trade for it?"

"Weed."

"You can't trade weed for coke," replied Messy as he walked outside.

"Yeah," replied Hecky, "you can. I worked with a guy up in Squamish who has a grow-op. I buy weed and trade it with a guy in Washington."

"Fuck off!" exclaimed Derek.

"Weed goes for a premium in California and coke is worth a shitload more here," said Hecky.

"We aren't getting into slinging, Hecky," said Derek. "We'll end up dead or in prison."

"Yeah, dude, this isn't smart," said Messy. "How did you even make the exchange?"

"In Abbottsford, there is a road that separates the U.S. and Canada. I drove down it, tossed a bag out of the window, while Steve tossed a bag in the side door of the van. I never got my speed below forty."

"Jesus Christ! That is so stupid!" yelled Derek.

"Stupid? I made us $300,000 profit in four hours of work," screamed Hecky.

"You put this whole house at risk! Money isn't so useful when you're in fucking jail."

"I would have taken the fall if I got caught," said Hecky.

"I would hope so, since you did this on your own," continued Derek.

July 2009
TWENTY-SIX

The boys went downtown for dinner and a night out a few days later. After dinner, they went to a nightclub for VIP and bottle service. Hecky was throwing money around and it was making the boys uncomfortable. He was putting a lot of eyes on them as they sat in their booth drinking Goose. Moments later, eight girls joined them.

The flashiness also caught the attention of some people they didn't want to be noticed by – the R.O.P. It was rare to see young men at a club, throwing around money that didn't acquire it illegally. The boys were no different. The R.O.P. saw through the charade.

Hecky was talking to a girl at the boy's booth when a member of the R.O.P. sat down next to him. The man had sleeves of tattoos on both arms, a neck tattoo and was disguising several tattoos under a black dress shirt. Hecky's body language changed within seconds of the man sitting beside him. He knew who the man was. Hecky slumped in his chair and the expression on his face went from delighted to terrified. Messy and Derek locked eyes from across the bar, almost as if to say, *what do we do?* Derek shook his head to say, *let this happen.* He hoped that a good scare would set Hecky straight. R-Luv watched on from a distance as well. Derek couldn't make out what Hecky and the man were saying to one another, but he knew that the R.O.P. member was trying to intimidate Hecky, and it was working. The man stood to his feet and lifted his shirt; he had a gun hidden in his waistband. He backed up, pulled his shirt down and walked to the exit with his crew.

The boys walked over to Hecky, whose pride was decimated.

"What was that?" asked R-Luv.

"They basically just robbed me," replied Hecky. "He said that if he sees us out, he'll make us pay again."

"We have to pick up their check?" asked Messy.

"Fucking cunt!" yelled Hecky.

"What do you expect? They're gangsters. They aren't about being nice and charitable. They take what they want; they don't ask."

*   *   *   *   *

Anna held her morning coffee as she rode the elevator up to her fourth-floor office. The door opened and Anna was greeted by a fellow officer, "Good morning, Anna."

"Good morning, Bryan."

"I think you'll want to see last night's R.O.P. footage."

Anna followed Bryan to a tech room and sat down in a folding chair across from a desk.

"What am I looking at?" asked Anna.

"You'll know when you see it."

*   *   *   *   *

Derek woke up at 11 a.m. He walked to the backyard; Hecky was outside on his lawn chair holding a coffee and a cigarette. "Heck, why are you up early?"

Hecky shook his head. "I was thinking about how to get back at that piece of shit."

"You need to let this go. These aren't frat kids, these are ruthless, put-you-in-the-ground kind of guys."

"He disrespected me, Sarge."

"He disrespected all of us, Hecky. So what? Who fucking cares?!"

"I care, Sarge!"

"Yeah, well, the rest of us don't. You want to be a respected corpse? 'Cause that will happen. These guys are everywhere."

As Hecky and Derek continued fighting, the doorbell rang. Derek answered the door to see Anna, and she was not happy.

"Anna, hey, what's up?"

"Were you out last night?" she asked as she barged her way into the kitchen. "I heard you met the R.O.P."

"Yeah, hey," said Hecky, caught off-guard. "We had a run-in with some pretty nasty characters."

"Riley, can I talk to Derek in private please?"

"Sure," replied Hecky.

Derek knew he was in for it. Hecky walked up the stairs and Anna began, "Can you explain to me why you were in a club with a bunch of girls hanging off of you?"

"I was out with the boys. Why are you spying on me?"

"Spying on you! I have a team following the R.O.P. Imagine my surprise when I see my boyfriend in the club surrounded by skanks."

"I never touched any girls."

"Derek, I can't keep doing this. Whatever we have and whatever we were ends here. I don't want to see you again, and I especially don't want to see you associating with the R.O.P."

Derek laughed. "Is that what you think that was?"

"What do you call it?"

"They threatened Hecky into paying their tab. If that's associating...Anyway, you've got me so wrong, Anna, but that's fine. I don't need jealous and insecure people in my life!"

Anna walked to the front door and slammed it shut. A second later, Hecky came charging down the stairs.

"Are you alright, Sarge?"

"I'm fine. Did you hear that?"

Hecky nodded his head.

"So, you know that they are untouchable right now," Derek continued. "Your little revenge plot ends here."

October 5th, 2009

Derek yelled into his phone, "Hecky, it's our house!"

"What? Who would be in our house?" asked Hecky.

"I don't know."

"I'm just rolling into town now. When I hear something, you will too! Get back here ASAP!"

"Okay, we will."

"Do we have anything there that will jam us up?" asked Hecky.

"Not unless you or Messy do."

"Nope, it's fine."

"Okay, we'll leave in an hour!" A cold shiver ran down Derek's spine; he knew they were in trouble. Messy looked over at him and took a deep breath. He knew too. They scrambled to pack their bags as quickly as they could.

Mandy was dumbfounded, "what happened?"

Derek knew he needed to feed her a line. "Something on our street." He took a deep breath, "I guess I will call you in the next couple of days."

"Okay, Derek. But, what happened?"

"Someone was murdered in our neighbourhood."

"Oh my God!"

"Yeah," Derek took another deep breath. "It's fucking awful. I'm really sorry."

"Okay, it's okay, Derek." Derek and Mandy kissed and she walked out of the room to her car.

Derek loaded the last of the bags into the car. He looked over at Mandy, who had yet to leave. She looked over at Derek and asked, "What's wrong?"

Messy came storming out of the motel room and slammed the door behind him.

Mandy looked at Messy and looked back at Derek. She asked again, "What's wrong?"

"It was in our house," said Derek.

"Oh my God, Derek. That's so horrible. Was it someone you knew?"

"I really have no idea, our roommate knew nothing." Derek tried hard to keep it together.

"Call me, please! When you get a chance. I want to make sure everything is okay."

"I will," replied Derek as they leaned in and kissed. He let her go and whispered in her ear, "I'll miss you."

Mandy smiled as Derek stepped back and turned to walk to the car.

*   *   *   *   *

Messy and Derek didn't speak until they hit Kamloops, and even then, they didn't say more than a few words. Derek went over different scenarios as to what might have happened in their home. He called R-Luv every hour on the hour; no answer. Derek wondered about his involvement. R-Luv hadn't been well; he hadn't been okay with the work they'd been doing, and he needed out.

What happened in that house?

August 2009

Hecky was still steaming from the R.O.P. incident at the club. He'd gone off the rails and insisted that the boys make a deal with Matty to traffic cocaine across the border. Hecky was buying weed for pennies on the dollar and wanted to trade it for cocaine; every five key run would net $150,000.

Derek's greed began to get the best of him. *Fuck five keys,* he thought. If he was going to do it, he'd do fifteen keys. He knew it would be the same sentence for five or fifteen keys – might as well make it worth their while. Derek knew that five runs multiplied by $450,000 per run worked out to $2.25 million. Each of them would walk away with over $550,000 and bring their total to just shy of a million dollars each.

Hecky had Derek convinced that the boys would have enough money to finally focus on making the truck a legitimate business. His plan was to pack the weed in duffel bags, drive to Zero Avenue in Abbottsford and toss the weed into a waiting vehicle in America. Down the road, another man would toss a duffel bag into Hecky's van, and they would press on without slowing down. It was low tech and high risk. Using Hecky's van meant exposing him to risk if someone caught a glimpse. They needed a truck. Nothing fancy, just a truck.

And they had to move fast. Doing these drops was risky and it was only a matter of time before someone spotted them making an exchange.

Hecky and Matty had an agreement: for the next two weeks the boys would supply wholesale cocaine to George in exchange for $2.25 million. If they were caught, they were looking at a decade in prison. If not, they'd be set for life. The plan was in place, they just needed R-Luv and Messy on board.

Hecky decided that the best thing to do would be to take the boys to Zero Avenue to see what the plan was. They piled into the Edge and drove to Abbotsford to see a home that was for sale. Derek and Hecky feigned interest in the property, but in all that seclusion they were really there to talk to Messy and R-Luv about becoming international drug smugglers.

Messy was curious as to why the boys were out in the valley. It was then that Hecky began his elaborate pitch. He pointed to the two roads running parallel to one another. One road was on the American side of the border; the other on the Canadian side. The roads were separated by a grass median no wider than ten feet.

"Boys, if you look at the road that is going the other way, that is the United States of America."

"Where's the goddamn border?" asked Messy, puzzled.

"That is the border."

"If that's the U.S., what's to stop us from crossing?" asked Hecky.

"I'm sure they have shit in place," said R-Luv. "Like geothermal."

"Let's find out," said Hecky. He walked across Zero Avenue into the States and stood on the U.S. side.

He waited a few minutes before he sat down on the ground.

"Big fucking response, eh, boys?"

The boys continued to wait, and wait, and wait. Finally, after a half-hour, Hecky walked back into Canada.

"What the fuck?" asked R-Luv. "That is frightening."

"Yeah, really," said Messy. "Is this where you did that?"

"Boys, I drove this and threw a bag of weed into the U.S. and had a bag full of Charlie tossed into my van."

"You are out of your goddamn mind," said R-Luv.

"Bullshit!" said Messy. "Hecky, do you know what the Afghan's went through to get product to the U.S.? And here you are telling me that dummies like us can walk it across. I'm not buying it."

"Boys, I did it."

"Why?" asked R-Luv.

"For 300 g's."

"That is fucked!" said R-Luv. "That is 'end up with gangs and cartels after you' kind of shit."

"R-Luv, do you think any of us want this?" asked Hecky.

"You do," replied R-Luv. "And it looks like Sarge does too!"

"Whoa, I'm just intrigued," replied Derek.

"I think we are staring into the abyss and we are best to back away."

"R-Luv, we have a chance to make $2.25 million in the next two weeks. Five trips – all we do are five trips. We rent a truck, two of us in the front, two in the back. Two guys toss the weed out into a waiting car in the U.S., and then catch the coke when it gets tossed back. We never stop; never slow down. We drive. You saw the response; its open season out here."

"Why isn't everyone doing this?" asked R-Luv.

As he finished talking, a helicopter flew over the boys' heads and dropped a large crate onto the ground in the United States. Hecky gave the boys the night to decide if they were in or out.

*   *   *   *   *

Derek didn't sleep a wink. A part of him was hoping that the boys would say no and he could press on with the truck. The greedy part of him was hoping one of them would say yes.

He crawled out of bed at 6:00 a.m. and walked downstairs. Messy and R-Luv were sitting at the table chatting.

"You guys couldn't sleep?"

"Nope," R-Luv said, while Messy shook his head.

"It's kind of frightening that Hecky is up there sawing like a chainsaw. All I could think about was my parents. It would destroy our community if I got caught pulling this job," said Messy.

"What do you really think, Sarge? Is this possible?" asked R-Luv.

"I don't know, man, that's for you to decide," Derek said, pouring himself a cup of coffee. "To me, a half million bucks is a lot of money. Is it worth ten plus years in jail? Maybe. I'm not sure."

"That's not an answer, Sarge."

"I don't have an answer, Messy. I really don't. I can't tell you what you want to hear. The truth is that I'm scared of the consequences. I'm scared of jail; scared of being killed. But I'm also excited about the possibilities. We could be completely free of all of this. Free of having to work jobs we hate. Free from relying on others. So, do I want the money? You're goddamn right I do!"

"I'm in," said Messy.

"Fucking eh!" exclaimed Derek as he and Messy high fived.

R-Luv's morality was getting the best of him. "I don't know. I really don't want to be in on this."

"We need four, R-Luv," said Derek. "We need your help!"

R-Luv took a deep breath, "We have been doing everything to keep the bullets out of the gun and now he comes in double barreled and points both guns right at us."

Hecky walked into the kitchen. "Did any of you guys sleep?"

"Nope," replied Derek. "You sure did though."

"Did you guys figure out what you want to do?" asked Hecky.

Derek pointed to Messy. "We're in, R-Luv's on the fence."

"What's your hang up?"

"Getting caught, getting killed, getting too deep into this whole thing and not being able to get out. And that's just off the top of my head."

"I can't force you. If you don't want in, then don't do it," said Hecky.

"We need a fourth," said Messy.

"We'll find one, and while we look, R-Luv can think about it."

After the meeting, Derek walked upstairs to his room. Hecky met him at his door.

"We're not looking for anyone else."

"No?" asked Derek.

"No, it's either him or no one."

That evening, the boys convened in the backyard at 9:00 p.m. Hecky had some maps and documents spread out on a table, detailing the moving parts of the plan. After he outlined details, he would shred the document and toss them in the fire pit. Near the end of their meeting, R-Luv opened the backdoor and saw the boys sitting on the couches.

"Hey, boys," said R-Luv.

"What's up?" asked Hecky.

"You guys busy?"

"Just working," replied Hecky. "Do you want in on this here?"

"Five times?" asked R-Luv.

"Five times, fourteen days."

R-Luv walked outside and closed the door behind him.

* * * * *

The next morning, the boys took a drive down Zero Avenue to get the lay of the land in the daytime. Hecky explained the landmarks that the boys needed to look for in order to know when to toss the bags. The kicker in the whole plan was that the guys on the other side tossing these duffel bags were catching them in the back of a truck bed as well. The plan required pinpoint accuracy and precise timing. They wouldn't squeak by being sloppy; they needed to be spot on.

Derek didn't understand how the U.S. didn't have a patrol or sensors protecting the border. Hecky explained that they have sensors for people crossing the border, but they mostly caught hikers who accidently crossed.

* * * * *

The following day, the boys prepped for their first run. Messy and Derek bagged up the weed and left it in the garage.

They began the drive to Abbottsford at 7:00 p.m. that evening. Hecky drove with R-Luv riding shotgun with Messy and Derek in the bed of the truck. The drive lasted around an hour and was pretty rough on Derek's back. Hecky pulled onto Zero Avenue and let the boys know they could get ready to throw the bags. Derek stood up and saw a truck driving toward them on the American side; they steadied themselves and prepared to throw the bags. As the truck approached, the boys slowed to 35km/h. Derek tossed the first bag over the border and the man on the other side made the catch.

Messy made two perfect throws in a row; Derek had to complete one last throw. He rifled the bag as hard as he could and watched it come up short. The man on the other side reached out and grabbed the bag by the strap. He yanked the bag into the cab and both trucks sped off.

Hecky drove a kilometer down the road. The boys had just received four duffel bags full of cocaine. Hecky hit the gas while Messy and Derek tucked the duffel bags away and hid.

Derek's heart was racing, his pulse pounding, his head spinning. He almost blew it! Despite his error, they had made their first exchange!

An hour later, Hecky pulled into the garage and they dumped the duffel bags into the switch bags. Hecky and Derek prepared to meet with Matty and George.

"What if these guys jack you?" questioned R-Luv.

"What?" replied Derek.

"What if they want to keep the coke and the money and decide to take both?"

"Got it covered," said Hecky.

"What's that mean?"

"It means we can handle ourselves," answered Hecky.

"Are you guys strapped or something?" joked Messy.

"We'll be back in an hour."

Hecky and Derek jumped in Hecky's Windstar and drove to their 9 p.m. meeting. Hecky pulled into the parking lot and parked beside Matty and George. Derek jumped out of the van and Matty jumped out of the other vehicle. They shook hands between the two vans. Matty handed Derek a cigarette; they smoked and began chatting.

Their positioning was by design: they stood blocking the view of any nearby patrons, ensuring that no one could see George and Hecky passing bags back and forth.

After the exchange, Matty and Derek continued to chat and walked into the café. They ordered coffee and walked out to the parking lot to smoke another cigarette.

After their smoke, they jumped into their vehicles and took off. Hecky and Derek drove to the storage unit and dropped the money off before heading back to the house.

In the midst of all of these crazy things, they were still moving. Between the food truck, packing boxes and bags of weed, they were spinning a pile of plates.

*   *   *   *   *

Two days after the first drop the boys made a second drop. This time Derek made the throw with a little extra mustard on it.

The next day, they made a third switch, three days after that, a fourth.

*   *   *   *   *

Between drop 4 and 5, the boys had to move to the new house. The best part of their move was that they would be out of their current house, which had become a hot place.

Hecky hired movers to allow the boys to focus on their last drop. They packed their belongings and were ready to go the morning of the move.

On moving day, the boys went for breakfast at the Brentwood Mall. The restaurant had a beautiful view of Burnaby below. The boys sat in a booth next to the window that ran parallel to the front of the mall. They ordered breakfast and sat quietly enjoying their coffee. Derek was happy to be moving to a place where no one knew them. It was a blank slate – exactly what they needed.

Derek looked out over the jam-packed parking lot and noticed a white, early 2000's model, Ford Explorer parked down the hill. It appeared to be occupied by at least four people, all of who looked to be male. Derek saw a commotion in the back seat. He turned his attention back to the boys who were talking about the house. His voice stopped the conversation, "Hecky, you see the white Explorer down the hill?"

Hecky glanced quickly at the vehicle and looked back at Derek and nodded his head. "You think they are here for us? Were we followed?"

"Who is that?" asked Messy.

"I don't know, dude. George's competition maybe?" Derek took another subtle look. "If they drive toward us, hit the fucking floor."

The boys nodded in agreement. A waitress stopped at the boys' table to top up their coffee. Derek kept an eye on the SUV; it began to move toward them. The driver navigated around a block of parked cars and pulled out onto the street that ran parallel to the restaurant. The SUV stopped in front of the restaurant and the windows rolled down.

Derek and the boys hit the floor as the shooting started, pop pop pop, the sound of automatic gunfire echoed outside the window as bullets and shattered glass rained down on the booth. They were under attack! Derek could barely breathe.

The shooting subsided quickly and the sound of squealing tires could be heard as the SUV peeled away. Patrons of the restaurant were screaming and yelling. Fortunately, no one was hurt. Messy had taken the waitress to the floor. Even she managed to avoid the hail of bullets.

Derek knew the boys were the marks of these not-so marksmen. Other than a cut on R-Luvs' face and shards of glass in Derek's arm, they were intact.

The police and paramedics were on the scene before Derek had even stood to his feet. A young male paramedic rushed over to R-Luv and began attending to his cuts. The police began investigating the incident, focusing primarily on the boys' booth.

Derek could see an older police detective asking patrons questions. All fingers pointed directly at the boys. The older detective looked at the boys, pulled out his pen and paper and approached them. He flashed his badge and introduced himself as Det. Ryan. He was about 6'4', 220lbs with a grey goatee and a crew cut. He was dressed in a knee length pea coat, shirt and tie.

"What were you boys doing here this morning?" asked Ryan.

"Breakfast," replied Derek, his hands shaking as he pulled glass from his forearm.

"You boys from town here?"

Derek continued, "Ontario and R-Luv is from Manitoba."

Ryan went from pleasantries to the unexpected "Do you guys have any gang ties?" he asked bluntly.

"I'm sorry?" said Derek. The boys snickered. "We run a food truck."

Derek's answer puzzled Det. Ryan. "You guys run a food truck?"

"Eat It and Beat It," answered Messy.

"Oh, I've eaten there before. Your sandwiches are great!"

"Thank you," answered Derek.

"Why eat here today?" he asked.

"We are moving to Point Grey," Derek responded.

"Business must be good," said Ryan as he nodded his head. "Do you have any idea why someone would be shooting at you?"

"Mistaken identity? I really don't know." replied Derek.

"Are you sure they were shooting at us?" asked Hecky.

"Well, if you were sitting here, then yes," said Ryan. "The gunfire is concentrated to this area."

Just when Derek thought things couldn't get any worse, Anna walked into the restaurant.

"Jesus Christ, are you guys okay?"

"Yeah, we're fine."

"You know them?" asked Ryan.

"Yeah," answered Anna.

Ryan looked at Anna and backed away from the boys. "I'll be back." Ryan walked away and began to talk with other officers on the scene.

Anna turned to Derek and began to freak out, "I knew you four were into something and now here we are."

"Whoa," Derek feigned surprise.

"Don't play dumb," said Anna, pointing her finger into Derek's chest. "You know what I'm talking about! I don't know if you did something to somebody, or for somebody, but I suggest you blow town!"

"Anna, the only thing we are into is the mobile food business. Why would we risk -"

"I don't know, Derek. Maybe your restaurant isn't all that you are making it out to be. Somebody wants you and your friends dead. I'd think long and hard for the reason why."

Hecky drove the boys to the old house afterward. It had already been emptied and the trucks were gone.

Messy and Derek jumped into the Edge; Derek drove them to Point Grey. He doubled back several times to avoid being followed.

They arrived at the new house, exited their vehicles and had a quick chat on the front lawn.

Derek began, "We have to assume they got eyes on us all the time. Every trip home is going to require a double back."

"Any thoughts on who put the bulls eye on our backs?" asked Messy.

"George?" asked R-Luv.

"No," said Hecky. "Why would he do that? We haven't fulfilled our deal."

"One trip left – we're a loose-end after that." suggested Messy.

"I don't see it," said Derek.

"So, if it wasn't George, who shot at us today?" asked Hecky

"I only saw shadows – windows were too tinted," said Derek.

"No one knows?" asked Hecky.

"The R.O.P.?" said Messy.

"Yeah, I mean, that's what I would think," said R-Luv.

"It would make sense. We had that run-in at the club. You know what happened to that other member. We are wholesaling to their competition."

"What can we do about it?" asked Hecky. "Didn't Anna say they had heat on them?"

"She did, but how hard is it to cut out on that shit."

"Surely, they're well-practiced in the art of ditching a tail," said Hecky.

"We need to make a point of not going out alone," said R-Luv. "We need a buddy system."

*   *   *   *   *

Two days after the shooting, the boys packed up the truck for one last drop Derek's biggest fear was getting so close to being done and then having it all taken away. They were almost done with all the craziness, and that scared the shit out of him.

The drive from Point Grey to Abbottsford was a little longer than what the boys were used to. The extra forty minutes took their toll on Derek's back. Messy could see him wincing in pain as he tried to shuffle his body into a more comfortable position. He settled on his side and felt okay. Hecky drove down a straight stretch and Derek could feel them getting close to the drop spot.

A few moments later, Hecky began cursing up front. The back window of the truck opened and Hecky began to speak, "Don't move, boys. We have a cop riding our ass."

"Lose him! The guys on the other side are going to toss the shit!"

"I know, but I can't floor it; we'll get pulled over," replied Hecky.

"Slow down," said Messy, "Slow right down. They'll pass."

"That'll seem suspicious," yelled Hecky.

"Nah, everyone slows down when they see a cop."

Hecky gently applied the brakes. The boys waited; it was boom or bust.

"He's not passing," yelled Hecky.

"Give it time!" yelled Derek.

After a few seconds, Derek heard the roar of the police car engine as it passed by.

Hecky yelled back to Messy, "Nice job. I'll let them get way ahead."

The cops ripped up the highway and were well in front of the boys by the time Derek threw the tarp off and stood to one knee. As he tried to get to his feet, he felt an immense amount of pain shoot from his back into his legs. He had pinched a nerve in his back!

"Jesus," he screamed in agony.

"What happened?" asked Messy.

"My back! I can't stand! Fuck!"

Messy reached for both bags while Derek lay back down on the driver's side of the truck bed. He watched from below as Messy tossed the bags. Messy fist-pumped and waited for the return bags. Seconds later he began catching the return bags and dropped them at Derek's feet. He caught the last bag, lay down and pulled the tarp over them.

"Hospital!" yelled Derek.

The boys drove back to the house and left the bags for the drop with Matty later that night.

Messy and R-Luv stayed at the house and waited while Hecky drove Derek to the hospital. Hecky helped walk Derek into the emergency room and sat him in a chair.

Over the next four hours, Hecky and Derek sat in the ER waiting and watching. Waiting for a doctor and watching other patients puking up their lunch.

After all the waiting, Derek was finally looked at. The doctor ran reflex tests, as well as tests on Derek's rectum, and sent him for an x-ray. After that was completed, the doctor loaded Derek up with painkillers and sent him home. He was happy to be high; it helped him forget that he was in agony. Hecky drove to the pharmacy and eventually back to the house.

The boys walked into the house. It was eerily quiet. Hecky moved much quicker than Derek as he walked through the house looking for the boys. He walked into the living room and cursed, "Fuck!"

Derek walked into the living room and noticed five very large intimidating men pointing guns at Messy and R-Luv. It was The Devil's Grip and the boys were in trouble.

October 5th 2009

Messy and Derek dropped the money and guns at their new storage unit and drove to the house. They now had two different storage units full of enough evidence to send them to jail for more years than any criminal would care for.

They pulled onto their street at about 7:00 p.m. A dozen or so police cars greeted them on the street. Derek parked a good distance from the house. As they climbed out, Derek could see Hecky's van in his peripheral. Hecky had already arrived. Messy and Derek continued to walk toward the house. Hecky walked up from behind them. "Let's get on the same page, boys."

"Talk to me," said Derek.

"It's hard to make a plan when we don't know what happened in there. We can't just feed them bunk."

"You think R-Luv set us up?" asked Derek. "Would he off someone and breeze with the case dough?"

"No shot," said Hecky. "No one is touching that unit. He'd be drifting off with fuck all."

"Let's just tell the truth," said Derek as he stopped walking. "Hecky, you were in Squamish. Messy and I went to Canmore and R-Luv was in Winnipeg. Problem solved, no?"

"Why would we go home and you guys to Canmore?" asked Hecky.

"Yeah, I feel like these guys will give us the third all day," said Messy.

"Just say we went there 'cause we hate going home," said Derek.

"We hate it," reiterated Messy.

"K, fine. Let's go see what happened," suggested Hecky.

The boys approached the house, now surrounded with yellow police tape and curious onlookers. Hecky was the first to approach the officer who was securing the entrance to the house. "Excuse me, who should I speak to about what happened here?"

"What's it matter to you, kid?" asked the officer.

"Well, the three of us live here."

"Oh, sorry." The officer stood up, looked the boys up and down and grabbed his radio. "Give me a minute to radio someone."

"Did somebody break into the house?" asked Hecky.

"No, kid. Do you think all of this chaos would be going on for a B & E?"

"Oh," replied Hecky as he feigned his surprise, "Did somebody die?"

"Look," replied the officer, "the detective will be here any second and he will fill you in on what happened."

A few seconds later an older man dressed in a suit came running over to the boys. He introduced himself as Det. Gugasian. He was a heavyset man, 6'1 and close to 300 pounds. "Gentlemen, if you don't mind, can you show me some ID just so I can verify that this is your residence."

"Sure," replied Derek.

The boys reached for their wallets and handed over their driver's license. Gugasian studied them and handed all three ID's back to the boys.

"Let's go around back and talk, okay guys?" gestured Gugasian.

The boys followed the detective into the back yard where they sat down at their patio table.

"What can you tell me about this man?" asked Gugasian, as he slid R-Luv's drivers license across the table.

"Fuck!" screamed Hecky.

"That's R-Luv," replied Derek.

"Is he inside?" asked Hecky.

"I'm afraid so, guys."

"Fuck!" screamed Messy.

Messy and Derek put their heads into their hands as they tried to process the news. *Why was R-Luv even here? That wasn't the plan.* Derek ran his hands through his hair and took a deep breath, fighting back tears. "Do you have any idea who did this?"

"I'm afraid not. Whoever did this got away clean, which is why I'd like to talk to you. Did he have enemies or anyone who would want to hurt him?"

"No, sir," said Derek.

Gugasian grinned. "You can cut the shit. I know you were targeted in Brentwood. But I don't know why."

Hecky stood up. "I'll give you one. A few months back we were out at a club, throwing some money around. Anyways, the R.O.P. didn't like it so they approached our booth, threatened us and made us pay off their tab."

"So, hold on," said Gugasian, "they want you dead because they threatened you into paying a bar tab, and you paid it?"

"Can I finish?" asked Hecky, as he held up a single finger. Gugasian nodded his head. "A week later, I was out and I saw one of them walk into a convenience store. When he walked out, I played the knockout game."

"You hit him? asked Gugasian.

"Is that so wrong? They humiliated us!"

"Well, kid, you got balls, I'll give you that," said Gugasian. "You might have gotten your friend killed though. These guys don't go anywhere alone. Chances are that guy had a lookout."

Hecky's story was bullshit; it was cover for what really happened. The Grip had killed R-Luv. They had taken the tax money and shot him anyways. The boys had a war on their hands, and Derek vowed that he wouldn't be caught off-guard again.

Gugasian went through the details of R-Luvs' murder. The house had been ransacked. Whoever was in the house was looking for money, product, or both. They had taken some of the more high-end items. Gugasian then went into detail about how R-Luv had been killed. He had been tied to a chair and tortured with a soldering iron for at least a day before he had his throat slit.

Immense guilt and sorrow hammered through Derek. R-Luv wanted no part of this, but he let Hecky talk him into it.

August 2009
TWENTY-SEVEN

The Devil's Grip had broken into the house and taken R-Luv and Messy hostage. Five Grip members stood behind them as they were sitting on the couch, their heads hung low.

Derek knew that the boys were in way over their head; this was his worst fear coming true. They'd gotten involved with biker gangs. They were owned, and he knew it.

The leader of The Grip was Dennis Bell – a large, menacing looking man. He was 6'7" with slick jet-black hair and a dark black beard with hints of grey. His obsidian-black eyes stared a hole through everything he looked at. His massive arms were covered with tattoos and he wore a leather cut and jeans.

"Your boys told us quite a story while we were clocking," said Dennis. "International drug trafficking, armed robbery, second story work. You boys have quite the flow."

"What do you want?" asked Hecky.

"Have you ever seen someone skinned alive?" Dennis retorted.

"No," answered Hecky.

"You want to?"

"Not really," answered Hecky.

Dennis pointed at Hecky, "Then think about that the next time you decide to sling in The Devil's Grip."

"We aren't slinging," said Hecky.

"No, new jack, you are bringing Charlie to my competitor."

"What do you want from us?"

"First thing, we are jacking this shipment. Next, we're taxing you."

"What kind of tax?"

"Two-hundred-fifty," he replied.

Hecky looked over at Derek with a look of concern. Derek nodded his head; he didn't care. They would still be well ahead of the game. He knew they would be out a few hundred grand, plus the four-fifty they would have made on delivery, but it was a small price to pay for what they had already achieved.

"Okay," replied Hecky. "How long do we have?"

"Fourteen days." replied Dennis, "or we come back here and really flex some muscle."

Jesus Christ, thought Derek. *This wasn't their muscle.* The Grip kept all eyes on the boys as they put their guns down by their sides and walked backwards out the door. Hecky freaked, "What the fuck happened?"

"They were lying in wait," said Messy. "They knew where we lived – where we had been."

"Jesus, we are out seven hundred grand! FUCK!"

"Who cares, Hecky. This is the sign that we are done. It's over. We pay them their money and we are fucking ghost." Derek continued, "We made our money; let's just move on and stop having to watch our six."

Hecky yelled, "I want to light these fuckers up like the Vegas strip."

"Well, we aren't going to do that. You want to go toe-to-toe with a biker gang? Are you fucked in the head?"

"They dissed us! Again!" yelled Hecky. "I'm sick of it."

"Would you rather be dead and respected or alive and wealthy?"

"Fuck off, Sarge. Don't play that Sophie's Choice shit on me. It doesn't work."

"What do you think will happen, Hecky?" asked Derek. "They have more men, more guns and more pull. We lose that war ten times out of ten."

"Fuck!" Hecky paced the room, "We'll pay the money," finally resigning to the fact that it was a fight he couldn't win.

That evening, the boys drove to the storage unit to collect the tax money. Derek navigated through heavy traffic during rush hour. They were a few blocks away when Derek noticed a suspicious GMC following three cars back. It had been there since they left.

"Guys," said Derek, as he checked his rearview mirrors, "we have a tail. Only one of you look. It's the Tahoe three cars back."

"Fucking great," said Hecky.

"I'm going to pull in and out of the parking lot to see if they follow."

Derek did a U-turn into a parking lot and pulled back into traffic. The Tahoe pulled into the parking lot as the boys pulled out. It was a tail.

"Fuck!" yelled Derek. "What do we do? We can't go into the unit!"

"We can't go home," said Hecky.

The boys were stuck between a rock and hard place.

"Let's get a hotel," suggested R-Luv. "If they tail us there, who cares."

*   *   *   *   *

They checked out of their hotel the next morning and jumped in the Edge. As they were headed back to the storage unit, Derek's gut told him to circle the facility to see if anything looked suspicious. He pulled into the parking lot and drove around the entire facility. Halfway around the building, R-Luv noticed a moving truck door slam shut from the inside. "Yo, you see that?"

Derek's first thought was Heat. Pacino and his crew lock themselves in a U-Haul while they wait for De Niro's crew to pull their heist. He knew that the cops would have seen them pull into the parking lot; they were sitting on the storage facility, and more importantly, they were sitting on the boy's only cash.

They had 13 days to come up with a quarter million dollars and no money to give. Trouble was brewing.

"Fuck sakes," said Hecky, "we need that money."

"It's not thorough, Hecky."

R-Luv spoke up, "Why don't we lure them out?"

"How so?" asked Messy.

R-Luv continued, "We rent a unit near our unit. We enter it, walk out with a duffel bag and find out whether or not this is a hot place. They'll grab us if they are; if they aren't, we'll know too. Then maybe, just maybe, if they are convinced we don't have anything, they will pull surveillance."

"It's worth a shot," said Messy

The boys drove around the storage unit to the front of the building and parked in front. Derek went inside and spent ten minutes signing up for a second storage locker three down from their original locker. He hoped that if the police were in fact sitting on the locker, they would see the boys leave the decoy locker and swarm them. Derek got his key and drove to their decoy locker. Hecky, Messy and R-Luv jumped out of the car, opened the locker door and went inside. Derek backed up against the unit door and parked. He jumped out of the Edge, lit a cigarette and paced in front of the locker. He played with his cell phone as the boys stood inside the empty locker, waiting with the door shut.

After a few moments, Derek butted out his cigarette and put his phone away. He looked both ways and opened the unit door. Messy, Hecky and R-Luv emerged with a duffel bag. R-Luv shut the door and the boys jumped back into the Edge. Derek started the engine.

"Cut the fucking engine!" yelled a police officer as he emerged from his hiding place, gun up, and ran toward the car. Nine armed officers quickly swarmed the boys and surrounded the car. The officer continued yelling, "Hands in the air! Open your door with one hand using the outside handle!"

The boys put their hands in the air and surrendered. They slowly opened their doors, exited the car and lay face down on the pavement.

One of the officers grabbed the duffel bags out of their car and set them on the ground. The officers frantically searched through the bags looking for money, dope or anything that could incriminate the boys. They searched the car as well. But the duffel bags were full of laundry; the car had nothing incriminating.

After ten minutes, Anna emerged from behind one of the banks of storage lockers holding a document in her hand. Derek could see her talking to one of the other agents. She walked over to the boys and dropped the paper on the ground for Derek to read.

"There's a warrant to search your locker."

"You can't do that!"

"It's already done," Anna said, as she motioned to one of the officers to cut the lock off of the locker. "Cut it."

The officer cut the lock and opened the door to show the officers and everyone else an empty locker.

"Fuck, fuck!" screamed Anna.

"We just got this locker this morning!" yelled Derek. "We just wanted to see how big it was."

Anna stormed over to Derek, "Get him up." Anna continued. "I know what you are up to."

"What are you talking about?"

"I know you are hiding something, and I will find it."

"We are putting our extra furniture here."

"Bullshit," said Anna as she paced. "You and these idiots are into something. I fucking know it."

"What you know and what you can prove are two completely different things," yelled Hecky from the ground.

"You know what, guys? That's fine," said Anna. "I'm going to keep a crew here 24/7. If you have something here, you will not get it back, ever. If I have to pay a security guard out of my own pocket, I will. Uncuff them."

The officers began to stand the boys up to their feet and they were let out of their handcuffs. Derek walked toward the Edge, which had been torn apart by the officers. The boys climbed inside and Derek drove them out of the complex. Hecky was about to say something when Derek interrupted him.

"Shut up!"

Derek figured there was a one hundred percent chance that Anna's crew had bugged his car.

Back at the house, the boys went to the backyard and began to talk.

"Okay," started Derek. "What do we do now? We have shit to cover and no fucking money!"

"We need work," said Hecky. "It needs to be lucrative and immediate."

"Jobs like that aren't just going to pop up out of thin air," said Messy. "We can't just walk into a bank and rip off a quarter."

"We could jack a tin can," said Hecky, jokingly referring to an armoured truck.

Derek remembered the truck in Renfrew, the one that no one would think to rob. He jumped to his feet.

"Boys, I have our fucking job!"

October 5th 2009

The boys finished their conversations with the police and left. Derek then drove them to a hotel where they checked in for the night.

The mood was somber; the boys had just identified R-Luv's body. With the hell he went through, he might have given the boys up. None of them would blame him if he did.

The police told the boys to stay in the hotel for a few days and put an officer on them while they completed their investigation. They were stuck in their rooms waiting for the police to shake the right tree and make an arrest. Derek felt helpless. He sat on his bed feeling sorry for himself when his phone rang. It was Mandy.

"Hey, Derek."

"Hey."

"How is everything?"

"It was our roommate."

"Oh my God! I'm so sorry."

"It's awful. Police are at our house and it's just a mess."

"Do you want me to come there?"

"I do, but not this week. We are stuck in a hotel. Police don't want us there in case somebody comes back."

Derek didn't want Mandy in that part of his life. He was falling in love and knew that the evil in his life would chase her away.

"You know," said Mandy as she hesitated, "they have hotels here."

"They do?" Derek asked, as he smiled. "I should come back, eh?"

"You should."

"Let me sleep on that, I think I might. I need out of Vancouver."

"Okay, Derek. Tell your friends I'm thinking of them. Good night!"

"Good night, Mandy!"

Derek hung up the phone and walked to the common area of the suite. Hecky and Messy were on the couch watching a ball game. The Yankees were playing the Angels. "Yanks are out West?"

"Yeah," answered Messy.

Derek walked to the kitchen and poured himself a scotch. He took his drink over to the living room and sat down on the couch next to Messy.

"You guys alright?" asked Derek.

"Nope," replied Hecky.

"I just keep thinking about R-Luv," said Messy.

"Yeah, I know," said Derek.

"What are we doing here, boys?"

"What?" asked Derek.

"I mean what are we doing?" asked Hecky a second time. "Are we dipping town? Are we waiting for The Five to slap bracelets on us? Or, are we going to murk these guys?"

"Murk who?" asked Derek. "We don't even know who to go after."

"The Grip," said Hecky.

"We don't know it was them," said Messy.

"Come on, Messy," replied Hecky. "Who else was it?"

"Maybe the police," said Derek.

"Why would cops do that?" asked Hecky, gesturing with his hand.

"Cause we made them look like goofs," answered Derek. "Look, it was probably The Grip, but we aren't going to flex with them. We don't have any help, money, guns or any access to any of the above. We paid the tax. We tell them we have nothing left to give. We don't have anything left to give."

"Fuck that," said Hecky. "We gave them $250k. R-Luv and I walked in there and gave it to them. We were done with it. They went back on the deal. I'm calling Matty to get help, or at the very least some protection."

September 2009

Derek put a sheet of paper on his living room coffee table and began to draw a map of the area he was talking about in Renfrew. He pulled up Google Street View to assist him. The boys looked on as he began to talk them through the plan.

"its pretty fucking simple, boys. Every Thursday morning around 11:00 a.m., a tin can parks on Raglan Street. One driver stays inside, and the passenger makes the exchange. I've checked a few times and there never appears to be a third man. The second man uses a dolly to carry cash and coin. It's stacked halfway to the top every time. But on the last Thursday before the 28th of every month, there is an extra bag."

"What's the bag?" asked R-Luv.

"Welfare," he replied. "Its an extra bag – makes it heavier and harder to move, but also more lucrative."

"How do we get the bags from him?" asked Hecky.

"I'll get to that," answered Derek. "There's a sidewalk that he has to lift the cart over. When he lowers his head, we bum rush him from his six. We park the car as close as we can. Passenger exits and approaches the guard, and another comes from behind the post office, across the street. You can see it here. Our passenger sprays the guard. Mace would work if we can get it. The other man watches the driver; if he exits, we mace him too. But he won't."

"Why not?" asked Messy.

"They are instructed in a robbery to keep their ass in the driver's seat, so they don't give up the whole truck."

"Makes sense," said Hecky.

"So, our driver pulls up at the back in the driver's blind spot and parks. Two of us load the car, jump in and we all take off down Renfrew Avenue. It runs perpendicular to Main Street. At the end of Renfrew is a trail that leads to another neighbourhood. That street is one street away from the highway. We will drive as far down the trail as we can, having a switch car waiting on the other side.

R-Luv raised his hand and Derek pointed at him.

"I got your question," said Derek. "Now, an issue is that the trail is obstructed by cinder blocks. We are going to move them the night before so we can slip through to the switch. Afterward, we will torch the original and drive the switch to our two rentals. We then torch the switch car and head West."

"Where are we getting the switch cars?" asked Messy.

"Good question. We'll have to steal them the day before."

"Do you know anything about boosting cars?" asked R-Luv.

"I don't, but I have a buddy who works at a dealership. I have his code and I made a copy of his work key from the last time I saw him."

"You've been planning this?" asked Hecky.

"This was my rainy-day plan, and, brother, it is pouring right now!"

"What next?" asked Hecky.

"We will take the cars the morning of, set the switch car up on the trail in the morning, ten minutes before we hit the truck."

"Won't they notice two new whips missing?" asked Messy.

"Maybe, but even if they check inventory first thing, that's not until 10:00 a.m. And if they do check right away, then most of The Five will be on the other side of town while we rob the truck. My guess is they won't notice them missing until later in the day."

"So, what do we do after we get into the switch car?"

"We take the switch to a back road and make a double switch – R-Luv and Hecky in one car, Messy and I in another. Cops will be looking for three or four guys, not two. Then we cruise to the 17, jump on the TransCanada and we're ghosts."

"If it's so easy, why has no one done it?" asked Messy.

"No one sees the angle. You know what it's like in a small town. No one expects it. Cops aren't prepared for it. If we end up in a firefight, they don't have the capacity to respond."

"How much money is in the bags?" asked Hecky.

"If my research is right, it should be a minimum of two hundred and fifty. Thousand. Four hundred max."

"Fuck, eh," said R-Luv.

"Questions? Concerns?" asked Derek, "all of the above?"

"When do we go?" asked R-Luv.

"Five days," Derek answered. "If we do this, we dip tomorrow. If you say yes, we need to get our shit together 'cause we got a lot of road to cover."

The boys nodded in agreement. They were in and it was on. Over the next 36 hours they put the wheels in motion. They packed up the guns, disguises and tools they would require to make their move.

*   *   *   *   *

On Sunday night, they left the city and began the 4,800 km journey from Vancouver to Renfrew. The boys would drive in four-hour shifts and only stop for gas. The less places that they showed their faces, the better.

*   *   *   *   *

Hecky drove them down Main Street in Renfrew after their fifty-four-hour journey. They cruised past a large grocery store and past town hall. Derek felt a warm nostalgic feeling fall over him. The downtown core of Renfrew had many cute boutiques and small businesses. They approached the corner with the bank.

Derek kept his head low; he had seen it thousands of times and knew the route inside and out. Hecky turned down Renfrew Avenue to the trail at the end of the road. He approached it slowly and the boys looked down the trail.

"That's a tight fucking squeeze, boys," said Hecky.

"You can make it," said Messy.

"Not driving a buck twenty I can't," he replied.

"Boys, if we plan this out right, we won't need to speed down here."

"Dude," yelled R-Luv, "you said they had cinder blocks here."

Derek looked at the trail and noticed they had replaced the barrier with a steel yellow gate.

"Fuck!"

"Are you kidding?" asked Hecky, "This is great. We'll drive right through it!"

Hecky drove the boys out to where they would park their switch car. It was a residential area surrounding the Renfrew Arena. They studied the trail as they turned the car around in a parking lot across from the arena. Hecky slowly drove the escape route. On Ma-te-way Park Drive they would have to deal with two stop signs before they could turn left on the road to freedom: Lisgar Avenue.

Hecky drove the four kilometers on Lisgar Avenue before turning right onto South McNaughton Drive – a quiet country dirt road. The first switch car would be parked there, a stone's throw from a garage.

Hecky drove two kilometers past the garage and turned right onto Butler Road, another country road. Three kilometers later he made a left onto Highway 60.

"Right on Price," said Derek. "Messy and I will switch here."

Messy and Derek would then take highway 60 to Haley Road and onto Highway 17. That would take them all the way back to Vancouver.

* * * * *

The boys woke at 3:30 a.m. Messy, R-Luv and Derek set out to steal two getaway cars, while Hecky drove to park their car on Price Road.

R-Luv arrived at the dealership just before 5 a.m., letting the boys off down the street. They wanted to ensure that their car wouldn't be picked up on any security cameras. The boys masked up and walked down the street perpendicular to the car dealership. They crossed the street and walked through the parking lot to a side entrance of the main building.

Derek opened the door and sprinted across the showroom to the alarm pad. He punched in the code as he remembered it. Accepted!

On a wall in the back of the showroom was the cabinet that held the keys. Derek ran over to it and grabbed two keys for Dodge Chargers. He threw one set to Messy and kept one for himself. They walked to the exit, Derek reset the alarm before they exited the building. He locked the door and walked to his getaway car.

They drove the stolen cars across town to Price Road. On his way out of Renfrew, Derek noticed that there was a demolition crew at the Renfrew Mall tearing it down. He felt fortunate that they hadn't planned to use that area as an escape route.

Derek met up with the boys in Cobden at 6:00 a.m. Hecky and R-Luv pulled an audible and elected to park their switch vehicle in Cobden – a small village twenty minutes West of Renfrew.

At 7:30 a.m., they finished breakfast and drove back to Renfrew. They pulled off the highway onto O'Brien Road and waited in a McDonald's parking lot. It was the longest forty minutes of their life.

October 5th 2009

Matty and George agreed to meet with the boys for coffee near the hotel. Messy, Hecky and Derek were leery about leaving the safety of the hotel, particularly at night. They were being hunted; anyone could take them down. The cops sitting on the storage unit meant that they didn't have any guns or means of getting one.

The boys arrived at the coffee shop first, walking inside and sitting down away from the windows. Derek chose a seat in the corner of the shop; any attacker would need to attack him head-on. Matty and George rolled into the coffee shop a few minutes later and sat down across from them. They weren't alone.

Derek got his first good look at George. He was 6'4 and in great shape. He had jet-black hair that was slicked back into a neatly kept bun. Tattoos littered his light brown skin; he had sleeves of images covering his bulging biceps and the word 'righteous' scribbled across his neck in large black writing.

Walking in behind Matty and George were two of the scariest looking men Derek had ever seen. They were covered head to toe in tattoos and piercings and were of Mexican or Columbian descent. They had teardrops on their cheeks and tattoos covering their skulls. They both dressed in white t-shirts and jeans and scared the shit out of Derek. He immediately greeted Matty and acted as if the other two men didn't intimidate him.

"Matty."

"Sarge," Matty replied, as he nodded his head. "Sorry to hear about R-Luv."

"You hear much chatter about it?" asked Messy.

"Just shit on the wire."

"You think The Grip had a hand in it?" asked Hecky.

"Yeah," said George nodding his head. "Them or The Five maybe."

"We thought that," said Hecky.

"You guys made them look fucking dumb," said George.

"Anna wouldn't," said Derek.

"Anna doesn't control the whole force," said Hecky.

"Listen," said George as he leaned forward, "you have a lot of heat on you right now, I am going to need to take air on this thing and let you figure this shit out."

"You have two cartel guys standing at your six," said Derek. "You aren't fooling us with that? Where the fuck did these guys even come from?"

"We aren't trying to fool you."

"This whole thing is Matty's fucking fault!" yelled Derek.

"How so, Sarge?" asked Matty.

"You came to us and floated this to Hecky. We set you up, and you've had flow of that shit since."

"Lines are dry now, Sarge."

"You think I can help you? We need some protection right now. Help us, please!" Derek didn't like begging; desperate times.

"Listen, man," George started, "my friends back there can lend you pieces for a price. And if you get a beat on them, we'll help there too. But my crew is not going to put people in front of you. It's just not going to happen."

"What price?" asked Derek.

One of the Cartel Men spoke, "The shit keeps changing hands on Zero."

"We keep the lines wet."

"Yeah," said George, snickering.

"Only you are going to run Tango and Cash," said the Cartel Friend.

"What's that?" asked Derek.

"Jackpot," said the Cartel Man.

Derek was confused. He shook his head, unsure of what they meant.

"Fentanyl, you dumb fuck."

"No idea what that is," said Derek.

"We'll be in touch," said George. "Give me your key. I'll leave it on the tire. Gear will be in the trunk."

Derek handed Matty his key and The Cartel Friend leaned into Derek and spoke quietly. "If you get any ideas on skipping, best think twice. All those decapitations and Columbian neckties ain't for show."

After a few minutes they stood up and looked outside before exiting. Derek walked outside first with Messy and Hecky following. They walked quickly to the car and Derek unlocked it. Messy jumped in the backseat and checked the trunk.

"Anything?" asked Derek.

"Duffel bag," replied Messy.

"Check it!" insisted Hecky.

Messy looked in the bag and sat back in his seat. "Probably about twenty pieces."

The boys had an arsenal, and all it took was a deal with the Devil.

September 28th 2009

The boys dropped R-Luv off at the switch car and drove toward the bank. Messy and Derek would be the heist men, Hecky would drive the first car, and R-Luv would man the switch. They had planned to draw straws for their roles. However, Derek volunteered to come across the street from behind the post office, since it put him at the most risk. He knew the town better than the others and felt comfortable in Renfrew. Messy had a tough gig as the one to ambush the guard.

Hecky and Messy dropped Derek off next to the post office at 10:55 a.m. He masked up and hoped like hell that no one spotted him in full heist gear. He kept his weapon in a black overcoat. Minutes later, Messy radioed him to say that they were in position. Derek stood in an alley, leaning on the wall for what felt like an eternity. In reality it was six minutes. At 11:01 a.m., Messy got on the radio, "They're here." Derek muted his radio and began to creep down the alley toward Main Street. He could hear police sirens ring out. Two cop cars turned onto Main Street and sped toward the bank. *Fuck, someone spotted me!* He took a few steps back and cocked his gun in case he needed to use it.

The police sped toward the bank and through the intersection right past Derek. They were heading to the car dealership!

The sirens distracted the guard who had just exited the truck. He walked around to the back of the truck and entered the back door, closing the door behind him. Derek stayed still in the shadows of the alley. The guard re-opened the back door and stepped outside; his cart loaded with bags. Derek watched Messy get out of the car and creep toward the guard. Messy shielded himself from the driver's line of sight.

The guard lifted the cart onto the sidewalk and Messy maced him. The guard reached for his eyes, releasing the bag into his waiting arms. Derek peaked out to see if the driver was aware of what had just happened. He was reading the paper! Messy grabbed the cart and pulled it to the back of the truck. The guard fell behind the truck, out of the driver's field of vision.

Hecky pulled the car out of his parking space and up next to the boys. He opened the passenger side door. Derek charged through traffic across the street. He grabbed the money and threw it on the floor of the getaway car and shut the door. The guard on the ground grabbed Messy's foot and reached for his pistol with his free hand.

Derek saw the guard at the last second and hit him with the butt end of his gun, knocking him unconscious. Messy opened the back door and he and Derek entered the car.

"Go, go, go!"

Hecky peeled out and made a right on Renfrew Avenue; the guard in the truck was still reading the paper! He raced down Renfrew Avenue and passed cross streets Argyle, Lochiel, and Bonnechere Avenue. He then passed a local high school where students were leaving early for lunch. He was doing 120 in a 40 when he raced onto Ross Avenue, hopped the curb and flew through the gates that blocked the Millennium Trail. He decelerated as they neared the switch car and nearly lost control on the trail's loose gravel, regaining control a few seconds later.

Derek could see R-Luv standing next to the switch car. Hecky skidded to a stop a few feet away. He popped the trunk and retrieved two full gas cans. R-Luv grabbed the money from the getaway car and loaded it into the switch. Derek poured gasoline into the car and lit a book of matches on fire. Messy finished pouring the gas and tossed the can into the car. The boys cleared out and watched Derek throw the match inside the car and run.

They loaded into the switch car with Derek driving. He raced toward Lisgar Avenue, running both stop signs before turning left onto the road out of town. In the rearview mirror, he could see dark black smoke from the switch.

He stuck to the speed limit as he drove down Highway 132 toward South McNaughton Road. His shoulder checks made the boys nervous, "What are you doing?" asked Hecky.

"Relax," yelled Derek, "no sense speeding. We are good!"

Derek turned onto South McNaughton Road and continued to drive the speed limit. He made a casual right turn onto Butler Road and followed it until he made a left onto Highway 60.

A short time later they pulled into Cobden. The car was silent as they pulled up to another switch. Derek's chest had stopped pounding; his palms were sweaty. He couldn't hear anything but the sound of the blood rushing through his ears. They had pulled off the impossible!

R-Luv and Hecky jumped out of the car. Hecky grabbed half the cash.

"Boys," said Derek, as they froze in place. "Be safe."

They smiled, nodded, and walked toward their switch.

Derek drove Messy and himself to the last switch car. Messy jumped out with the last of the money and followed Derek in the switch car as they drove out of Cobden toward Pembroke. The car had to be ditched in an out-of-the-way place.

Derek spotted a desolate country road and turned onto it. He drove a kilometer off the main road and pulled over. He caught his breath before he grabbed the gas cans and doused the car inside and out. He took a deep breath of the gasoline-stenched air and lit the match. It burned in his fingers for a moment before he tossed it in the car, igniting it.

Messy peeled out before Derek was even in the car; Derek struggled to shut his door as they raced away. He watched in his rearview mirror as the brand new car burned, and then exploded into a ball of fire.

A few hours later, they pulled into a gas station in North Bay. Messy sat quietly in the driver's seat.

"What did we just do?" he asked.

"We saved our asses."

"This whole thing," he continued, "it just keeps snowballing."

"No, bro," answered Derek, "snowballing is what we are going to do when we roll into Canmore."

"I'm tired, Sarge. I'm tired of this. When we get back, I'm out. We pay our debt, then I'm coming home."

"To do what?"

"Open the hobby shop."

"Wow, you're done with Van?"

"Fuck Van," said Messy.

Mid-October 2009

Messy and Hecky shielded Derek as he carried the duffel bag into the elevator of the hotel. The weapons and accessories weighed the bag down and he was struggling to carry it.

They exited the elevator on their floor; Hecky ran ahead to open the door. Derek dragged the bag into the room and tossed it on the couch.

Hecky unzipped the bag to unveil the haul. In the bag were three Bushmaster XM-15 M4's, three TMP's with silencers, three Beretta 9mm's, three SigSauer 1911 pistols, three Glocks and what appeared to be a single AR-15. They'd also included three sets of body armour, along with both smoke and hand grenades and other incendiary devices. At the bottom of the bag were extra ammo and accessories.

The boys looked at each other in awe. They now had the arms to protect themselves. They had one problem though; they still needed to find out where The Grip hung out.

"This bag has to be worth a hundred G's," suggested Messy.

Hecky looked at the bag and shook his head. He walked to his laptop, sat down and began typing.

"What are you doing, Hecky?"

"Research," he replied.

"On what?" asked Derek.

"A guy on set told me awhile ago that there is a site online that outs gangsters and their hangouts."

"In Vancouver?" asked Messy.

"Yup," Hecky spun his laptop around and showed it to Messy and Derek. It was a picture of The Grip's hangout with the address.

A few hours later, they were parked in a rental car a block from The Grip's clubhouse. They watched as members came and went. By 5:00 p.m., 25 members had arrived; none had left. They were having a meeting.

"Let's toss fucking grenades inside!" yelled Hecky.

"And then what?" asked Derek, "have a firefight in the street?"

"Hecky, be easy," said Messy. "We aren't tangling with these guys."

"They will catch up to us and take us down like they did R-Luv." said Hecky, with conviction.

An hour and a half later, the large clubhouse doors swung open and thirty members of The Grip spilled out onto the sidewalk. They jumped onto their bikes and left.

*   *   *   *   *

Over the course of the next week, the boys watched the clubhouse every day, and every day at 5:00 p.m. the clubhouse was full.

Hecky had dreams of blowing into the clubhouse guns-blazing and killing every member. They knew that wasn't a realistic option. They might kill a few but would almost certainly be taken down in a hail of gunfire.

After seven days of spying, the boys met in their hotel room to discuss their options moving forward. Messy suggested they take the week to decide what to do. He'd planned a trip to Pembroke to visit his family and suggested Derek and Hecky do the same. Hecky took the week to go to Squamish, while Derek visited Mandy in Canmore.

On his way out of town, Derek ditched the guns in the second storage unit and grabbed ten grand. The cash was getting low; they would be cash poor until the cops stopped watching the storage unit. Eat It and Beat It had been sitting idle for weeks and the boys' bank accounts had become a series of zeros with a zero out in front.

Derek knew that the time away from Vancouver would do them good. He hoped that by going away it would make each of them realize that they needed to get away. Permanently. Messy was mapping his way out of town and Derek knew he should follow suit. But going home broke was not an option. Derek didn't have a plan for the future. All he knew was that he wanted Mandy and to get out of Van. He had his windows down and the sunroof open as he drove into the interior of B.C. At the halfway point of the trip, he received a call from Dannick. "Hey bud, how's it going?"

"Good, buddy. How are you?"

"I'm good. Did you hear about the bank robbery in town?"

"Someone posted about it on Facebook. What happened?"

"A group of guys robbed an armoured truck on Main. They burned their cars on the way out of town!"

"Holy shit," replied Derek, "that's crazy! Did they catch the guys?"

"No. The cops are everywhere, but I haven't heard anything."

"Well, you guys would be the first to know if they caught the guy"

"Perks of being the local media."

"So, what's up?" asked Derek.

"Well, my boss wants me to cover the Olympics in Vancouver."

Fuck! thought Derek. N*ot good.* "That's awesome!" he replied.

"Yeah, man. Only issue is, my station doesn't have money to put me up anywhere. So...-"

"So, you want to know if you can crash at my place?" asked Derek.

"Yeah."

"I guess you could. Only issue is I don't know where I'll be. Messy is talking about moving and I might too."

"I thought things were good!"

"They are," replied Derek, "but we got some offers on the truck, so we might sell and start something else."

"That's awesome!" replied Dannick. "Well, buddy, think it over. We'll try to arrange something if you are still there. Let me know."

"I will, buddy. I love you! Can you put Dad on the phone?"

"I love you, broseph. I'll get him."

"Bye, Dannick." Derek waited.

"Hey, son," said Peter.

"Hey, Dad, what's new?"

"Oh, not much. Going to Pittsburgh next week for business. Other than that, not a lot."

"Make sure you check out a Penguins game!"

"We are seeing two!"

"That's awesome!" shouted Derek. "Hey, what did you make of that robbery Dannick was talking about?"

"Shades of Zagadka."

"These guys that good?"

"They torched all the evidence and hurt no one. Pretty impressive."

Derek smiled to himself.

"Anyways, this is your dime. I hope all is well. We miss you."

"I miss you too! I love you!"

"Love you too, Derek."

Derek hung up and received a phone call from Hecky.

"Hey, dude."

"Hey buddy, how's the drive?"

"It's okay. You at your Dad's?"

"Yeah."

"Nice, I dropped off my bags and grabbed ten."

"K, I did too," replied Hecky.

"Shit's getting low, eh."

"I know," replied Hecky.

"I think we should sell the truck," suggested Derek.

"You want to give up the truck?"

"No, I'm just suggesting it."

"Okay. Are you looking to get out of Vancouver too?" asked Hecky.

"It would be nice to get away. Leave with something in our pocket."

"Do you want to see if those offers are still doable?" asked Hecky.

"I would. Yes, please!"

"I'll put out feelers. I want to move back to Squamish. Fuck Van."

"Fuck it!" replied Derek.

October 3rd 2009

It was evening when Messy and Derek rolled into Canmore. Their eyes had grown weary after driving for thirty hours straight, three breaks aside. They were ready to check into a motel and get off on happy dust.

They drove to a local liquor store to stock up on scotch and beer. They then scoured Canmore for a place to score.

It wasn't long before they were set up. After scoring, they checked into a motel, where they poured Johnny Blue and busted a bag of blow all over the coffee table.

Derek sat down on the bed and watched Messy set down his Visa, roll up a fifty and take a bump. Messy passed the bill to Derek and he did the same. They were criminals, gangsters, bank robbers, international drug traffickers. Just a couple of small-town boys who became big time criminals.

Derek felt good about going back home and living a quiet life without the chaos. He knew that if they sold the truck, he would have a nice chunk of money to buy a cottage and live quietly. He'd stopped caring what he did for money; he could work in a factory and live comfortably. It had taken a long time to realize that he just needed to be among his friends and family – those who could keep him on the right path.

The blood and the blow rushed to Derek's brain like sprinters toward the finish line. He took a sip of his scotch and watched Messy take another bump. Derek noticed that there were little piles of coke all around the room. Messy was out of control.

"Better put the DND sign out front," Derek said.

Messy nodded his head. Derek took another hit, then another. Another scotch. A hit. Fast and loose. He needed to stop. He stood up, gained his faculties and walked to the bathroom. He locked the door behind him and looked in the mirror.

Derek Sierzant was not who he once was. In fact, he'd become a lot of things that he never wanted to be: a drug addict; an alcoholic; a mess of a human being. The only thing he held onto was that, despite all of the craziness, he had never killed anybody.

November 2009
TWENTY-EIGHT

At about 3:00 p.m. local time, Derek checked into the Best Western in Canmore. He walked to his room, dropped off his belongings, took a shower and poured a scotch. His hands were shaking; his nerves had him sweating so bad that he drenched his shirt. He needed another shower.

Derek left his hotel and drove through Canmore, one turn after another, before making his final turn onto Riva. He pulled up in front of Mandy's house. It was a tiny two-story home with wood siding and a one-car garage. It was cute, just like Mandy. He turned off the engine and collected himself. He took a deep breath, stepped out of his car, walked up to the door and knocked. Seconds later, Mandy answered, dressed in a teal dress with a bird pattern. It was simple yet adorable.

She smiled and it blinded Derek. "Hi," she said, as she stepped forward and wrapped her arms around Derek. Derek closed his arms around her and squeezed. He felt a breath of her perfume fill his lungs.

Derek pulled away to allow her to lock her door. She stepped in front of him and walked down the stairs.

"How are you?" asked Mandy.

"I'm great, Mandy."

She looked back and smiled. Derek took a deep breath. He could feel the air as he breathed in her hair; the smell of flowers and honey tickled his senses.

They climbed in Derek's car drove through the quiet suburban streets of Canmore. "How has it been?" asked Mandy.

"It's been weird since R-Luv."

"Do you want to talk about it?"

Derek looked over at Mandy and feigned a smile. "Not really, it's just, I don't know, it sewered all the good we had going on. It's tainted, you know?"

"I could see that. It's hard to lose someone – familiar surroundings always remind you of what you had."

Derek pulled into the Crazyweed parking lot. Mandy was very excited about Derek's choice of restaurant.

"You did your homework," she said, squeezing Derek's hand.

They walked inside and were seated in a booth along the wall, in front of a large window. Derek ordered a beautiful red wine to start. For entrees, Mandy ordered the Alaskan King Crab Risotto and Derek had the Chipotle Crust Alberta Sterling Rib eye.

"I've got a surprise," said Mandy.

Derek laughed, "Oh?"

"It's nothing major."

The waitress brought the wine to the table. Derek sampled a glass and nodded his head. He poured Mandy a glass and then poured one for himself.

Mandy continued, "Any guess?"

"Clueless. Do I get a hint?"

"Nope," said Mandy with a smile. She paused. "Ok, one hint. It's an activity."

Derek looked up. "That's vague."

"It's a fun activity," said Mandy, taking her first sip of wine.

"Oh, I don't like fun. What else?"

Mandy finished her sip of wine and nodded in approval. "It's an activity where I get to wear a ball cap."

"Are we helping someone move?"

"Rude," said Mandy with a smile. "Okay fine, no more hints!"

"Oh, come on!"

"No, unless you buy me dessert."

They finished their meal and drove to a local theatre for a drink. Mandy grabbed Derek's hand and led him inside. They sat in an empty booth and placed a drink order. Derek studied his surroundings. It was calming for him to finally be out of Vancouver. No one was hunting him down – that craziness didn't exist in his world with Mandy.

He took a sip of his Glenlivet and smiled at Mandy. She smiled back.

"Are you always so happy?"

"I try to be."

"I wish it wasn't so far, Derek. I miss you all the time."

"What if I told you I'm moving?"

Mandy smiled and looked intrigued. "Where will you go?"

"Anywhere!" replied Derek. "We're selling the truck."

"Wow, that's amazing!" A hush fell over the table. Mandy sipped her drink and Derek debated telling her his plan for the future.

"I want to come here."

"You do?" asked Mandy.

"I do." Derek felt himself rushing but he couldn't control it. "All I do is think about you. I count the minutes until you and I are together, and I hate it."

"There are a lot of places around here to start a restaurant."

"I don't know if that's my end game. I liked the restaurant, but I don't think it's for me. We'll see. I will take my time to decide."

"That's great, Derek! I'm so happy for you!" Mandy leaned in and kissed Derek on the cheek.

"What do you want from life?" asked Derek.

Mandy smiled and thought about the question for a moment. "I want to be a mom."

"Yeah?"

"Yeah, more than anything else. I want to have a girl so I can be as close to her as I was to my Mom."

"God, you are so selfless."

"I'm really not, Derek. I want a child for selfish reasons too. I want the purpose of raising someone the right way."

"The way you were raised?" asked Derek.

"No," replied Mandy. "I mean, not really. My parents raised me right eventually. But it wasn't easy."

The open mic host addressed the crowd, looking for someone to play a song. Derek looked at Mandy and raised his hand. Mandy smiled as Derek finished his drink and walked toward the stage.

On stage, Derek sat at the piano and adjusted the chair. He began to play a slow instrumental before he sang.

Sip my coffee at the diner bar, there you were.
I washed my clothes in the light of day, there you were.
I stared at you and caught your eye, there you were.
I think of ways to exaggerate.

Derek sang to Mandy in front of a room full of people. They locked eyes; she smiled and watched him. He finished the song and stood to a loud applause. He walked off stage toward Mandy. She stood up, pulled him in close and gave him a kiss.

A short time later, they left the bar, hand in hand, and drove back to her house. Derek pulled up in front of her house, helped her out of the car and closed the door behind her.

"Thank you. You might be the last true gentleman in this world."

Mandy leaned in and kissed Derek. He kissed back and enjoyed the cherry taste of her lips. She pulled away slowly, turned and walked up the stairs to her house. Derek watched and smiled. She stopped at the top of the stairs and turned to face him.

"Hot Springs tomorrow?"

"My surprise," said Derek.

"10:00 a.m. Pick me up!"

* * * * *

The next day, Derek woke up, had breakfast and drove to Mandy's.

She walked out of her house dressed in jeans, Air Jordan high-tops, a leather jacket and a backward Blue Jays hat. Derek had never seen anyone make high-tops look sexy.

She climbed into the car and they drove to the Banff Hot Springs.

Derek took a deep breath of the crisp mountain air. The views were spectacular; the Hot Springs were nestled into the side of the mountain and looked out over them. Fog lingered over the mountain peaks and the air had a chill.

Mandy led Derek into the café. After a coffee, Derek walked to the change room and switched into his trunks and robe. He was feeling self-conscious about his tattoos. Some, like the Pittsburgh Penguins logo and the eye from Tool's Lateralus album, were easy to explain. Others, like his Kray twins and Dillinger tattoos, wouldn't be.

Derek walked onto the deck and climbed into the warm pool. He hoped that if he were quick enough, she wouldn't see all the tattoos. He stood in the heated pool and looked over the side to the mountains below, where the fog still lingered overtop.

Derek heard a door open and watched Mandy walk out onto the deck. She removed her robe and shook her sable black hair. She drew a stare or two from men in the pool as she showed off a blue and white two-piece bikini that contrasted her olive skin beautifully. Her petite body drew Derek's stares; he couldn't believe how perfect she was. She walked toward the pool's stairs and climbed down. Derek felt his heart race inside his chest as the mountain air filtered through her summer hair. He couldn't handle her; his heart was going to explode. She walked over to him and began to kiss him on the lips. He kissed back and began to blush.

Mandy pulled back, smiled and ducked into the water. Derek liked this side of Mandy. She walked to the edge of the pool and smirked.

"What?" asked Derek, curious as to what she was dreaming up.

"Nothing," she replied, "just thinking of something."

"Care to indulge me?"

"I'm thinking of you," she said as she smiled, "cooking me dinner."

"I'd love to cook you dinner."

"Naked," said Mandy with a grin.

Derek didn't know how to respond. Mandy walked over to him and kissed him.

"Are you blushing?" she asked.

He grinned, blushed again and lowered himself into the water, swimming over to the pool wall. Mandy followed and they looked out over the mountains, snuggled close.

They lounged for a few hours and had lunch before Derek drove them back to Canmore. They stopped for groceries before returning to Mandy's house. Her home was ultra-modern, complete with high-end finishes and trendy furniture.

Derek unpacked groceries in the kitchen while Mandy showered. His cell phone rang; the ID said Hecky.

"Hey, buddy. What's going on?"

"I did it, Sarge. I sold the truck!"

"Holy shit! Really?"

"Yeah, buddy, for real!" yelled Hecky. "We have to sign the papers and that, but someone is offering three hundred for it. We're out!"

"Holy shit! Nice job!"

Before he even had a chance to decipher the news, Mandy walked into the kitchen wearing only a towel. She didn't speak; she looked Derek in the eyes and smiled. She reached for his hand, took it in hers and walked him into her bedroom.

Mandy took a step into her room and paused. She looked up at him and a tear streamed down her face.

"What's wrong?" asked Derek.

Mandy started to cry.

"Babe, what's wrong?"

She didn't answer him, just brought her hands to her face. Derek wrapped his arms around her and she withdrew. She walked over to her bed, sat down and cried into her hands while Derek stood in the doorway, stunned.

"Derek, I can't"-

"Can't what, babe?"

Mandy wiped the tears from her face. Derek walked over to her nightstand, picked up a box of Kleenex and handed it to her. She wiped away her tears.

"I haven't had sex in three years."

"That's okay."

"Oh my God, I'm such a mess."

"It's okay."

"It's not, Derek."

"What is it?"

"Derek, I can't...I haven't been naked in front of anyone in forever."

"Why is that? Did something happen to you?"

"No. Well, I mean, kind of."

Derek's world rattled. He felt his throat close and his fists clench. He stared blankly for a moment. Mandy looked at him and attempted to smile. Derek teared up with her.

"Derek, I've had an eating disorder for the past five years." Mandy choked back the tears and continued, "I don't see what you see when I look at myself." Mandy wiped away tears as Derek massaged her. "I promise I'll be able to eventually. I just can't right now."

"Babe, it's fine. We won't do anything that you aren't comfortable with." Derek wrapped his arms around Mandy and hugged her. He then pulled back. "I don't understand, how were you able to walk in front of everyone in a bikini today?"

"I felt fine until we came in here and I saw myself in the mirror. I see this monster in the mirror."

Derek winced; he couldn't relate. He saw a monster in himself because he was a monster. Mandy wasn't.

"Derek, I survived this thing that tried to take me down. I didn't let it define me, even though the scars from it are all over me."

Derek stared blankly. He had no idea what to say or how to react.

* * * * *

The next morning, Derek was up first and made coffee. He sat down with his guitar on Mandy's couch and began strumming and then picked at the strings. His fingers worked their way into a song and the lyrics soon followed.

"You are fade out on your bed, you feed pills –" Derek spotted Mandy across the room and stopped playing.

"You okay?" asked Mandy.

Derek looked up at see her standing in the doorway.

"I'll be okay," he replied.

"We'll be okay, Derek."

They had breakfast and exchanged goodbyes. Heading to Vancouver, he called Hecky as he pulled into town later that evening.

"Hey, buddy, where you at?"

"The house. Cops cleared us to go home. I grabbed all your shit."

Derek re-routed himself and drove back to the house. He arrived home and was greeted by Messy and Hecky, who were relaxing and enjoying a ball game on TV. Derek grabbed a beer from the fridge and joined them on the couch.

"What are you guys doing tonight?" asked Derek.

"Drinking," said Messy.

"You got plans?" asked Hecky.

"Not really," Derek replied as he stood up. "I feel trapped already."

"We are trapped," said Messy. "Prisoners in our own fucking house."

Derek settled in and tried to relax in front of a ball game with the boys. He couldn't.

"When do we meet the lawyer?" he asked.

"Tomorrow," answered Hecky.

"Not soon enough," said Messy.

The next day, the boys met with their lawyer downtown to sign the documents. It was a done deal – a hundred thousand dollars each less legal fees and taxes! They could barely contain their excitement as they took an elevator to the lobby.

"Nothing keeping us here now!" shouted Messy with excitement.

Hecky held the door for the boys and they walked outside. Derek felt the warmth of the sun on his face and a calm come over him. He was on his way out – finally. The sun caught him in the eye; he was startled as the windows and doors around him began to shatter and fall to pieces.

Bullets flew from a black SUV across the street. A machine gun fired shots out the passenger side window at the boys. Derek hit the ground as soon as he heard the glass shatter. He had his bulletproof vest, but his gun was nowhere near him.

The bullets continued to fly as tires squealed and the SUV took off down the street. Derek stayed low to the ground as he crawled over to Messy and Hecky to check on them. They had a few bumps and bruises, but, incredibly, no one had been hit.

Within minutes of the shooting the police arrived on the scene. For the second time in two months Derek and the boys were the intended target of a drive-by shooting. There was no escaping it this time. The police and The Grip were onto them.

The officers approached the boys and questioned them. They gave the same canned answers they had given at each of the previous shootings. This time, there was no covering up their involvement in the world of crime. The police knew that the boys were into something deep and they weren't about to let it go; they asked that the boys come in for questioning. The boys complied and walked from the crime scene to a nearby parking garage. They jumped into the Edge and drove to the VPD station.

Derek had long suspected the Edge of being bugged; the boys were dead silent the entire ride. The shooting, coupled with the constant bulls eye on their back, had them thinking about their own mortality.

Derek slowed down near a grocery store and pulled into the parking lot; he wanted to have a discussion before they went to the police station. They jumped out of the car and shut their doors.

"Don't talk within earshot of the car," suggested Hecky. They nodded at each other and walked across the parking lot.

"What are we going to do?" Messy asked.

"We should find a shyster," replied Derek.

"We'll look guilty," said Hecky.

"We are guilty!" shouted Derek. "A lawyer keeps us out of bracelets."

"We were just at a lawyer's," suggested Messy.

"Yeah, he's not right for this," said Derek. "We need a criminal lawyer – somebody who got school with this kind of shit."

"Why don't we see what the PoPo want first? If we stick to script, we might not need anyone." said Hecky.

Messy and Derek nodded their heads in agreement.

"Fuck this town. We are done here!" shouted Derek.

"What about Matty's new six's?" asked Hecky.

"We're going to skip on those motherfuckers!" shouted Derek.

"I don't think we can, Sarge," said Hecky, cautioning Derek.

"Let's just deal with the cops first and move on from there."

Messy and Hecky nodded their heads as they turned away from Derek and began to walk toward the car. Derek called out, "Hold on, boys. Are you off-script or do we need a refresh?"

Messy and Derek turned around to face Derek. They both nodded their heads and turned to walk toward the car. As they took their first steps, the Edge exploded into a ball of fire.

"Jesus Christ!"

"What the fuck?" cried Messy.

"That's it!" Hecky exclaimed, stomping around the parking lot. "They want to keep coming, we're going to end them!"

The boys stood in the middle of the parking lot, watching flames shoot out of the car.

"Fuck," said Hecky, "I had smokes in there."

"Well I guess the cops will come to us," suggested Messy.

Messy was right; within five minutes the same police that the boys had spoke to earlier had arrived on the scene. This time the boys were driven to the police station.

Derek sat in an interrogation room by himself for three straight hours. He knew the police wanted him to sweat it out. He also knew the police had nothing to hold him.

The door swung open and Anna walked inside holding a dossier. She set her folder on the desk, took off her jacket and rolled up her sleeves.

"You can cut the theatrics."

"I'm hot, Derek. Don't read too much into it." Anna sat down in her seat, "I don't expect you to talk, so I'm not going to try. I'm just going to show you what you are in for."

Anna began pulling pictures from the folder and setting them on the table. They were mug shots of The Devil's Grip members. She began pointing to each picture.

"This guy here has killed five people, but I can't prove any of them." She pointed to the next picture. "This guy killed seven – same thing. I can't prove shit." She pointed to the next picture. "This guy killed nine, and I can't prove a goddamn thing. Do you see?"

"I see that you are terrible at your job," joked Derek with a smirk.

"You and your boys are a blip on the radar to these guys – a speed bump. You are the thing until their next thing. So, good luck. I have nothing to offer you except one piece of advice: find someone who will help you, because I won't, and The Grip won't stop until you and those two idiots are squashed."

Derek sat in his chair for a few minutes. He knew it was time to go underground, to hide out and to go unnoticed until he and the boys could deal with their issues with The Grip, which was now much more difficult. It was a certainty that their clubhouse would be sat on; extinguishing that flame was a fantasy. They needed another way at them, and they needed it now. They were a man down and The Grip was looking to punch their ticket.

That evening, the boys stayed at a high-profile hotel in the heart of the downtown core. The Grip would be hard-pressed to attack them there. They slept, guns in hand. They were done taking chances; The Grip was coming at them hard. Hecky brainstormed a way to do one of two things: go into hiding and hope they weren't found or end The Devil's Grip. Option 2 meant putting it all on the line and killing the entire Devil's Grip.

"I wonder if they meet outside of the clubhouse?" asked Hecky.

"Like at a bar?" asked Derek.

"Or a house. You'd think that if they always meet there, they would have been bum rushed by now."

"Yeah," Derek replied, "maybe."

"That's where we have to hit them," said Messy, with conviction.

Derek went to bed. He lay there, thinking about how far he'd set himself back. He did everything for freedom and liberty and here he was boxed into his hotel. His phone rang; it was Mandy.

"Hello?"

"Hey, babe!" said Mandy in her perky, sexy voice. "You okay? You were quiet when you left."

"I'm okay, babe." Derek paused.

"What are you up to?"

"I'm just hanging out with the boys. We are celebrating a bit. We signed the papers today for the sale!"

"Wow, that's awesome! When do you move here?"

"Soon! I get my money in a month, then we'll see what happens!"

"I really think you should open a brick and mortar restaurant. We have plenty of places; I'm sure we could find something suitable."

"I don't know if I have it in me to open another restaurant. I don't really know what I want to do. Right now, I just want to be with you."

"Me too, Derek. I want you out of that city. It seems like there are shootings every day."

"It is ridiculous. Even going to the bar is worrisome. You don't know if it's safe." Derek took a deep breath. *How long could he keep this up*?

"Did the police say anything about your friend?"

"No, they are still investigating."

"I'd like to see you again, Derek. Maybe I could meet you halfway?"

"What's halfway?"

"Kamloops?" asked Mandy.

"More like Salmon Arm, I think."

"Yes!" exclaimed Mandy. "Meet me there at noon tomorrow?"

"Okay!"

Derek rented a VW Passat, fueled up on coffee and set out on his four-hour journey. Mandy was the only thing in Derek's life that he liked to think about. Every other thought had become a worry: about being shot, about being caught, about losing his life, his freedom, his family, or his friends. But then there was Mandy. She was a vacation Derek took. The idea of having a life with her was the only good Derek could think about. He was feeling again – he hadn't felt in a while.

*   *   *   *   *

Derek returned to Vancouver and the boys gathered for breakfast in the common area of their hotel room. Hecky had news. He took the boys outside to a rental car; they jumped inside and drove deep into the West Vancouver suburbs. The homes in West Van had manicured lawns, beautiful gardens and mature trees.

He turned onto a quiet street where the boys sat silent for twenty minutes. He said one word, "Watch."

They watched.

Minutes later, six large black SUV's pulled up in front of the house.

Members of The Grip began to pile out of the vehicles onto the sidewalk. They stood around waiting and smoking. Their President arrived and led them into his home.

Hecky turned to the boys and smiled. "Every month they have a BBQ here. This is where we do it!"

"We do what?" asked Messy.

"You know – it!"

"You mean we blow in there and shoot up the place?" asked Derek.

"No," said Hecky, "we go in there and put out the fire."

"What are you talking about?"

"I'm going to rig the BBQ."

"Rig it to do what? Blow you up?" joked Messy.

"I'll exchange their tank with a modified one. Then we walk through the front door and punch their ticket."

"Can you do that?" asked Messy.

"I think so," replied Hecky. "I've done way more complicated shit than that on set."

"It's not totally stupid," said Messy.

"It's pretty stupid," replied Derek. "We walk in like there like hatchet men and put them down? What about their family?"

"They aren't there."

"What about any hangarounds?"

"No hangarounds at the house," replied Hecky.

"Do you have a better idea, Derek?" asked Messy.

Derek thought for a moment. "I just don't want to end up on the negative side of a zero-sum game."

"It's us or it's them, Sarge," said Hecky. "I don't love the idea, but its time to throw lead their way. These guys aren't going to stop coming."

"Can I really kill someone?" asked Derek out loud.

"You'd be surprised what you can do when someone won't stop shooting at you," replied Messy.

*   *   *   *   *

Hecky began to work on a way to rig a propane tank to explode. As the week went on it became apparent that rigging the propane tank would be above their heads. Hecky gathered with the boys in the common area of their hotel and began talking about alternatives.

"Boys, I can't rig this fucking thing."

"Then let's just go," said Derek. "Let's blow town!"

"I have another idea," said Hecky. "I want to use an explosive with an RFID chip."

Derek and Messy didn't understand what Hecky was talking about; he went deep into detail.

"I think I can replace one of their dinner plates with a modified plate that we would place on the BBQ. It would look like any other plate – only, in the middle of it, would be a small amount of C-4, a wireless receiver and a RFID chip. I would need a few days to build some and test them."

"Dude, you are going to blow yourself up," said Derek. "Where did you learn this shit?"

"It'll be good," promised Hecky. "I do this shit on set all the time!"

"On film sets?" asked Messy.

"Yeah, I mean, it's more controlled, but I got tips from Matty's Cartel Guy. He calls this a Boyuyu."

"What's that?" asked Derek.

"It's chaos in Spanish. He said they use it all the time down there."

"They use a Spanish name for a device used in Mexico?" asked Derek.

"Fuck," replied Hecky, "I guess so."

"Where are you going to get C-4?" asked Messy.

"I got a hookup," replied Hecky.

"A hookup?" Derek pressed.

"Jesus fucking Christ, Sarge. Yes, a hookup."

That evening, Dannick called Derek to check again if he had a place for him to stay during the Olympics.

"What's going on?" asked Derek.

"Not much, bro. Can you talk?"

"Yeah, what's up?"

"You able to house me while I'm out there for the games?"

"Shit, man. The boys and I rented out the house. I booked a hotel out in Abbottsford though. It's far, but you are welcome to stay there."

Derek's lies weren't enough to dissuade Dannick from coming out West. It was great exposure for him, and Derek understood his side of things. He just didn't want him there.

"Awesome, bud. Love you!"

"Love you, bro," Derek answered.

Seconds later his phone rang again; it was Mandy.

"Hey, Derek!"

"Hey, babe. What's up?"

"Not much, just sitting at home. What did you do today?"

"Not much, just had lunch with the boys and hung out. You?"

"I worked and had dinner with my Dad."

"That's awesome!"

"We're going to come visit next weekend if that's okay!"

"Ah," Derek had to think quickly. "Shit! The boys and I just booked a trip down to Pittsburgh to celebrate."

"Oh, sorry, I didn't know!"

"We just planned it! Sorry! We'll figure something out soon. Maybe you won't have to go anywhere to visit!"

"I hope so, Derek. I hate this!"

"I do too. You are every single star in my sky!"

"Babe, stop!" Mandy giggled.

"My will is strong, and my feelings are intense. I won't hide it."

"I know you are passionate, Derek. I want to see that side of you."

"You will."

"I'll be honest – sometimes I wonder if I will know you."

"You will. We will."

November 2009
TWENTY-NINE

A few days later, Hecky drove Derek and Messy out to a field outside of the city to test plates. It was there that they disposed of a police car a year ago.

Messy and Derek waited for Hecky to finish tinkering. Hecky stood up and walked toward them. Seconds later he set the charge and BOOM! The plate exploded behind him and a huge smoke bomb entered the sky. The charge left a four-foot crater in the ground. Hecky looked at Messy and Derek and smiled. "Satisfied?"

"Wow, I'm good. How many have you done?" asked Derek.

"I set three charges; they all went off with no delay. We are good to go here. The range is good too."

"Now we just need to learn how to shoot," said Messy.

"Dude, if this works there will be nothing left to shoot," joked Hecky.

Over the next week, the boys practiced shooting every day. They were in a life or death situation; nothing could be left to chance.

Messy had basic military weapons training and worked as an instructor for Derek and Hecky.

*   *   *   *   *

After a week of work with the guns, they had become quick and accurate. They all had pretty good hand eye co-ordination to begin with; it was a matter of learning the intricacies of the guns.

Mandy called Derek every night. She wanted to join him on his trip to Pittsburgh. He had planned to go alone after the boys backed out but welcomed Mandy to tag along.

After the last day of shooting practice, the boys left on their trips. They would come back, re-group and spend one last week preparing for their attack on The Grip.

Derek flew to Pittsburgh and Mandy met him there. It was their first trip together and his first time in the 412.

Mandy booked a room at the Renaissance Pittsburgh hotel on 6th street. The Renaissance was an upscale hotel that overlooked the Allegheny River. It had the feel of an old American east coast hotel.

Derek arrived at 11:00 a.m. Saturday and met Mandy in the hotel lobby. She wore a bright sundress that turned the head of every man she walked past. She spotted Derek, ran to him and planted a kiss before grabbing his hand and walking to their room. She unlocked the door to their room and Derek scooped her up in his arms and carried her inside. He walked her over to the bed and set her down gently. He kissed her and stood to his feet. He noticed two Pens tickets on the side table.

"What's that?"

"Tickets to the game tonight." "Shit, we're going to a game?"

"Right behind the bench!"

"That's too much, Mandy!"

"Hey, I'm just going 'cause it's hat night."

Derek smiled and planted a kiss on Mandy's lips.

They left their hotel room and took a cab to 18th Street in the Strip District. Mandy had heard from a Yinzer about a famous sandwich shop called Primanti Brothers. It opened in 1933 and was iconic in the Steel City.

They walked inside and were seated in the back corner. The walls were covered in a mural of customers enjoying Primanti sandwiches.

Derek and Mandy both ordered a beer with a black angus steak sandwich. The sandwich arrived topped with provolone cheese, tomatoes, homemade coleslaw, fresh cut fries all on fresh Italian bread.

Derek took a bite of his massive sandwich and smiled; it was amazing! He finished his sandwich quickly and waited for Mandy to finish.

They paid up and exited to the street. As they took a step outside onto the sidewalk, a group of bikers parked their bikes across the street. They were wearing cuts displaying their gang's emblem. Derek couldn't quite make out their emblem, but as soon as he heard the roar of the motorcycles, he nearly hit the ground.

It was clear that no matter where he went, he would always look over his shoulder for The Grip. Derek knew that The Grip had to go. They had to go where they couldn't haunt him or anyone he cared about.

That evening, Mandy and Derek walked from their hotel room to the Mellon Arena on Fifth Avenue. They both dressed in their black and Vegas gold Pittsburgh Penguin jerseys. As they approached the arena, Derek could see the large igloo-looking arena. He'd seen it a million times on television, but never in person.

Across the road from the Igloo he could see the Penguins' new home arena nearing completion. The Consol Energy Centre was set to open in less than one year.

They walked inside the Igloo and were handed a promotional Penguins ball cap. Derek was full of anticipation as they walked through the curtain into the arena. He smiled ear to ear.

"Awww, babe. You are so happy!"

Mandy pulled out her phone and took a picture of Derek smiling.

"Excuse me?" asked Mandy as she turned to a young black teenager who was walking with his girlfriend. "Can you take our picture?"

The young man took Mandy's cell phone as she and Derek stood together for the photo. The young man took a few photos and handed Mandy back her phone.

"Thank you so much!" she shouted.

"No problem," replied the young man. "Go Pens!"

"Go Pens, baby!" yelled Derek as he and the young man fist bumped.

They took their seats in the lower level, behind the Pens' bench. Derek looked around in awe. It was a dump, but to Derek it was iconic.

The game began and Sidney Crosby quickly took control.

"If he gets a hat trick, I'm keeping my hat," joked Mandy.

"You are not!"

"I am, but I'll throw yours!"

"If he gets a hat trick, everyone here will be tossing their hat."

Midway through the third period, Crosby buried his third goal past goalie Steve Valliquette. Derek tossed his hat onto the ice and turned to see Mandy put both hands on her head.

Derek laughed and yelled over the sound of the goal siren, "It's okay, babe. I think he's got enough!"

Derek looked up to watch the Penguins fans litter the ice with the ball caps. "Only Sid would net a hatty on hat night."

"I can't wait to see him play for Canada," said Mandy.

Derek looked upwards and watched hat after hat fly over his head and felt everything slow down. He was in his happy place; he grew up idolizing Mario Lemieux and the Pens. They were larger than life – heroes of his youth. He couldn't believe he was finally there in their town.

He relished the last few minutes of an 8-3 Penguins win. He sat in his seat after the game soaking it all in.

"This was the most fun I've ever had."

"I'm glad you enjoyed it, babe."

For the remainder of the trip, Mandy and Derek did all the touristy things that people do in Pittsburgh. They went to The Church Brew Works, Market Square, The Warhol Museum, Carnegie, and Mount Washington. They got lost a million times in the confusing streets of Pittsburgh, but Derek felt at home. He felt safe, away from the chaos of Vancouver.

*   *   *   *   *

Derek returned to Vancouver and found out that Hecky had installed a high-end security system in the house to keep out any unwanted visitors. He also had bars installed on the doors and windows. Derek couldn't tell if he lived in a home or a luxurious prison.

He walked into the house and left his luggage at the door. Hecky walked over and gave him a hug.

"Feel safe now?" he asked.

"I feel like I'm in jail already."

"It's just temporary. In a week there will be no one left to hunt us."

"A week from now I'm leaving town – for good."

Over the next week, Messy provided weapons training to Hecky and Derek for eight-plus hours a day. They became accurate enough to shoot a moving target with each class of gun.

It was time. There was no running, no turning back, no other move to make. The boys were going to try to wipe out The Devil's Grip.

*   *   *   *   *

At 3:30 p.m., on a warm December day, the wife of Devil's Grip president Dennis Bell took the kids in her SUV and left her house.

Hecky grabbed his bag and walked up the street toward the house. Messy and Derek hung back in a stolen car as lookouts.

Fifteen minutes later, Hecky emerged from the backyard and casually strolled back to their stolen car. He placed his bag in the trunk and grabbed the bag of guns. Inside the car, Messy and Derek had each already armed themselves with weapons and body armour. Hecky put on his gear and readied himself.

The Devil's Grip arrived at the house a few minutes later. They lined up their bikes on the street, parked and entered the house. One by one they arrived, thirty of them in total.

Hecky, Messy and Derek took one final breath and exited the car. They separated from one another and crept through the streets until they were a few houses down from their target. They lowered themselves into a crouched position and prepared for the inevitable bang.

Hecky nodded his head to the boys and pulled out his remote to arm the bombs; he looked at Derek and pressed the button three times.

Bang, bang, bang – three separate violent explosions echoed throughout the neighbourhood! Derek looked up to see debris litter the sky and fall to the ground in a heap. He wondered why there had been three explosions; he looked to Hecky for answers, but Hecky was already running toward the remains of the house. Derek followed him with Messy right behind him.

"What the fuck?" yelled Derek, his body charged with adrenaline.

"I set three charges!"

"Jesus Christ! Look at this fucking place!" yelled Derek.

"Come on!" Hecky yelled back, as he raced toward the charred remains of the house. Messy and Derek followed him into the backyard. Derek shoved aside the ashy remains of the wood fence. Messy began to check for survivors. One by one he would look at the bodies then shake his head no to Derek and Hecky.

Hecky began to feel for a pulse on each body; he found none. He walked over to check one last body; the man was a tall man, at least 6"4. His blood-soaked face was half missing and both of his legs had been blown off in the blast; he choked on his own blood as he struggled to breathe. Hecky stood over him, listening to him cough up blood. Hecky waited before he pointed his gun and fired a bullet into the man's brain, ending his suffering. Hecky turned and nodded to Derek and then looked to Derek's left and pointed with urgency.

Messy and Derek turned around to look and heard another loud bang. It was a member of The Grip; he had arrived late to the party. His gun fired as Derek turned. The bullet caught Messy in his right cheek and dropped him to the ground. Hecky returned fire and hit the man four times in the chest.

Messy and Derek fell to the ground as blood splattered through the air. Messy's face began gushing blood and he struggled to breathe. Derek tried to clot the wound with his hands, but there was no way to stop it without medical equipment.

"Get the fucking car!" yelled Derek and Hecky took off and raced out of the backyard down the street. Derek could hear police sirens heading toward them. They had to go now!

Messy tried to use what strength he had left to assist Derek in getting him up to his feet. Messy's legs were like two spaghetti noodles; he was dead weight leaning on Derek.

Hecky charged back into the yard and grabbed Messy on the other side and they walked him to the car. Derek opened the back door and helped Messy inside. Hecky ran around the car and jumped in the driver's seat. Messy and Derek sat in the back while Hecky sped away from the scene of the crime.

Derek grabbed a hoodie from the backseat and pressed it on Messy's face. Blood continued to leak all over. Hecky drove erratically through the neighbourhood as he tried to help them escape to their switch car. Derek could feel Messy's breathing become shallow; Messy looked up and attempted to speak, but his face was in too much pain.

"Don't speak, we're going to get you help."

"What are we going to do, Sarge?" asked Hecky.

"Go to a hospital!"

"And say what?"

"Say someone shot at us! We've already been shot at twice!"

Messy began to convulse in Derek's arms as he choked on blood.

"Ah, fuck! Hold on, Messy! He's not going to fucking make it!"

"We're nowhere near a hospital!" yelled Hecky. "I don't even know this fucking part of town."

"Hold on, Messy! Hold on!"

Messy took one last look at Derek and let his eyelids fall.

"No, no, no, no, Messy, stay with me, bud!" Derek tried to shake Messy as he pleaded with him. He leaned in and listened for breathing; his breathing had stopped. He was gone.

"Fuck!"

Hecky turned back and began smashing the steering wheel and screaming. "Fuck, fuck, fuck!"

"What do we do with him? We can't bring him in the switch."

"We have to leave him."

"They will know, Hecky. They'll piece that together in two seconds."

The boys were nearing their switch car that was parked a block away from The Grip's clubhouse.

"I have an idea," said Hecky. He pulled the car in front of The Grip's clubhouse, jumped out and helped Derek pull Messy's body out of the car. They stabled his lifeless body and approached the door. Hecky shot out the lock and kicked the door open.

The boys walked inside and carried Messy over to a wooden chair in the corner of the clubhouse. They sat Messy upright.

Derek looked at Messy keeled over in the chair and had all emotion come over him. He tried his best to fight back tears; the last thing he needed was his DNA all over the place.

"Keep it together," said Hecky, as he tossed a rope to him. "Tie him up."

There was no time to ask questions. Doing as he was told, he tied Messy up. Hecky walked back into the room with one of The Grip's automatic weapons and shot Messy's corpse a few more times.

"What the fuck?" yelled Derek.

"The Grip did this – now the cops will know they did. Come on."

Hecky passed Derek and walked toward the exit. A few steps from the exit, Hecky stopped and took a step inside a room just off the hallway. Hecky spotted a safe.

"Holy shit, that's their safe!"

"So what? Let's go!"

"So that's our way out of here."

"There's no time," said Derek.

"Give me time," said Hecky.

Derek peeked out the window of the doorway. "Three minutes," he said, as he walked out of the room. He stood at the front door watching for anything suspicious. Every second felt like an hour.

Two minutes later, Derek heard a loud BANG.

"You okay, Hecky?"

"All good!" shouted Hecky.

Derek walked toward the room and noticed smoke billowing out into the hallway.

"What happened?"

"I set a charge," replied Hecky.

Hecky had blown up the safe door; through the smoke Derek could see stacks and stacks of money – some torched, some still good. Hecky looked at Derek.

"Open your bag."

Derek opened the zipper of his duffel bag and Hecky frantically stashed money into it. He packed all the money they could grab and even grabbed a few stacks in his hands.

The boys exited the building and ran to their getaway car. Hecky drove one block to their switch. Once there, Derek piled the bags of money into the switch car while Hecky wiped down the getaway car.

"How do we torch it?" asked Derek.

Hecky held up two grenades, one in each hand. "With these."

Hecky pulled the pins on each grenade and dropped them in the car. He ran toward the switch car and Derek jumped into the driver's seat. Derek hammered on the gas pedal and they sped away, screaming at the top of their lungs.

Derek drove cautiously through the streets of Vancouver until they reached the second storage unit, pulling the car up front. They exited the car, picked up their bags of guns and money, walked inside the unit and shut the door behind them.

Once inside, Hecky and Derek looked each other up and down. They were covered in Messy's blood. They changed into clothing that were left in the storage unit. Hecky dumped the duffel bag's contents out onto the floor and began to count the money.

Derek changed while Hecky counted.

"$485,000."

Hecky then began to count the second bag while Derek counted the loose stacks.

Derek finished, "$170,000."

"$545,000," said Hecky.

Derek quickly counted the last bag of money, "$515,000."

"Holy shit, dude," said Hecky. "This is ridiculous!"

Derek stacked the money on a travel case and tried to temper his enthusiasm. He'd just lost his best friend. It didn't feel right to celebrate.

Hecky was amped though, and he paced the empty room, unable to stop his heavy breathing. Derek took a deep breath and walked over to the door.

"We need to go," reasoned Derek.

Hecky followed him as they shut off the light, shut the door and locked the unit.

Derek drove them back to the house and parked the rental car. Hecky walked inside as Derek sat in the car, thinking about all that had just happened.

A few minutes later, Hecky walked out of the house with Derek's cell phone in his hand.

"It's Mandy."

Derek took the phone from Hecky.

"Hey, babe, how's it going?"

"I'm good, Derek. Did you forget your phone somewhere?"

"Oh, I left it inside, I'm just out in the garage."

"Oh. Did you see the news?"

"No, I haven't had the TV on all day. What's up?"

"There was a huge explosion in Van – a house was blown to bits!"

"Oh my God, really? Turn on the news, Hecky!"

Hecky ran ahead into the house and Derek followed. By the time he arrived inside, Hecky had the TV on the local news station.

"I'm looking at it now. That's craziness!"

"I just wanted to call and make sure it wasn't your neighbourhood."

"All good, babe. We are nowhere close to that!"

"Okay. I'll call you tonight!"

"Okay, babe. I miss you!"

"Miss you too, Derek!"

Derek hung up and turned his attention to the news.

"Jesus Christ," exclaimed Derek. "There is fuck-all left! Why did you set three charges?"

"So it would look like this," replied Hecky, as he sat down on the couch and leaned back.

"You can't tell me we aren't their number one suspect."

"Do you think that they would believe we have the capability of doing this?"

"Maybe – you do blow shit up for a living."

"These guys had a long list of enemies – most of whom are more than capable of doing something like this."

The newscasters were making obvious assumptions about what caused the explosion. An overhead view showed bits and pieces of the house strewn across the street and other nearby properties. A shot of the house showed multiple bodies covered by white sheets on the ground in the backyard. The television station cut to a different shot almost immediately while the announcers pondered what could have happened.

Hecky and Derek looked at each other. They'd gone too far. Way too far.

For the next three hours their eyes were glued to the television. Derek knew the police would show as soon as they discovered Messy's body.

Hecky and Derek waited – and waited and waited. At about 10:00 p.m. they grew tired of waiting.

"We should go out for dinner," suggested Hecky.

Food was the last thing on Derek's mind. He was sick over what happened to Messy, but he couldn't sit and stew for another minute.

"Yeah," replied Derek, "let's go. I need to get out."

They piled into Hecky's van and drove to a local pub. For the first time in months, Derek stepped out onto the street without feeling like he was being hunted.

They ate dinner, had a beer and drove back to the house. Hecky pulled the van onto their street to see police cars parked in front of their house. He pulled into the driveway and parked. As they jumped out of the van, Anna and two plain-clothes police officers approached them.

"Derek!" shouted Anna.

"Anna!" Derek shouted back, attempting to be aloof.

"Where were you guys today?"

"Here, mostly – did some groceries and had dinner. Why, what's up?"

"Have you seen your friend? The tall one?" asked Anna.

"Messy? He left earlier."

"He say where he was going?"

"Gym, maybe? I didn't ask."

"That house that blew up belonged to Dennis Bell."

"What house?"

"Save it," said Anna. "I know you did this – you and him." said Anna, as she pointed past Derek at Hecky.

"Me?" asked Hecky, feigning surprise. "What the fuck did I do?"

"Stop! The shit you pulled got another one of your friends killed. Hope you're happy, boys," said Anna, as she turned and walked to her car.

"Wait," asked Derek. "What?!? What happened to Messy?"

Anna turned back to Derek.

"Fuck off, Derek. You and that idiot already know."

"Know what?" asked Hecky, as he continued the charade. Anna walked to her car, climbed inside and slammed the car door shut.

December 15th 2009

Derek boarded a plane to Ottawa. It was his first trip home since the bank job. He was excited to not have police eye balling his every move.

He arrived in Ottawa and picked up a rental car at the airport. He knew his parents would have questions about Vancouver and business. They didn't know Messy, his family or any of the other boys for that matter; Derek hoped his life on the West Coast would remain a mystery to them.

At 6:00 p.m., he arrived home and was greeted at the front door by his family. They exchanged pleasantries and sat down for dinner and drinks.

Derek answered all his parents' questions as truthfully as he could without hesitation. Dannick even had questions about staying at the house and getting into the city to cover events. Dannick was happy to know that he would get free run of the house; The Grip threat was gone.

Derek spent the next two weeks with friends and family. He spoke to Mandy every night; she was happy that he would be moving soon.

December 28th 2009

Derek ordered a ticket for Mandy to fly from Calgary to Ottawa the following day.

He met her at the airport gate. Derek could see her face shine bright as he ran toward her and scooped her up in his arms. He kissed her hard and she kissed him soft. Derek set her down.

"Welcome to Ottawa."

They arrived in Renfrew shortly after 4:00 p.m., checked into a hotel and drove to his parents' house for dinner.

They walked into the house and were greeted by the dog. Dannick walked into the front foyer to pick up the dog and noticed Mandy.

"Whoa."

Mandy laughed, "Hi, I'm Mandy."

Dannick extended his hand and stared blankly at Mandy. Derek looked at his Brother and snickered. He brushed past Dannick and led Mandy up the stairs to the kitchen and living room area. His Mom was working in the kitchen.

"Mom, "I'd like you to meet Mandy," Derek said, gleaming.

"I've heard so much about you. It's wonderful to finally meet you."

"Likewise," replied Mandy, as they shook hands. "Would you like some help with dinner?"

"I'd love for you to pour us some wine and tell me about yourself."

The ladies talked in the kitchen while Derek and Dannick watched a World Juniors hockey game on television. Minutes later, Peter walked in from his shop and they sat down to dinner. Peter began razzing Derek, then Dannick joined in, and Mandy started too. The jokes ranged from jabs about Derek being an unemployed Voluntaryist to being unable to commit to anything. It was the kind of thing he was used to. Little did they know.

Derek's parents loved Mandy – everyone did. Her smile lit up a room and her personality made even the most guarded person open up and spill their guts. Derek knew that he was lucky this girl even looked at him, let alone let him be with her.

The following day, Derek took Mandy into Ottawa to see the sites. They visited the Parliament buildings, the canal and the Byward Market before heading out to dinner in the trendy Westboro neighbourhood.

December 31st 2009

On New Years Eve, they attended a party at a friend of Derek's; it was a tradition among his Ottawa friends. Every New Year's Eve they would party at the McShane farmhouse. It would freeze rain and multiple cars would get stuck in their 400-metre-long driveway while trying to go to Finnegan's. This year was no different.

Mandy and Derek arrived around 8:00 p.m. She fit in with his friends right away and threw drinks back with the best of them.

By 10:00 p.m., Derek could feel a buzz coming on; he excused himself from a game of flip cup to step outside. He stood outside in the snow, taking a piss and staring at the stars. The snowflakes fell like diamonds. He couldn't help but wonder where Messy and R-Luv were and how they felt about him now. He didn't like himself much; he couldn't imagine they did either. He felt a tear freeze to his face.

Mandy opened the door and stumbled outside. She was drunk.

"Were you peeing?" she asked.

Derek nodded his head yes and Mandy turned up her nose. "Gross!"

"You do it too!"

"And you're smoking too!"

"You know I smoke."

"Derek, I'm really drunk!"

"I know, babe, me too!"

"Will you stay with me tonight?"

"I will."

"Every night?"

Derek smiled, "Every night."

He grabbed Mandy's hand and kissed it as they walked into the house. McShane announced that cabs were coming to take them to the bar.

An hour later, the entire party had shifted scenes to a downtown Renfrew bar. Derek fist pumped to techno on the dance floor with Mandy and his friends. After a few dances he walked outside. On his way to the exit, he walked through a crowd of people he grew up with; he had a lot of memories running through his mind. He couldn't figure out if he was in a better spot than the previous New Year's Eve when he nearly overdosed.

On the surface, he appeared to have everything going for him. He had a beautiful girlfriend, money and lived in a world-class city. He had all of the things that any vain person would value. But deep down, he knew that he was in trouble: trouble with the law, trouble with other criminals and trouble keeping track of his own lies. He had built a house of cards and all he could do was live in it and enjoy it while it was still standing.

Derek began to sweat; for once he wasn't coasting like a snowbird. He had made a clean sneak – many clean sneaks over the last two years. He knew that he needed to enjoy all of this; his friends had sacrificed so he could have this. He had sacrificed his friends so he could have this. He stood in the parking lot and smoked. He blew smoke rings into the cold night air and stared skyward. After a few minutes, he went back inside. Mandy met him at the bottom of the stairs and dragged him onto the dance floor. They tore it up for the next hour and were hammered when the ball came down.

McShane leaned in to whisper in Derek's ear, but he yelled, "How much coke have you done?"

Mandy's face said it all; she'd heard it. Everyone in the bar heard it. Derek felt Mandy's hand let go. She backed away and left the club. He quickly ran up the stairs and out the door; Mandy was outside smoking. Derek approached her slowly. "You don't smoke."

"I used to."

Derek lit a cigarette and looked at the sky.

"You know I didn't do any coke tonight. Or since we met for that matter. But I did have a life before we met. I did shit I'm not proud of." Derek took a drag of his smoke. "I won't hide from my past; it made me who I am."

"Sometimes I wonder if I will know you, Derek."

"Look, I've made mistakes."

"Are you still making mistakes?"

"Everyone makes mistakes," Derek took another puff of his cigarette. "I still screw up, I just don't make those kinds of mistakes."

"How are you able to drink and not have it escalate to other stuff?"

"I'm just able to shut it out. I spent years coked out. Years! And I am not about to go back to it. I won't."

"Derek, I'm not looking for a reclamation project. I am a reclamation project. I thought you had your life together."

"I do! Look, last New Year's was a huge eye opener for me. That guy O'Connor that you met, he balled his eyes out in front of me because he thought I was killing myself."

"You were."

"I was." Derek took a puff of his smoke, "but I've found reason to live."

"I hope so, because I won't hang around. My friend's husband did this to her and I won't have you do it to me."

"He was a junkie?"

"No, but he did bad things and he paid for what he did. He lost his friends and family. I don't want that. We have a good thing going. Please think about that."

"I do. I always do."

"There is a place for you inside of my heart, Derek," said Mandy. Derek smiled at Mandy and wiped a tear from her face. "I love you, Derek."

Derek's jaw hit the ground, he could barely answer, "I love you too!"

He softly put each hand to Mandy's face and kissed her.

They returned to their hotel room minutes later. Derek kicked off his boots and took off his jacket. Mandy jumped into his arms and tackled him to the floor. She lay on top of him and kissed him.

"You have a beautiful soul, Derek. It's dark and damaged, but I know it's full of good."

Derek couldn't reply. He knew that he was damaged and dark, but he couldn't find any goodness. He hadn't been able to find it for a while. He knew that he was robbing Mandy of meeting someone much better than him. He knew that his bad would eventually infiltrate her world.

"We'll grow, Derek. Together we will grow."

Mandy kissed Derek passionately and they made love.

*   *   *   *   *

Derek put Mandy on a plane back to Calgary the next day and jumped on a plane to Vancouver. Derek arrived around 2:00 p.m. Vancouver time. He grabbed his luggage and walked to Hecky's van outside the airport doors. Hecky had been in Whistler with his Dad for the past few weeks and had just rolled back into the city.

"So, the cops came by the house again," said Hecky.

"What did you tell them?"

"I told them we are grieving."

"I am grieving," replied Derek.

"So am I."

"Any weird shit around the neighbourhood?" asked Derek.

"All quiet except for the cops."

"That's good. How's Squamish?"

"I'm going back after the Olympics. I want to hang around for that and tie up loose ends."

"It'd be nice to get our stash."

"I don't see any way of us getting at that," said Hecky. "We've got over a million each. It's a head start."

"I hope I can stretch it."

"Are you going to Canmore?"

"That's the plan." replied Derek.

"Good for you, bro. I'm happy that you're happy."

"Thanks, Hecky."

They arrived home, unpacked and got dressed to go out. Hecky wanted to go out downtown. They had dinner and walked to a small pub on Commercial Drive. They sat in a corner booth with a bottle of high-end bourbon, chatting about the future. Derek was optimistic that once he escaped Vancouver, he could leave the city behind for good.

Hecky kept checking out the crowd behind Derek. As the night went on, Derek became more on edge with every look Hecky took. Then it happened; he recognized someone.

"Good evening, boys," said Anna as she approached them.

"Hi, Anna," replied Hecky.

"We're going to ask that you leave here for the night and go home."

"Why?" asked Hecky. "We are just sitting quietly having a drink."

"Well, we are part of a joint task force whose goal is to keep gangsters like you out of places like this."

"We aren't gangsters!"

"You might not have a criminal record, but you most certainly are. Now get out and don't come back."

Derek stood up and turned around.

"You know what? You had me wrong from day one, and you still do."

"Good thing we are leaving town eh, Sarge?" said Hecky.

"Good thing, bud," replied Derek.

Hecky and Derek stood up, walked quietly to the door and left the bar, walking to Hecky's van. Hecky started the van and pulled out of the parking lot. As Hecky started to drive, the boys were surrounded by four police cars. Multiple officers jumped out of the squad cars with guns drawn and rushed toward Hecky and Derek. They threw their hands in the air.

"Get out of the car!" yelled one of the officers.

Hecky and Derek slowly reached for the door handles and stepped out of the van. The officers rushed the boys and pinned them against the side of the van. Anna walked toward Derek with a piece of paper in her hand and a smile on her face.

"Derek Sierzant and Riley Heckman, this is a search warrant for your vehicles and your residence. Read it if you like, but I'll tell you what it says. It says we can look wherever we want, for whatever we want."

The officers stood the boys to their feet, walked them to a squad car and put them in the back of it.

They watched Hecky's van get torn apart. The cops checked every square inch of it. Derek and Hecky grinned at each other and looked over at Anna; she grew frustrated once again.

The cops finished tearing apart the van and waited for the search of the house to be complete. After a half hour, an officer approached the car and opened the door. The boys were let out and had their handcuffs removed. Anna approached the boys, clearly angry.

"You two think you are so smart. Last men standing. What about your friends?"

"What about 'em?" asked Hecky.

"Doesn't it make you sick to know you killed them?" asked Anna.

"I don't see how," replied Hecky. "If they got in over their heads that is on them."

"You know at some point the government is going to audit your little food truck venture."

Derek laughed. "That's fine, you can send that group of crooks to us."

"Yeah, do you want to check our parents' houses too?" asked Hecky. "Maybe you can have a look at our accounting or our bank statements?"

"What do I need to do to prove to you that you are chasing ghosts?" asked Derek.

"You can't, because I'm not."

"Is this about something else?"

"Don't flatter yourself, Derek."

"Don't project things onto me because I ended things with you."

"Dream on. Now go home and don't come back down here!"

Anna walked away and Hecky smirked at Derek. "Anyone want to make a quick twenty bucks helping me put my van back together?"

The officers all shot dirty looks at Hecky.

The boys returned home. Over the next week, they only left the house to get cigarettes and groceries.

January 2010
THIRTY

Mandy called Derek every night asking how many days left. Derek was counting the days as well. *Get through the Olympics,* he thought. *Just get through the games and leave town like all the Olympians.*

After a week of living like Howard Hughes, Derek was starting to lose it; Hecky too. The police certainly weren't sympathizing with them. Every day they would show up to ask the boys something new.

Finally, the police knocked on the door and asked the boys to come with them. They were going to ask more questions at the station.

Hecky and Derek were brought down to the police station in the back of separate police cruisers. The cops took the scenic route to make sure the ride took as long as possible. The more time the boys had to think, the more time their minds had to wander.

Derek knew that the police had nothing on them and would need one to turn on the other to make a case. They had gone over their story a million times and covered every scenario that could trap them.

The cars pulled into the parking garage and two officers each walked Derek and Hecky from the cruiser into the building, where they were led into separate interrogation rooms. They were left alone in the tiny rooms for over two hours.

A detective walked into the room to speak with Derek. He was dressed in a suit and tie and brought Derek coffee and a donut.

"Evening, Derek. I'm Det. Smith. I want to thank you for your cooperation in this matter."

Derek was curious as to which interrogation model the police would attempt to use. He and Hecky had become students of crime. Derek knew of the Reid Model, which was almost confrontational right off the bat. The PEACE model was more of a dialogue between the interrogator and the suspect.

"Tell me about yourself, Derek," Smith started.

"I was born. I lived. I'm here."

"Okay, I get it – vague question gets a vague answer. Why move to Vancouver? Was it the restaurant?"

"Money, to both."

Smith laughed to himself. "Derek, you lived with two men who were murdered, and you've been shot at multiple times. How would you view this if you were me?"

Smith caught Derek off guard; he wasn't prepared for a hypothetical line of questioning. He improvised by providing hypothetical's of his own.

"You have kids, Detective?"

"I do."

"Do you ever worry they could get mixed up with the wrong crowd?"

"Of course."

"That shit doesn't change when you're my age. Just because the guys I'm friends with do bad shit doesn't mean I do. People make mistakes and pay for them. Messy and R-Luv made their beds, and now they are lying in them."

"Big coincidence, no?"

"Coincidences still happen, don't they? You don't believe they exist?"

"I believe in coincidences; I've just never seen a cluster of coincidences quite like this."

"Just because you don't see them doesn't mean they don't happen."

"It doesn't help me believe," replied Smith.

"Do you believe in God?"

"I do."

"Have you ever seen him?"

"Indirectly."

"You've seen God indirectly?" asked Derek.

"I've seen God's work."

"So, you believe in God, even though you've never seen him?"

"Yes."

"Well, I believe in coincidences, and I've seen them."

"Derek, you haven't answered the question." Smith took a moment to collect his thoughts. "How would you view it if you were an outsider and someone you knew had two roommates murdered?"

"I'd probably think they should find some new roommates. Which is exactly what Riley and I are doing."

"Where are you moving, Derek?"

"Fucktown."

"Why are you moving?"

"Because all my friends here keep getting killed."

"Where is Riley going?"

"Ask him. He's two doors down."

"What was your involvement in your friends' affairs?"

"None – no involvement – other than being used as target practice."

"You know what I think, Derek?"

"I bet you're going to tell me."

"Listen, I've seen a thousand kids like you before. I'd say 90% of them are lying in the ground now."

He paused.

"I think you and Riley are the ringleaders of this whole thing. And I think you and Riley were the targets. Jyoshi and Ryan were your fall guys."

"I think you give me too much credit. You really think I could do this – why haven't they kept coming?"

"Probably because you and Riley wiped out their whole organization. Was that your idea or Riley's?"

"You can try to rattle me, but there is nothing for me to give, and nothing for you to get. So, keep wasting your time if you want, but you're chasing ghosts."

"Derek, you can go. But know that once you walk out that door, I won't be here to help you. If you come back, I won't have a deal for you to cut, so you can take half your punishment now or all of it later."

Derek looked out the door and quietly walked toward it. Hecky was sitting in the hallway with an officer. He stood up the second he saw Derek.

"You good?" he asked.

"All good buddy."

"Let's get the fuck out of here!"

*   *   *   *   *

A week later, Derek left the house, climbed into his rental car and drove to the grocery store. He hadn't left the house in a week. The fridge had been bare for two days and he was hungry.

He returned home from the store and noticed a familiar car in the driveway. Matty and George were visiting Hecky. Matty met Derek at the door and gave him a hug.

"Sorry to hear about your boy."

"Are you?" asked Derek, catching Matty off guard.

"Yeah, man! We ain't so close now, but we still boys, homie."

"We aren't boys anymore, Matty. What we did, we did for us. Not you and your cartel buddies."

"Goddamn, Grip man," snickered Matty. "So glad they are chilled and buried."

"You know you set this shit in motion. Without you coming by the house that day, Messy and R-Luv would still have their voices echoing inside these walls."

"Careful what you say, Sargey. I'm the reason you have these walls."

"You think I give a shit about that? We were doing fine without you, and we'll be fine when we're gone."

"I heard you're leaving soon."

"Gone and not coming back."

"You think the Cart Guys are going to let you skate? I'll miss you, but they won't!"

"You threatening me, Matty?"

"Not at all, but those guys will. You made a deal: guns for your work. They've got their hooks in you."

Matty walked back into the living room and sat down with Hecky. He looked back at Derek.

"They might violate your little non-aggression principle."

Derek knew there was no way he was going to hang around with them. He walked outside to his rental car.

Just as he was about to open his car door, a female voice call his name.

"Derek, Derek!"

He looked back and saw Anna emerge from a car. "Hi, Derek."

"Hey," replied Derek. Anna smiled and Derek half-smiled back, "You know you are trespassing."

"I've got city property under my feet."

"If you say so," Derek turned and began to walk toward his car.

"I see your boy is associating with known gangsters," Anna pointed to Matty's car.

"Matty?" asked Derek.

Anna nodded her head yes.

Derek scoffed and snickered to himself, "Are you joking?"

"Are you?" asked Anna.

Derek shook his head.

"I know you think you've got it all figured out, but if you continue down this path you will end up just like your friends."

"I'm not choosing their path, Anna. I'm not in that life, nor do I plan to be. I'm gone in a month, and I'm not coming back."

"Just because you run doesn't mean the life won't find you. It will come crashing through your door like a no-knock warrant. It will take everything you care about."

"I'll be fine, Anna. I appreciate your concern." Derek turned and walked to his car.

"Your boy is pretty plugged in with some cartel guys, just know that. The guys he's connected to are connected to the worst of the worst."

* * * * *

Over the next week, Hecky would come and go with no regard for his own well-being. He was making moves and didn't seem to care if he drew the attention of Derek or the police. Derek sat tight at home, bored and alone. He missed Mandy and couldn't wait to leave Vancouver. Mandy and Derek continued talking every night. If they weren't texting, they were talking; if they weren't talking, they were texting. Derek's mind was on Mandy 24/7.

* * * * *

Dannick arrived the day before the Opening Ceremonies of the Vancouver Olympics. Derek picked him up from the airport in a rental car and drove him back to the house.

Walking through the house, Dannick was blown away by the décor of the home; he had never seen anything like it.

"This place is unreal! Business must be good!"

"It is, buddy. Life is good!"

"Can I have a job?" asked Dannick, jokingly.

Fuck no, thought Derek.

They had an early dinner and then took a cab downtown to The Bar. Derek hadn't gone out in quite a while but let Dannick twist his arm.

They arrived at 10:00 p.m. and circled the inside of the bar a few times looking for a spot to relax. Derek didn't want to be out, but with the Olympics in town, Dannick wanted to get out and have some fun.

Dannick walked out to the dance floor and began dancing with a girl. Derek stood at the bar and watched the DJ spin records up top. He took a look around the club; he knew that the people in the club were just like him, pretending to be something they weren't. He was trying to hold together the perception that he was normal and successful. He then noticed Anna and her crew walk into the bar. They were dressed in the same jackets they were wearing when they tossed him out of a bar the week before.

Anna and her partners circled the bar; Derek had nowhere to hide. Anna spotted him and pointed directly at him. He stood in place, defeated and alone. Anna walked toward Derek and stood in front of him.

"I thought I was pretty clear, Derek."

"You think I want to be here?"

"Well, you are here."

"Yeah, yeah, I'm leaving."

Derek began to walk toward Dannick, but one of her partners stopped him.

"Listen, crop top, I just want to go," said Derek.

Anna pointed to the officer.

"Let him go."

The officer stepped aside, and Derek began to walk toward the exit.

Derek walked past Dannick who was still talking to the same girl. He slid Dannick $100 in twenties and smiled.

"Hey, buddy, I'm being kicked out. Stay and have fun!"

Dannick looked at Derek, confused. "Are you sure?"

"Yeah, buddy, I'm good." Derek walked toward the exit.

The next morning, Derek woke up to the sound of laugher in the living room. He threw on jogging pants and a t-shirt and walked downstairs. Dannick, Matty and Hecky were chatting. They looked like they all just came home from a night on the town.

Hecky grinned at Derek. "Baby Bro is just like you eh, Sarge!"

"Yeah, he's his Brother's Brother," said Matty.

"That girl?" asked Derek.

Dannick nodded. Derek was sad that his Brother was treating women the way he'd treated women. He didn't want that for him.

Hecky and Matty chatted for a bit, then broke off from Derek and Dannick and went out. Derek poured himself a coffee in the kitchen and walked out to the living room.

"How's Mandy?" asked Dannick.

"She's good, man. She's excited."

"Only a few weeks away eh, bud?"

"I can't wait. I'm a different person when I'm with her."

"I can tell," said Dannick. "You're better with her."

"I hope you find someone like her. You deserve that more than I do."

"You deserve it too, Derek. With all the shit you had to go through, you seem good."

"I am."

"I'm glad. It makes me happy to see you happy."

*　*　*　*　*

Over the next two weeks, Derek was a tourist in Vancouver. He attended hockey games and other Olympic events. He was in Whistler when Alex Bilodeau won Canada's first gold medal on Canadian soil. He was there when Sidney Crosby buried a shootout winner on Jonas Hiller to lead Canada over Switzerland.

Every night he would return home to find Hecky and Matty hanging out in their living room. Some nights they were doing coke, other nights they were doing worse. Derek would beat Dannick to the house and banish them to Hecky's room. He didn't want Dannick to see that.

Dannick was having the time of his life. Every night he would return to the house with stories of who he met, who he interviewed and what he had seen that day.

Every story made Derek jealous of Dannick. Derek longed for his life, an exciting job, close friends and normalcy. Derek's life was everything but. His normalcy was Mandy.

February 26th 2010

The games began coming to a close. The city was buzzing as Canada had made it to the Gold Medal game in men's ice hockey.

At 10:00 p.m., Derek arrived home. Once again, Hecky and Matty were in the living room doing drugs. It was a drug Derek had never seen before. He looked at the boys and shook his head.

"What the fuck are you doing?"

"It's blow." replied Matty.

"Matty, I've seen more blow than Bogotá – that isn't blow! You idiots are going off the fucking rails!"

"It's fine, Sarge. We're all good!"

"Hecky, you're yelling!"

"Am I?"

"Can I talk to you in here?"

Hecky walked toward the kitchen. Derek followed.

"What the hell is wrong with you?" asked Derek.

"What?"

"You're doing fucking crystal now. Are you that snowed up? You are already fucking nuts – do you need to feed that insanity even more?"

"It's one time, Sarge. Chill! I'm sure the youngin' has seen it before."

"You and that idiot get the fuck upstairs and don't come out when Dannick gets here. I don't need you freaking him out."

"You twisted, Sarge. You think you are always fucking right and I'm always fucking wrong!"

"Hecky, what the hell are you jawing about? I'd love to fucking know what happens in that lifted, warped brain of yours. Smarten the fuck up!"

Hecky walked past Derek and yelled at Matty.

"Grab that shit and move upstairs!"

February 27th, 2010
THIRTY-ONE

The next morning, Derek woke to crashing and banging noises in the kitchen. He walked downstairs to find pots and pans all over the floor. Hecky was lying there laughing.

"Jesus Christ, what the fuck are you doing?"

"You want breakfast?" asked Hecky.

Derek knelt down next to Hecky, who looked up and laughed.

"Are you okay?" asked Derek.

"I'm fucking great, Sarge!"

"Hecky, I'm seriously worried about you. You are off the rails, man."

"I'm good, bud."

"No, Hecky, you aren't. Matty is not someone you should be hanging out with. He's bad news."

"Was I so bad for you, Sarge?" asked Matty, who had quietly entered the kitchen.

"Oh shit!" shouted Hecky.

"How much good did you bring into my life, Matty? For real."

"I brought a lot of money into your life. Don't forget that!"

"Should I forget that Hecky and R-Luv are dead because of that?"

"Collateral damage, Sarge."

Derek stood to his feet and put his hands together as if he was saying a prayer.

"Matty, what happened to you? You were this nice, polite kid and now you are this."

"You know why, Sarge."

"Matty, please leave. I need to straighten Hecky out. He is going off the deep end and you're not helping."

"He's a big boy, Sarge. He can do whatever the fuck he wants."

Hecky spoke up, "Yeah, Sarge, fuck off!" Hecky pushed Derek back and he stood back quickly.

"Stop trying to run things," said Matty. "I thought you're supposed to be against coercion."

"Alright, you guys do whatever you want. I'm an Ancap, what the fuck do I care! Just make sure your fist ends where my head starts."

Derek stormed off to his room and packed a bag, then went to Dannick's room and woke him up.

"Pack your shit, buddy. We're going to a hotel!"

Getting a hotel in the city during the Olympics was impossible. Lucky for Derek, he found a couple on Kijiji who listed their hotel for the weekend. They had booked it for the entire Olympics and were leaving town early. The price was jacked up, but Derek didn't want to spend his last days in Vancouver worried about Hecky and Matty going crazy on Crystal.

They checked into the hotel. Dannick grabbed his gear and headed out to work. He was happy to have a shorter commute downtown.

Derek lay down on the bed in his room and turned on the television. He was finally able to rest. It had been a crazy two years of running from one place to another, one play to another. As he drifted off to sleep his phone rang. He looked at the caller ID; it was Mandy.

"Hey babe," answered Derek.

"Two days, sweets!"

"I know, babe. I can't wait!"

"What is your plan for moving? Did you get your friends to help?"

"I hired movers and then I'll drive the truck to Canmore."

"I cleared out a pile of space for your stuff. I can't wait for it and you to be here with me!"

"Neither can I, babe. I already packed most of my stuff, so I checked into a hotel with Dannick. We're going to watch the gold medal game downtown on the big screen."

"That's so fun! I wish I could join you guys!"

"We do too!"

"I'm going to visit my friend tonight. I'll give you a call tomorrow."

"Sounds good. Have fun!"

"You too, Derek!"

Mandy hung up and Derek rolled over and took an afternoon nap.

*   *   *   *   *

Derek woke up in the evening and ordered room service. While waiting for his food he looked over his missed texts and calls. Mom, Dannick, Mandy and Hecky had all texted. He read through them, ignoring Hecky. He was annoyed; calling Hecky a friend was becoming increasingly difficult.

After reading all his texts he gave Hecky's text a read: *Sorry I was such a dick. Matty and I want to take you out tonight, meet downtown?"*

Fuck that! thought Derek. He was done with both of them. He would stay in and avoid all the bad in Van. Derek texted Hecky back, saying he wasn't feeling well and checked into the hotel. Derek spent the night watching a movie.

February 28th, 2010
THIRTY-TWO

Derek woke at 9:00 a.m. and went out for breakfast. He returned to the hotel to find Dannick getting ready. The plan was to go down to the screening area early to get a good spot. Derek went alone, allowing Dannick to finish his interviews.

Derek arrived at the screening area at 11:00 a.m. People crowded around him as he stood sipping on a coffee. He and Mandy texted while he waited. *One more day* he thought.

The crowd had filled in when Derek texted Hecky to join him and Dannick at the game. It was Derek's one last nice gesture to him.

The puck dropped at 12:15 p.m. local time, with Sidney Crosby taking the opening face-off for Canada. Dannick was late arriving at the screening area and narrowly missed the puck drop. He brought Derek a beer.

They watched Canada take a 1-0 lead late into the third period. The crowd waited in anticipation of a celebration that would surely consume Canada.

With just over a minute left, Zach Parise broke the hearts of Canadians everywhere when he buried a shot past Roberto Luongo. The air had been let out of the entire country.

The game went into overtime and with every chance, for either team, the crowd worked into a frenzy. Canada needed this; they needed to win this game. Then it happened.

Sidney Crosby took a pass from Jerome Iginla inside the left face-off circle and buried a quick wrist shot underneath Ryan Miller. GAME OVER. CANADA WINS!

The crowd went nuts! Dannick and Derek screamed out loud. Derek couldn't hear his own thoughts. All he could hear was inaudible screaming from thousands of fans.

"Fucking Sid!" yelled Dannick, as he high fived total strangers. The cheering continued as Dannick and Derek became separated in the crowd. Derek spun around looking for his Brother; he was gone. The crowd filled in the area where Dannick once stood.

Derek pulled out his phone and tried to call Dannick. He answered, but all Derek could hear was undecipherable yelling on the other end of the line. Derek hung up and took another look around. Nothing. He wasn't worried; they'd meet back at the hotel.

He began to make the long walk back to his hotel. He pulled a cigarette from the pack in his pocket and lit it.

The crowd was still in a frenzy. Derek couldn't help but enjoy the moment; a gold medal for Team Canada punched Derek's ticket out of town.

Walking with the crowd, he could feel somebody rubbing against him from behind. He didn't turn – he figured everyone in the crowd was rubbing against everyone else. The bumping continued until he felt something blunt poke into his back.

"Hey, Sarge," said Matty from behind. He'd snuck up behind Derek and shoved a gun into his spine.

"What are you doing, Matty?"

"I heard you got a huge stash of money and the only key."

"What about it?" asked Derek.

"You're going to take me to it."

Derek kept walking. "You going to shoot me in the middle of town?"

"If I have to."

"Nah, I don't think you will."

"I've got this thing buried so deep that no one would even hear it."

"Why are you doing this, Matty?"

"Money. I owe it – you have it."

"The cart guys."

"Something like that."

Derek and Matty walked forward until they approached a crosswalk with the flashing hand and a countdown at four. Three, two, one, Derek leaned back and smashed Matty in the face as hard as he could with his elbow. Matty's head flung back, stunned. Derek pushed through a group of people, jumped out onto the crosswalk and ran across the street. He weaved through the thousands of people in the streets, trying to get to his hotel. He spun around in every direction. Matty was gone.

Derek walked the streets until, twenty minutes later, he arrived back at the hotel. He walked calmly through the lobby as he attempted to call Dannick on his cell phone. He had to get Dannick out of town and get himself gone. His belongings meant nothing; he didn't need them. He wasn't going home. He wasn't seeing Hecky again. Matty had turned against him and he needed to get out of Vancouver and on with his life.

Derek took the elevator up to his hotel room and calmly stood in front of it. *How was he going to explain to Dannick that he had to take him to the airport right now?* He would need to think of something on the way. Then it hit him – Hecky turned on him. He was the only person who knew Derek was downtown. He dimed.

Derek calmly opened the door and walked into the room, "Dannick?"

Dannick peered out from around the corner, "Hey, bud!"

"Pack your shit, buddy. Change of plans – I have to take you to the airport tonight. I'm leaving too!"

"What's up?" asked Dannick.

"Nothing, man. I just want to get going to surprise Mandy."

"You guys are so cute," said Dannick as he smiled.

"Why?"

Derek walked toward Dannick. As he turned the corner, he saw Mandy sitting on his bed, as beautiful as ever. She'd made the trip to Vancouver. *Fuck!* thought Derek.

"Hey, Derek," said Mandy.

"Oh my God. What are you doing here?" asked Derek.

"I thought I would spend your last night here with you."

Jesus, this is terrible, thought Derek. "I was coming to see you!"

"Now you don't have to!"

Mandy stood up, walked over to Derek and gave him a kiss. He knew they were in trouble; they had to go right now!

"I would still like to drive tonight. I have a beat on a job and I would like to meet the guy tomorrow."

"Job isn't going anywhere, bro," said Dannick.

"It could. I need to go."

"What's wrong?" asked Mandy.

"This city, man. I just…" Derek rubbed his head in frustration. "We just, we need to go right fucking now."

"Are you okay?" asked Dannick.

"I'm not."

"What is it?" asked Mandy.

Derek grabbed Dannick's suitcase and opened the door to set it outside. He took one step outside and was greeted by a fist to his face. Derek stumbled back into the corner of the wall and fell down. Mandy screamed as George walked in with his gun drawn. Matty stood behind him.

"Hey, Derek," said Matty. George and Matty both revealed their guns.

Matty had come for the money; his prize was the key to the first storage locker which Derek wore on a chain around his neck. Derek looked at Matty who fired a shot that knocked Derek to the ground. Derek clutched the bloody bullet wound on his right thigh. The blood leaked through his fingers as he screamed in agony.

"Shut the fuck up!" Matty pointed his gun at Mandy and Dannick. "You two, on your knees."

Dannick and Mandy watched Derek, terrified, as they dropped to their knees in the middle of the room.

Derek crawled toward Mandy. "Don't do this, Matty," pleaded Derek. "Take the fucking money and go."

"I know you'll come after me."

"Just fucking take it and go!"

"Derek, who are these guys?" asked Mandy.

"I'm Matty."

"Just go!" yelled Derek.

"Why are you doing this?" asked Mandy.

"Let me give you the 411 on Derek Sierzant. Derek has grinded out seven million dollars in the last year, and I'm here to take it from him."

Mandy looked at Derek. "What does that mean?"

"Means that he's been slinging."

"What?" asked Dannick.

"Your bro is the best criminal I've ever seen. No one runs like him."

Derek hung his head in shame; he had nothing to say. He could feel the harsh looks from Mandy and Dannick as they knelt down across from him.

"Derek, I never planned for any of this to happen, but I need to pay the cart back."

"What did you do to Hecky?"

"He's comfortable."

"Your friend Hecky? Is he dead?"

"Jesus Christ, Sarge. You really shut her out. They are all gone."

"My God, Derek. Who are you?" yelled Mandy.

"He put his boys on this path."

"You piece of shit!" screamed Derek. Matty looked down at Derek and grinned. Derek took a deep breath and spit a tooth onto the carpeted floor. He looked up at Dannick; his eyes were full of fear and confusion. His world shattered in a matter of seconds. Derek's world had finally collided with someone he loved.

"Sargey, there is seven mill out there, and I'm splitting it two ways."

Bang! Matty shot Dannick in the back of the head, splattering Dannick's brain all over the berber carpet of the hotel room floor.

"Jesus Christ!" screamed Derek. "Fuck!" Words weren't coming; rage and anger was. Derek picked up Dannick and held him. His little Brother, his best friend, limp, lifeless and gone.

Mandy went pale, her face blank. Derek looked into her sparkling blue eyes; she looked back, as a single tear streamed down her face. Derek couldn't move as he looked at Dannick's lifeless body lying in his arms.

"Don't do this Matty. She didn't do shit!"

Mandy looked at Derek again. His perfect angel had been brought into Derek's world of horror. Tears streamed down Derek's face as he thought about all the things he couldn't erase from his life. He took a deep breath and stared straight ahead at Mandy. All he could do was mouth the words *I'm sorry* to her. She cried as he looked her in the eyes, a bullet from Matty's gun pierced the back of her head and ended her life. She fell facedown to the floor. Gone were his dreams of top-down rides along the coast with the girl he loved.

He'd done it; Matty had killed the two people Derek loved the most. Derek couldn't move and he had nowhere to move to. Mandy, Dannick, Messy, and R-Luv – all gone. Derek had nothing left except the air in his lungs and he didn't want it anymore.

Matty stood near the bathroom and George stood in front of the entrance into the room. They towered over Derek as they cocked their guns.

As they were about to pull the triggers the door burst open; police officers piled into the room. George was right in front of them as the officers fired. Multiple rounds hit George in his face, chest and arms. His bullet-riddled body trembled to the floor. Dead.

Matty took off running into the bedroom and locked the door. Several officers attempted to kick the door open and, after a few tries, they opened it.

They entered the bedroom to discover that Matty was gone. Derek could hear them call out that the bedroom window was open; Matty had used the fire escape to do exactly that.

Anna was one of the last officers to walk in the door. She knelt down beside Derek and rubbed his back while the paramedics looked at his leg.

"Is he gone?"

"He's gone, Derek. They are too."

Derek began to sob. He lay on the ground, shaking and sobbing. It was over; he had nothing left. No home. Nowhere to go. No one to talk to.

The paramedics patched him up and assisted him onto a stretcher. Derek looked down at Mandy and Dannick. Both were lying in a pool of blood, executed right in front of him. The paramedics wheeled Derek out of the hotel to an ambulance. He could see the coroner's van parked down the street. They were in the midst of loading three bodies inside.

His head swiveled around, looking for Matty. Derek wondered how much of the ambush was him and how much was driven by desperation to pay back the cartel.

The paramedics closed the door to the ambulance and Derek began to fade – sleep was approaching.

March 1st 2010
THIRTY-THREE

Derek woke up in a hospital bed the following morning. Anna was sitting in a chair by his side; he woke up, groggy from the painkillers.

"Derek?"

"Yeah?"

"Do you want to me to get the nurse?" asked Anna.

"No, it's fine. Where am I?"

"You're at the General. They removed the bullet from your leg."

"Jesus, that actually happened."

"It did, Derek. All of it happened."

"Did anyone come to see me?"

"Your parents came to get Dan."

"Where are they?"

"Here. Your Mom had a spell. Did you know she has glioblastoma?"

"I don't know what that is."

"It's brain cancer, Derek.

"Fuck." Derek let out a deep breath and laid back in his bed and began to cry. "Pile it on."

"Derek, stop feeling sorry for yourself. You did this. You set all of this in motion. No one did this to you." Anna paused for a moment and then continued her verbal assault. "You'll have to live with this; there is no one left for you but you." Anna walked toward the door and let that set in. Derek continued to cry. "You wanted everything for nothing, Derek."

"Anna, I'd do anything if it meant even an hour without this feeling." Derek paused for a moment and stared at the ceiling. "I can't believe that he did that."

"Crazies will be crazy, but it's my job to limit the damage they can do."

"It's not working, Anna. The war on drugs, what you do. None of it will ever work. George goes in the ground and ten more of him pop up."

"Derek, stop! All you've done is why you have nothing left. It's nothing I did or didn't do. It's not the war on drugs. I tried to keep you out of the firefight and you jumped in and aimed all those weapons at everyone you love."

Anna faked a smile and walked out the door. Derek lay back in his bed and stared blankly at the ceiling. Sleep came once again.

A few hours later, Derek was checked by the doctors and released. An orderly pushed him out of the hospital in a wheelchair and he was left to sit. No one was coming; no one cared anymore. He hoped that Matty would drive by and finish him off.

*   *   *   *   *

The next morning, Derek woke up at home, alone. He put on the morning news; he was all over it with Matty, Mandy, Dannick and Hecky. His life was over. Anywhere he went and anyone that knew him would forever dub him that guy.

By afternoon he rented a car and drove by the first storage unit. He knew that the last time the boy's left it there was still four million dollars inside. Untouchable money. The police were likely still looking at it. If they weren't, Matty had already cleaned it out.

Derek drove his rental car methodically past the unit three separate times, each time checking for a cube van nearby. It was still there.

He knew Anna suspected he'd go after the money. They were both right. He turned the car around and drove away as quick as he could. He began to drive aimlessly through the streets of Vancouver, debating his next move.

He drove up the Sea to Sky Highway to Squamish, wondering if Hecky's parents would know anything about his whereabouts. He had disappeared without a trace and the police were looking for him.

He pulled into Hecky's parents' complex and parked in front of the house. He entered in the garage code as he remembered it and it worked. He stepped into the garage and used the garage door to enter. The house was eerily quiet.

He made his way up the stairs and onto the main floor. There was a meal prepped on the kitchen island; it stank up the entire floor. Someone had left in a hurry.

Derek walked upstairs and called out, "Mr. Heckman?" There was no response. He opened the door to the master bedroom and on the other side of the bed he could see feet on the floor. He approached the body slowly and looked over the bed. Mr. Heckman had been badly beaten and was now dead.

Derek turned and opened the door to the master bathroom. He took one step into the bathroom and nearly stepped in a dry pool of blood. He looked up and saw Hecky handcuffed to the shower rod. His body was beaten and bloodied; he'd been tortured for a long time. Derek knew how Matty was able to find him – he'd beaten it out of Hecky. Hecky didn't turn. If anything, he did all he could to protect Derek.

Derek sat on the edge of the bathtub and looked around the room. That was it, now he had nothing left.

February 28th 2010
THIRTY-FOUR

Matty drove in panic through the suburbs of Maple Ridge. His plan had gone to shit, he was scrambling. He was covered in the blood of Dannick and Mandy.

He drove over his parent's front lawn as he pulled his car into the driveway. He scrambled into the house, packed a bag, grabbed his Mom's makeup and walked to the garage. Approaching his Father's BMW 535, he opened the door and climbed inside. He knew that every cop in B.C. would be looking for his car. He peeled out of his parents' garage and drove frantically toward the Greater Vancouver city limits.

He arrived at the boys' second storage unit and quickly scouted it for police; there wasn't a suspicious car in sight. He grabbed the keys, an empty suitcase and walked to the boys' unit. Once inside the unit, Matty packed his bag to the brim with cash. He wheeled the money back to his Father's car, jumped inside and drove until he found himself in downtown Kelowna. He abandoned the car a few blocks from a motel. He paid cash and checked into a room.

He lay on his bed looking at his open suitcase filled with cash. He'd ended his own life – the life he knew anyway. He couldn't go back to his family or friends. Vancouver and all he knew would be a distant memory. He killed all of it and left it for dead in Derek's hotel room.

Matty holed up in his motel room for the next three days, waiting for the heat to turn down so he could go back for the other storage unit. He needed it to pay back the cartel. The two million was for him to start over.

Matty's plan to get the second storage unit had been compromised. His original plan was to use George as a decoy while he jumped in and out of the unit. On his own, Matty knew he would be hard-pressed to make a clean sneak. He mulled over his options while he waited for his beard to fill in so he could alter his appearance. All he needed was time.

* * * * *

Three days later, Matty looked like a different man. His beard had filled in and he'd died his hair jet-black. He used makeup to cover up other features and wore blue contacts. He was prepared to return to Vancouver to scoop up Derek's four million dollars. He needed a car first, but he couldn't rent one. He couldn't buy one either. He would have to steal one.

Matty grabbed his luggage, put on his hoodie and ball cap and walked back out into the world. He looked around the parking lot; there wasn't a car in sight. He roamed the streets in search of the perfect car to take him to his destination.

He walked down Water Street past the Delta Grand hotel and spotted a parking lot full of cars. It was the Prospera Place Arena, home of the Kelowna Rockets.

Matty kept his head low as he surveyed the parking lot for a vehicle to steal. He spotted an early 2000's model Audi A4 with the windows rolled down. He approached the car and peeked inside. The car was littered with food wrappers and other garbage.

He opened the door and tossed his bag inside. He fidgeted with the car's steering column and worked along the dash to wire the car to start. The sun became a nuisance; Matty flipped the drivers visor down and keys fell into his lap. He laughed. *Kids are such idiots*, he thought. He started the car and drove onto Water Street. Within minutes he'd escaped Kelowna and was driving toward Vancouver.

Matty arrived and drove straight to the storage unit. He parked in a spot where he could see the unit and the surveillance van at the same time. He watched for the remainder of the day and well into the evening. He needed to see a shift change; he needed to know whether or not the police were still watching. Throughout the evening and overnight nothing happened. Matty grew antsy.

The following morning, he began to consider opening the door. Then, at 8:00 a.m., the van door opened and two officers jumped out. A ghost car pulled up and two men jumped out, trading places with the men in the van. Matty smiled. They were there, and he knew how to get to them. He sat in the car for a few more hours. He had plenty of firepower to take the officers down; he just needed the cover of night to do so.

Night came and Matty grabbed his two guns and stepped out of his car. He approached the cube van from the back and prepared himself. He pulled out his automatic weapon and sprayed the back door of the cube van until the bullets ran out. He waited for the door to open; it didn't. The men inside were dead.

Matty approached the van door and opened it. The computers and equipment inside the van were smoking. The officers were slumped over in their chairs with blood pooling beneath their feet. Matty had killed them both. He shut the door and ran back to the car. He drove into the storage unit parking lot and pulled up in front of the door to the unit. He exited the car, smashed open the lock and walked inside.

Inside the unit were bags and bags of the boy's money. Matty opened the rear doors of his car and began transporting the cash from the unit to the car.

Moments later, he stacked the last of the money in the car and looked it over – millions of dollars. He paused and took a deep breath. He still had to run; the cops would be coming even harder. He had chalked up two more bodies.

Matty locked the unit door with a new lock and turned to walk to his car. He caught a glimpse of a shadow and was quickly struck in the face with a wooden baseball bat. He fell to the ground, rattled and stunned.

He watched the shadow emerge from the darkness and approach him. He recognized his masked assailant.

Derek had been watching the watchers and Matty walked right into it. He looked up at Derek and spotted a second shadow. A man, shorter than Derek. *Who was this?* Derek hit Matty in the face a second time, knocking him unconscious. He grabbed Matty by the arm, flipped him over and zip tied his hands behind his back. The second man pulled a sedan next to Matty's car. Derek and the second man picked Matty up and tossed him in the trunk. After closing the trunk, Derek walked to the driver's side of Matty's Audi, opened the door and climbed inside. He drove away with the second man following.

They drove toward Squamish. Derek made a left-hand turn on a dirt road and drove toward the water. The road opened up to an area that was all too familiar. It was where Derek and Hecky had disposed of a detective.

They parked close to the water and exited their vehicles. Derek opened the door to the backseat and grabbed Matty's bags.

Across the parking lot was an additional vehicle. Derek unlocked the car with a fob and opened the trunk. He tossed the luggage and money in the trunk of the additional car and walked back toward Matty's car. He popped the trunk to Matty's car and opened it. Matty attempted to climb out of the trunk but stopped after meeting Derek's fist. He slumped back into the trunk and Derek pulled out the remaining bags of luggage. Derek walked over to the other car and dropped the bags into the trunk. He then picked up two large gas cans and walked back toward Matty's car. Matty's lip and nose bled profusely down his face.

Derek set the gas cans on the ground and pulled out a pack of cigarettes. He took two out of the pack and put them between his lips. "Do you want a smoke, Matty?"

"Kind of hard to smoke it."

Derek lit both cigarettes and placed one between Matty's lips. They both took a drag and exhaled. Derek then reached in and took the cigarette from Matty's lips. Matty attempted to bite him; Derek moved quickly and slapped Matty in the face.

"Fuck you, Sarge. Do your fucking worst!"

Derek took his cigarette and put it out on Matty's cheek.

"Ahhhhhhh, fuck!" yelled Matty.

Derek picked a pop can off the ground and stood back up. He took another drag of his cigarette.

"Matty, I don't need to tell you that you took everything from me."

"You set yourself up for that. If not me, someone else would have."

"Then I would have done to them what I'm going to do to you."

Derek dropped his cigarette into the pop can and set it on the ground. He stood back up and picked up the first gas can, uncapped it and soaked Matty head to toe in gasoline. He grabbed the second can and soaked the inside of the car. Derek tossed both gas cans in the back seat and shut the door.

Matty began to yell, "Help! Help!"

The masked man punched Matty and he slumped back into the trunk. Derek stood over him, looking down.

"You know we ripped off your parents."

Matty looked up at Derek. "I know. Hecky told me."

Derek pulled out a gun, pointed it at Matty and stood over him.

"How fitting, Sarge? You killing me the way I killed your Girl and your Brother."

Derek paused and looked at the gun, "Hecky too."

"I never shot Hecky."

"I did," replied Derek. "He wasn't dead when I got to his folks'. He laid there for three fucking days, choking on his own blood. He asked me to put him down." Matty nodded his head, remorseless for what he'd done. "You took that from me too. I'd never killed anyone."

"You better hide that gun well. The cops would love to shut the door on the three murders tied to it."

"Two murders," replied Derek.

"What?" asked Matty.

Derek wiped the gun down with a rag and dropped it into the trunk next to Matty. Matty's eyes became large as Derek pulled out a Zippo and lit it. Matty watched Derek toss the lighter into the trunk and screamed, "Fuck you!" The trunk became engulfed in flames. Derek turned and walked away from the car while Matty screamed in agony as his body began to burn.

Derek and the masked man walked toward their getaway car. They climbed into the car and Derek started it. He turned the car around and took one last look at Matty's car. He could still hear screams; Matty wasn't dead yet. Derek drove up the dirt road toward the Sea to Sky Highway. As he was about to turn onto the highway, he heard the car explode. He made the turn and disappeared.

*   *   *   *   *

The following day Matty's stolen getaway was discovered outside of Squamish. The emergency response was large. Matty's torched body was discovered in the trunk of his car.

Anna arrived on the scene hours after investigators had started their search for clues. The torched car was still smoldering as fireman tried to put it out. The search had already begun for the car that Derek and the masked man had used to drive from the storage unit.

Anna spoke with a plain-clothed officer. "Who's the vic?"

"Our best guess is that it's your suspect in the downtown double."

"Someone finally caught up to him," said Anna.

"Looks that way."

"Anything from either car?"

"Well, your burner was stolen out of Kelowna a couple of days. This one was taken out of Burnaby yesterday."

"Anything in it?" asked Anna.

"We got a pretty good partial. We'll run it, see what we get."

"Let me know," said Anna, as she walked back to her car and drove back to Vancouver. She was done for the day. It would take days to get information from the crime scene.

The car near Squamish was out of her jurisdiction, but the overall scope of her case against Derek and the boys allowed her to coordinate with other police and task forces.

*   *   *   *   *

Anna walked into the police station three days later and made her way to her cubical in the bullpen. She'd spent the past two days waiting for results on the partial fingerprint. At 10:00 a.m., she was approached by a lab technician and handed an envelope that contained the results from the partial fingerprint.

"Your fingerprint analysis," said the young lab tech.

Anna opened the envelope and found a single sheet of paper.

"What's this?" she asked.

"It's the weirdest thing. I ran it through the database and nothing came up. But it got a restricted Interpol hit."

"What?" asked Anna, shocked.

Ten minutes later, Anna was handed an envelope with the information about her victim in the burned up car. She looked down at the second envelope; Matty was her victim. She knew it was Derek.

Anna walked to her desk. She was staring at the envelope when two male Interpol agents approached her.

"Miss Johnson?" asked the taller of the two agents.

"Yes," she replied.

"We'd like to speak to you."

"What is this about?"

"In private, please."

Anna stood up from her seat and walked the two detectives to an interrogation room. She shut the door and sat across from the two men.

"What can I do?" asked Anna.

"Miss Johnson, we'd like to know a little more about the prints you ran."

"Gang murder near Squamish. It was gang retaliation. The victim killed the perp's Brother and Girlfriend."

"How old is this perp?"

"24," replied Anna.

The men looked at one another, confused. "Hmm, okay."

"What?" asked Anna, her curiosity now stoked.

"It's just not our guy," replied The Agent.

"Are you sure there isn't an older man involved?"

Anna furrowed her brow, "An older man? No."

"Okay."

"Okay, seriously. What's going on? Why are you interested in this?" asked Anna.

"Miss Johnson, this stays here."

"Okay," replied Anna, as she leaned in across the table.

"Your partial belongs to a Polish thief named Zagadka. Interpol has been after him for 30 years."

"Who is he?" asked Anna.

"He may be the greatest thief who ever lived. No one has ever even had a look at this guy."

"How do you have his prints?"

"He was pursued and nearly caught in 1983. A suitcase he dropped had his fingerprint on it. He went underground and then silent, which brings us to today."

"This guy waits 30 years to surface and pops up in B.C. to off a kid on a dope beef?" Asked Anna.

"I doubt it. Zagadka never killed. That's what made him so good – his crimes were all non-violent."

"Maybe it's coincidence," said Anna. "He could have driven that car another time."

"This Sierzant kid, he's Polish?" asked the Interpol agent.

"He told me he was Kashubian."

The two agents looked at one another and the shorter one said, "We need to bring him in."

April 2010

Derek's eyes grew tired. It was 4:00 p.m. and he had been driving for ten straight hours. It was the tail end of a 40-hour drive from Squamish to Pennsylvania. He turned left on Grandview Avenue in the Mount Washington neighbourhood of Pittsburgh. Derek shook his passenger awake and locked his eyes back on the road. His passenger shifted in his seat and began to wake up.

Derek drove past the Duquesne Incline and felt all emotion come over him. He'd lost everything: his Brother, his Mother, his friends and Mandy.

He pulled off on the right-hand side of the street and stopped the car.

Derek stepped out and walked into Point of View Park, on the side of Mount Washington. Wyatt followed him and sat down beside him. He looked out over Heinz Field, Carnegie and Downtown Pittsburgh. He thought back to his days there with Mandy. They had stood in that very park imagining a life together. Derek held back tears as he thought about Mandy and how unfair life had been for her. He managed to do the thing he promised he wouldn't: he let his world ruin hers. He had it all, and yet nothing. He was on top of the world and at rock bottom. He had his freedom, his guilt, his money and his Dad.

Derek turned to his passenger and smiled. His Dad smiled back. The statue depiction of George Washington and Guyasuta was a perfect analogy for Derek and Zagadka. Their weapons down, finally meeting face-to-face, showing each other who they really were. Neither proud of what they were, but accepting of the prison they have built for themselves. Derek was his Father's son. He was a master thief and an escape artist.

ACKNOWLEDGEMENTS

This novel was started on January 22nd 2009. It was the day I started to clear my head and my heart. It was the day I made the decision not to continue down a path towards darkness.

I was in debt, broke and jobless. I didn't have a place to live and I didn't feel good about my life, or myself. I put pen to paper and began to map out a story of where I couldn't let my life go.

I chose light that day, and I persevered through a lot of things to get this story out into the world.

I have a lot of people to thank for making this book possible. Amanda. My wife. My best friend. She encouraged me, and let me know that I could do this. She's been a rock for me and I couldn't have done it without her love and support. She encouraged me to keep going countless times. So if you hated the book, it's mostly her fault. Babe, I love you. Thank you for letting me nap on the days where I stayed up writing until 3 a.m. and thanks for giving me answers to a lot of questions I had about my own writing.

To my two daughters, it is so easy loving you and being your Dad. There is no way I could have finished my story without learning about myself through fatherhood. My sun rises and sets with both of you.

Thanks to my family for bailing me out, and letting me come home with my tail between my legs. I love you all very much.

Thanks to Patsy and Marce. You're always there to help us at the drop of a hat. We love you both so much, you mean the world to us.

Thanks to my pooches Ricky and Bella for being by my side for the last eight years. They say writing is very isolating, but I've never felt that was as long as I had my furry co-pilots who'd stay up all hours of the night with me. Bella passed away a few days before my book release and I miss her dearly. She was the sweetest little thing.

Thanks to Kevin Davidson for combing this girl's hair over and over. It took a year to find you but everything you did for this book was worth the wait.

Thanks to Mike Yantha for the fantastic cover. You took my words and brought them to life, visually. I'm incredibly grateful.

Thanks to Jordy, Alex and Graham for assisting with the cover.

Thanks to Jordan and Graham for test reading this thing and giving me the feedback I needed to make the necessary improvements.

Thanks to Corey Leckie for being an advice machine, I couldn't have kept this train on the tracks without you. Thanks for shooting the social media commercial as well.

Thanks to the LPMC. Heise and JS communicate in a way that makes me wish I were a better communicator. Thanks to you both for always making time for me.

Thanks to Lee for the three-hour phone call to point me in all the directions I needed to go. I would have been lost without your guidance.

Thanks to Rory, Gez and K-Fed. You three kicked off the adventure with me and kept me going when Vancouver got tough. Rory, I'm forever in your debt.

Thanks to Fraser. Fraser passed away a few years ago and he was somebody I really admired. He was the most talented musician I've ever seen and was also one of the few people who had genuine interest in my book. He was an amazing human being.

Lastly, thanks to all of you for reading my words. I never thought this could actually reach readers, but it has. I hope you enjoyed reading it as much as I enjoyed creating it.

ABOUT THE AUTHOR

Joshua Cybulski was born and raised in Renfrew, Ontario, Canada. He became a published poet at the age of 13. It was this achievement propelled him into pursuing a career as a storyteller.

Joshua currently lives with his wife and two young daughters in Ottawa, Canada, where he works as an instructor and a broadcaster.

CPSIA information can be obtained
at www.ICGtesting.com
Printed in the USA
LVHW101821090622
720911LV00011B/118

9 798686 6184